RIPPLE EFFECT

Kristin Mayer

Ripple Effect
Book One of The Effect Series
Copyright © 2014, 2015 by K. Mayer Enterprises, Inc.
Cover Designer: Lisa Jay
(http://lisajaystudio.com/)
Interior Designer: JT Formatting
(http://www.facebook.com/JTFormatting)
Editor: Nichole Strauss with Perfectly Publishable
(https://www.facebook.com/perfectlypublishable)

Ripple Effect / Kristin Mayer – 2nd ed.
Library of Congress Cataloging-in-Publication Data
ISBN-13: 978-0-9899913-7-7

VISIT MY WEBSITE AT
http://www.authorkristinmayer.com

I dedicate this book to
my *Uncle Chris*.

Your **STRENGTH**

knows no *bounds*.

Adam

I HAD A major fucking problem to deal with. Someone was taking pictures of members at my club and then sell-ing them online. Earlier this evening, I had been informed of the leak when Mark Robertson brought me a picture he had seen of his girlfriend, Sam, on his football teammate's cell phone. Supposedly, other pictures with the same background were being sold on this exclusive site.

I stared at the pic of my old fuck buddy, Sam, in the cat mask, red wig, and black leather outfit. Sam was now going to live the life of merry commitment and white picket fences with Mark. I was glad she'd found someone. She deserved to be happy. Mark seemed like a decent guy. When Sam and I had been together, we had both known the score no attachments, just sex. It'd worked for us, and we had both known our arrangement would end one day.

My phone rang. It was my partner and best friend, Brandt.

I answered, "Did you pull the footage from last Halloween?"

"Yeah, I've got it all cued up and I'm reviewing it. We'll catch this asshole, Adam. I'll keep you posted. Everything else looks good in both areas of the club."

"Thanks. I'm going to make my rounds. Let me know when you find something."

"Will do."

We both hung up the phone.

Brandt and I had been friends since we were kids. We'd spent the first few years after high school working odd jobs here and there, not having a fucking clue as to what we wanted to do in life. We'd decided to attend college where some of our friends were going. After trying one year, we'd known college life wasn't for us, and we'd opened up a bar Club Envy. In the beginning, it had started as a regular bar that had a band and a dance floor.

After being open for more than a year, Brandt and I had gotten smashed one night after turning a decent profit for the bar. During one of our many shots, we had come up with the idea of expanding and adding an exclusive sex club in the back of Club Envy. We hadn't given the sex club a different name since we didn't want to draw attention to it necessarily. We had met a patron at our bar who helped spread our name among those people who were interested in the sex-club scene.

Walking out of my office to make my rounds while Brandt looked at the footage, I glanced around. The crowd was sparse tonight, as I'd expected, since it was Tuesday.

The main entrance was across the club. There was extra security on that side, and paperwork was needed each time a patron entered.

I went to see Trigger, the bouncer who guarded the club's side entrance used by employees and VIPs only for the sex club. The bar side had a completely different entrance on the other side of the building. Trigger was about twenty-two with brown eyes and messy blond hair. He was stacked and could throw a hell of a punch. The girls seemed to like him, and on his nights off he took pleasure in what the club had to offer. Trigger was what we called a free lover. He didn't do the exclusivity thing. He wanted to float from girl to girl.

Trigger gave me a nod as I walked up.

"All's good, Adam. The new girl you cleared came in with Nora, and she's at the bar. Snake is currently with her, like you requested."

Nora was the club's bartender, which is why Ainsley, the new girl, was allowed to enter the club for the first time without Brandt or me.

"Thanks, Trigger. Let me know if anything comes up."

Trigger gave me a nod, and I walked off toward the bar of the sex club. This side of the club was completely different than the bar side. The sex-club side was retro in style with frosted glass tables and multi-colored lights of red, green, purple, yellow, and blue that illuminated the room with a sexy glow. Odd-shaped chairs sat around the tables. There were high tables, low tables, lounge areas, and the bar area. Behind the bar area were rooms where different scenes could take place, depending on a member's desires. If all the rooms were booked, there was a communal room and an exhibitionist room anyone could use.

Unless members were in one of the rooms, Brandt and I required them to be dressed. We didn't mind the main area getting a little hot and heavy, but discretion needed to be used.

All the members here tonight were seasoned patrons and generally abided by the rules.

As I approached the bar, a bright pink wig caught my attention. It had to be Ainsley Pearson, Nora's friend and the potential new member. Her back was to me, but she was laughing and talking with Nora.

Ainsley's questionnaire had intrigued me. She wasn't the typical person who would seek membership at my club. From the picture I had of her, she was beautiful with long chestnut hair and pale blue eyes. Nora had asked for a favor to fast-track Ainsley on the visitor list. It normally took longer than two weeks to get a visitation night. Brandt and I didn't want any riffraff from the street coming into our establishment, and I needed time to complete the screenings. When Nora had shown me Ainsley's picture, I had wanted to meet her myself for some reason. Generally, I always went with my gut instinct on those types of decisions.

I walked up slowly and nodded to Snake, another security guard, who stood about four feet away from Ainsley. He had short, spikey, black hair with a snake tattoo winding up his neck. With a tip of my head, I gave him the signal that I would watch Ainsley for a bit.

As Snake strolled off, I saw him take his walkie-talkie from his back pocket. He was probably talking to Brandt to see where he needed to go next. I hated those damn walkie-talkies, but Brandt had insisted we get them for all the personnel. I never carried mine. If there were a problem, security would find me. If I had to get involved, whoever caused the problem would wish like hell that he or she hadn't started anything.

Next, I checked Ainsley's wrist to make sure she had on the black bracelet. Nonmembers weren't allowed to engage in sexual activity while in the club. Membership fees weren't cheap, and I needed to make sure potential members were serious before they benefited from the pleasures the club could offer. Per the reports I had received, Ainsley didn't have much money in her account, and she worked part-time at the university's library. Sometimes, the fees weren't important, and I had a feeling that Ainsley would fall into that category.

I leaned up against the bar. "Hey, Nora. How about a beer?"

Nora gave me an endearing smile and went to get my standard brand of beer, Guinness. From the corner of my eye, I could see I had Ainsley's attention. She was watching me with her head cocked slightly as if she was trying to figure me out. I wasn't ready to look at her yet. Nora popped the cap off my Guinness and handed it to me. I liked Guinness better in a bottle and had it brought in special even though it was on tap. I took a swig of beer and turned toward Ainsley.

Nora had said that she and Ainsley had become good friends during their sophomore year of college, and they were seniors now.

Ainsley was even more beautiful than her picture. Her chestnut hair hid beneath the wig. Her makeup seemed heavier than the more natural shot I had of her in my office. She gave me a sly smile, and I was instantly hard. She had the perfect mouth, and I wanted those lips wrapped around my cock. The moment our eyes connected, my dick wanted inside her. I looked around, making sure no one could hear me. I wanted to see how she would react. The one thing that hadn't been clear on her questionnaire was why she wanted to join a sex club. Her answer had been vague, and in this case, it had only intrigued me more. Normally, if I wasn't able to get a clear picture from the paperwork, a visitor pass would not be issued.

I tipped my beer her way. "Ainsley, right?"

Her smile dropped, and her eyes darted around the bar. She looked surprised as she said, "Do I know you?"

I extended my hand. "I'm Adam Ryker, owner of Club Envy."

Her features relaxed as she extended her hand. "Nice to meet you. Thanks for letting me visit tonight. Are you the person I talk to about becoming a member?"

She was direct. I liked a woman who didn't beat around the bush.

I took a swig. "Let me show you around, and then we can talk."

Ainsley glanced toward Nora, who nodded.

So, Little Miss Pink Wig is the cautious type.

Most women who came here were outgoing and didn't care if someone knew who they were. They strictly wanted to find a partner. I liked that Ainsley wasn't like that.

She slid off the stool, and her tight skirt went up slightly. I had to stop myself from running my hand along her inner thigh.

"Sounds good. Lead the way, Adam."

Her head came to the top of my shoulders. I was just over six foot, so she had to be five-five or five-six. Ainsley was a petite little thing and insanely gorgeous. She adjusted her tight skirt back in place.

We walked, and her perfume heightened my desire to fuck her against the first available surface club rules be damned.

Fuck, she's hot. Shit, I need to beat my pansy ass for not being able to control my dick right now.

She asked, "So, how does one get into the sex-club business?"

My eyes went to hers. In the four years I had been running the sex-club, no other female member had ever asked me that. They were here for pleasure and the details of my life were of little interest.

She seemed genuinely curious as she continued to look around at everything, absorbing the atmosphere.

She must have sensed my surprise as she clarified, "I'm a business major at the University of Georgia, and I was curious. You probably already know that though from the background check. I'm taking a summer course on marketing, and my mind thought about how, in your case, sex does sell."

I laughed as we approached the private rooms that people had to reserve in advance. I took another swig of my Guinness as I thought about how to answer.

"Well, my business partner, Brandt, and I started the bar five years ago. One night, almost a year after we opened, we got drunk and talked about fuck pads. From there, we came up with this." I shrugged.

We stopped in front of one of the doors. A slight blush crept across Ainsley's cheeks as she looked at the door. Each of the doors had a sign. This particular one said:

Brandt and I had gone with the names of the shots we had taken that night as we schemed up our new adventure together.

Ainsley looked at the sign and murmured, "Afterburn?"

I replied, "Shot names."

"Makes sense and goes with the atmosphere. So, Adam, tell me about the club and what lies behind the Afterburn door?"

I started into my standard speech. "As you might have noticed, the main bar area requires clothes. All members can have a tab, but the balance is due on a weekly basis. This is where the private rooms, six in all, are located. The other side has two separate rooms. One is a communal room, and the other is set up for those who like exhibitionism. Since it's the middle of the week, two of the private rooms aren't booked tonight, so I'm able to show you what one looks like. Each room is styled differently, but the apparatus and toys are all the same. After each room is used, everything is sterilized and cleaned prior to the next usage. Generally, rooms are booked for full evenings. Any questions so far?"

She was calmly taking it all in. I was having a hard time figuring her out. One minute, she would blush, and the next, she would ask business questions, but she wasn't trying to screw the first thing with a cock between their legs walking her way. She was a puzzle to me, and I was drawn to her.

What is she after?

She shook her head. "No questions right now. Show away."

I opened the door, and she walked in, looking around from floor to ceiling.

There was a tall bed, some sex chairs, a dresser full of toys, and a few other pieces of furniture that made for some fan-fucking-tastic sex. Club Envy had two rooms centered around BDSM, and they were equipped with whips, chains, shackles, and the like. I had tried it a few times, but it wasn't my style.

Ainsley walked farther into the room. Her tall heels helped emphasize her toned calves. She turned back my way. "This is different but intriguing. If interested, how does someone find a partner?"

She cocked her head to the side as she looked at me. I thought she was trying to read me as much as I was her. She wasn't going to let me get away with shit, and I liked it.

I took another swig of my beer. "I'd wager that you wouldn't have any problems finding someone if you were interested. Once that black bracelet comes off, it's like dating. People approach you, and you either agree or don't agree to take the next step. Just because you come to a room with someone doesn't mean that you have to follow through. You can leave at any time. If you ever run into a problem, you can come find me, if I'm not already there. We'll talk more about all this in my office."

She bit her lip and looked down. Thinking about her in this room with all the ways I could pleasure her made my cock so hard that it was as if it were turning to stone. I knew my body, and it had never reacted this fast to someone. I needed to get her out of here and make sure she understood how this worked before I made a move. She wasn't ready for that step.

I walked backward toward the door. "Why don't we go to my office and talk some more? We can discuss your thoughts and go from there."

She came my way as she said, "Sure. I have some questions now that I'd like to ask when we get to your office."

"Sounds good."

I motioned for her to step out of the room, and I followed. Music from the club surrounded us. Ainsley paused, and I took the lead as we went toward my office. I generally found that people got nervous around me when I was quiet. They would start chatting up a storm, divulging information I hadn't been able to get from the questionnaire. But Ainsley was silently taking everything in. Her wheels seemed to be constantly churning in that beautiful head of hers.

We walked into my office where the lush decorations continued. I had a glass desk, black leather desk chair, and two square black leather chairs in front of the desk. Ainsley's eyes drifted to the door in the back. That door led to my private quarters where I would stay the night if needed. No girl had ever been back there.

Ainsley took a seat in a chair as I went to my desk chair.

In between the two chairs in front of my desk was a funky vase sitting on a glass Z-shaped table.

She looked at me again with those inquisitively sharp eyes. "How would I stay anonymous if I were able to afford the monthly fees?"

"We'd give you another name to use for checking in. You could continue to wear wigs or any other disguises you wanted. If you wear a wig, keep it on, even in the rooms. Otherwise, people will be able to spot you in public."

Ainsley's right hand went to her pink wig, and she played with the strands. "How many members do you have?"

I took the last sip of my Guinness. "Currently, we have a few hundred members, but a little over half are regular attendees. Twenty people are on the waiting list to get in. I like to slowly introduce new members to the club in order to maintain control and balance of the atmosphere."

"How did I get in so fast?" Her response wasn't challenging. It seemed to come from mere curiosity.

Ainsley seemed confident and collected. From the questionnaire she'd completed, Ainsley had confirmed she wasn't a virgin. Virgins were a no-go for the club. Nora had mentioned that Ainsley had a steady boyfriend through college until recently. I figured the breakup was a part of what had driven her to try this scene. Nora had stressed that Ainsley had a no-bullshit policy, and she shot straight. This was the part of Ainsley that I found most intriguing about her wanting to visit the club. It was the swaying factor in moving her ahead on the waiting list. She didn't seem to have some fucked-up part in her that I could see in people who came here. There was a pocket of our members who were unable to have relationships outside of the sex-club walls. The majority of the members, it seemed, would use sex to escape some reality they needed to face.

Hell, I should know.

Leaning forward in my chair, I thought about the best way to respond. There was something about her that I craved to taste. I wanted to take her off the market before the sharks out in the club could have a chance to feel her, touch her, pleasure her. My heart beat faster. It was time to get my proposal out in the open. If she rejected me, I wasn't sure what I would to do. I hadn't feared rejection in years, and the thought unnerved me.

Stop being a pussy and put it out there.

In the extended silence, she didn't begin to fidget. She calmly sat there as if she embraced the silence. She took me by surprise.

I found it best to always turn the question back on the person until I knew what he or she wanted. Years of being deceived had taught me that. After being burned by my own asshole of a brother in the worst possible way, I always protected myself.

"Why do you ask?" I responded to her question about getting into the club so quickly.

Ainsley's delicate fingers grazed the vase. "From what I can tell, you run your business on stringent rules and guidelines. Everything seems to have order and a procedure. After being here tonight, it surprises me that I was moved ahead. From the background check you did on me, you know that I don't have a substantial bank account. I'm a simple college student with scholarships and a part-time job. When Nora told me I should try Club Envy, I put the thought aside for several weeks before applying. When I did apply, I thought it would take months. Then, to fast-track my application when you know I wouldn't be the most profitable business decision doesn't make sense to me."

She was good, really good. I wasn't ready to start answering her question on why I had fast-tracked her application without having a little more information about her. Her questionnaire only said that she was a business student but hadn't directly answered in detail on why she wanted to join the club. Normally, I rejected vague questionnaires, but I'd had to meet her. It was what she didn't say that peaked my curiosity.

"I know you're a business major, but what is your emphasis?"

Her pale blue eyes met mine again. "I think it's only fair you answer my question before I answer yours."

She held her ground, and it turned me on even more.

Putting my hands behind my head, I responded, "Fair enough. I'm intrigued by you, Ainsley. From the moment I saw your picture, I wanted to meet you."

The reflection from the light danced off the silver tinsel sporadically placed through her wig. Interlacing her fingers, she responded, "I changed my emphasis to analysis. That's why I've doubled up on summer classes in order to be sure to graduate on time."

That explained her observations of the finer details of everything and why the background check hadn't had that information.

Not giving her time to ask anything else, I went right to the heart of the matter. "Why do you want to be a member of Club Envy?"

She sat straighter in her chair. Her eyes became slightly sad. "I want to do something with no strings attached. I want to live, be a little rebellious, and be in the moment. I've always done things according to the rules. Nora and I were talking, and she suggested this place. I've never done anything like this before."

Her eyes flickered slightly to the left, an obvious tell, and I knew she wasn't telling me everything. Years of watching people had allowed me to read them better than most. I continued to watch her as she penetrated me with her pale blue gaze. I wondered if she meant it when she said she wanted no strings. I was able to do no strings. However, people said they were able to do it, but in reality, they were trying to tame the wild part within me that refused to settle down.

My dick ached to feel her, but I wouldn't go there if I thought us sleeping together was going to end up with fucking hearts being drawn around our names. Hearts and love were overrated. I should know since mine had been ripped out...gruesomely.

I hoped to be the in-between guy who worshiped her body the way it deserved to be touched.

We sat there in silence. She never tried to fill the uncomfortable gaps with conversation. Hell, at this point, it seemed like she could outlast me with the silence.

"What type of guy are you looking for?"

She crossed her legs, and my eyes were drawn again to

how toned they were.

"Before we get to that, I think we should discuss the membership fees and any additional rules or information that didn't come with the visitation packet. I don't want to waste your time if I can't afford to be here. In fact, after seeing the place tonight, I know I can't afford it. I hope I didn't waste your time."

Normally, the first questions from potential members were all related to sex and what the rules were. She was definitely different. If she did join, she'd be one of the younger women here, and fuck, she would get attention.

I needed to think about how I wanted to handle this. The thought of her walking out of Club Envy and wrapping her legs around someone else pissed me off. From the moment I'd approved her visitation, I had doubted she would be able to afford the fees, but I hadn't cared. The only possibility I had wondered about was that she might have a trust fund of some sort or an allowance from her parents.

Leaning forward, I thought about how to best approach Ainsley to be my new fuck buddy. From what I could sense, she wouldn't take handouts. My last partner, Sam, hadn't been able to afford this place either, and I had waived her membership fee for her exclusivity. I never shared partners. They were mine, and I was theirs until we parted ways.

I wanted Ainsley bad. The worst thing she could say at this point was no. *Shit, I want her to say yes.*

"Ainsley, I want to propose something. The rules are the same as the packet you received. The confidentiality agreements that you signed will still apply. All the STD tests you took will be put in your permanent file. If there's no change in the information you already provided we will use your existing questionnaire."

I paused, and Ainsley nodded.

"The reason I want to know what kind of guy you are looking for is because I want to be your partner while you're a member here. Some members want multiple partners, but that's not how I do it. We can discuss fees later, but it would be something within your budget. I don't want you to feel demeaned by my offer, but I think you and I can give each other what we need."

She played with a ring on her right index finger. She turned it around and around again while watching me. She crossed her legs in the other direction. By the slight squirm, I knew she was attracted to me. She was doing a damn fine job of masking it though. I sat there with no emotion on my face even though my dick jumped for joy at the thought that she wanted me inside her.

She moved her head to one side. "I'm not a submissive. I don't know the ins and outs of all that, but I know that's not for me."

She was all business, and I liked that about her. She wasn't doing all that lovey-dovey giggle shit.

I relaxed my posture in my seat since she hadn't said no. "I'm not asking for a submissive. We'll both give each other what we need on equal ground. We'll never do anything you are uncomfortable with."

She let my words absorb. My eyes kept going to her top. It was a low-scoop green silk shirt. The club was cold, and as she shifted, I could make out the faint outline of her nipples.

Ainsley also relaxed her posture slightly as she leaned back in the chair. "And what do you need, Adam?"

"To fuck you hard, countless times, to be buried so deep inside you while you scream in pleasure that's what I want out of this, Ainsley. Lust and sex, that's it."

I heard her intake of breath, and her eyes became clouded. She looked me over. She twirled her ring again. Her breathing was a tad quicker. To the normal observer, she would still appear unaffected.

"So, how does that work? We make appointments to have sex?"

Letting out a small breath, I knew I was making ground and could feel the deal getting closer to being finished. I was going to have to kiss her tonight before she left. I needed to touch her. And if I were lucky, I was going to take her against my office wall.

Keeping my voice calm, I responded, "More or less. We work out times to give each other pleasure, and then we return to our normal lives. There are no strings, no complications just sexual gratification. What do you think?"

She stood, tall and confident. Without wavering, she said, "Yes."

Ainsley

MY INSIDES FELT like they were shaking as I looked at Adam sitting behind his glass desk while I stood resolute after giving my answer. My mind was still trying to comprehend that I had agreed to a sexual arrangement for lust and sex only. This was definitely outside of the box for me, but I needed a change in pace, something different. Hopefully, this was the distraction I was looking for to move on from the breakup with my ex, Jarrod.

Jarrod and I had dated since I was a freshman in college. He was a business major also and had graduated this past summer. During his last semester of college, everything changed. Jarrod had begun trying to force me to reconcile with my father, whom I despised. When I'd refused, he'd become angry, broken up with me, and dated a good friend of mine whose father also had connections. I had later found out he had been cheating on me with my supposed friend. Even the promise of love would not send me to my father's doorstep.

Being used had hurt, but I would be okay. Jarrod hadn't been the one, and I thought I had known that all along during our relationship. It had been easy being with him at the time.

Sometimes what you think is the good choice ends up being a wolf in sheep's clothing.

Focusing back on the moment, I looked over at the man sitting behind the desk. Adam was attractive and had that bad-boy appeal to him with his tatted arms.

I wonder what tattoos are beneath his shirt.

His brown eyes were warm, and his dark hair was short but done in a messy way. I had never been with a bad boy. Normally, I always went for the safe guy. However, my last safe guy had turned out to be a power-seeking asshole.

From the moment I had seen Adam at the bar, a primal instinct in me had called out, *I want to have sex with him.*

Adam stood. He was in a tight-fitting blue T-shirt and jeans. The moment I'd said yes, something had changed in his eyes. The atmosphere had charged with a sexual energy. My insides wanted to combust, but I remained calm and collected on the outside. He walked over to me like a predator after his prey, and I stood firm. He wasn't going to feel like he had the upper hand on me. He stopped within inches of me. I slowly looked up and cocked one eyebrow.

"You have no idea how much we are going to enjoy each other, Ainsley. I'm going to make you feel pleasure beyond your wildest dreams and I'm going to touch your body like it deserves." As he spoke, his breath invaded my senses.

I took a shallow breath, hoping he didn't see how his words affected me. "I've never done anything like this. I don't know what the next step is."

"Let your body be your guide."

I licked my lips, and Adam's head slowly moved toward mine. His eyes searched mine in what I assumed was to see if there was any hesitation on my part. To give him my answer, I moved my head up toward his.

Hell, I agreed to have sex with this man with no strings attached, so what is a little kissing at this point?

I was nervous since I had never done anything like this before. Hoping he couldn't see it or sense my feelings, I tried to stay as calm as possible on the outside. His eyes continued to dart back and forth across mine. We were mere inches apart as I could feel his breath on my lips. My body wanted to close the gap, but I refused to appear desperate. I was going to make him kiss me first.

The anticipation kept building as we stayed locked in this position, not moving.

"I'm going to kiss you, Ainsley. I want to taste you."

Adam closed the gap and pressed his lips against mine. One hand went to my hip, and the other went to the lower part of my neck. There was heat in his touch, and it warmed my veins. I opened up to him the moment his tongue pressed against my lips, and I let my body take over.

In that instance, everything changed as our kissing became hungrier. I wanted to claw my way inside of him, and he seemed to feel the same way. He pulled me closer to his body, to bring me flush against him. Both of his hands went to my ass as he walked us backward until I was against the wall. Something inside of me broke free as I became bold and wrapped one of my legs around his waist, causing my skirt to ride up indecently high.

He groaned in approval. He backed away slightly, putting

space between us, as his hand went to the place right above my knee and slowly traveled up to my inner thigh. When he reached the bottom of my skirt, he was just inches from my core. My hips rocked into his hand. Adam leaned back into me and we kissed like wild animals.

Adam's fingers reached the edge of my panties and dipped beneath. I let out a small whimper as someone knocked on the door. I disengaged, but Adam pressed his body against mine, keeping me still.

"They'll leave. We need each other, Ainsley. Please don't stop this."

"I want this, too."

He pushed his lips back to mine, and I was lost in the moment. Adam pushed his finger inside me, and I pressed against the palm of his hand for more friction. My body tingled and heated from his touch.

From the door came another knock and a voice. "Adam? Are you in there? I found something. You aren't picking up your phone."

Considering I was in this position with an almost complete stranger and someone potentially coming into the room, I gently pushed against Adam's chest. He backed away a couple of inches, but he held on to me until I was steady on my feet.

His eyes searched mine as he called out loudly with a slight agitation lacing his voice. "Just a second, Brandt."

From the information he had shared a few minutes before, Brandt was his partner. Brandt sounded like he had a barely-there British accent.

My body was still worked up as I gazed into Adam's eyes. I was shocked I had let myself go like that.

Adam gave me a soft kiss. "I'll be right back. We're dealing with a problem. I can't wait to continue this." He gestured between the two of us.

I was a little breathless at this point as I melted from the sweet gesture of the kiss. "Take your time."

Adam's brows crinkled, but then he strolled confidently toward the door. Looking down, I saw that my skirt was above my panties, and I quickly smoothed it out.

Oh my, I melted at the kiss. I need to get a grip on this situation. This is a pleasure-only situation.

My mind had a hard time reconciling the charming, tender side of Adam, like the kiss he had given me, with the no-attachment relationship he adamantly wanted.

No, it's what we both want.

Adam cracked the door open enough to talk through. His arm muscles stiffened and his voice became rougher as he spoke to Brandt. I walked back over to the chair and grabbed my purse. This would convey the message I was leaving without me being rude. As much as I wanted to roll around with this guy, I wanted to be an official paying member. After the confusing feelings I'd felt from the kiss, I needed to make sure a business transaction took place in order for me to keep it all compartmentalized.

This is pleasure only, not a relationship.

Adam closed the door, turned toward the wall where we had been, and then whipped back around to where I was, surprise evident on his face. "Are you leaving?" He sounded shocked. "You don't have to leave."

Standing tall and taking a deep breath, trying to squelch my desires, I responded clinically, "Yes. Will you be here tomorrow? I can come at eight, if that works. Before we start being each other's pleasure buddies, I want to be an official member."

Adam swallowed, and I glanced down at his crotch. There

was definitely a bulge going on behind the placket of his denim pants. Looks like we were both going to end up having to take care of business on our own tonight. He walked toward his desk, and then he stopped and looked at me. I gulped. He went to speak, but then didn't and continued toward his desk. I turned and followed his movement. His masculine cologne still invaded my senses from where we'd touched earlier. Barely glancing my way, he pulled out a drawer and then a white band.

I remembered from the packet that a white band meant the member was taken and exclusively with someone. They were off-limits like the black bands for visitors. The sight made me excited, but I pushed it down.

This is pleasure only.

He walked toward me. "Will one hundred dollars a month for your fee work?"

I protested, but he cut me off. "Ainsley, yes, the fee is much higher than that normally, but any exclusive partner for Brandt or me is generally free. However, I have a feeling that you won't accept a free membership even though I don't want to take your money."

Adam stopped right in front of me. We spent so much time looking into each other's eyes, trying to get a glimpse of what the other person was thinking. There was no way I would take a free membership as that would make me feel cheap.

"I'll bring a check tomorrow when I come at eight. Is there anything else I need to bring?"

Adam's brows creased again, but a smile formed as he held up the white bracelet for me to take. "Be sure to wear this when you come. It says you're taken and will keep anyone from approaching you. I don't do relationships, but I sure as hell don't share either."

I took the bracelet and gave him back the black one. "Does this mean that you won't be sleeping with anyone else while this arrangement lasts? I won't share either. You'll find that I'm not a pushover, Adam. I like an even playing field."

His grin grew wider. "I won't be fucking anyone else besides you. I'm hard as a rock from thinking about how many different ways we are going to have each other."

I liked playful, hot Adam. The way he threw sex out there so casually turned me on since it had always been more clinical in my past relationships.

"Good to know. I can't wait to start this little adventure. I'd better head out. It looks like you have a problem to take care of, and I have a paper to finish up for school." My voice was steady and unaffected even though my body felt like it was hanging on by a thread.

Adam put his arm on the small of my back. I wanted to look at the intricate details of his tattoos that encased his arms, but I only glanced at them prior to looking ahead. The words *Carpe Diem* were done on the inside of his right bicep that I had seen earlier while we were in the Afterburn room. I wondered what the story was behind all his different tats.

As we made our way to the door, Adam talked, filling the silence. "When you get here tomorrow, if I'm not at the side entrance, have Trigger find me."

"The guy who was at the door with the blond hair when I came in with Nora?"

"That would be him. He'll be aware you're coming. Don't enter without him or me. I need to make sure everyone knows you're mine."

Those last words were exactly the reason I needed to be sure to pay for a membership. The word *mine* had several meanings. I had a feeling the definition I was used to attaching was not the same as Adam's. He opened the door for me, and we entered the sex club again.

As the hour grew later, I could tell things got a little steamier out in the open. Couples were now cozied up on the couches, whispering to each other with hands roaming. The interior designer had done a good job of setting the mood as the iridescent lights cast faint hints of color on the frosted glass. Low, mysterious music played that had me wanting to make out with Adam.

Nora was behind the bar in full bartender mode. She saw me and gave me the call-me signal. I gave a little nod her way, confirming I would. I loved Nora's free spirit and how she always went with the way the wind blew. Some people thought she was a little much, but she was one of my best friends. Nora was about my size, but she had enough gusto to seem like a linebacker on a football team. Her blonde hair was done up messy, but I could still see the streaks of purple that she had added last week. She would change her hair color frequently, depending on her mood.

Nora and I had met at the library where I worked part-time. A few years ago, I had helped her find some books she was looking for, and from there, we'd become friends over time. It took me a while to open up to people and trust them. Nora was the most loyal friend I had ever had besides my mother. Plus, she never pushed me to talk if I didn't want to. She liked to keep her feelings below the surface, too, not exposed for all to see what was going on.

Adam and I approached the door, and Trigger gave me a slight smile.

I said, "Night."

He responded, "Night."

I figured Adam would say good-bye to me at the door, but

he continued out into the night.

I broke the silence between us. "I'm in the lot across the street. You don't have to walk me to my car." Escorting me to my vehicle had more of a date feeling than was necessary given our arrangement.

Adam's hand flexed against my back. "I know. It's something I want to do. With the drunk crowd from the bar area, I don't want you running into any problems. Just because we aren't dating doesn't mean I don't want to make sure you're safe."

My head hurt from the conflicting statements. Those were things a boyfriend would say.

Focus on the facts, Ainsley. "Thanks. Do you have many problems on the bar side?"

We crossed the street to my old silver Camry. It wasn't new and flashy, but at least the car was mine. My mom had cosigned the loan for me as I'd refused to have anything to do with my dad.

Adam still hadn't answered my question as we made it to my car.

He turned me and leaned toward me, causing my back to touch the driver's side door. "Normally, no, we don't have many problems. You're gorgeous, Ainsley, and I don't want you to be harassed by some horny ass who's had too much to drink. You're exclusively mine, and I protect what's mine. I run a tight establishment here, but that doesn't mean sometimes people don't step over the line, especially where alcohol is involved. Always make sure I know when you're coming, so someone can be on the lookout for you, okay?"

What the hell am I supposed to say to that?

I reminded myself that he wasn't the bring-you-flowers kind of guy. We were using each other's bodies, and that was

25

it. I guessed that didn't imply he had to be a total asshole. He could still be a gentleman.

"Okay. I'll let you know prior to coming over. I'll need your cell phone number. Or do you want me to call the club?"

His fingers came underneath my chin, and he raised it until my eyes met his. "I'll text you with it in a bit. I'll see you tomorrow. If you can come sooner than eight, then text me. I'll clear my schedule for you."

"I'll try. I don't get off from the library until five, and then I'm helping a friend out for an hour, so I won't be available until a little after six."

Without warning, his lips came down on mine, and he kissed me again. My body automatically reacted to him. I arched into him as the need from earlier came back full force. Adam's hand went to my hips, and he pushed his erection against me. I was two seconds away from asking him to take me back inside when his phone vibrated. He pulled back from the kiss and leaned his forehead against mine. We were both slightly out of breath.

"Fuck. I need to get back into the club. I can't wait to spend time with you tomorrow, Ainsley. It's all I'll think about until then."

I smiled big. "Me, too. Good luck with your problem."

Adam stepped away and I opened up the car door.

"I'll see you tomorrow," he said.

I gave him a shy smile and said, "Tomorrow."

He closed my door and jogged back across the street. He stopped and turned around as I cranked my car. I pulled out of the parking lot, and I could see that he continued to watch me until I was no longer visible to him. This type of arrangement was definitely foreign to me. He was thoughtful, and I believed he was going to be a generous lover. The problems were making sure I kept it businesslike and didn't read too much into the small gestures. My heart had already been bruised from being used and cheated on by Jarrod. Now I needed to make sure I kept it safe because Adam was the more dangerous type to have feelings for. He could permeate my mind, my every thought, my existence.

I reminded myself, *he was a lay. We're pleasure buddies. This is no-attachment sex.*

That was what I kept telling myself as I made my way home to my apartment.

Adam

AFTER I WATCHED Ainsley's brake lights disappear, I turned and went into the club.

Fuck me, I want her.

The way she'd responded to me as I'd kissed and touched her was incredible.

Shit, I need to stop thinking about her.

I never thought about a woman for this long after I had sex with her, and I hadn't even had Ainsley yet. She was invading all my thoughts and I'd have her tomorrow night. Right now, I needed to get my head in the game and focus on the problem at hand the picture-taking prick.

I walked back to the door and spoke to Trigger. "Let Brandt know I'm on my way."

"Will do, Adam."

Trigger pulled out his walkie-talkie when I stopped and turned toward him again. I looked around and noticed a few people were standing about.

"The new girl will be back tomorrow. Don't let anyone lay a hand on her. She has a white bracelet. She's going to be anonymous and hasn't picked her name yet."

He gave me a smirk. "I figured you'd end up wanting her. I'll make sure either Snake or I have her until you're able to get up here. She's a hot piece of ass. Hell, I was going to go after her the minute that black bracelet came off."

"Don't, Trigger. Don't ever talk about her like that, or you and I are going to have problems. She's taken. End of fucking story." The growl in my voice was evident.

Trigger raised his hands in a surrendering motion. "I meant no disrespect, man. It won't happen again. I know the rules."

I nodded and then made my way back to the security office where we kept all the monitors. My mind worked on overdrive as I thought about my outburst of possessive behavior. I scrubbed a hand down my face.

Why the hell did that comment from Trigger bother me? I need to figure it out.

As I walked through the door, I saw Brandt sitting at the computer desk. He practically lived in this office, refusing to use his own. A video was pulled up on the large screen mounted on the wall. Front and center on the screen was some fucker with a black masquerade mask.

"Is this the asshole who's causing us shit?"

Brandt turned my way. The ladies liked him a lot, but he had kept to himself. I thought they liked his bad-boy appeal with his messy, long blond hair. He had a few tats, not as many as me, but they were evident.

He cracked his neck from side to side. "What's eating you? You look like you've got a stick shoved up your ass. Did that new girl turn you down?"

What is wrong with everyone tonight? First, Trigger, and now, Brandt is getting all insightful about my sex life.

I went and stood in front of the screen and continued looking at the man in the mask.

I need another drink.

"Ainsley's claimed, Brandt. Quit dicking around, and tell me what you found."

Brandt slightly chuckled from behind me, and it pissed me the hell off. Ainsley knocked me off balance, and these bastards could sense my weakness. At least I'd be the one pleasuring her, and that was all that mattered. Anyone who wanted to give me a hard time could fuck off.

After some clicking of the keyboard keys, the video played.

Brandt explained what he had found. "Whoever this asshole is, he didn't take his mask off the entire night. I've got the footage pulled up to where we can see him taking the picture underneath his suit jacket with what looks like a high tech little camera."

Whoever this prick was, he had taken the picture subtly. I would have never noticed it if I were doing surveillance. The camera barely stuck out from this angle. It wasn't uncommon for some members to wear masks to keep up with the fantasy in the club, but they had to log it into the system when they arrived.

Walking up closer to the video screen, I asked, "Did you see how this asshole got past security?"

The screen went black, and another image was cued up.

Brandt explained, "I think he was connected to Roach.

Watch this, and see for yourself."

The next video played. Roach, the security guard who had quit without notice, checked in everyone before they were buzzed into the actual club at the main entrance on the sex-club side. Roach had never sat right with me, but it had been a favor to Brandt, who tried to help a friend. Roach had two kids, and had no job and needed something steady. Brandt had hoped the security position would help keep Roach out of drugs, so he could stay with his kids.

Everyone needs a second chance, Adam. I know I did, Brandt had said to me.

I had capitulated to Brandt's request, but those words of agreement burned like acid now since I went against my gut. Roach had passed all the normal background checks, but something had rubbed me wrong about the guy.

Next, the unidentified asshole in the black mask walked up. Roach gave a slight nod of his head and buzzed him through no paperwork, no sign in.

My eyes darted back to Brandt. We'd had several heated disagreements about why Roach shouldn't be hired.

Hell, the nickname he had given himself was enough of a damn clue to me.

My gut had told me Roach would be a problem, but I'd ignored it for Brandt. Now, because of it, we had a problem on our hands.

Brandt put his hands up and looked contrite. He knew I had gone out on a limb for him. "Hey, man, I get it. I'm sorry. I thought he wanted a fresh start, and I couldn't turn someone away. If everyone had turned me away after everything I did, there's no telling where I would be. I'm fucking pissed that I asked you for a favor, and he backstabbed me. This is my mess, so I'll clean it up."

I looked up at the ceiling for a second. "I know, Brandt. I get it. I think we should talk to Hampton first. The moment we play our hands, it's all out there. For now, Roach and his accomplice have no idea that we know what they've done. Let's see how many times this bastard got into our club and who all was here those nights. We need to determine what kind of liability we're looking at."

Hampton did all our background checks for the club. He was also a private investigator.

"Sounds good, Adam. I'll have Hampton investigate Roach deeper, and we'll see what turns up. Roach's exgirlfriend picked up his kids and moved to Florida, so I'll have Hampton check to see if he's joined them. In the meantime, I'll start combing through the footage and let you know what I find." Brandt ran his hand through his hair.

He was as pissed as I was. He just didn't show it like I did.

I walked out of the room. "Thanks, man. I'm going to go check out the bar side. The Thrillhammers are playing tonight, and the crowd gets a little wild every time they play."

He yelled after me. "Take a damn walkie-talkie with you, and I'll let you know if I find anything."

I went to the door and passed by the walkie-talkie basket. *I hate those damn things.* They were a distraction as I worked. On one or two occasions, the button had been held down while someone was getting a piece of ass. I didn't need to hear that shit.

I called over my shoulder, "Call my cell phone."

As I closed the door, I could hear Brandt chuckling.

Bastard.

I made my way to the only internal door connecting the sex club with the bar. The main outside entrances were on opposite sides of the building. Only Brandt, Trigger, Snake and I had the key that opened the door up into our bar side office. This go-between office stayed locked. We didn't want drunkards accidentally wandering into the sex club, and it was damn near impossible to get in on the sex-club side unless a slimly bastard like Roach let the person in.

As I made my way into my other office, I locked the door behind me. The pulse of the music vibrated through the walls. I could hear the crowd going wild as The Thrillhammers went into their opening song "JESCO." It was going to get crazy out there tonight. We had hired them about six months ago. Since then, their popularity had exploded, and they could pack a house.

I left the connecting office and locked that door behind me before making my way out to the bar area. The bar was decorated how Brandt and I liked. Old street signs and neon beer signs filled the rustic-metal walls. It was a fun bar with a dance floor.

As I entered the bar area, I made eye contact with Chris, the guitarist for The Thrillhammers. He gave me a nod that told me all was good. I walked toward the main entrance to check on everything. Our bouncer, Jethro, was a bald heavy-set man. Sitting on a stool, he looked like a giant teddy bear, but that motherfucker could throw down if he needed to. Jethro had been with us since we had opened the place nearly five years ago.

I walked up and slapped him on the back. "Hey there, man. Anything happening?"

Jethro rubbed his slick head and said, "Nah, it's all good so far, man. We're at ninety percent capacity. I'll start the waiting line when we get to ninety-five."

I slapped him on the back again. "Thanks. Let me know if

you need anything."

Jethro nodded as a couple walked up to him with their IDs. I made my way to the bar as The Thrillhammers were playing "Jesco White, where are you tonight?" and working up the crowd.

Jenney, another employee who had been with Brandt and me since the beginning, worked behind the bar tonight. She danced with the beat of the song, her strawberry-blonde hair bouncing around. When she saw me, she grabbed a Guinness. She popped the top off and handed it to me. "Here you go, Adam. It's a full house tonight."

I tilted my beer toward her. "Thanks, Jenney. It's because The Thrillhammers agreed to do a midweek set versus their normal weekend ones."

She tapped the bar twice as she called out, "I like it. Means the tips are going to be flowing in."

Jenney shimmied over to her next customer, and I laughed. She was a funny girl full of spitfire. I respected her as she never tried to cross the employer-employee boundaries.

I dragged a hand down my face and headed back to my office. I was tired, and I wanted nothing but to be buried in Ainsley.

Shit, why can't I stop thinking about her?

This had been a long day, and I was ready for it to be over.

After making sure I locked each door, I entered the sex-club side again.

I peeked back in the security office where Brandt sat, watching videos.

Brandt turned as I spoke, "I'll be in my office. I need to get Ainsley set up in the system. She's requested to be anonymous, so I'll let you know what name she chooses."

A smile spread across his face, and then he pointed to the screens. "I bet it's eating you alive with how much she's affected you. I saw all I needed to see to know it's true even if you deny it."

I flipped him the bird and walked toward my office. Low mood music played, which made my dick ache for someone I hadn't even had yet.

Shit.

I took a seat behind my desk and grabbed my phone from my pocket. I pulled up Ainsley's number from her file and texted her.

Me: It's Adam. Did you make it home okay?

She responded almost immediately, which made me smile.

Ainsley: I did, and now I have your number. I hope your problem is getting solved.
Me: It's ongoing. I'll see you at eight. If you can come sooner, let me know.
Ainsley: Will do. I'll see you tomorrow, PB.
Me: PB?
Ainsley: Pleasure Buddy.

I chuckled. *She was ever surprising.*

Me: I can't wait. I'll do my best to fulfill that nickname.
Ainsley: You'd better, or I'll have to nickname you DB.
Me: DB?
Ainsley: Defective Buddy. We need to work on your acronyms.

I took a swig of beer that Nora had brought me, and nearly choked.

Me: Challenge accepted.
Ainsley: Good. I'll see you tomorrow. I have to finish my paper. Night.
Me: Night.

I frowned at the phone. Part of me was disappointed that she had ended the text. Being each other's fuck buddies didn't mean I couldn't be friendly with her.

Being comfortable with each other only increases the moments of pleasure.

Shit, I sound like some fruitcake talk show.

Taking another swig of beer, I looked at the mountain of paperwork I needed to complete.

Instead of working, I opened Ainsley's file again. She was beautiful, and I couldn't wait to see what she looked like without the wig and additional makeup. I pulled up the computer to make sure I still had a room reserved. Brandt and I always kept at least one room reserved for our use, and we'd release it the day of if it wasn't needed. As of late, I hadn't seen any action, and my dick was ready for it.

Tomorrow night could not get here soon enough. Forcing thoughts of Ainsley aside, I closed the file and pulled everything I could find on Roach from my files.

Ainsley

I TURNED ON the radio, trying to calm myself as I made my way to the club. I wasn't a virgin, but tonight felt different. I felt like I was about to embark on a journey, for better or for worse. I hoped it wasn't the latter. The time was ten till eight, and I was going to be a few minutes late. Nora had a younger sister, Emilyn, who I adored and helped watch some days when their mother wasn't able to get off work and Nora had to bartend at the sex club. Between Nora's school tuition and their mother's medical bills, I knew things were tight, and I did what I could to help.

At the stoplight, I texted Adam.

Me: Hey, I'll be there after eight. My obligation ran long. Sorry.

Adam: It's fine. Thanks for letting me know. I'll be out-side, waiting for you.

Me: Okay, PB or DB. Your name will be decided at the end of the evening.

Adam: Oh, it'll be APB!

Me: We shall see.

Adam: Don't you want to know what the A stands for?

Me: Awful?

Adam: No! Get your ass here, and we'll find out.

Me: It's on its way.

I smiled at the thought of him making up acronyms. I considered the possibilities amazing, awesome. My mind drew a blank at other A words. For some reason, creating a semi-friendly rapport helped me bridge some semblance of knowing him prior to having sex with him. I had never had unconnected sex before with a stranger, and I wondered if I'd freeze in the moment. My mind needed to connect the dots and somehow make it non-prostitute like.

At five after eight, I pulled into the parking lot and looked one last time in the mirror.

My pink wig from last Halloween and my heavier makeup helped hide what I looked like. When I looked back out the front windshield, I saw Adam jogging out the door and across the street to me. He had on a white branded T-shirt and jeans. My mind tried to make my body get out of the car, but I couldn't stop staring at his body as he made it to my window. I wanted to trace every tattoo on his arms and figure out what each meant.

The moment our eyes met, we smiled at each other, and that small gesture helped ease my nerves.

We do have some sort of connection—physical at least.

On the outside, I knew I looked calm and collected. It was how I had survived all those years of hearing my dad beat my mother from down the hall. Each night, I would dread when the sun went down, wondering if that night would be a silent night or one filled with muffled cries and screams. After the beatings, my dad would always come to my room to see if I was awake. I would lay there, motionless, giving the impression I was sound asleep, fearing what would happen if he thought I was awake. Then, each morning, my mother and father would pretend to be a happy family. My father would tell us what his plans were for the day as my mother would limp around the kitchen. Finally, out of the blue, my dad had found greener pastures after receiving a huge promotion at work. He'd left us for a younger woman, and I was grateful for it because I hated him. I never felt weaker and more pathetic in my life for not fighting, protecting, or standing up for my mom. It was an eternal regret I would carry forever. My mom still didn't know that I was aware what had happened to her all those years.

Adam opened my car door, and I stepped out.

His eyes shot down to my wrist to see the white band. "You remembered."

"Of course I did." I dug through my purse for the check I had written out prior to leaving my apartment. Pulling it out, I handed it to Adam. "Here's my first month's membership fee. Do I need to sign anything else?"

Adam looked at the check in my hand with almost contempt. Keeping a passive face in place, I pushed it forward slightly. He went to speak and then closed his mouth. We were in yet another silent standoff.

I am not going to lose this round.

We stared at each other for a minute. The silence didn't

39

bother me like most people. I embraced it. Silent nights had meant that my father left my mother alone and wasn't hurting her.

Adam grabbed the check and stuffed it in the front pocket of his jeans. His chocolate eyes searched mine as he said, "You're officially a member. Are you ready?"

"Lead the way, Pleasure Buddy. I hope I don't have to re-name you."

He chuckled. "It's highly unlikely."

I smiled, and the inner tension within me lessened. He grabbed my hand and walked me to the side door that Trigger guarded. It was Wednesday night, and the place was busier than it had been last night.

As we approached the door, Trigger gave us both a nod. "All's good, Adam. I'll let Brandt know if I run into any problems."

Adam nodded. "Thanks, Trigger."

I glanced over into the bar area where some people were making out while others were drinking. One guy had his hand creeping up a woman's leg so I glanced away. The sensual music had my pulse climbing, and I looked back. We had stopped without me realizing it. Although watching the couple touch each other felt like I was invading their privacy, I wanted to see how far they would go in public. My eyes were drawn to the couple as the man's hand drew closer and closer to the edge of the woman's skirt.

Adam's mouth was at my ear as he whispered, "Does that turn you on, Ainsley?"

The sensual tone in his voice had me swallowing hard and closing my eyes briefly. I never knew that would be a turn-on as Adam had said those things to me. Feeling off-kilter, I didn't respond. Instead, I turned and looked up into his eyes.

We both stared at each other again. That seemed to be something we did when neither of us knew what to say.

What does my lack of a response say to him?

Without another word, he tightened his grip on mine and led the way to the exclusive rooms at the back of the club. We came to the same room I'd seen last night, and I read the door again.

Adam's hand reached for the door, and then he turned back to me. "If anything makes you feel uncomfortable, Ainsley, I want you to tell me, and it stops. We are equals. There's never any pressure to finish anything we start. Understood?"

I squeezed his hand. "Yes, I understand."

Adam nodded and took me inside the room. The room had changed subtly. Last night, the sheets had appeared to be a sort of red cotton, but tonight, they were black silk. The lights were turned down.

The inquisitive side of me came out. "Did you have the sheets changed to silk?"

Adam let go of my hand and turned me to face him. "Yes, I did. I think you'll like how the silk feels against your skin as we fuck each other senseless." He took a step closer. "Ainsley, I need you to be honest with me. How adventurous have you been in the bedroom prior to tonight?"

A slight blush crept up my face.

Hell, he's about to see everything, so what's the point in being modest?

He'd be able to tell I was not adventurous in my sex life the moment we slept together. "I've had sex, and I use a vibrator. I've never used other sex paraphernalia."

"That's all I needed to know. We'll take this slow."

"I'm a big girl. You don't have to treat me with kid gloves. I'll tell you if it gets to be too much."

This was beginning to feel more clinical, causing my internal nerves to rise. I had to have some type of connection. I wasn't a receptacle. I shifted on my feet and played with the ring on my right hand.

Adam slowly walked toward me. "Ainsley, let your body take over. Stop thinking so much. This is about two people enjoying each other without all the other bullshit in life. We are about to learn each other intimately. All the other shit doesn't matter. Just focus on how your body wants me because I sure as hell want you."

His hands went to the top button of my purple fitted blouse, and my breathing became slightly deeper.

Keep it together, Ainsley.

Maintaining eye contact, he undid the top button, and my mind eased … a little.

He went to the next button. "Is this okay, Ainsley?"

"Yes." My words were soft but confident as I kept eyes focused on his. *I want to try this.*

He continued undoing one button at a time. Reaching the last button of my untucked blouse hanging over my A-line black skirt, he pushed open my shirt and exposed my bra. I had specifically chosen this black lace bra as it was one of the nicest ones I had.

Adam groaned in appreciation as he slipped the shirt off my shoulders. "You are beautiful. Do you want to take your wig off?"

I shook my head. "Leave it on."

His brows crinkled for a moment before he touched me at the top of my bra. He dipped one finger under to feel my breast, and I gave a small whimper as I closed my eyes, trying to let my body take over. My sex clenched in anticipation. A finger trailed between my breasts to my navel, leaving a tingling trail. When he made it to the top of my skirt, he traced the edge around the back until his hand found the zipper in the back and dragged it down. My skirt lowered to the floor, and I stepped out of it. Adam stepped back, and my eyes opened as my body lost the connection of his touch.

His hands went to the bottom of his T-shirt. When I walked forward, he stopped, and I touched the hem. For a brief moment, I closed my eyes, summoning my inner sexual being. Next, I opened my eyes and pulled his shirt up. I focused on the skin I exposed, feeling his muscles moving under my touch. Below his navel, there were no tattoos. I continued pushing his shirt up. As he lifted his arms and helped me to get it over his head, I saw that his sleeved tats on both of his arms continued on to the top part of his chest on each side. The inquisitive side of me wanted to ask him all about them, but I might potentially lose my nerve if I stopped now. Instead, my fingers trailed back down his stomach to the top of his pants where I unbuttoned them. Adam's hands came on top of mine as he helped me push them off his waist. He kicked off his shoes, and then his jeans were discarded to the side. We both stood there, looking at each other. He was gorgeous and toned. I let my desire for him invade every part of my brain, consuming all my thoughts.

His raspy voice broke the quietness of the room. "Are you ready, Ainsley? You can stop this anytime you need to. We'll start off slow. Focus on the sensation."

I wanted to get this going before my mind had too much time to overthink anything. Looking Adam straight in the eyes, I responded, "I'm ready. I'll tell you if I want to stop. I'm not a pushover."

His hands reached for my hips and brought me to him. I could feel his erection against my stomach. His mouth came down toward me. The moment his lips touched mine, any reservation I had about this arrangement vanished, and my body came alive, like it had last night. All thoughts evaporated as he consumed me. He turned us and walked backward. I felt silk against my upper legs and knew we were at the tall bed.

Adam's tongue expertly stroked mine, and my hands went to his hair. He nipped my lip, and a moan escaped without warning. My body felt as if it were on fire. His hands went to my back and unsnapped my bra. Breaking the kiss, he stepped back and brought my bra down. I took a deep breath, which caused my breasts to rise.

"I can't wait. You're a fucking dream come true," he whispered. "First, I want you to touch yourself."

I froze. I had never masturbated in front of anyone before. Getting myself off was always done in the privacy of my bedroom in the dark. Without a word, hands went to my black lace boy shorts, and he shimmied them down my legs.

"I don't think—"

He leaned back in and took one of my nipples into his mouth. He sucked it to a point where pleasure mixed with pain, and I had never felt that sensation before. His hand came on top of mine. My mind was a haze as it guided down and fingers brushed over my sensitive areas.

My breath came faster. My mind only sought to increase the sensations of pleasure.

Adam switched nipples, repeating the intense sucking, and pressed my hands harder into me. My hips flexed into the pressure seeking more. I threw my head back and rubbed myself with abandonment.

"Oh, Adam."

My hand was pulled away seconds before I would have orgasmed. Irritation built inside me. My mouth was about to let loose on Adam as he looked at me with hunger in his eyes.

"Lean back on the bed, baby. I want you coming for the first time on my mouth. There will be plenty of time for me to watch you finger-fuck yourself."

Adam's words caused my anger to fade and be replaced by the fire that had tried to consume me before. I did as he asked. Soft silky material grazed my bare skin. Adam knelt before me, and his hands spread my legs open. Adam devoured me and my legs spread open without hesitation.

"That's right, Ainsley. Focus on how good my tongue is going to feel pressed against you."

Adam's head moved between my legs and his warm tongue found my sex. Any reservation I may have had about this arrangement left in that moment. The heat of his mouth combined with the pressure of his tongue on my clit had me breathless.

He pulled back. Right as I was about to scream at him in frustration, he returned to my core. His tongue did a circular thing that had ecstasy engulfing me as he made me come.

"Did that feel good, Ainsley?"

"Yes…"

My body had needed a good orgasm for a while. It unwound itself from all the pent-up tension I hadn't realized I had. My mind was fuzzy as Adam stood and removed his boxers. His erection sprang free, and with the size of him, I knew it was going to feel unbelievable when he entered me. He came over on top of me, and our mouths found each other again. The silk felt fantastic as he scooted us up the bed. The sensation was indescribable. I was lost as he kept bumping the tip of his cock on my clit. My body was ready for another orgasm. My legs instinctively wrapped around him, and I tried to pull him inside me. Adam's arms left my back when we stopped moving, and I vaguely heard a ripping sound above my head. The way his tongue traced the veins of my neck had me bowing off the bed.

"More. I want more, Adam."

"You're about to get more."

Next, I felt the tip of his erection at my sex. My mind came back to life as I said, "Condom?"

Adam's mouth was at my ear. "It's already on. Never worry about me using protection. I always will. Lose yourself in this, Ainsley. Let me take care of you."

His words touched something deep within me. His hardened length breached my entrance, and my body tried to pull him inside me. Adam pushed in slowly, and we both made noises of pure satisfaction.

"Shit, you feel fantastic."

I brought his mouth back down to mine as I said, "You, too."

He moved, and my hips rocked into him for maximum friction. The climb was incredible as he thrust in and out, quicker and harder with each penetration into my body. My hands went to his shoulders, and I held on as the feeling of my orgasm spread through my body. Adam sunk into me one more time as he reached his own climax. We were both panting hard as he rolled off to the side. I was barely aware of him taking the condom off and tossing it somewhere beside the bed as I came back down to reality.

Adam covered our bodies up to our hips with a silk blanket. I needed that escape more than I'd known. I loved how free this felt. Everything I had ever done in the sexual realm had been straitlaced while I was in a relationship. Having sex with nearly a complete stranger was liberating and totally against my normally analytical brain. As the fog cleared, I rolled onto my side, pulled the blanket up above my breasts, and looked him in the eyes. He mirrored my position, and we stared at each other for a bit. Adam seemed content to lay here, which made me smile.

After some time, I broke the silence. "Can I ask you some questions?"

He looked at my face and then gave me a grin in return. "Of course."

My mind tried to ensure that I kept my distance. To avoid developing feelings for Adam, especially after sleeping with him, I needed parameters to work within. I decided to go for the straightforward approach, like I generally did when I was curious. It seemed to serve me better.

"I don't know what I'm supposed to do after we have sex. Do we do it once, and I leave? I know this isn't a relationship, and I don't want my questions to make it seem like I think it is. I truly understand this is a consensual pleasuring session. At the same time though, if we both get up and go to separate corners until we have a desire again, it seems too detached. Now that we've had sex, I guess I don't know how the arrangement works between those times. Does that make sense?"

Adam appeared to be thinking about his response as his brows crinkled. His voice was low when he spoke, "I under-

47

stand what you're saying, and I should have explained it more thoroughly. I've been dying to get my cock in you, and that's all I could focus on. When we are in the club, I will treat you as if we are together. It's a buildup of feelings. If I didn't tease you and bring anticipation into the picture, the orgasm would be mediocre at best. Most of those desires—the want, the lust, the need—come from the foreplay. It's all an essential part of making the moment when we join our bodies the best feeling possible. We were both still worked up from last night."

"However, when either of us leaves the parking lot, the attachment we show each other in the club becomes nonexistent, but the exclusivity part stays intact. If we keep sex to the club, then it stays in that frame of mind when you walk through those doors. If I saw you, let's say, at a grocery store, we would say hello and continue on our way unless we wanted to talk about our next meeting at the club. There would be no foreplay outside of the club. Does that help?"

My mind thought about each sentence as I assimilated it all. "Yes, I think so. It's different, but I think I understand it. Basically, in here, we are in a committed relationship, for lack of a better term—meaning we can flirt, play, and have fun with each other, but all the serious things in life are checked at the door. Outside of the club, we are acquaintances. Is that right?"

Adam smiled. "It is. We give each other the benefits of a relationship without all the drama and attachment. We'll continue to learn each other and get more comfortable with what the other likes."

I turned over, looking at the rest of the room, and the sheet exposed my back. Adams fingers lightly traced unidentifiable shapes across my exposed skin causing a satiated warmth to spread through my body. There was a chaise lounge, what looked to be a sex swing with straps hanging from the ceiling, a large beanbag, and a chest of drawers.

"Will we use more of what's in this room? Or will we only have sex in the bed?" The longing in my voice wasn't lost on me. A part of me apparently wanted to explore my sexual side.

Adam's hand crept down to my hip bone and then made its way down to my clit under the sheet. He scooted closer until his body was against mine and his lips were at my ear. "Ainsley, I'm going to fuck you so many ways, and it won't just be in the bed."

He expertly touched me, and I closed my eyes as I moved my hips to gain some friction.

"Would you like that, Ainsley?"

Little moans escaped me as he pressed against me harder, delaying my response.

I tried to focus. "Yes. Yes, I want that."

His voice was a low, sexy growl. "I want to take you from behind."

My body responded as I turned to lay on my stomach. Moving behind me, I heard a foil packet tear. Adam raised my hips and entered me in one movement. The way he moved in and out felt like my world was being altered by something amazing. It was unbelievable. His thumb moved back to my clit, and I bucked at the feeling. *Oh, that felt good to push back as he pushed in.*

"Oh, Adam, faster, harder."

He complied as he said, "I've got you, baby."

Those words sent shivers through my body. After several more thrusts, I called out an incoherent cry of ecstasy. We both collapsed as Adam pulled out of me before lying on his side. I lay there as I bathed in the languid feeling from sex.

I turned to face him and smiled. "I think I'm going to like

this a lot, Pleasure Buddy. You are definitely not a Defective Buddy. Your nickname has been decided."

I giggled as Adam brought me to him, looking triumphant.

"Can you come back tomorrow? I want to try the Tantra Chair."

"Tantra Chair?"

Adam moved closer, nipped my lip, and then pointed. My head turned and followed to where he pointed at the chaise lounge I had noticed earlier sitting off to the right of the door.

"That chair right over there is going to keep us busy tomorrow night."

I turned to face him, moving closer to where our lips were almost touching. "Sounds good. Can I ask you something else?"

He rubbed his nose against mine. "Ainsley, you can ask me whatever you want. It's the only way we'll learn to trust each other, and you'll be able to relax more when we're not in the heat of the moment."

I took a deep breath. It was hard being vulnerable. "Did you still enjoy it even though I'm obviously not as experienced as your previous partners?"

"Ainsley, it was perfect. Don't ever compare yourself to a past partner. You were incredible, and we will form a bond that works for us. It will be ours. I'm going to have fun showing you things while learning your body." He spoke the words soft and seductive.

My fingers went to the tattoos on his arm, and I smiled. It felt good to hear that my sexual abilities weren't being scrutinized and he had enjoyed it as much as I had. I traced the words *Carpe Diem* on the inside of his bicep, and then I moved to the tribal design with the word *Strength* intertwined in the symbol.

"Do each of your tattoos have a story behind them? I'm fascinated by your ink. I don't have any tattoos."

Adam's hand went to my hip. "Have you ever thought about getting one?"

I noticed that when he wasn't ready to disclose something about himself, he would turn the question back on me.

Standing my ground, I responded, "You first."

A smirk played on his lips. "They all have a meaning of some sort. The word *Strength* written inside the tribal design is to remind me that strength always comes from within. That's why the design spirals out from there." Adam gave me an expectant look since he had shared.

"I've thought about it, but I don't know if I could choose something that I'd love on my skin for my entire life."

Adam stroked my skin. "You have beautiful skin, Ainsley."

"Thank you."

His hand touched my hip, drawing lazy circles on it. "What time can you come tomorrow?"

"I can be here at seven, but I need to leave by midnight." The thought of doing things in the Tantra Chair caused me to bite down on my lip.

He pressed his lips to mine. "Perfect."

Adam

I LOOKED AT the clock, and it approached five. It had been a long day of waiting for seven to come. Ainsley had me wanting more. Last night had not been enough, and the experience had only heightened my desire for her. I had kept the fucking to a few times last night as I needed to learn her body. The way she'd responded to me was perfect. She was tight and she'd squeezed my cock to perfection.

What I wouldn't give to feel her bare...

I needed to stop having those thoughts. Ever since Ainsley had left last night, my focus had been shit.

Ainsley was confident and tough, but I had seen a vulnerable side to her. She needed a closer connection than any of my other fuck buddies had needed, and without thinking, I had given it to her. I had never laid there and talked before or after having sex. None of my previous partners had wanted to be close, or it would have ended. Surprisingly enough, I had enjoyed myself, and I wanted to learn everything I could about what made Ainsley tick. Just because this wasn't how I did my typical exclusive arrangements at the club didn't mean this couldn't work. I believed Ainsley wasn't looking for anything more. She seemed like a straight shooter.

My phone beeped. It was my sister, Jessica.

Jessica: Hey, Adam. Our parents' anniversary is coming up. I want us all to celebrate together. They'd never push you, but I know they'd like it.
Me: Will he be there?

I barely acknowledged my brother's name anymore. He had moved in on my future and stolen it from me. I'd never forgive him or Selena for their affair. Jessica tried to stay neutral, but it was a delicate balance with how everything stood.

Jessica: Yes. Adam, please come.
Me: I'll think about it.
Jessica: Thanks for considering it.

There was a knock at the door.

"What?" My voice was agitated. It seems like it had been since I got here right before lunch.

The door opened, and Brandt strolled in, wearing a T-shirt and jeans. He took a seat where Ainsley had been the night before last.

"Hampton is looking into Roach. I sent him all the information you'd provided to me. He'll follow up with us tomorrow at the latest."

"Good. He'd better not dick around."

Brandt cocked his eyebrow. "When has Hampton ever screwed around? What's eating you? You've been on edge since you got here. You need to chill the fuck out."

I let out a deep breath and scrubbed my hand down my face. "I'm fine. I want this problem solved and behind us."

He kept staring at me, and it irritated the shit out of me.

"Is Ainsley coming back tonight?"

Shit, here we go.

"Yes." I kept my answer short and clipped.

He stood and stretched. "Good. Maybe she'll be able to get you out of your foul mood. Until she gets here, you might want to take a nap in your hidey-hole room back there. You've been snapping at everyone."

I ignored his comment. "All the books are caught up, and I approved a new visitor for next Wednesday. His name is Tyler Helms, and he does not want an anonymous identity. He's a junior partner at the law firm we use."

We had the best law firm in town, S&P Associates, LLP.

"Good to know. I'm headed over to the bar side to make sure they've got everything they need. The Thrillhammers are playing again tonight, so the house should be packed." Brandt walked toward the door. "Take my advice, man. Go hide in your room."

I had been a little short with him—well, with everyone today. He might have a point.

"Let me know if you need anything."

"Will do." With that, he left.

Maybe a quick nap before Ainsley got here would be good.

I walked back to my room where I stayed from time to time when I was at the club late and didn't want to drive home.

It had all the essentials—bed, dresser, closet, and bathroom. I had slept like shit last night, and I was exhausted. Some rest would do me good, so I wouldn't be a dickhead to Ainsley. I fell face-first on the bed, and pictures of Ainsley from last night were the last things I remembered.

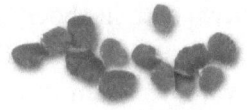

"Adam…"

Ainsley's voice invaded my thoughts, but she wasn't due here for a bit.

"Adam?"

The bed dipped, and I felt a small hand on my arm. It was Ainsley's touch.

Hell, this is going to be the best dream I've had in ages.

"I'll come back tomorrow. Sleep tight, Adam."

Lips brushed my forehead and then the bed rose again. I heard footsteps.

Shit, she's here. I pushed off the bed and called out hoarsely, "Ainsley, wait."

She stopped and turned. "It's okay, Adam. I can come back later. You're exhausted. You need your rest."

I kept blinking the haze away. She was in white capris that hugged her slim figure, a tight blue T-shirt, and that damn pink wig.

Hot. As. Hell.

She played with the ring on her right finger. I was pretty sure that meant she was unsure of something.

Shit, I don't want her to be unsure about staying with me.

I did the first thing that came to mind. I walked straight

up to her and kissed her. The small gasp right before my lips touched hers, told me she hadn't expected me to come after her like this. Her body needed to take over her brain that was probably telling her that I didn't care if she were here or not. That was the furthest thing from the truth. Her being here with me was all that I had thought about through the day.

Ainsley opened her mouth in shock, and I took advantage by pushing my tongue inside. By her rigid posture, I could tell she was still thinking with her brain. It was obvious when she let the moment take over. She became clay in my hands as her body took control. I needed her in that place, so she wouldn't try to leave right now.

I need this. I want her.

My hand went beneath her shirt and grazed her nipple. The contact relaxed her. The moan that escaped her mouth as we kissed had me hard as a rock.

I pulled away from Ainsley and looked into her pale blue eyes that were piercing me. "I can't wait, baby."

"Please, hurry. I can't wait either."

We stripped in a mad dash. The sound of fabric tearing filled the room. I needed in her again. She shimmied out of her panties as I ditched my boxers. I closed the distance and reached for the snap of her bra in the back. I wanted to be the one to unveil her breasts. I was out of my mind, needing to have her right now. I pulled her bra off her body. Her breasts were perky and perfectly sized. I loved how her rose-colored nipples darkened in anticipation.

"Adam…"

Her plea spurred me to pick her up, and she wrapped her legs around my waist. I loved hearing my name leave her lips, sounding as if I were the air she needed to breathe. I raised her up high enough to bring her nipple to my mouth where I sucked it in hard, and she threw her head back. The moment we met the bed, I laid her down and spread her legs. My cock was about to be right where it was supposed to be—in Ainsley. Her eyes connected with mine as I barely pushed my cock in.

"You feel amazing, Ainsley."

Her body went rigid, and her eyes went round. "Condom?"

Shit.

Shit.

Shit.

I pulled out. "Fuck. I'm so fucking sorry, Ainsley. I never forget. Damn it."

She was supposed to be able to trust me so she wouldn't have to worry about it, but I'd screwed that up.

Breathlessly, she responded, "Get one. Hurry. Purse. Side Pocket."

She squirmed beneath me, obviously needing an orgasm. I moved down her body and sucked her bud into my mouth. She was tight, warm, and ready. Massaging her walls with my fingers, I added the slightest bit of pressure to her clit with my tongue, which had her moaning in the sweetest way. Her eyes rolled to the back of her head as I gave her what she needed.

While she came down from her high, I went to get a condom from her purse. It seemed we both needed this. Rolling it on, I went straight back to that beautiful girl who had agreed to be exclusively mine. Taking my earlier position, I lined myself up and pushed inside her with a hard thrust. Ainsley moaned in response.

"Too much, sweetheart?"

"No. I need it fast, hard, rough."

That was music to my ears. "You've got it."

I hammered into her over and over again. Loving how her

pussy quivered around me, I twisted my hips.

Ainsley shook her head back and forth. "I'm so close, Adam. So close."

Going all the way in three more times had us both calling out at the same time. The surge of raw power that came through me was magnificent. I felt territorial, like I needed to mark her entire body with me. We had been desperate for each other. Pulling out and discarding the condom in the wastebasket beside the bed, I realized where we were.

My safe haven. My room. The place where I never brought women.

I'm losing my damn mind around this woman.

I turned back and saw Ainsley watching me with a shy smile on her face. The last thing I needed to do was become a dickhead because I had broken one of my rules. She hadn't broken my rule.

Shit.

I moved back to Ainsley. I brought her closer to me as we lay facing each other on the bed, and her legs entwined with mine. This was what she needed, and I needed to provide it to her while this lasted. I was still shocked at myself because I never broke one of my rules. However, I maintained my even breathing, so she wouldn't suspect that something was wrong with me.

I need a drink.

"I'm glad you decided to wake up from that deep sleep you were in." She giggled.

I couldn't help but smile at the sound. "Me, too. I was out of it. My damn phone was supposed to go off. What time is it?"

She looked at a delicate gold watch on her wrist. "It's almost seven thirty. I was a few minutes late. My obligation ran long."

I slowly trailed my hand up and down her arm. "Do you mind if I ask, what is the obligation you keep referring to?"

Ainsley lifted her head and looked at me. "Of course not. It's how we'll learn to trust each other in the club. I help watch Nora's sister, Emilyn. Sometimes, Nora and her mother's schedules overlap, so I offer to help watch Emilyn to save them money in sitters."

"That's nice of you. I'm sure they appreciate it." I hoped this didn't take away from our time together. *Shit, I'd look like a clingy bastard if I said anything.*

"They do. They're a wonderful family. Emilyn is seven, and she's precious. Did you have a long night last night? You seem tired."

I scrubbed a hand down my face. "I didn't sleep for shit. It happens from time to time."

Glancing down at Ainsley, she looked me over, watching me, as if she could see deep within me.

Before she had a chance to delve deeper into the reason behind my sleep deprivation, which happened to be her, I asked, "Want to head to the bar and get a drink? I believe we still have a date with the Tantra Chair."

She looked up at the ceiling, and I noticed she twirled her ring on her right finger.

"Can I ask you something first? But I don't want you to think I'm looking for compliments?"

"Ainsley, you can ask me anything."

She took a deep breath and looked toward me. My guard went up slightly as I wondered what she was going to ask. It was still hard to read what went on inside that head of hers.

"Am I handling this okay? This is completely out of my element, and I want to make sure I'm doing this right. You won't hurt my feelings if I should be doing something differently with the whole sex-without-strings angle."

This was her insecure side, and I wondered what had made her that way.

"How do you feel right now? How does what we're doing make you feel?"

Her pale blue eyes got a faraway look in them as she thought. Her focus shifted to me as she said, "I can't think of anything but amazing, more than amazing actually. I can't describe it, but it's the freest I've ever felt."

"Then, you're doing it perfectly. When you're here, think about the now. Nothing outside these walls matters. The here, the now, our connection, our pleasure—that's all that matters. This is our escape from reality."

She rose and gently pressed her lips to mine. "Thank you."

The kiss felt too intimate to me, and I pulled back quickly before settling down on the pillow. "Did anyone bother you tonight? I'm sorry I wasn't there to meet you in the parking lot."

"No, no one bothered me. Trigger had Snake show me to your office."

"Good."

She yawned, and it was contagious as I followed. My eyes felt heavy. Listening to Ainsley's even breathing had my eyes shutting, and I drifted off to sleep. I was still so tired.

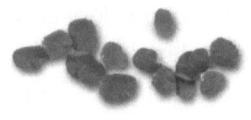

"Adam? What time is it?"

My body was wrapped around Ainsley's. Peering over to the clock, I groggily said, "It's after one."

She moved, and I automatically pulled her closer to me.

"Adam, I need to go home. I was supposed to leave at midnight. I have to be at work at nine."

Realizing what I was doing, I let her go. *Shit, I was cuddling. I might as well put a pink pansy-ass bow on my head.* I turned on the lamp.

Moving off the bed, she went to gather her clothes in the dim light from the lamp I'd turned on. I followed to find my own clothes. We dressed to the sound of the ticking clock.

Ainsley was about to put on her T-shirt when she giggled. "I think I'm going to need to borrow one of your shirts, Adam. Um…I guess we were a bit excited." She giggled again as she held up her shirt.

It was torn up the middle.

I had been crazed out of my mind to get inside her. "Shit, I'm sorry. Let me find you something."

Heading into the small closet, I grabbed a red T-shirt off the hanger. "This will be a little big, but it will keep you covered."

She took it from me and slipped it on. "Thanks. I need something to get home in. I'll wash it and bring it back to you."

"That works. I'll get you a new T-shirt."

She bit her lip. "It's okay. It was fun having you want me like that."

I grabbed her hand and we left the room. We made our way through the club that was still alive.

Her insecure comments from before still bothered me.

Did whatever asshole she was with before not make her

feel desired and wanted? Fucking moron.

Trigger stood post at the VIP door.

As we walked past, I said, "I'll be back in a bit. Let Brandt know."

"Sounds good, man. I will."

Three loud assholes were hanging out in the parking lot. They were eyeing Ainsley as we walked by. Instinctually, I pulled her closer to me in a possessive manner. Over my shoulder, I looked them over as we walked. It looked like one was about to say something until he made eye contact with me.

Good choice.

As we approached her car, I veered us to the passenger side. "Let me take you home." I was going to try to take the nondemanding route, but in reality, that wasn't an option.

"It's okay. I'm only about twenty minutes from here. I'm a little tired, but I'll be okay. College student, remember?"

She rummaged through her purse and pulled out her keys.

Lightly placing my hand on hers, I said, "It's late, and I'll feel better if you let me. I'll have a car come by and pick me up."

Ainsley yawned again and nodded, releasing the car keys to me. Opening the door for her, she got in and laid her head back. She was exhausted. Going to the driver's side, I got in and cranked her small car. It smelled like her, and my dick livened up.

Down, boy. We are not inside the club.

Ainsley hit a few buttons on her GPS. "This will take you right to my apartment. I'm in unit nine. You can park in either parking spot for my apartment."

She yawned again and closed her eyes. Ainsley fell back asleep before we even left the parking lot.

After following the directions, I found she lived in a typical college housing unit. Buildings of bland colors with no shrubbery were lined up side by side in the complex. I pulled into the lot. Her unit was on the ground floor. Without waking her, I first went to her apartment door and found the door key on her key ring. Walking through the door, the place was slightly illuminated by the stove light she had left on. The living room, kitchen, and eating area were all one room. Looking down the small hallway, a bathroom appeared on the right side, and her bedroom was on the left. There was nothing extravagant in the simple apartment.

Heading back to the car, I got her out and carried her into her home. Being careful not to bump Ainsley into anything, I went to her bed. The covers were already pulled back from not making the bed this morning.

Gently, I set her down. "Ainsley, baby, I'm going to take off your pants so you can sleep better, and I'll set your alarm for seven thirty."

"Mmmkay."

She was gone. I took off her shoes and then slipped her pants off her body. Seeing her like this had me wanting her again. I had wasted all my damn time with her tonight sleeping.

Son of a bitch!

Covering her up, she moaned and said, "Thank you, Adam."

Just the sound and knowing how I could have her screaming in pleasure was enough to make me step toward her.

Shit, I'm in her home. I can't do this in her home. We can only fuck at the club.

I turned and walked out of the room, needing to break the connection. I had almost broken one of my cardinal rules.

Sex is to only happen at the club.

It was what kept partners from getting all dopey-eyed at the thought of having something more. I pulled up the app on my phone to call a cab and put in the info. Locking the door from the inside, I stepped outside to wait. At least if I was locked out of her house, I wouldn't be tempted to say screw it and bury myself in her.

Shit.

I paced as I waited.

I was going to have to work on redrawing the boundaries that I had let blur.

Ainsley

MY ALARM BUZZED. Blindly reaching over, I hit the snooze button. Pushing myself off the bed, I went to my bathroom across the hall and flipped on the light. I wanted more sleep. Grabbing my toothbrush, I put the toothpaste on it and leisurely brushed my teeth. When I glanced in the mirror, I saw Adam's shirt on my body, and I froze, remembering him bringing me home and kissing me good night. Confusing emotions swirled within me as I rinsed out my mouth. At times, over the last two days, it'd felt like what Adam and I were doing began to become more.

No way. He was clear. This is fun. No attachments.

Turning on the shower, I pulled off his shirt and set it aside before getting underneath the cascading hot water. I'd refused to smell the T-shirt because I knew it would smell like

Adam. I was glad I had been half gone to the world last night when he brought me home. Knowing how badly I'd wanted him, I might have tried to do something to have more sex with him while being outside of the club walls. That was against his rules, so it had been for the best. The way he could make me feel was beyond anything Jarrod had. Jarrod had always been more concerned with himself versus me. Most of the time, I had been left unsatisfied, and I would have to finish myself off. After being with Adam, I could feel the difference in how he would take care of my needs.

Getting out of the shower, I combed through my brown hair. Next, I put on a little blush and mascara. Normally, I used very little makeup, except for when I would go to the club. My hair was straight as a board, so I normally didn't use a hair dryer. It looked the same, regardless if I'd dried it or not. Then, I put on a light summer dress.

My phone rang, and I was slightly disappointed when I saw my mom's name flashing across the screen. I had hoped it would be Adam, but I quickly pushed the thought aside.

"Hey, Mom."

"Hey there. I haven't heard from you in a couple of days, so I decided to check up on you."

There was no way I was telling Mom about what I'd been doing at Club Envy. It was one of the reasons I had not called her.

"Just studying and working, you know me." I gave a little shrug even though she couldn't see it.

Her clock chimed in the background. "Yes, darling, I do. Did you get the invitation to Donna's party?"

I rolled my eyes. Donna Stevensons was a backstabbing bitch, who had been pretending to be my mom's friend.

"Yes. I'll see if I can work my schedule so I can come.

I've got to run though. I don't want to be late for work. Love you."

"Love you, too, Ainsley. Come home whenever you can."

"I will. Bye."

"Bye."

I hung up the phone and took a deep breath as I grabbed my keys. I avoided going home as much as possible. She still lived in the same house as I had when I was a child. I hadn't been home since my mom's birthday. I would go visit her twice a year for her birthday and Christmas. Otherwise, Mom always came to my place as I used the excuse of being busy with school and work. I loved her, but the memories of what had happened in my childhood home were too painful. Every corner reminded me of something bad.

My mom and I were close, but we both kept secrets from each other. With the club, I had added another secret to the pile. In the end though, she had always been there for me, and she had never let my father touch me. Anytime I'd aggravated my dad, he would take it out on my mom that night. I'd learned to do as I was told, and I never questioned him. Sometimes I wondered if he'd known that I knew what he did to her.

I hate him.

I got in my little car and drove to the campus library. As I pulled into the parking lot, my phone beeped with a text. It was Nora's mom, Nancy.

Nancy: My boss has asked if I can take clients out at the last minute. Can you watch Emilyn until ten? I know it's Friday. If not, I understand.

Me: Of course I can. I'll pick her up from school.

Nancy: You're a lifesaver. Thank you!

Me: You're most welcome. I love watching her when I'm able to.

My day officially sucked. I wanted to see Adam again. I liked the escape and the freeness he could give me from the real world. But Nancy and Nora needed my help more than I needed another orgasm. Plus Adam and I hadn't made plans tonight, and I refused to put my life on hold for him.

I walked the campus, lost in my thoughts. The old stone steps to the library came into view, and I went inside to clock in. Since the campus was nearly deserted, my task for the last few weeks had been to make sure all books were in their proper place. The project was about halfway completed. It was a mundane task, but it paid the bills. I noticed my manager, Maria, was not at her desk, so I left her a note and headed out to the floor to begin today's sorting. It was going to be a long day, but the smell of books consoled me and wrapped me in a comforting blanket.

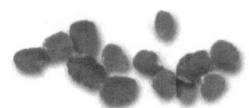

I was headed over to pick Emilyn up early from the kids program she went to during the summer while school was out. It was a little after three as I pulled up to the old red-brick building. I rolled down the window and waited as freshly cut grass invaded my nose.

I had completed another few aisles of books at work today, and my head was tired after alphabetizing all day long. On top of everything, I hadn't heard from Adam, which bothered me more than I wanted to admit.

Maybe he got his fill of me for a couple of days?

It was ridiculous for me to think that we would see each other every day. A teacher escorted Emilyn to the back passenger side of my car. Emilyn threw her backpack across the seat as she got in with a smile.

"Hey there, Squirt. How was your day?"

Emilyn had black hair, like her mother, and a petite frame, like Nora. Her eyes were an emerald green that had so much fire and spark in them.

We smiled at each other in the rearview mirror.

"It was good. Mrs. Thompson showed us how to make a liquid tornado in a two-liter bottle during project time. I made mine with purple liquid."

I pulled away from the curb. "Oh, that sounds fun. I remember doing those as a kid. How does spaghetti sound for dinner? If that sounds okay, I need to stop by the store to get hamburger meat and noodles."

"Sounds great. I love spending time with you, Ainsley."

Her sweet little voice warmed my heart and lightened my sour mood, distancing Adam from my thoughts.

"Me, too, Squirt."

We drove to the local grocery story and got out of the car. After paying the club fee to Adam, I had exactly fifty-two dollars and sixty-seven cents in my bank account. Things were tight, but I could make it on my own. I would get another check from the library this week. My academic scholarship covered my tuition, rent, and utilities. As long as I didn't go crazy spending money, I could get by comfortably. There wasn't extra money each month, but I was on my own, and that was what mattered.

I grabbed a shopping basket, and Emilyn and I headed back to the meat department.

"What movie do you want to watch tonight, squirt?"

I already knew the answer before Emilyn responded.

"Can we watch *The Last Unicorn*? I love Prince Lir. I asked my mom for that movie for my birthday."

Her birthday was coming up in December, and I had already asked Nancy if I could get the movie for her. She had fallen in love with it when we watched it at my house one of the first times I had kept her. Watching that movie with my mom was one of my fondest childhood memories.

"I think that sounds like the perfect date."

We grabbed some wheat noodles on the way to the meat section.

"Can we get some garlic bread, Ainsley?"

I grabbed a small thing of hamburger meat. I had a huge can of tomato sauce in the cabinet at home that I had bought when it was a two-for-one deal.

"I have some regular bread at home. We can put butter and garlic salt on it. It'll be cheaper. Does that sound good?"

"Yes, that sounds fun. Ainsley, why is that guy staring at you?"

Emilyn took her little hand and pointed to someone behind me.

Crap. Now some guy knows we're talking about him. How am I going to handle this suavely?

Slowly, I peered over my shoulder and froze when my eyes met those brown ones that had been in most of my thoughts as of late.

Adam.

I gave him a shy smile, and he walked toward us. He had on a baseball cap, T-shirt, and jeans. The way he looked me over had me melting. I turned to face him fully, and I drank in the sight of him.

He spoke first. "Hey there."

"Hey."

He is gorgeous.

I knew I had that look of lust in my eyes with how he quirked his mouth, but I didn't care. It was hard to believe last night we had been intimate with each other.

A little set of hands pulled on my elbow as Adam and I continued to be locked in a trance.

"Who is he, Ainsley? Who is this guy smiling at you funny?"

I pressed my lips together. Adam seemed to be at a loss for words, too, as he looked down at Emilyn.

"Um…this is Adam, my, um…he's, um…my man-friend. Yes, he's my man-friend at the grocery store. He's, um… shopping."

Oh geez, I'm an idiot, a total non-loquacious, blabbering imbecile.

"Man-friend? What's a man-friend, Ainsley?"

Adam raised an eyebrow at me and chuckled. I wanted to slap his chest for not helping in this matter. At least Emilyn was only questioning his title versus how I had stumbled through that explanation.

Little Emilyn's voice pressed on with a question. "What's a man-friend?"

I looked down at her, trying to get my thoughts together. "Well, it's a man who's a friend. Adam, this is my friend Emilyn."

Please let this awkward moment end. Kill. Me. Now.

Adam crouched down to be at eye level with Emilyn. "It's nice to meet you. Ainsley has told me how much fun you have together. What are you doing tonight?"

Emilyn pointed to the basket. "My mom has to go out to

71

dinner with people tonight, so Ainsley is watching me. It's going to be fun. We're making spaghetti and then watching *The Last Unicorn*. It's cheaper to make garlic bread out of bread at home, so that's what we are going to do."

"I bet it is." Adam stood up. "Is there anything else you need to get?"

His voice was deep, and it curled my toes. I had to keep reminding myself that a seven-year-old was beside me, and Adam and I were outside the club walls.

I looked in my basket, making sure I had both things I needed since my mind was a scrambled mess. "I've got everything."

"Good. I'll walk you up to the front."

I wanted nothing but to spend a little more time with him. I actually missed him after seeing him for the last three nights.

No, I miss the sex. That's what I've missed. Yes, I miss the sex.

We walked, and Emilyn was a few feet in front of me. Adam leaned in to my side, and his nearness made me want him so badly.

"Will I see you tonight?"

I shook my head and looked up to his features. He appeared slightly frustrated at my nonverbal answer.

I spoke softly so that little ears wouldn't hear. "No, I didn't hear from you today, so I thought we weren't meeting. Then, I was asked to watch Emilyn, and I told her mom I was free."

His brows pulled together as we approached the cashier. The cashier was an attractive college-aged guy with blond hair and blue eyes. According to his name tag, his name was Joel. I handed my basket over, and Joel rang up my two items before putting them in a bag.

Emilyn asked, "Ainsley, can I have some money to ride the car over there?"

Before I had a chance to respond, Adam handed Emilyn a dollar. "There you go."

"Thanks, man-friend," Emilyn sang as she skipped to the ride.

I took a deep breath at the term Emilyn was sure to start spouting to everyone. I gave Joel a smile and handed him my coupon for the noodles.

Joel took the coupon and scanned it as he said, "Nice nickname for your friend. She's adorable. Is she your sister?"

"No, I watch her sometimes." I gave a polite smile.

The new total of fourteen dollars and thirty-three cents flashed across the screen of the cash register. I handed the cashier my debit card. Adam hadn't said a word, but he was practically scowling at the cashier. He seemed to be on the verge of hostile.

What is his problem?

As Joel handed me back my card and receipt, he said, "Would you happen to be free this weekend?"

Adam wrapped his hand around my waist. "What the fuck do you think *man-friend* means? I'm standing right here, asshole. She's off-limits."

Joel and I both looked shocked. I was mortified.

Trying to salvage this situation, I calmly said, "I appreciate the offer, but I can't. Thanks, Joel. Have a good day."

Of course, Joel only gave me a tentative smile. I didn't blame him for not saying anything else with the Neanderthal standing beside me. As Adam and I walked toward the ride where Emilyn was, my temper flared, and I stepped out of Adam's embrace.

"Come on, Emilyn. It's time to go," I said sternly.

"I have one more ride. Please, Ainsley." Her pleading voice got me almost every time.

I nodded at her to continue, and she gave me a huge grin.

Adam put his hand on my waist. "I'm sorry. I shouldn't have done that."

I let out a slow breath and prayed for patience. What had happened did not sit well with me. "No, you shouldn't have. Do you not trust me? If you weren't here, guess what? I still would have said no. I'm not going to break our agreement and cheat on you. Plus, we are outside of the club. We're supposed to be acquaintances per your rules."

Adam's hand returned to my back. "I trust you. I'm on edge because I don't get to see you tonight. I should have texted you earlier, but I didn't want to crowd you. Last night, I wasted my time by sleeping, so I'm pissed at myself."

My heart softened at his words. I glanced at Emilyn, who was lost in her ride, and then I turned to Adam.

"I forgive you. It's weird seeing you outside of the club. I didn't expect to run into you so quickly in my normal daily life. I wasn't prepared, and I'm having a little difficulty with compartmentalizing this with how you're acting."

His hand came out and grabbed mine. "I understand. I feel the same way. I didn't expect to react that way."

His words confused me.

Emilyn walked up before I had a chance to ask him to clarify.

"It's over. Thanks, man-friend, for the dollar. Are we ready to go, Ainsley? I'm excited to cook with you."

"Yes, Squirt."

It was still warm outside, and the faint smell of grilled food wafted through the air. My insides were all knotted up, not knowing how I was supposed to feel. Adam had become possessive of me in public, and part of me liked it even though he'd overreacted. On the other hand, he had gotten borderline hostile with someone.

Would he hit me if he lost his temper?

I always feared I would be drawn to someone abusive like my mother had been.

"Hey, Ainsley's man-friend?"

I corrected Emilyn. "His name is Adam."

"Hey, Adam. Do you want to come make spaghetti and watch a movie with us?" She jumped, looking hopeful.

My eyes darted to Adam's, and he looked as perplexed as I felt. The last thing I wanted was for him to feel like he had to come. Plus, I needed to wrap my head around what had happened.

This is casual sex. Per Adam, that's it. It's what I agreed to. We need to stick to his rules.

However, a big part of me still wanted him with a ferocity I wasn't aware I had within me. My mind felt wishy-washy as different emotions fought within me.

To save Adam from the awkward moment, I answered, "Squirt, Adam has to get to work. He's more than welcome, but he has a lot to do."

Emilyn gave a disappointed huff and hopped in the backseat of the car. When I turned around, Adam was closer than publicly appropriate for friends.

"Will I see you tomorrow? I want to see you tomorrow, Ainsley."

Again, my brain should not have been so happy to hear that from him, considering what we were doing.

"I think so." Then, I remembered my agenda for tomorrow. "Wait, I have a group project meeting tomorrow. It's been scheduled for a week. I'll text you when we confirm a time. I may not be able to."

"I'm anxious to get back inside you." His voice was deep and gruff.

My insides turned into liquid molten lava. "I want that, too."

We stood there, staring at each other. Then, a car honked from across the parking lot and broke our trance, causing us each to take a step back.

He leaned in and gave me a kiss on the cheek. "I'll see you later, Ainsley. I love your real hair. You're gorgeous. I hope you let me fuck you next time without your pink wig," he whispered.

When his stubble rubbed against my face, I turned into a raging mess of hot hormones. His words caused my fingers to ache with the need to touch him.

"I'd like that. I'll see you later," I said.

He swallowed hard. "I can't wait."

A child screamed in the distance and he shook his head as if clearing his thoughts. Without a word, Adam jogged off to a black motorcycle where he got on and cranked it in one fluid movement. He turned his baseball cap backward, looked my way, and gave me a wink. My heart thudded loudly in my chest at the sight. In the next moment, he was gone, and I leaned against my car, wondering if I was going to survive this adventure.

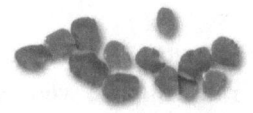

Emilyn and I were in the kitchen, adding the last of the sauce to the meatballs. We let it simmer as the noodles boiled on the stove. It was a simple recipe with sauce, meat, and ore-gano. We were making a lot, which would give me leftovers for a few days. It was better than ramen noodles, which I lived off of frequently.

Emilyn had on my pink polka-dot apron as she helped me. "This smells good, Ainsley. How much longer until it's ready?"

I stirred the simmering sauce in the pot. "About ten more minutes, and it should be done. Oh, we forgot to make the bread. We should do that. It won't take too long."

The doorbell rang.

"Don't touch anything. I don't want you to get hurt, okay?"

"Okay. I promise, Ainsley."

As I headed the short distance to the front door, I could hear Emilyn taking deep breaths as she continued to smell the spaghetti.

I called over my shoulder. "Don't hyperventilate in there, Squirt!"

Emilyn giggled as I peeped through the hole. I gasped when I saw Adam holding what looked to be a loaf of French bread in a silver oblong package.

What is he doing here? We're only supposed to see each other in the club.

My mind was going in a million different directions as I tried to compose myself. I opened the door but made sure that Emilyn could not see my man-friend.

"Hey there." He stood there, nervously looking at me.

"Hey."

His brown eyes washed over me, and he smiled. "I was invited by Emilyn, and I was never given a chance to re-spond."

"You're here for dinner?" My voice sounded shocked and incredulous, not my normal composed self. His eyes dipped to my legs and I remembered I had on my short shorts I had changed into once we had gotten back to my place.

He grabbed my shirt and pulled me slightly forward. When my face passed the doorway, he pressed his firm lips to mine. I went to deepen the kiss when he pulled back.

"I'm here for dinner, if I'm still invited. I can't go without having you tonight. When Emilyn leaves, maybe we can re-draw some lines, if you're okay with it."

Redraw lines?

My mind raced with the possibilities.

I opened the door wider for him to enter. "Okay, come on in and after she leaves, we can talk about it."

My insides were jumping with anticipation. I was going to have sex with Adam tonight, and he seemed like he maybe wanted more. I wanted more, too. Just how much more I want-ed was still a mystery to me. I needed to keep my heart in check because this dangerous game I played would get me hurt if I didn't keep it all in perspective.

In the end, I was a Pleasure Buddy.

Pleasure Buddy—that's it.

Nothing more.

Adam

THE MOMENT AINSLEY let me into her apartment, I wanted to strip her down and taste every inch of her. Her long chestnut hair was thrown on top of her head. My cock ached for her.

From the kitchen, Nora's sister, Emilyn, called, "Hey, man-friend. You came to dinner. I could tell you wanted spaghetti."

Man-friend. I didn't know whether to curse the name or not.

When that shithead at the grocery store, Joel, had tried to ask Ainsley out, I'd wanted *man-friend* to mean a hell of a lot more than it did. My unexpected thoughts and behavior had shocked the hell out of me. After leaving the grocery store, I had driven back to the club where Brandt had basically kicked me out for my attitude.

His words echoed through my head. *Adam, go find Ainsley. Who gives a shit where you two sleep together? Get over your own fucking rules and enjoy each other. You're not promising forever by having sex with her outside of these walls.*

Holding out my peace offering of garlic bread, I said, "I did, if it's still okay. I brought you some garlic bread. A little birdie told me that you might not have any."

Emilyn came bounding up to me. "You brought garlic bread? Ainsley and I forgot to make it. Will you be my man-friend, too?"

Ainsley coughed, and I wanted to laugh. There was no telling where Ainsley had come up with the term, and each time it had been said, a slight blush would appear on her cheeks.

"How about we become good friends? That's a step above man-friend."

The little energetic girl gave me a hug. "I like that a lot." She pulled away and bounced.

Where do kids get all this energy from?

"Will you stay for the movie, too, Adam? I want you to stay. We're watching *The Last Unicorn*. Ainsley and I need someone to sing Prince Lir's parts."

I looked toward Ainsley to bail me out of the situation I had somehow gotten myself into. Ainsley gave me a sweet smile in return.

Oh, I'm going to get her back.

I crouched down to Emilyn's level and touched her nose. "I think I will stay for the movie. I'll have to watch it this time, so I can sing next time. Sound good?"

Emilyn clapped. "Yes! Yes! Yes! It's my favorite. You're going to love Prince Lir."

"I bet I will."

I stood up and walked from the living room toward the kitchen. I went over to where Ainsley stood while she'd watched the exchange. She barely contained her amusement. On purpose, I invaded her space. I liked how her body responded to my proximity. Her pale-blue eyes were searching mine. This was brand-new territory for me. *It still didn't mean we are going to have anything more, but why should we limit ourselves?* Brandt had a point. Ainsley seemed like she could keep the boundaries up in her mind. We both might as well enjoy it as much as possible while this lasted.

"It smells delicious. What can I do to help?" I asked.

Being this close to her, I could smell her perfume, and blood rushed to the muscle I wouldn't be able to exercise for a bit. As she stood up on her tiptoes in her short shorts, I knew I was going to take her while she bent over something this evening. Her body was perfectly toned. I had to adjust myself as my dick pressed against my zipper. This would be a long evening of waiting for Emilyn's mom to get off work.

Emilyn called out, "Ainsley, I'm going to the bathroom. I'll be right back."

Ainsley opened up a cabinet door. I ran my hand up her leg, and she gasped.

"Adam, Emilyn is here."

The door to the bathroom closed.

"Shh…I'm listening. I just need to feel you."

I slipped my finger inside her, and she leaned against the counter. There wasn't much room, but I was still able to get soft little moans of pleasure from her, even with her shorts on.

She spread her legs wider and involuntarily sighed. "Oh, Adam."

The bathroom door opened, and I withdrew my hand and

brought Ainsley back to a standing position.

"Tonight, I'm going to take you over the back of your couch. We're going to go at it like animals."

Her body shivered at my words. Just above a whisper, she said, "Please."

Emilyn walked back into the room. "Are we ready to eat?"

Ainsley took a deep breath and turned toward Emilyn. Ainsley appeared unaffected, except for the slightly fast rise of her chest. "Yes. Adam was about to get the glasses down. I'll take the noodles off the stove and drain them."

The opened cabinet door showed the location of the glasses. I pulled three down. Ainsley and I gave each other a knowing smile as she drained the noodles. Fire burned in her eyes, and I was going to stoke that fire every chance I got tonight.

I definitely made the right decision to come over here. Here's to hoping she accepts my new proposal.

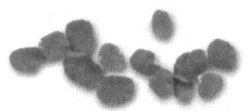

We sat on the couch with Emilyn between us. She had insisted that she be in the middle. Ainsley had giggled at my failed attempts to put her in the middle. I couldn't keep my eyes off of her while she and Emilyn sang along to this white unicorn movie.

Ainsley is enchanting.

It was obvious the girls had watched this hundreds of times with how they would keep saying the lines out loud. Throughout the entire movie, the heat between Ainsley and I kept building whenever we glanced toward each other. Each time our eyes made contact, images of her bent over this couch would flash through my mind.

I imagined being inside her again and mouthed to her, *I can't wait to fuck you.*

Her face reddened, and she glanced down at the otherwise engaged Emilyn.

Looking at me again, she mouthed back, *Me either.*

That did it. I was officially at a raging hard-on state during this movie.

Prince Lir needs to get on with it and stop pussyfooting around with whatever her name is.

Where the hell is Emilyn's mom?

Emilyn was a cute girl, but right now, I felt like I was being cockblocked. I was five minutes away from giving Nora a paid night off.

Ainsley's phone pinged. She picked it up from the edge of the brown cloth sofa.

"Hey, squirt. Your mom finished early and will be here in twenty minutes."

Hell yeah! My night is about to get a lot better.

"Oh, man. I wish I could stay the night." Emilyn's voice sounded hopeful. "Maybe we could all play a game, and then you could take me home, Ainsley."

Shit.

Ainsley glanced at me and pressed her lips together before she reached over and hugged Emilyn, who giggled in response to loving the attention.

"Not this time, squirt. But we'll plan something soon, okay?" Ainsley kept squeezing her.

Emilyn responded, "Okay." She sounded disappointed.

There was guilt at the cute little girl's pleading voice, but it wasn't enough to change my plans. My dick was definitely in charge at this point.

Ainsley squeezed Emilyn harder. "Hey, turn that frown upside down. I got you all day today. Your mom will want to spend a little time with you tonight. We'll have a girls' night with Nora sometime soon."

Emilyn gave Ainsley a big hug. "You're the best."

Ainsley was incredible with kids. I was impressed.

We finished the movie, and there was a knock on the door a few minutes later.

"That's my mom." Emilyn took off toward the door.

I looked around Ainsley's apartment without being obvious for places we could have sex. The walls were sparsely decorated. Everything was minimal but comfortable.

Emilyn opened the door. "Hey, Mom. Ainsley's man-friend came over, we ate spaghetti, and then watched a movie."

Ainsley let out a deep breath.

I mumbled to her, "It's your fault. You're the one who came up with it."

She threw a pillow at me. "You were no help. Desperate times called for desperate measures."

Emilyn let her mom into the room as I gave a low chortle.

Ainsley stood. "Hey, Nancy. Hope your dinner went well. This is my friend Adam. Adam, this is Nancy."

I stood and crossed the room to shake Nancy's hand.

She eyed me over and then gave me a smile. "Nice to meet you, Adam."

"Nice to meet you also."

Nancy looked at Ainsley. "Thank you. You're a godsend. I'll be in touch. Emilyn, grab your backpack so we can get home and read some more of Swiss Family Robinson."

Emilyn bounced around on her toes, making her black hair sway. Then, she ran straight to Ainsley. "Night. I can't wait to see you again."

"Me either, squirt."

Next, she came running up to me. "I like you. Will you come over again sometime? My mom is trying to set Ainsley up with a guy named Joe, but I like you better than him."

My initial instinct was to set everyone straight that I was the only man in Ainsley's life, but I tempered my emotions. Ainsley had awakened a possessive side of me that had been asleep for years. I only had exclusive partners, but the possibility of them going to someone else had never bothered me as long as they ended it with me first. If they did move on before ending it with me, we would be history anyway, so it wouldn't matter. They had all been a way to pass the time while getting off and having fun.

I gave Emilyn a hug back. Then, I pulled back and winked. "Well, I guess I'll have to make sure I stay on your good side so you keep liking me better than this Joe. We can go for ice cream sometime, if that sounds good." The words were out before I'd had a chance to process what I said.

This was all part of redrawing the lines. It was okay to be here, to be a part of Ainsley's life in this sense. I swallowed, trying to find my balance in all this again. It was like taking a detour and not knowing when I'd end up back on the route I was used to.

We said our good-byes. At the sound of the door clicking, I waited for a few seconds and then turned to Ainsley.

"Ainsley, we need to talk."

Her face dropped from the teasing smile she'd had and her eyes got wider.

Then, it sank in how I had worded it. Those were the

dreaded four words to any relationship.

"Shit, I don't mean it like that. I meant I want to change some things about our agreement. I'd like to extend the borders of where we have sex, if that sounds good to you."

She sat back on the couch and I followed. While she twirled her ring, I could tell she was still cautious.

"What kind of new borders? What made you change your mind?"

That's a fair question.

I was about to change everything up and she deserved some answers, especially since we had only started this a few days ago.

"Honestly, Ainsley, I like fucking you—a lot. If we both understand the score, it shouldn't matter where we do it. Why not make it easier on ourselves? The concept still stays in place."

She cocked her head at me. "So, basically, we're going out together in public now, but everything is still with no attachments."

My hands moved through the air to emphasize my point. "No attachments. Just pleasure anywhere we want it."

"Then, what happened at the supermarket today?" She was obviously analyzing the situation.

Why, oh why, couldn't I keep my cool today? Who am I kidding? I went ballistic thinking someone else was trying to move in on what was mine—for now.

"Honestly?"

She folded her hands in her lap. The no-nonsense Ainsley I liked was here in full force.

"Are you anything but honest with me? Yes, I want to know what the honest answer is. Adam, I don't need an attachment, but I do need to know that you're being honest with me. I can't handle lying."

I felt like I was screwing this up all to hell, and I needed to get this back on track. "Ainsley, I am always honest with you. I won't lie to you. I didn't expect to see you at the store today. I had wanted to text you all day. Then, I saw you and all I could think about was you naked beneath me. When that ass-hole tried to get a date, something that I wasn't aware was still in me came to the surface. It's why I normally refuse to take what I do outside of the club. I'm territorial, Ainsley. I don't share what I consider mine, and I wanted to beat the shit out of that guy for looking at you the way he did."

She visibly flinched and stood up before going across the room. I could feel the emotional distance she had put between us. The feeling left me bereft. I wanted her to be connected with me again.

I stood and walked toward her. "What did I say wrong? Talk to me, Ainsley."

She froze, and for some reason, I needed to touch her to console her. She was as stiff as a board, and she looked around the room as if she were plotting her escape.

"Are you a violent man, Adam?"

"What?" My voice sounded confused as I tried to process everything.

"You said you wanted to beat the shit out of the cashier. Are you normally violent? I need you to be honest with me."

I touched her face. "Hey, look at me, Ainsley."

She slowly glanced up, and the worry in her eyes cut through me.

What happened to her?

I needed her to trust me. "I would never hurt you. I've been in fights and broken up fights, but I've never nor would I ever hit a woman. Have I ever made you feel uncomfortable until now?"

She shook her head. "No, I feel safe and protected when I've been with you. Your reaction today shocked me. What came to the surface today? What did you mean by that?"

Double shit.

The last thing I wanted to do was explain my fucked-up past. I brought my thumbs to her shoulders, and I rubbed them. "I'm glad you feel protected when you're with me. I want you to feel that way." I stopped and Ainsley continued to look expectantly at me. *Hell, might as well tell her.* "In high school and for a few years after that, I had a serious girlfriend—or what I thought was a serious girlfriend. To make a long story short, she cheated on me several times. It's why I keep things to the club. There's no need for all the extra bullshit and wondering who might be moving in on your girl."

I had to know what had happened to her. Right now was not the time to ask. If I pried too deep it would open up a two-way street I wasn't prepared to reciprocate. The need to fiercely protect her surfaced and I was trying to squelch it. This wasn't part of the arrangement, but thinking of her ever being with another man pissed me off. She was mine.

I mentally added, *For now.*

She leaned up on her tiptoes. "I don't want to talk anymore. I want our escape from reality. Make me forget. You free me in a way I never thought possible."

"Whatever you want, it's yours."

She looked desperate to get out of whatever memory tormented her. She stood back, pulled her shirt over her head, and shimmied out of her shorts. I ran my hands along the sides of her ribs.

"I want to forget. Please," she said.

I pulled the condom out of my back pocket, unbuttoned

my pants, pulled my cock out, and put it on. I snapped her barely there panties off of her and picked her up by her ass.

Hell, I'd buy her a hundred pairs to rip them off her body.

Within seconds, I pushed into her, feeling relieved to be inside her again. The inner beast that had been roaming, trying to obliterate all in its path, quieted. Tonight, she'd forget everything but the pleasure I would bring to her body. Her back was against the wall as I moved in and out of her, pushing my dick along her throbbing walls. I bit her perky nipple and then sucked it hard as she cried out in pleasure. She knotted her hands in my hair. I wanted it quick and fast before I took her over the couch and lost myself in her. I'd draw it out more later.

"I'm almost there, Adam. Harder."

I did as she'd wished and let go of her nipple to increase the movement. I sank deeper and deeper into her. Her pussy clenched, and I knew she was close.

Pure heaven.

Her eyes rolled back in her head as she called out, "Yes!"

She was warm and tight as she lost herself in the sensation. I had to focus on not losing my load in her. I rode out Ainsley's wave of ecstasy. As her head fell to my shoulder, I walked toward the back of the couch as she continued to pulse around me.

I pulled out of her, set her down on her feet, and turned her to face the back of the couch. "Baby, lean over."

She complied as I spread her legs. She was still high from her orgasm. Lining up my cock, I rammed myself into her. Ainsley gave a sound of bliss as her head lay on the back of the couch. Inch by inch, I pulled out and then ran my cock up her cleft. Another moan escaped. Lining back up at her entrance, I thrust in so deep that she screamed as her body perked back to life.

"Does that feel good, Ainsley? Do you like it hard?"

"Yes! Again!"

I repeated the motion, but this time, she squeezed me tight, and I had to close my eyes to focus on not coming. I knew I had hit that spot within her again.

She was nearly panting as she bucked into me. "Adam, I need—"

The twisting motion of my hips stopped her mid-sentence. "I've got you, baby."

Holding her hips firm, I quickened my pace. Ainsley tried to use her arms as leverage to push back and meet me, but I didn't allow her to move. Three more thrusts and she collapsed on the couch, calling out incoherent words. I let the sensation release my own euphoric orgasm through me. As I pulled out, Ainsley slipped to the floor. I quickly picked her up before she dropped too far down and cradled her in my arms. She was limp as I carried her to her room.

I need to get this damn condom off.

"Did that give you what you were looking for?"

She nestled further into my chest at my words, but then she stopped. "Are you leaving already?"

I liked hearing the regret in her voice. She didn't want me to go. I didn't want to go.

"No, baby, we're just getting started."

She giggled. "Good."

I laid her on the bed and then went to the bathroom across the hall to clean up before returning back to her. Shedding my jeans and shirt, I crawled into the bed with her.

She turned to me. "I like the new boundaries. It'll make things easier with school and work. Is it bad that you're not at the club on one of the busiest nights of the week?"

I trailed my fingers down her stomach. She had at least one more orgasm in her before I would let her rest.

"I've put in my fair share of hours. Last year, Brandt took off for a few months and then slowly came back to the club. He and I will work it out."

I made contact with her clit, and her mouth formed an O. She was ready to go. I looked up and saw she had a headboard. It was time to try something a little different.

She moved her hips. "Adam, please. I don't know how you do it, but I need to go again."

I liked that her pussy was shaved clean. It was going to add to the sensation. "Ainsley, I want to taste you again."

Her lips moved to mine, and I obliged even though that wasn't the kind of taste I craved.

"Ainsley, I want you to sit on your knees, face the wall, and grab the headboard."

I withdrew my hand, and it took her a few seconds to process, but she did as I'd asked with no questions. When she let her body take over, the analytical Ainsley would leave, and a wanton creature came in her place.

I spread her legs and positioned myself underneath her. Her pussy was a glorious pink, wet from the moisture of our pleasure. "Don't let go of the headboard. Absorb the sensation."

She nodded. I put both hands on each side of her hips and brought her down to me. I licked and sucked her core, working her, as I brought her to the point of no return. She tasted the perfect combination of sweet and salty and I probed her deeper. The sensation of my stubble on her bareness caused her to grind further down on my face.

I fucking love it.

She rode me and screamed out. I couldn't get enough of

her as I devoured all she gave me. Ainsley was getting the escaped reality she had asked for tonight. The escaped reality we both needed.

"I'm so close. It feels so good."

I went up to her clit and gave it a small nip, which had Ainsley falling apart. She collapsed and I brought her to my side as she caught her breath.

I traced the area around her nipple, and she shivered.

"I like how you make me lose myself," she said softly.

"Back at you, baby."

We laid there for a few moments in silence as we slowly touched each other. Ainsley's hand reached up to one of my tattoos on my upper shoulder. It was the words, *This Too Shall Pass*.

She was inquisitive. "I find your tattoos fascinating. What's the significance behind this one?"

"It reminds me that regardless of what I'm going through, the situation will come to pass. I'll survive and come out stronger in the end even if it's not what I want."

She traced the words with her index finger. "I was cheated on, too. My ex didn't think I'd get him far enough in life, so he went elsewhere. I know what betrayal feels like."

I had the urge to pummel the shit out of the dickwad who had done that to Ainsley. "When did you guys break up?"

"A few months ago. When were you cheated on?"

It was only fair that I answered her question. I wanted to answer her. "I found out the one and only year I went to college. Once everything surfaced, I found out her affair had been going on for some time."

She nodded. I didn't think either one of us wanted to delve deeper as we reflected.

"So, you drive a motorcycle?"

I liked the subject change. This was easy, not personal. "I do. I like the speed and freedom it gives. Do you like to ride?"

She laid her head on my chest. Being close to Ainsley like this felt natural.

"I've never been on one. They look fun."

"I'll take you sometime. You'll love it."

She yawned. "I'd like that."

We lapsed into silence, and I listened to her breathing even out. I'd let her rest before I took her again. Looking down at her, I realized so many feelings were unearthing themselves with this new arrangement. They were stronger than what I remembered and scared the shit out of me.

I thought back to the end of my first year of school and a night when I had come home to my apartment to find my now ex-girlfriend, Selena.

Pulling up to the apartment I shared with Brandt a few blocks from the college campus, I noticed that Selena was already here. My girlfriend was a senior in college whereas I was a freshman. Brandt and I had dicked around for a few years before deciding to give college a try. To pay the bills, Brandt and I worked as bartenders at a local club.

Selena and I were heading out tonight to celebrate our five-year anniversary, and I was going to propose to her. I knew she wanted to get engaged even though I thought we should wait. But hell, I wanted Selena to be happy. I loved her.

I walked through the door and saw my gorgeous girl sitting at the table. Her short black hair and green eyes got me every time. By the way she chewed on her bottom lip, I knew something bothered her. Hopefully, after tonight, she'd be on cloud nine for weeks as she showed all her friends her ring.

"Hey, sweetheart. What's got you troubled?"

Selena turned to face me with a blank expression on her face. "Adam, we need to talk."

Oh shit.

Those were the worst words anyone could hear. I walked over to sit at the table, and I put my hand on Selena's knee, but she moved away from my touch.

"What's going on, Selena?"

She cleared her throat. "Adam, this isn't working for me anymore. I need more out of a relationship. I need to know that my life isn't going to be a string of keg parties. I'm a senior, and you're starting school. I need someone who is serious about his future."

What.

The.

Fuck.

My body was frozen as everything I'd planned shattered and dissolved into a million pieces.

She gave me a smile and continued on. "I hope we can still remain friends. It's been fun, Adam. I do want you to know that I did believe I loved you until my eyes were opened."

My voice came out cold. "Have you been cheating on me?"

She stood. "I got all my stuff earlier. I'll see you around. I wish you the best, Adam. I really do."

"Did you fucking cheat on me?" I practically spit the words.

She walked to the door and put her hand on the knob. Before turning it, she turned back. "I didn't want it to happen this way. I didn't want or go looking for it. He loves me like I deserve. He's ready to give me a future. I'm sorry."

The door opened, and she walked out. My life had walked out the door. She was going to another man. Selena had taken my heart and obliterated it, leaving nothing left.

I will never put myself out there again. Never.

Taking the vase that was filled with flowers she had purchased off the table, I threw it against the wall. "MOTHERFUCKER!"

That memory is what kept me from allowing myself to get close to anyone. With all this additional time I spent with Ainsley, I would need to remind myself about it over and over again to make sure the lines wouldn't get blurred into something that wasn't meant to be. Ainsley sighed in her sleep and wound her arms a little around me. I liked the way she made me feel, and I would enjoy it while it lasted.

This is temporary. It won't last.

My phone beeped.

Brandt: I know you're with Ainsley. Hampton is heading over to let me know what he's found on Roach. I can handle it if you want.

Me: I know that, but I want to hear it, too. I'll be there in twenty.

Brandt: Sounds good. We'll wait for you.

I slowly extricated myself from Ainsley and then laid my phone on the bed while I got dressed. Finding a pad of paper and pen in the kitchen, I scrawled out a note, letting her know where I went. I laid it on the nightstand and then hurried out of her place after locking the door from the inside. I was anxious to get this whole thing with Roach and whoever this picture-taking prick was behind us.

Bending down, I gave her a light kiss on her forehead. Her eyes danced behind her eyelids and a small involuntary smile played out across her lips. As I watched her breathe in and out, looking like an angel, I decided that I wanted to do this different than I had other fuck buddies in the club. No relationship, but I didn't want to go straight to the toys and games. I wanted to learn her body, appreciate the basics with the most exquisite woman I had been with. Changing that wasn't going to alter the fact that we would one day go our separate ways. However, I was going to savor the time we did have together.

Ainsley

AN INCESSANT VIBRATING noise near my ear awoke me from my sleep. Prying my sleepy eyes open, I glanced at the screen lighting up only inches from my head. It wasn't my phone.

Adam. Where is Adam?

I flipped on the lamp and saw a note.

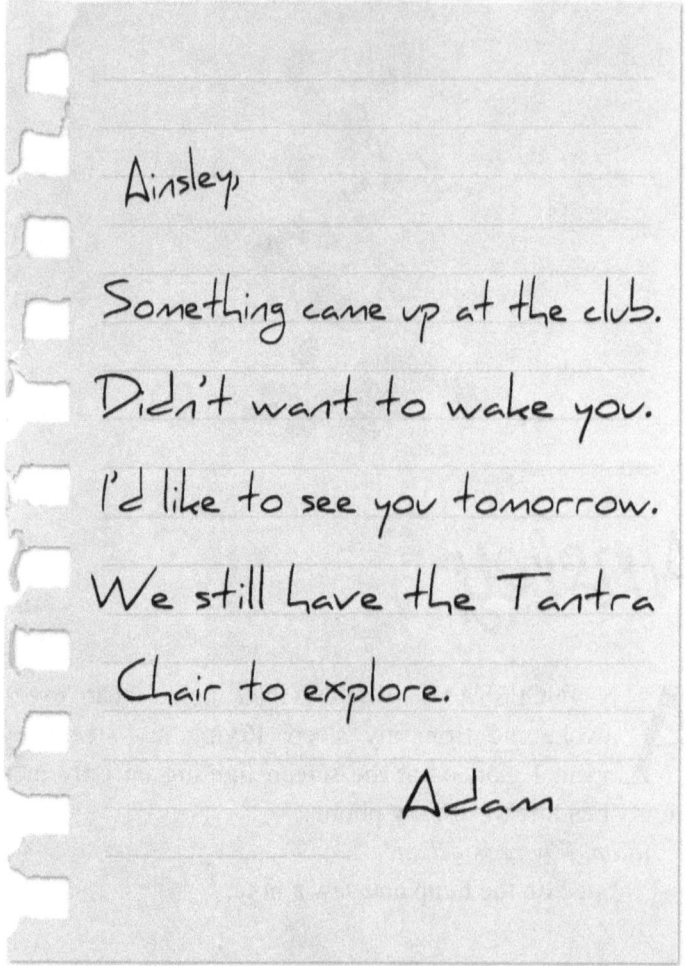

Ainsley,

Something came up at the club.
Didn't want to wake you.
I'd like to see you tomorrow.
We still have the Tantra
Chair to explore.

Adam

I glanced at the phone and saw several text messages flashing on the main screen. I didn't open the phone, but I caught a glimpse of a few of the texts. They were from different guys that I assumed were all employees of the club.

Trigger: All's good, Adam.
Snake: Headed to the bar side. Crowd getting excited.
Jethro: Thrillhammers playing last song. Full house to-night. It's all under control.

The clock read after three in the morning. If his employees kept in touch with him via text, I was sure he'd need his phone. I sat there, debating on whether or not I should show up at the club. After a few moments, I decided to go ahead and head to Club Envy. Fact was, deep down, I wanted to see him again. Part of me wanted to feel what it was like to wake up to him even though I knew this was not a relationship.

Adam brought out a side of me that I never knew existed. What I had done tonight, holding on to the headboard as he tasted me, was something I'd only fantasized about. I wanted all the sexual experiences I could get with Adam before it ended.

Putting on my yoga pants and T-shirt, I put his phone in my purse. Right before I made it to the door, I remembered I needed my pink wig. My hair was thrown up haphazardly before I loosely put the wig on.

Leaving the apartment, I got in my car and drove over to the club. I was wide-awake as I thought about seeing Adam again. Pulling into my normal parking spot I noticed the club side was shut down. A few people milled around their cars. I got out of my car and hastily made my way across the street when someone called after me.

"Hey there! Come over here, gorgeous. We could have some fun." The words were slurred.

I wanted no part of this situation. It would only lead to trouble. I didn't respond and picked up my pace as I crossed the street to the main parking lot of the club where the side door I always entered was. I knocked and no one answered.

Where is Trigger?

The same guy called from across the lot. "Darling, come back over here. We could all go to my place and have some fun."

I knocked louder as I took deep breaths, trying to prepare my mind. Peering back, I saw three guys were walking this way. If they crossed the street and made it into this lot, I would take off running. They were drunk, and I could run for miles. I had my phone, so I could call a cab as soon as I was away from them.

Yes, that's what I'll do.

The taller one wearing a baseball cap was the one who had spoken to me, and he was halfway across the street, coming closer to me. I banged louder on the door.

This is why Adam wanted me to call before I came here.

Please someone answer the door.

I looked back at the guys that were across the street and now in the main parking lot with me. Ten more feet and I would have no choice but to take off. My pulse quickened under my skin. The guys kept walking closer. My heart was pounding in my ears as I secured my purse on my shoulder. I banged louder on the door. They were almost to the point I had set mentally to take off. I turned, preparing my body to run. Adrenaline coursed through my veins. I was about to begin sprinting, but then the door opened, and I pushed past Trigger, needing to find Adam.

"Hey, wait up!" Trigger called from behind me.

I stopped.

"Were those guys bothering you?"

"They were drunk. I have something for Adam."

I wanted away from this. The thought of fighting made

me nervous. It reminded me too much of my dad. I avoided it at all costs. Trigger's brown eyes looked me over. He was attractive in that preppy-boy-gone-bad sort of way. He had on low-slung jeans with a faded T-shirt that had the number forty-four printed on it.

"I'll walk you back there. Are you sure you're okay?"

I nodded. "I'm good."

We walked, and Trigger talked to me. "How's your night been?"

It felt as if he was still trying to assess if I was actually okay. My insides were all shaken up, but I would be okay. They were drunk, and they hadn't done anything.

"It's been okay." I kept it simple.

"Have you decided what you are going to be called? I don't know your name."

My mind was still connected to the scene outside as I spoke. "I'm Ainsley."

"Nice to meet you, Ainsley. I like that name. Most people who go the anonymous route choose more out-there names like Tooty Fruity or Voluptuous Raptor. They're ridiculous names half the time."

He chuckled about his comment, and I was now nauseous. My head felt like all the blood rushed out at the same time. I had forgotten to keep my name a secret. In the stress of the situation, I had slipped.

Shit.

We passed by a guy with coal black hair and Trigger called to him.

"Hey, Snake. I left my walkie-talkie at the bar with Nora when I was radioed by you that Ainsley was at the door. Send someone to check the east side. There are drunks out there and they got a little aggressive, I think."

Trigger tipped his head toward me, and Snake's eyes widened a little bit. I felt humiliated that they were making a big deal out of what had happened, but I kept my mouth shut, not wanting to make a bigger deal out of it.

"Will do," Snake replied as he walked at a quicker pace.

This was getting worse and worse. Everyone was going to know my real name now. The incident outside was getting blown up. We were at Adam's office door and Trigger opened it. I hurried inside, and then I quickly realized I had walked in on a meeting with two guys and Adam. Everyone stopped talking and looked at me.

This night is officially horrible.

Trigger spoke from behind me. "Hey, Adam. Sorry, man. I thought you guys were in Brandt's security office. Ainsley came by and I was going to let her stay in here until you were done."

Adam looked as shocked as I felt as he glanced between Trigger and me. I felt for my ring on my right hand. It had been my grandmother's. At times, it felt like a security blanket. It was the only piece I had of her. My dad had thrown out most everything else, except for what my mom had been able to hide in the basement.

Trying to get out of this awkward situation, I grabbed his phone out of my purse and walked confidently but briskly to him. "You forgot your phone, and I thought you might need it." I handed it to Adam. "I'm going to head home now. I'll talk to you later."

I turned to the other two men in the room. One was a slightly older white-haired man with an athletic build. The other man looked to be Adam's age with messy long blond hair and a few tats. I assumed he was Brandt, Adam's partner.

"Have a good evening. I apologize for interrupting." I

walked back to the door.

I should never have come tonight. I should never have come.

As I was getting close to the door where Trigger still stood, Adam called, "Wait."

I stopped.

"Hampton, is there anything else we need to discuss tonight? If not, I'm going to talk to Ainsley."

I stayed facing the door.

A gruff older voice said, "No, Adam. I'll be in touch with what we discussed. I'm glad you guys are letting me handle this."

I faced the room again. Hampton stood and shook Brandt's hand first and then Adam's.

"I'll be in touch, boys. I can show myself out." He walked toward me. "It was nice meeting you, Ainsley."

My eyes darted to Adam's, and they were penetrating me hard. It was one of the few times I had seen him lose his composure. The tension in the room was rising, crackling like a new log being thrown on a fire.

"It was nice to meet you, too, Hampton."

Brandt followed Hampton and he gave me a friendly wink before everyone exited the room. Adam and I were now alone, and the silence was deafening. I had no idea what he thought about all this.

His phone vibrated, and he looked at the screen before turning back to me. He typed out another message. "Did someone bother you outside of the club?"

My night is getting worse by the second.

Someone had texted him about what had happened.

"I'm okay. There were some drunk guys and no one was at the door. I'm okay."

He scrubbed a hand down his face. "Ainsley, that's why I asked that you always tell me before you come, so something like that wouldn't happen." His voice was laced with agitation.

"I had your cell phone, and I didn't have the club number. I honestly wasn't thinking." My tone was tired. I had messed up, and I realized the gravity of the situation.

The wig started to itch my head, so I took it off and threw it to the couch. It didn't matter now anyway.

"I obviously made the wrong decision, and yes, before you ask, I slipped with my name. It was my fault. Trigger asked what to call me, and I answered with my name."

His phone vibrated again. As Adam read the text his face darkened into a glare at the screen. He typed back a message.

Adam walked toward me, his face softening instantly. "Are you okay? Don't give me the surface answer. Are you okay? Trigger said you looked shaken on the video when I asked them to rewatch the footage."

That's what he had been texting about. I took a deep breath. "I was nervous. I'm okay now, I promise. I've handled worse."

Triple shit.

I had slipped again. Adam's brows drew together, and I avoided his penetrating deep gaze.

I continued. "I'm tired. I shouldn't have come. I was trying to help and I keep making a mess of everything. I'm going home now."

He took a deep breath. "I still need to handle a couple of things. I can't follow or take you home right now."

I started to speak, but he raised his hand.

"I know you're capable, but I have other plans for us, if you're game. What time do you have to be at work or school?"

Adam appeared as tired as I felt when I looked into his

eyes.

"I don't have work or school. It's Saturday."

He gave me a small smirk. "Finally, something has gone our way. Do you want to come with me? Or would you like to sleep in the back room? I should be less than an hour."

If I went back to his room, I'd toss and turn. "I'll come with you."

Adam nodded and then looked down at my wrist. "Where's your white band?"

Sighing heavily, I responded, "I left it in my car. I can't believe all the mistakes I've made tonight. I just…I thought…I wanted…I don't even know what I'm trying to say. I'm normally not like this. I woke up, and I was trying to help. All I've done is make mistake after mistake."

He walked over to his desk and sternly spoke. "Ainsley, the rules of the club are to keep *you* safe, too. I don't want you to deal with unnecessary shit. Keep that in mind anytime you come. I know our agreement altered today, but nothing with the club has. Do you want to put your pink wig back on?"

There was that word—*agreement*. Part of me hated how that sounded. After he'd come to my place earlier tonight, I'd acted like a girlfriend. He would have figured out where his phone was. He had my number, and he could have called it when he realized.

I am such a moron.

I'd sort through everything and compartmentalize it all later.

"Honestly, I'm tired of wearing that wig. I don't want to be anonymous anymore. I'm horrible at lying, and if someone did call me something like Tooty Fruity, I'd never answer. I'll go by Ainsley and not share my last name. It'll make things easier." I ran my fingers through my hair to untangle it.

"I think you'd make a great Tooty Fruity."

The smirk on his face let me know that we had moved out of the tense waters of this conversation. That was definitely a benefit of our *agreement.*

I mockingly hit his shoulder as he handed me the white bracelet.

"Be quiet. Tooty Fruity is much too bland for my taste. I think I'd go by something like Sparkling Candy Apple."

We were smiling at each other, and he leaned down to kiss me. My body responded when the kiss deepened. His tongue worked my mouth. He had a powerful presence that overtook me.

He pulled back. "I need to go home after this to check on my dog. Do you want to come home with me since you don't have anything today?" He looked down at my right hand. I followed his gaze and saw I was playing with my ring. "What's going through that beautiful mind, Ainsley? Talk to me."

I searched his eyes as his searched mine. The straight honest truth was always best. "I don't want to come off as clingy by saying yes. I don't want you to think it's expected. I truly understand what this is, and I don't want you to feel obligated to invite me if you want to keep your personal space... well, personal, for lack of a better term."

His hand came on top of mine. "I wouldn't have invited you if I wasn't comfortable doing so. I wouldn't have redrawn the boundary lines if I didn't think you could handle it. If it gets to be too much for either one of us, we can talk about it and change it as needed. This isn't meant to stress you or me out. It should make it easier to have fan-fucking-tastic sex."

I bit down on my lip. "I like your plan. I have plans this evening with Nora. She's picking me up at eight. My group project plans were cancelled."

A brief look of disappointment flashed across his face, and then it was gone. I would be lying if I said I didn't like that look.

"What time do the different clubs of Club Envy close? I'm curious since it seemed like the place was thinned out."

He took out his phone and texted someone as he spoke. "Through the week, the dance side closes at two, and the sex-club side closes at three. On weekends, the dance side closes at three, and the sex-club side closes at four." His phone beeped. "That's Brandt. He's got things under control. We can go ahead and leave."

"Okay, sounds good."

We both walked out of the club. It was after four, and the place was vacated. I could hear cleaning machines working in the background.

"Is anyone still here?"

"Snake is on this side, making sure the place is locked up. Brandt is meeting with Jethro on the bar side to make sure all the paperwork was done from an incident that happened earlier over there. I thought I was going to need to do that, but they're handling it."

We passed through the door, and Adam locked it behind him. Quickly, I searched the parking lot, but there was no one there. The guys had left.

Adam mumbled under his breath, "Good thing those ass-holes left."

Part of me warmed at his possessive side, but I was still leery, wondering if Adam could control his anger. My dad had imprinted a fear on me, and I was afraid of repeating my mother's mistakes.

I focused on Adam's earlier words.

I would never hurt you. I've been in fights and broken up fights, but I've never nor would I ever hit a woman.

As we stepped into the street, I asked, "If you don't mind me asking, what incident happened?" I pulled my keys out of my purse.

Adam took them and unlocked the door. "Some guy got pissed when our bartender cut him off. He threw a glass at her. She's okay, but the cops had to come, take a report, and all that shit."

Just thinking about the fighting had my stomach turning a little.

Adam continued. "I'll program my address into your GPS in case we get separated as you follow me to my house."

I nodded as he sat down in the car, cranked it, and typed what I assumed was his address into the portable GPS on the dash of the car. Getting out of the car, he stood beside it until I was seated and buckled in.

He pointed toward the club. "My motorcycle is parked right across the street in the same lot as the club. It should be easy for you to follow me at this time of night. I'm about ten minutes away. You know you can park next to the club, right?"

"Yeah, I like this spot. I'll see you there."

For some reason, I liked parking in the second parking lot across the street. It didn't make sense to me why I preferred this, but I was too tired to think about it. Adam gave a quick kiss and took off across the street. Revving the engine, he pulled out. He looked my way and nodded. There was something hot about a man with tatted arms on a bike. I followed him and watched him drive it easily, commanding the machine between his legs. Just seeing this side of him had desire blooming through me.

The GPS said we were less than a minute away when we pulled into a neighborhood with nice normal-sized houses.

Turning left onto Lilly Drive, we pulled into the last house on the street. It was a brick home with a landscaped yard. Adam pulled his bike into the garage, parking next to a black Camaro. There was a canoe mounted on the far wall.

Adam was organized, and I was impressed.

I parked behind his car in the driveway, grabbed my purse, and made my way over to where he hung up his helmet. I watched him from behind. My body was alive and on fire with want as we entered his home. He turned around to speak to me, and I was unable to control myself as I launched my body into him. I kissed him, and he picked me up as I wrapped my legs around his waist.

"My body needs you, Adam."

He groaned in approval. "I'll take care of you, baby."

I loved how I didn't feel self-conscious around him, especially after riding his face as if I would never get an orgasm again. Adam brought out an uninhibited side I hadn't known existed.

He held me as I pulled my shirt over my head. Then, I worked on getting his shirt off before I leaned down and start kissing him while he walked us somewhere. His strength never wavered as his arms held me.

The moment he put me down, my pants and underwear were gone, and I worked on freeing him. Insatiable at the moment, we couldn't keep our hands off of each other as we reached a lounge chair in his room.

He lay back on the curvy end. "Instead of my face, this time, I want you to ride the hell out of my dick."

His ass was in the dip of the chair with his member at full attention. A slight heat graced my cheeks, but I complied and slid on him. The sensation felt so good. The angle caused an incredible friction as I moved up and down on him. My feet were on each side of the chair, and I used them to propel myself up and down. My hands went to his chest as his lips went to my nipples. He rolled them in between his fingers. The feeling was amazing as I rode him faster and harder. A light sheen of sweat coated our bodies, slickening them as they touched.

My core heated. *One more time and I'll orgasm.* On the upward motion, Adam's hands came out to the side and held my hips in place. My body tried to fight against him and slam home. I was so close.

"Adam, let go of me!"

"Absorb the need, Ainsley. Feel it building within you. You're close. I can feel your trembling walls."

He pushed his dick in an inch and took it back out. I bore down on him trying to use my strength to get me near the edge orgasm. It was so close, but so far away.

"That's right, baby. It's building. Can you feel the tip of my cock twitching for more?"

His words stilled me as I closed my eyes and did what he asked. My sex pulsed around Adam, on the verge of erupting. His dick moved within me, seeking more. Really feeling my body caused everything to become more sensitive.

Without warning, he let go of me and it was a race to the finish for both of us as we met each other's bodies. The sound of skin slapping filled the room. Adam leaned forward and took one of my nipples into his mouth. He bit it while he pinched the other one hard. That action mixed with the built up wave of pleasure caused me to go into a state of complete bliss.

I called out, "Yes! Yes! Yes!"

At the same time, Adam called out, "Fuck!"

We both reached the peak of ecstasy, riding it out, until we both collapsed, breathless. My mind had a numbing haze invading it as I sat there and felt his dick twitching inside me.

The only thing that I could think to say was, "I love this chair."

Adam chuckled. "Baby, this is the Tantra Chair. You're going to get very acquainted with this chair. I don't bring girls here, but I love this fucking chair so much I had to get one anyway."

For some reason, I felt giddy knowing we had a place that hadn't been infiltrated by countless women. It made me feel special. We lay there for a while until the fog cleared from my head.

Lying back, I giggled. "I didn't recognize that this is the same chair from the club until now. You had me a wanting mess earlier."

His hands went up and down my thighs. "Whatever I did, I'm going to have to repeat it because that was some out-of-this-world fucking."

I liked how I affected him. My body was drained, and I yawned. Without thinking, I said, "Just ride your bike, and I'll ride you."

He thrust in me a little deeper. "I'll remember that."

I pulled off of him and something warm trickled out of my body. I froze. Then, I looked down at the substance at the same time as Adam did.

Condom. We didn't use a condom.

In all my life, I had never been more thankful that I was on birth control. I had insisted on getting on the pill when Jarrod and I became sexually active our first year in college. We had actually fought about it. Jarrod hadn't thought I needed to get on the pill. The first month, my pills had gone missing, so I had gotten the shot. After that, I had kept taking the shots. It was easy. After Jarrod and I had broken up and I had seen the true Jarrod, I wondered if he'd wanted to trap me into something in order to get closer to my dad.

"Hell, Ainsley. We didn't use a condom. I've broken more damn rules this week for you than I have ever done in my life."

His tone turned me off completely. I got up from the Tantra Chair and put on the closest discarded shirt I could find. It smelled of Adam. Mine was somewhere in his house, lost during our lust-filled quest for each other.

I went to speak, but he continued. "Please tell me I'm not going to be on baby watch for the next month. Son of a bitch! I know better. I hope to hell you're on birth control."

He ran his hands through his hair. I was upset, too, that we'd had unprotected sex, but we were both clean. It was a rule of the club to be tested prior to becoming a member.

"I'm on birth control. I have been for about three years. You don't have to worry."

"Damn it all to hell. This is why sex should only be at the club." His words cut through me as he scrubbed a hand down his face.

I found my underwear and pants and put them back on. Trying to keep my voice calm, I worked on bringing rationale back into the conversation. "Neither of us were thinking. We'll have to be more mindful of it in the future. I don't like it any more than you do, but it'll be fine. You know I'm clean, and from the way you're reacting, I highly doubt you've had unprotected sex with anyone for a while. Let's calm down."

He moved his hands from his face. "Ainsley, this isn't a relationship where we calm down and talk through our shit. You come around, we fuck, and we go our separate ways."

"Don't treat me like that, Adam. I'm not a doormat." My tone was reproachful and my blood boiled at how he was acted.

Yes, we screwed up, but hell, it was a mistake.

This animosity made me nervous on the inside, but I stood my ground.

Without a word, he stood up, walked to the bathroom, and turned on the shower. The sound of the water filtered out into the bedroom.

Asshole.

I gathered my purse where I had dropped it at the door of the garage and went to my car. I refused to be treated that way. For all I cared at this point, he could go back to his damn club and his rules and screw away to his liking. I pulled out of the driveway and hastily wiped a tear away.

I will never let someone treat me like my dad did my mother all those years. He made my mom feel as if she wasn't important and her feelings didn't matter.

I refused to be made to feel...worthless.

Adam

I TURNED OFF the water after taking a hot shower to clear my head. My world altered constantly, and I felt out of control as a swirling of emotions battered inside me. The asshole side of me had won in the bedroom, and I was a prick for the way I'd acted to Ainsley.

Hell, I was the one who changed all the rules. I told her she would never have to worry about me wearing a condom. Fuck.

Ainsley had taken the high road, and she hadn't even thrown my own words back at me like I deserved. It was time to go face the music.

Grabbing the towel, I threw it around my waist and walked out into my bedroom to find it empty. I jogged through the house.

"Ainsley? Where are you, Ainsley?"

No answer.

My golden retriever came running up on alert. "Hey, Lindy, is there anyone else here?"

She sat. If Ainsley were here, Lindy would have gone to her. I peered out the front window.

Shit, she's gone. Of course she left after the way I had treated her.

I ran to get my phone and called her. She rejected my phone call after the second ring. I tried again, and I was rejected again. A third time, I tried and was still rejected.

I was furious with myself for treating her that way. There was no way I was ready to end this, and I knew she wasn't ready to either. I would have to grovel to get her back, and that wasn't something I was used to doing.

Ainsley is worth it.

She was worth being the exception. If I showed up at her place, I had a feeling she wouldn't answer the door, and it would only hurt my chances of getting her back. This was going to require creativity. I'd text her for now as I thought about how I was going to get her to talk to me.

Me: Ainsley, I know I fucked up. I'm sorry. Call me. Please. I didn't mean it.

I sat there, racking my brain on what to do, when a return message popped up.

Ainsley: I'm not a whore. I never asked for any rules to be changed. Being your FUCK BUDDY does not mean treating me however you want.

While I had her attention, I typed out a quick response.

Me: I know that. I'm sorry. I would never think of you as a whore. You're much more. Please call me.

Ainsley: I need some time to think everything through. I'll call you in a few days.

Me: Please don't give up on what we have until we talk.

If I could beat my own ass for making her feel like a whore, I would. I deserved to be knocked into next week. I had a feeling she wouldn't respond. She had said she would call in a few days. I needed another plan of attack to get her back with me as soon as possible. A few days wasn't going to cut it.

As I dressed, I pulled up Nora's phone number. She was probably sleeping since she had gotten off not too long ago. At this point, I didn't care.

Nora answered on the third ring. "Hello? This had better be good. You woke my ass up." Her voice was agitated.

I sounded desperate. "I need your help."

"You messed up with Ainsley, didn't you?"

"Yes."

Now, I hoped that Nora would help me out. If things went how I planned, I'd have Ainsley back with me and in my bed later tonight.

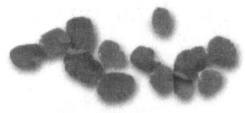

A few hours later, I paced my office like a caged tiger. After wasting the morning away with meaningless tasks at my house, I went ahead and came into the club.

Nora had agreed to bring Ainsley to the bar side of Club Envy. After highlighting what had happened to Nora, I had endured a lecture from hell from her. I never would have guessed she was that feisty.

Hell, she could pack a verbal punch.

Everything was set with Chris from The Thrillhammers. They were playing again tonight. I had lucked out that they had agreed to do both a Friday and Saturday set this week. Chris wanted me to listen to a group called The Divas, so we could use them during the week since The Thrillhammers' schedule had more bookings. To keep them on the Friday and Saturday schedule, I had offered his band a raise to play. They always packed a crowd, so it had made sense.

Brandt strolled into my office, closing the door after him, wearing a Club Envy T-shirt. "Dude, with as much sex as you're having you should have a shit-eating grin on your face. You're strung pretty tight. So, either Ainsley is a horrible lay, or something else is eating you. What the fuck gives?"

"Don't talk about Ainsley that way, Brandt. I know you don't mean it, but don't talk about her like that. I majorly messed up, and I'm working on getting things straight again."

Calmly, Brandt sat down in a chair across from my desk and put his arm over the back of it. "What happened?"

I continued to pace. "I broke another one of my rules today, and I lost it on her. I treated her like shit, and she walked."

A smirk appeared on Brandt's face, and it pissed me off.

I spoke harshly to him. "What the fuck are you smirking at?"

His British accent became a little thicker when he chose his words. "Adam, I'm going to give you a piece of advice. Forget your damn rules. You're not promising forever. If you keep talking about your boundaries and shit, she's going to bail. I have a feeling you've made it pretty clear on where you stand on the relationship thing. A relationship doesn't mean you're going to marry her. From what I can tell, you've been pushing Ainsley for more, and then you get all pissed off and moody for things you've done. You need to chillax and be with her. What does it matter if you have an actual girlfriend? It doesn't mean that she's going to want marriage if she knows you can't give her that. Has she pushed you for more?"

"No, she hasn't, not at all. I don't want to lead her on. I can't promise her anything. You know what happened to me. I don't want to put myself out there again after what I went through with Selena." My mind raced as I relived those last moments I'd had with Selena. My pacing picked up as the inner beast in me wanted to roar.

Brandt held up his hands. "I know that, and you don't have to. But fighting for what you want and then wrecking it for no apparent reason is being an idiot, Adam. I should know. Don't make the same mistake as me. You obviously want more with her than you've got. Normally, you couldn't care less when things end. Enjoy it, and have fun. Be happy. I think she's good for you. I already like her because she doesn't put up with your shit. Ainsley is not Selena."

My mind relaxed … some. *Brandt is right.*

Ainsley and I didn't have to conform to anything. It would be up to us. All that mattered was that Ainsley and I were okay with what we had going on. She was her own person, and I was mine. Neither one of us would have to give up who we were, like I had to do to make Selena happy.

I slapped Brandt on the back as I walked past him. "Thanks man. I get what you're saying."

Brandt stood. "I've got it under control at the club tonight. Go get your girl back. I'll touch base with Hampton to see where he's at on the Roach investigation."

I stopped, remembering I had responsibilities at the club. "Call me if you need something."

He walked passed me. "Adam, I've got this. I owe you for all that you did for me when I had to take off. When's Ainsley supposed to get here?"

I took another deep breath. "She's supposed to get here in a couple of hours."

As he opened the door, he said, "Focus on that. I'll handle the business."

Brandt closed the door, and I paced again, thinking about the picture problem we had with the club. Whoever the fucker was had taken a shit-ton of photos and was slowly releasing them on the website. Club Envy wasn't the only club on there. Hampton worked with tech specialists to track down a contact to get the site taken down. Finding Roach was the first step in all this. In addition, Hampton worked on trying to find the owners of the other clubs posted in the pics on the site. The asshole who took them was good and didn't leave many identifiable features in the pictures.

Looking at the clock, only five minutes had passed. I worked on getting my mind ready for tonight. It was going to be an uphill battle.

Ainsley is worth the fight.

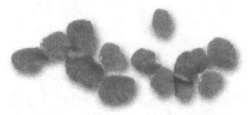

I was in my office that connected the bar side to the sex club side that I never used. I had the camera feeds pulled up, and I watched every person who walked through that front door. Nora had said she would come in through the front entrance. Jethro had been told to text me the minute he saw Nora. I wanted my bases covered. The time approached eight thirty, and they should have been here.

What is taking them so long?

My phone beeped with two text messages.

Jethro: I see Nora getting out of her car.

Nora: You owe me big time. I had to lie to get her in here for a few minutes while I supposedly get my paycheck. She's fighting me because she thinks you're here. Don't forget what I said. I'm not afraid to crunch your nuts if you hurt her. Are you picking up what I'm putting down?

I texted Nora back.

Me: Yes. I'll make it up to you. I promise.

Nora: You better.

I rubbed my hands down my pants and watched the screen intently. It was almost go time. Nora appeared in the view of the camera, and Ainsley followed. She was gorgeous in her fitted dress. I had saved them a table near the dance floor. Snake guarded the area to keep the table from getting used. Jethro let them pass, and Ainsley looked everywhere around the bar.

Hell, I hope she's looking for me. A spark ignited within me when disappointment crossed her face at not finding what she was looking for.

Nora said something and Ainsley laughed. The plan was to talk Ainsley into sitting and listening to a couple of songs from the band before they left for their girls' night out.

They made it to the table, and they spoke to Snake, who rolled his eyes. Then, he headed to the bar. Nora was probably giving him shit, and Snake knew to do whatever it took to get them to stay. It was almost time for me to make my way out there as The Thrillhammers finished their current song, "On Fire" from their *Long Story Short* album.

I left my office and headed to the bar. When I entered, some cocksucker was already talking to Ainsley. She smiled politely at him and shook her head.

I took a few deep breaths as I walked toward her. This was not the time to lose my cool with her. Confrontation made her nervous. When I was about three feet away her eyes made contact with mine. Lust burned beneath the fire in her pale blue eyes. She still wanted me, which was a good thing. That would make convincing her to give me another chance a lot easier. The guy continued to talk to her, but she paid him no attention.

Stupid fucker needs to leave now.

Snake set the drinks down on the table. Nora picked hers up and gave me a smirk before looking at the guy who tried to take my girl.

That's right. I'm about to claim her publicly as mine.

I knew I'd look like a contradictory asshole, but some-times, it took losing what I had to put everything in perspective. I kept reminding myself to stay calm, but I couldn't help that Ainsley brought a protective beast out of me, and I protected what was mine.

I made it to the table and spoke in the tone I used in the bedroom. "Dance with me."

Ainsley took her drink and gave it a small sip. She didn't answer as she glanced back and forth between me and the other guy. I guessed she was seeing if I would lose my cool again, but I wouldn't.

I held out my hand. "Dance with me, baby. I need to talk to you. Please."

My plea at the end seemed to soften her as she placed her hand in mine and stood. She looked back at Nora, and I gave the asshole she had been talking to a fuck-off look. He turned and left.

Nora laughed. "I'll be good. Go talk to your guy."

I brought Ainsley to the middle of the dance floor.

Chris from The Thrillhammers said, "This next song from our *Highway 369* album goes out to Adam's special girl."

Ainsley's eyes looked at mine, and she swallowed hard. She went to speak, but I pulled her to me and gave her a light kiss to silence her.

"Let's dance, and we can talk afterward in private."

She laid her head on my shoulder as The Thrillhammers sung "Better Days."

I've seen better days
Lying on the beach
The tide just creepin' in
I've seen better days
But to tell you the truth
Right now I don't know when
Sky so blue, it almost hurts my eyes
I see you and again my love's reprised
If I were to live for only one more day
Could I close my eyes and say
I've seen better days
Driftin' down the stream
Your fingers running through my hair

I've seen better days
Well maybe that's not true
But right now I just don't care
Sorrow times don't mean that much to me
I've just been left with these flawless memories
But all that pales to me and you this way
Oh I can remember
The fire and the embers
But your love burns hotter today
I've seen better days
And if I only had a few
You know I'd spend them all with you

The song ended and Ainsley stood there clutching me as the band rolled into their next song, "Girl to Queen." It was fast-paced, and the crowd moved in on us as we stood still, frozen in time.

I whispered in her ear, "I'm so fucking sorry. Will you give me a second chance? Before you say anything, can we talk first? I want you to have all the facts before you give me your answer."

She nodded her head against my chest.

Thank goodness.

I held her for a few more seconds until she pulled back. Her eyes were slightly watery. Turning toward the band, I nodded my thanks. Chris returned the gesture as The Thrill-hammers continued working the crowd.

"I need to tell Nora we're leaving."

I had her back and in my arms, and nothing else mattered right now. I gave a reassuring smile. "Okay. Sounds good."

She walked up to Nora and spoke. Nora pointed to a guy who stood across the bar area and gave her a wink. Ainsley gave her a hug and then walked back to me. The place was jammed, but all I could think about was that I had Ainsley back. She had agreed to talk to me. Waiting for this moment to see if I would get another chance had made this one of the longest days. I took Ainsley back in my arms and made my way toward the exit. I had brought my car today, so Ainsley and I could talk as I drove.

We passed by the bouncer.

"See ya, Jethro. I won't be back tonight. All communication should go to Brandt."

"You got it. Have a good one."

"You, too."

Ainsley and I walked in silence to the car and I opened the passenger side for her to get in. I jogged over to the driver's side. When I got inside, I noticed she slid her ring up and down her finger, showing she was nervous.

"Are you ready to go somewhere and talk, baby?"

"Can we go someplace where we can actually talk? Maybe we could stay in the car, so the console is between us. We can go anyplace where we won't end up naked."

Car sex was going to be on our agenda at some point in the near future. A console wouldn't keep me from having her. She was going to see how much fun we could have in this machine.

How could her previous partner not show her the pleasure she deserved?

"Sure. We'll go to a nearby park."

At my words, Ainsley relaxed a little bit.

I put the car in drive and headed to the park that was about ten minutes away. My car began to have that floral smell of Ainsley, and I liked it. I glanced over, and she was busy watching the outside world pass us by as she twirled that damn ring. Well, that ring was the only indicator of what she thought in moments like this.

Never mind, I love that damn ring.

Tonight on the dance floor was the most vulnerable and exposed I had seen Ainsley. She had taken those words and listened to them, felt them, and understood them.

Moments later, I pulled into the parking lot of the park and put the car in park. The gear shifting seemed to echo through the car.

She took a deep breath and turned to me. "Adam, I can't keep doing things how we've been doing them, especially after today."

Shit.

My heart sank. Afraid she would bolt, my initial reaction was to hit the door lock button so she couldn't get out.

She took another deep breath and continued. "I don't need a promise of forever. I know that you have no interest in getting married. I get that. I really do. But I need a stronger connection. I need to know what we have is meaningful to you. I don't want to hide and be someone's dirty little secret. When you said what you did this morning, I felt dirty and used. It was horrible. It's how my father treated my mother. I don't need a label, but I do need to feel that what we're sharing is more than pleasure buddies. I want to be more than a lay for you. I thought I could do the no-connection thing when I started the sex club, but if that means experiencing what happened today, I can't do that. Today changed a lot for me."

She stopped and took a few steadying breaths. This was my moment.

"Ainsley…" I waited for her to look at me.

Slowly, her eyes came to meet mine.

"Ainsley, I've thought a lot about this today. Even before

you said what you said now. I wanted to propose we take away all the rules and see where this goes. Right now, I don't see myself going toward that fairy-tale ending of marriage with the white picket fence, but I do want what we have to be meaningful. I'll give you all that I can and we can see where that leads us."

She gave me a questioning look and stopped fidgeting with her ring. She searched my eyes as she asked, "So, what does all that mean?"

"That we're together, and we'll see where it takes us. We'll publicly date and try the relationship thing."

A small smile graced her lips. "Can we still have fun at the sex club?"

"Abso-fucking-lutely."

She laughed and then seriously added, "I won't push you, Adam, for more than you're willing to give as long as you respect us and what we have. I don't need titles. I never have. You have to communicate with me too, though if there's something you need. It's a two-way street."

I reached over and grabbed her hand. "Thank you for giving me a second chance."

"You're worth it, Adam."

A huge weight lifted off my shoulders. "Can we go back to my place now, baby? I want you to stay the night with me."

"I'd like that as long as you still plan on pleasuring me."

I cranked and gunned the car out of the parking lot. "I think I can manage that."

Ainsley

MY MIND TRIED to process everything that had just happened. Adam was willing to try a relationship. That had never been my plan, but the hurt from this morning had shown me that there was no way I could personally disconnect from a person I was having sex with.

Adam grabbed my hand as he drove like a crazy man through the streets on the way to his place. For the first time in as long as I could remember, I was happy. Jarrod had never made me happy like this. He had become more of a security blanket, so I wouldn't be totally alone. At the time, I hadn't realized that was the case until our relationship was over. Jarrod had used me.

Adam pulled into his garage, and I got out of the car. He grabbed my hand and walked quickly toward his bedroom. A golden retriever lifted its head as we walked by.

Adam issued a command. "Stay, Lindy."

Lindy's head went back down.

Adam's house was what I would expect a bachelor pad to look like—brown leather furniture, a large television, and a few pictures on the wall.

Adam closed the door behind us. I stood there, letting the moment take over, as I wondered what approach he was going to take. I shut my eyes. Moments passed. Time stood still. Soft music played, and Adam placed his hands on the back of my dress and slowly unzipped it. My dress dropped to the floor. I stepped out of it and kicked off my shoes.

His hands went to my hips and he slowly peeled my panties down my legs. He leisurely traced his fingers up the back of my legs to my ass and then to the clasp of my bra. He unhooked it, and I let it slide off my arms. My breath quickened as he pressed himself against my body and I realized he was naked, too.

Adam walked us forward, toward his bed covered in black satin sheets. His hands worshiped my body and worked their way to the apex of my thighs. His lips trailed kisses along my neck. Softly, his hand brushed against my clit, and I whimpered.

He turned me around and looked me in the eyes. "I want to make love to you, not fuck, with no barriers. Are you okay with that?"

"But when we forgot today, it seemed like it was a big deal to you."

I needed his reason for wanting this before I said okay. It was something I wanted, but going without a condom was a big step, and it had come like a freight train on the heels of Adam deciding we should have a relationship.

We maintained eye contact as he replied, "I know I've seemed like a wishy-washy asshole in the last twenty-four hours, Ainsley. Feeling you was incredible, and the first time we make love, I want it to be only us. I trust you."

Those words had meaning on so many different levels. "I trust you, too." I stood up on my tiptoes and pulled his head down to meet mine. I kissed him gently and then whispered, "I don't want there to be any barriers either."

Laying me back on the bed, he crawled on top of my body. Adam used his strength and slid us up toward the top.

I love satin.

The silky blanket caressed me. Adam kissed me with more passion than I'd thought possible. Our tongues met each other in a sensual dance, colliding and entwining. Over these last few days, Adam had held so much back from me. He was capable of more passion than I'd known was imaginable.

In this moment, I gave him everything I had, every ounce of myself, as I ran my nails along his back. My legs opened as his tongue went down my neck and then across my right nipple. Sensations were spiraling out from his touch as his hand made its way down to my navel and continued on to my sex. My hips moved in anticipation of what was to come as his tongue continued to assault the tight peak my nipple had become.

Adam watched my every movement as his finger lightly skimmed over my clit. My breathing increased, and his eyes pooled with desire. He pushed two fingers in.

"Adam…"

"Shh…"

Soft, barely-there kisses moved upward, away from my breast. When Adam's lips made it back to mine, I could feel the tip of his hardened length near my entrance.

"Please, Adam."

He entered me, and I gasped at the sensation as he looked into my eyes. It was intense as he filled and became a part of me. Making it all the way inside me, he stopped and leaned down to start kissing me all over again. My legs wrapped around him needing him closer.

His body rocked in and out as we found a sensual rhythm that hit all the right spots. It wasn't heated or desperate, but slow and savoring. My body felt revered, and something formed between us, unifying us as a true couple.

Reaching its peak, my body released a powerful euphoric wave that crashed into my system. It was mind-numbing how marvelous it felt. Adam got harder. Then, I felt his warmness fan out within me. He continued pumping into me while maintaining eye contact as his heat spread within my body. I felt as if I had been claimed. We completely belonged to each other.

Adam collapsed to the side and then pulled me closely to him. The after-sex smell was a heady combination as I entwined my legs with his. We had made love.

"You're amazing, Ainsley. That was indescribable."

He kissed my neck, and I turned to kiss him. My heart blossomed at feeling this different side of Adam brought out. He gave a piece of himself to me for safekeeping, and I knew it was a piece he hadn't given in a long time. I wanted to ask more about his past, but I didn't want to ruin the moment. This was our moment.

Lowly, I whispered, "Thank you for fighting for me."

"Ainsley, you are worth fighting for."

His hand stroked my shoulder, and I smiled into his chest.

Some things are worth fighting for. Adam is one of them.

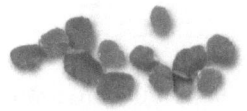

Sunlight hitting my face caused me to awake. Images of Adam making love to me over and over again trickled into my consciousness. Forgetting to shut the curtains, the moon had cast its glow over our bodies while we had made love. The sex had been unimaginable.

Adam was sound asleep beside me, dead to the world. I carefully slipped out from under his arm and headed to the bathroom where Adam had taken a shower yesterday. After freshening up, I slipped on one of his shirts. His shirt hit me mid-thigh, so there was no reason to find my underwear. I walked out to the garage, and I got my phone from my purse in his car.

Being in Adam's home, roaming around while Adam slept, was slightly uncomfortable. I felt like a stranger, as if I were intruding in his territory, but he needed to sleep.

I went back to the living room and sat on the couch. Taking a moment to myself, I glanced around to take in my surroundings. Decorations were at a minimum and his house was immaculately cleaned. Peering down at my phone, I noticed I had missed a few calls from my mom. It was a little after nine on Sunday morning. My mom was an early riser. It was our ritual to talk on Sunday mornings, so she would keep calling me until she reached me.

The reminder that I had missed three calls over the last few hours flashed across the screen and caused a smile. Every time I saw my mom's name, I remembered the connection her name had to mine. She had wanted me to always have a piece of herself, and she had used her first name as my middle name,

Christine.

As I was about to hit Send, Lindy walked through the door. I loved dogs. When I got down on the floor and leaned my back against the couch, she came up to me.

"Hey there, girl. You sure are pretty. I heard your dad call you Lindy last night."

She was a gorgeous golden retriever. Lindy nudged my hand to start petting her, and I complied.

"You're a good girl."

I stroked her ears, noticing her soft fur.

"I'm going to call my mom real quick, so you have to be quiet, okay?"

Lindy laid her head on my lap. I had always wanted a dog that cuddled with me. A flashback from my father came crashing into my mind.

"Mommy! Mommy! Do I get to keep her? She's so sweet." I held a cute little black puppy my mom had given me for my birthday.

We were going to be the best of friends. I would have something to hold on to at night when my daddy did things to my mommy that made her cry.

"Yes, sweetheart. Let me get the glasses down from the cabinet and pour the drinks before your dad gets home. We got back late, and I'm running a little bit behind." With her brown hair swinging behind her in a ponytail, she rushed around the kitchen, trying to get things ready as fast as possible.

It was Wednesday, and my dad always wanted meatloaf on Wednesdays. She remembered to push play on the CD player, and Mozart's classical music played. We listened to it every night while we ate. I hated it.

My dad came into the house in his normal grouchy way

and slammed the door. I moved to the far corner of the room. He threw all his stuff on the floor and looked at the bare table.

"Where's my dinner, Christine?"

My mom sweetly walked up and gave my dad a kiss on the cheek while wiping her hands on her apron. "Welcome home, Gerald. It's almost done. We got caught up in traffic. Have a seat, and I'll serve the salads."

He went to take his seat when my puppy made a noise.

His head snapped in my direction. "What is this, Christine?"

My mom put the smile she had perfected from the years of abuse on her face. "It's Ainsley's birthday. We had discussed that I could get her a puppy, so we went to get it today."

"Is this why my dinner is late?" His dark tone matched his coal-black hair and empty-looking dark eyes. I was convinced he was a horrible man.

It was two minutes after six. Dinner was always at six o'clock sharp.

My mom carried the salad and laid it on our black tablecloth. "We ran into traffic. The salad is ready."

"This mutt is the reason my dinner is late, isn't it?" He walked my way, and then he took the puppy from me.

I ran after him, crying. "Daddy, Daddy, please no. I'll be good. I'll help with dinner all week."

He tossed the puppy out the front door. "If it's still there in the morning, then it's a dog worth keeping. Go to bed for talking back to me. No birthday celebration for you." He turned back to my mom. "Christine, you and I need to talk this evening."

I turned and ran up the stairs as tears streamed down my face. My heart was broken. I couldn't protect my puppy against my dad just like I couldn't help my mom. In the morn-

ing, he'd act like nothing had happened and we were a perfect family.

When I awoke the next morning, the puppy was nowhere to be found.

My phone vibrated again as I stroked Lindy's hair. It was my mom calling, and I tried to rid my voice of any emotion as I hit Talk.

"Hey, Mom."

"Hey, sweetie. How are you doing?"

I focused on combing my fingers through some of Lindy's hair. She was a good dog as she sighed contentedly.

I responded, my voice sounding distant. "I'm good. I slept in this morning and I need to work on some things, but I was about to call so you didn't worry."

My mind wasn't in the right place to talk to my mom. When I thought about memories like that, it was hard not to ask her why she hadn't fought for me to keep that puppy. I never even had a chance to name him. I knew the answer though. She had been fighting her own battle each and every night against my dad. Knowing that still didn't take away the sharp memories I had that sometimes cut me like a jagged piece of glass. I always wanted to ask her why she hadn't taken me and left. My questions sometimes made me feel guilty because I loved my mom.

She broke through my thoughts. "Did you hear me, Ainsley?"

"I'm sorry, Mom. What did you say?"

She had the patience of a saint as she responded, "Don't forget about Donna's party. You promised you would come. I let her know that you'd be bringing someone. It's proper for someone your age to have a date at these upscale celebrations."

"I'll figure something out, Mom. I'll talk to you later. Love you."

"Love you, too, sweetie, so much."

I hung up the phone and put my head back on the couch. The deep cleansing breaths I took helped rid my head from all the cobwebs trying to set up shop this morning. I felt a body sit beside me, and I cracked open my eyes.

Adam sat there in his boxers, looking me over. "Is everything okay?"

I loved his tatted, muscular body. He was beautiful.

I looked down at Lindy, who then stood up and walked over to lie between our legs. I resumed petting her.

"It will be. I talked to my mom, and sometimes it's tough for me to think about the past." I cleared my throat. "Did you sleep well?"

Adam's brows drew together, and his hand came down to meet mine. "I'm not pushing for answers, Ainsley, but you can talk to me if you need to."

"Thanks. I will. I don't plan on inundating you with drama. You don't have to worry about that."

I remembered Adam talking about all the outside stuff a relationship could bring, and I didn't want to scare him off.

He picked up our entwined hands and looked at them for a few minutes. "My ex, Selena, broke up with me the night I was going to propose to her. She had been cheating on me for months. After that, I decided I was never going to go down the road of marriage and supposed happily ever afters. Since that night, I haven't put myself back out there until you. You changed my way of thinking, Ainsley. I want this and all that comes with it." He paused.

After a few moments of silence, I looked up.

He continued. "Ainsley, you don't have to tell me, but when you're ready, know that I put the drama out there first. I'm here if you need to talk. I want to be here for you."

Both our heads were lying back on the couch. I liked that Adam hadn't asked me to give him something I wasn't ready for. I guessed that made sharing a two-way street for both of us without judging.

"My ex, Jarrod, promised me forever. He wanted me to reconnect with my father in order to fast-track his career. When I refused to play my part, he went out and slept with my friend. Her dad is some bigwig at a company. Last I heard, they broke up, but he had a job, and he's been rising through the ranks."

"Ainsley, I won't ever push you toward someone you don't want to be near. I'm going to protect and support you."

I kissed him. "Thank you."

Lindy whimpered.

Adam turned to his dog and patted her head. "Are you hungry, girl? Let's go get you fed."

Lindy jumped up and raced toward the kitchen area.

Adam got up off the floor. "Let's eat, too. Do you like omelets?"

"Yes, that sounds great. I haven't had an omelet in forever."

Omelets with all the extras were expensive. I usually had plain eggs, but that was it.

Standing, Adam threw me up and over his shoulder. We made our way to his kitchen as I squealed in delight. I smacked his ass, and the next thing I knew, I had a finger sliding inside me, rubbing and working me. The tingling feeling invaded my body, and all I could focus on were the tantalizing sensations.

He walked over to a doorway where there was an exercise pull-up bar with rings extending a few inches down.

"Do you want to try something?" he asked.

His sex-ridden voice and his touch had me in an incoherent state.

I slapped his ass again, and he pushed two fingers inside me, causing me to moan.

Before the torture became unmanageable, I responded, "Yes, I'll try anything at this point. You're not playing fair."

My voice was needy as he kept working me into a wanton state.

He set me down in front of him and took his shirt off of me. He pinched my nipples as he said, "Ainsley, we'll do a real sex swing at the club sometime, but for now, we'll do this. When I pick you up, grab those rings up there. I'm going to shove my cock so far inside you while you hold on. Okay?"

My brain would not let me focus as he continued pulling my nipples to tight little points. I nodded because I was honestly up for whatever. He lifted me up, and I grabbed the rings, squeezing them. He supported me underneath my thighs, which helped me hold on to the rings better. He lined himself up and teased my clit as he looked into my eyes.

"Adam, stop screwing around and fuck me already." My voice was frustrated.

Adam's grin spread wider. Bringing his erection back to my entrance, he said, "I like when you talk dirty. I'm going to let that dirty mouth suck me off soon."

I let out an aggravated sound, and he sank so deep inside me that I screamed out. He was a madman as he swung me on and off him, hitting that magical spot that I craved. We maintained an intense eye contact as he continued to strike in and out. My arms were getting tired, which only added to the sensation building within my inner core.

Adam brought me to the point of no return, that place of pure bliss. My orgasm seared into my being as it hit. My grip loosened, but I held on as Adam came within me. Each time he'd poured himself into me felt like something between us deepened. Adam finished with a satisfied grin on his face. I wrapped my legs around his waist, completely spent, as I released the rings while he held me.

He nuzzled me. "Now, that was some fan-fucking-tastic sex."

"I would say it was sexilicious." My voice sounded completely satisfied.

He chuckled. "I would have to agree. That was sexilicious. Let's get you fed. By the way, we're eating breakfast naked. I might need a second round with you on the bar stool."

I kissed his neck as he set me down on a chair. He got some food out for Lindy, filling the automatic dog food dispenser, and then got out ingredients for the omelets. I noticed a large doggy door that led outside. That was probably how Adam could keep such strange hours and not be home every night.

"What can I do to help?"

Adam glanced up and gave me a sexy grin. "Just relax. I'm cooking you breakfast this morning."

He moved around the kitchen like a seasoned pro. He diced and chopped onions, mushrooms, tomatoes, and green peppers before cracking the eggs for the omelets. I watched in awe as he made me freshly-squeezed orange juice. He was a man of many talents, and my mouth watered. The smell of food filled the kitchen.

I remembered my mom's earlier request to bring a date to the function for her friend, Donna, whom I couldn't stand. Adam going as my date would be easier than debating with my mom on what was considered proper or not in the present day.

"Hey, Adam. Can I ask you something? And feel free to say no."

He glanced at my hand before he poured the egg mixture in the pan and a crackling noise commenced. "Of course. Ask me anything. I'll always shoot straight with you, Ainsley. I promise."

I flexed my hands on the countertop as I prepared my question. My insides were nervous from the fear of rejection, but I would accept whatever he said and be okay with it. "So, my mom has requested that I go to a function for one of her friends next weekend. She has it in her mind that it's proper for me to bring a date. If you're willing to go, it would be easier than me expending the energy to talk her out of why it's not necessary for me to have someone there. I mean, I want you there, but I don't want you to feel pressured to go."

The corner of his mouth tipped up. "Yes, I'll go. If she's worried about proper etiquette on bringing a date, what's your mom going to think of me all tatted up?" There was a note of concern in his voice as his brows drew together.

I shrugged my shoulders. "If you make me happy, that's all my mom cares about. It's one of the areas she doesn't meddle in at all. She trusts my judgment."

He nodded to himself as he slid the omelets out of the pan. "Breakfast is ready. Do you want to go anywhere today?"

He set the plate down in front of me. We ate and the omelet was delicious. Flavors burst in my mouth.

I took another bite while I thought about it. "This is delicious. Honestly, after the last few days, I could use a down day, but I'm flexible."

"I think that sounds like a good idea. But no *Last Uni-*

corn."

I giggled. "You're expected to sing the Prince Lir parts next time Emilyn comes over to watch it."

He smirked. "I'll figure out a way to talk her out of it. I'm not worried."

Adam oozed confidence, and I had no doubt that he was right.

"I think I figured out something I want to do today," I said.

"What's that?"

"Figure out a few more positions on the Tantra Chair."

A devilish grin spread on his face. "I think my day just got filled with lots of sexilicious sex."

I giggled, and I took another bite, thinking about all the orgasms to come.

Adam

JUST UNDER A week had passed since Ainsley and I had started officially dating. It was Friday, and Ainsley was on her way to the club.

Brandt needed me to be here tonight since he was going camping with his brother in Stone Mountain. They did it every year, the two of them, to remember their father who had been killed in Afghanistan. Their dad had died when Brandt was ten and his brother, Logan, was seven. Brandt's dad was American, and his mother was English, which was the reason Brandt had the slight accent at times. His parents had met and fallen in love on one of his dad's tours. After his dad had died, his mom had debated about moving back to Europe. In the end, she hadn't wanted to take the boys from the only home they could remember with their father. They had been fortunate not to have to move through the years.

My sister, Jessica, still bugged me about coming to my parents' anniversary party. I still hadn't decided. I wasn't sure if I could go. I wanted to spend some uninterrupted time with Ainsley tonight and think about all this shit tomorrow. I still had a while to decide on what I was going to do. After having lunch with my parents today, guilt plagued me for not agreeing to go. My mom had said something that was still on my mind as I waited for Ainsley.

I walked into the deli where I would meet my parents once a week for lunch. The place had a green awning with the words Something Sweet to Eat *written in white. I met my parents inside at our usual table. Baked goods lined the counter and sugary smells filled the air.*

My mom was slender with blonde hair and hazel eyes. She was short at just under five foot five. I towered over her. I was the exact image of my dad. Add twenty-five years to me, and I'd look exactly like him but with tattoos.

As I sat down, the waitress came up to the table and asked, "Same as always?"

My parents and I all said at the same time, "Yes, please."

She turned and walked away with a smile on her face. She was the owner's daughter and worked at the deli in the summer.

My mom started off with, "How's the club doing? I saw The Thrillhammers made the paper again, and it looked like they were playing at Club Envy."

I chuckled. My parents had actually cosigned the loan for the club. When Brandt and I had broken the news that we were expanding into a sex club, they had been supportive but shocked. After the details had been thoroughly outlined, they had accepted the direction we would be taking the club.

"It's going good. Pays the bills, so no complaints."

My mom gave me a gentle smile. "What's been going on in your world since we met last week?"

Ainsley came to mind, but I wasn't ready to mention her yet. Out of habit, I reached up and felt the scratch of my whiskers. I had forgotten to shave again. "Nothing much. You know, working and trying to stay on top of everything."

My dad wore one of his old Falcons T-shirts. He wore old ones during the off-season. It was one of those sports superstitions he and his buddy Marty would do to bring the team luck during the next year.

Our lunch was delivered. I had a Reuben sandwich with chips. It was the best sandwich in town.

My dad chimed in. "Your cousin, Lori, had her baby. She's coming to visit at Christmas."

I talked around the bite I had taken. "Oh, good. I'll have to make sure to see her."

Even though my brother, Jake, and I didn't talk, this worked for my parents and me. It allowed us to stay close. We never mentioned him. I would never force my parents to choose between us even though he was a lying, cheating bastard.

My mom watched me intently having that knowing look on her face. She was about to say something that was going to make me uncomfortable. My mom laid her hand on my free one. "I know you're going to find your true love one day, Adam. She's going to come in like a bright comet and change your world, leaving everything altered. I know you don't like talking about this, but I can sense something changing in you. I know it's a little off topic, but I needed to say this."

I had no words as I stopped mid-bite, thinking of the

brown-haired, blue-eyed woman who had been plaguing my every thought as of late.

My phone beeped, stirring me from my memory.
Finally, she is here.

Ainsley: I'm here.
Me: I'm on my way out. Stay in your car until I come to you.
Ainsley: Yes, sir!

I went to the entrance and then jogged across the lot to my girl. She gave me a sweet smile and a wave from the driver's seat. Things were easy between us. I liked holding her in public and showing her affection without any pressure to change who I was. Ainsley didn't push me for what I wasn't able to give. She let us exist and be without the normal bullshit relationship pressures, like what our future might look like and all that other crap.

I still wondered what was so troublesome from her past. In time, perhaps she would open up about it. There had been a few times this last week when I'd thought she wanted to tell me.

I opened the car door. "Hey there, baby."

As she got out of the car and locked it, she responded, "Hey. Sorry I'm a little late. Nancy's hours are changing, so she's not going to need me as much. Emilyn was upset, but she's better now that I promised to still see her. Nancy also asked me if I could help watch Emilyn the next few Friday nights. I guess Nancy has a new boyfriend."

Mentally, I said a plea that Ainsley had said no. I knew I was a bastard for thinking that, but right now, I wanted all of

Ainsley's free time. I was a selfish prick when it came to her, and I didn't care.

I grabbed her hand as I walked. "What did you end up telling her?" I tried to keep my voice casual.

Ainsley was in those super-short shorts and the tank top she had worn that night when I had come over to her place for spaghetti.

Hell, I'm going to have an issue with guys keeping their eyes where they belong.

I was on security tonight since Brandt was gone. There would be no sex for us until after the club closed, which would be at four in the fucking morning since I'd have to monitor everything.

Ainsley gave me a sad face. "I told her that I'd help her out. I didn't have any plans anyway."

I froze near the entrance of the sex club. My mouth gaped open. "Are you serious? Ainsley, I'm your plans when you're available."

She leaned up and nipped my lips. "Gotcha."

"You...you..."

She rocked my world with the smallest actions that wouldn't make sense to anyone. Ainsley was real. She wasn't conniving or caught up in money and prestige. Ainsley wanted to be happy and cared for.

I went to her ear. "I'm going to fuck you hard for that."

She tilted her head and kissed me. "That's what I was hoping for."

Ainsley walked toward the door where Trigger stood his post. She was saucily swaying her ass at me, and if I could pound into her right now, I would. I'd have her screaming for my cock. She knew I wasn't going to be able to do anything for a bit.

I jogged up behind her and put my arm around her shoulders. She looked up at me and gave me a beautiful grin as the slow hum from the sex club took over. Just having her in this environment had me envisioning all the possibilities. Her pale-blue eyes danced with happiness, and I liked being the one who had made them do that.

The crowd grew thicker as the night darkened. It would be a full house tonight.

We were headed back to the security office when my cell phone rang.

"This is Adam."

"Adam, Hampton. Do you have a second?"

I looked down at Ainsley, who watched me. I headed for the bar and she followed. I had to take this phone call.

"Hampton, can I call you back in five from my office?"

"Sure thing, Adam."

"Thanks."

I hung up the phone. With Brandt and two of our bouncers being gone, we were short-staffed from our normal head count.

Ainsley popped up onto a bar stool. The movement caused her shorts to ride up a little further.

Shit.

I looked over to Snake and nodded toward Ainsley. He knew what I wanted even though he was swamped with his own duties tonight.

Ainsley is more important.

I spun Ainsley around and kissed her hard, making sure all these assholes knew she was mine. When I pulled back, desire danced in her eyes.

Desire only for me. Good.

I looked down at her wrist to make sure she had on her

white bracelet. I liked seeing that white band on her. I liked the thought of her being taken—by me. It was a deep satisfaction.

"Baby, I need to go talk to Hampton. I'll be right back. Order whatever you want. It's on the house."

She gave me a light kiss. "Don't worry. I'll stay right here and talk to Nora. Go handle your business. I'll be okay."

I turned and went to my office. One of my old fuck buddies, Jasmine, hung out near my office door. She was beautiful with her short pixie-like dark hair and green eyes. She had wanted to get more serious, so I had walked. The noise of the club made it hard to hear everything as Jasmine spoke.

Her tongue swept across her bottom lip. "Hey, Adam. Are you busy tonight?"

I held up my wrist. I had on a white band also. "Jasmine, I'm taken. Our arrangement ended a few years ago. Excuse me."

She pouted her lips as I pushed past her. There was no need to say anything else. She meant nothing, and I had been crystal clear before we slept together.

Shutting the door, I dialed Hampton.

He picked up. "I think I've found Roach. He's in a small apartment in Alpharetta. I should have confirmation over the next day or so."

Finally, we're making headway.

"What do you need from us, Hampton?"

Hampton cleared his throat as papers rustled. "Do you want this guy pressed for information? I have a friend named Bane who knows people. If needed, I can call him to get some references of who we should hire."

I scrubbed a hand down my face. "Let's first see what Roach is up to. From there, we might need to get in contact with this Bane guy."

"Sounds good, Adam. I'll be in touch."

"Thanks. Let me know what you find out."

"Will do."

We hung up, and I sighed a breath of relief. Hopefully, this mess would be behind us soon. So far, no one's face had been visible on the pictures that were posted.

I went to my computer screen and glanced at all the video feeds from the club. The bar in the sex club came up. The new member, Tyler Helms, talked to Ainsley, and Jasmine walked toward her.

Fuck.

Just because Tyler was a rich trust-fund baby, and he was the son of our lawyer didn't mean he could write his own laws here. He was a cocky bastard.

My club. My rules. My girl.

Tyler had that look of lust on his face.

Motherfucker.

I could tell he wanted Ainsley.

Where is Snake?

And I knew Jasmine was going to cause problems.

I went straight to my office door and to the bar, nearly knocking someone over in the process.

That shithead is about to learn a lesson.

Wait.

I needed to maintain my composure. Ainsley didn't like fighting, and this was not how I would normally handle it in the sex club. Confrontation was a faster solution for the bar scene, so I generally chose that method. I needed to calm my inner-beast that always tried to surface. I didn't have an anger issue. I liked problems to be dealt with quickly at my club.

The music was low and sultry. Tyler touched Ainsley's shoulder as he spoke to her. My fists balled up, and then I relaxed them, reminding myself to stay calm. I could easily get my point across another way. Ainsley pulled away and scooted a little farther back from Tyler.

Asshole.

I made it to Ainsley and wrapped my hands around her waist. Jasmine stood behind Tyler, watching us.

"Hey, baby," I said.

Ainsley leaned into me at my term of endearment.

I looked over to Tyler, who watched the exchange. He was clearly surprised.

That's right, asshole. She's mine.

Tyler glanced at Ainsley's tits before looking back to me. I forced my fingers from their natural inclination to tighten into fists around her waist.

Tyler spoke almost condescendingly. "Hey, Adam. Good to see you again. Ainsley and I were about to have a drink."

Ainsley went stiff in my arms, and her head shot over to Tyler. Stiffly, she said, "I said I didn't want anything and that I was waiting for Adam, my boyfriend."

He gave a cocky smile, and I was three seconds away from revoking his membership.

As I held Ainsley closer to me, I spoke directly to this asshole with ice in my voice. "Tyler, I suggest you read the manual and know that white bracelets mean off-limits. Ainsley's mine. Don't make that mistake again. I'll revoke your membership next time any rule is broken, regardless of who your father is."

That sobered Tyler up.

Good.

He stared at me as if he tried to intimidate me. I looked him back in the eyes as I gave a smirk. Tyler downed his drink and slammed the glass on the bar before turning and walking away. I noticed that he hadn't acknowledged my earlier comment. If Ainsley wasn't here, he and I would be having a serious talk, but I didn't want to leave her alone for a second longer. He'd be here at some point when Ainsley wasn't.

With one problem down, another scooted closer to us. Ainsley looked away as Nora gave Ainsley an air high-five.

Jasmine took a long sip of her drink and then said, "You know, Adam and I used to fuck like rabbits. He's been through most of the girls here. We could try the three of us."

Ainsley's head snapped to the left. Before I had a chance to say anything, Ainsley said, "And who are you?"

Her voice held as much ice as I'd had in mine when addressing Tyler.

Jasmine gave a smirk. "I'm Jasmine. He said I was the best lay he'd had in years."

I interrupted. "Jasmine, I suggest you watch yourself. We haven't fucked in years. You'd bett—"

Ainsley held up her hands. I was strung tight and getting pissed off at the nerve of this bitch.

Ainsley calmly but sternly spoke with enough heat to melt Antarctica. "Jasmine, I'm not sure what you planned to accomplish, but if you think I don't know Adam has been with several people in this club, then you're delusional. I'm sorry you apparently haven't gotten over your fuck-buddy relationship, which I'm sure he made abundantly clear was over. I suggest we not speak anymore, or I'm going to ask Adam to revoke your membership for not respecting the white-bracelet rule."

My girl had a backbone, and I supported her. "Don't push it, Jasmine. If you bother Ainsley or myself again, you're gone."

Jasmine grabbed her drink and left the bar.

Problem two had officially been dealt with. Ainsley had shocked me with her reaction. She had been rational, and she'd let the past stay where it belonged—in the past.

I turned her around on the bar stool. "Are you okay?"

She stood up. "Yes, I'm okay. I've honestly been expecting someone like Jasmine to approach me with some sort of jealousy. Your past is more colorful than mine, but we've both still slept with people. It's a nonissue for me as long as they stay in the past."

"I promise, Ainsley. That's where they all are."

She reached up and gave me a gentle kiss. "Then, that's all that matters."

"Are you ready for our night on security camera duty?" I kissed her again.

Ainsley grabbed my hand and squeezed it. "I have my eagle eyes ready to spot anyone misbehaving."

"Good. You're going to need those for security."

She paused for a second and then glanced over her shoulder seeing Tyler on the other side of the room. Ainsley turned back to me. "Who is Tyler's father?"

"He's our lawyer's son."

A look of disgust went across Ainsley's face. Nora set a Guinness on the bar and then went to the next customer. Ainsley looked over her shoulder as I grabbed my beer and gave Nora a wave before she was out of sight. This week, Nora's hair was black with red tips. She wagged her eyebrows up and down while giving us one of those shit-eating grins.

Leaving the bar, we made it to the security office as several other people watched us. I knew people probably thought I had lost my marbles with how I acted with Ainsley, but I didn't care.

Ainsley had been in here when I gave her a thorough tour

of the place the other night. I closed the door behind us and motioned toward the couch.

"Make yourself comfortable, baby. I'm sorry I have to work tonight. I'll make it up to you."

Instead, she sat in the chair next to me. I liked that she wanted to be close to me.

"I'm going to hold you to that." Ainsley bounced her leg like she was nervous, and her shorts rode up slightly higher.

My dick ached. It was going to be a long night.

She twirled her ring and that was my sign that something was up. I planned on giving her a few minutes before I asked what was going on.

Then, she talked. "To pass the time while you watch the screens, do you want to play a game?"

Scrolling through all the screens quickly, it seemed like there weren't any impending problems. I checked the queue, and no one had hit their button to say they needed help.

I responded, "I'd be up for a game, I guess."

"I think we should play Twenty Questions."

I leaned back in the chair. We knew the basics about each other at this point. I was curious to see where she was going with this. I began to trust her more about not trying to push me somewhere I either didn't want to go or wasn't ready to go.

"I'm game."

She rubbed her hands together as I glanced at the screens again. Tyler and Jasmine had found each other.

Good. They would be a great match. Arrogant asses.

"I'll ask first." She tapped her finger to her mouth. "When did you lose your virginity?"

I chuckled. "Sixteen. It was in the back of my mom's pickup truck. You?"

"My senior prom in a hotel room. It was not memorable

in the slightest. He was drunk and passed out after the deed was done." She shook her head. "It was not fun. Okay, next question. What's something you want to do with me, but you haven't yet for whatever reason?"

I ran my hands down my jeans. I liked this game more and more, but she made security detail difficult.

"Tie you up while I fuck you senseless in the Tantra Chair."

She squirmed in her seat.

"What's a fantasy you've always wanted fulfilled?"

"To do naughty things together in a public place. It seems like it would be exhilarating."

Now, I enjoyed this little game a whole hell of a lot. I could easily do that for my girl. I made a mental note. She spread her legs slightly and a blush crept on her cheeks.

She's up to something.

She ran her finger up the inside of her leg. "Will you ever masturbate in front of me?"

My mouth gaped slightly at that question. I had not expected that. "Um…yes, *we* can do that."

She cocked her head to the side as I watched her face.

"Would you want me to do that, too?"

"Finger-fuck yourself while I watch?"

She nodded.

"Hell yes. I'd be right there, coming with you."

My girl was getting more and more sexually open each and every day, and I loved it. She was comfortable with me, and we could talk about almost anything.

Ainsley stood and dropped her shorts. She didn't have on any panties.

I swallowed hard. "Hell yes. Did you plan this, baby?"

"Yes."

That one simple word had my dick at full attention. I sat back in my chair and undid my pants, showing her how turned on I was. Quickly, I glanced at those stupid-ass screens again.

We're hiring someone for security tomorrow.

She sat back in the chair and licked her lips as she arched her back and pulled off her shirt and bra. She sat there in a chair, naked, for me. Her hand trailed toward her center, and my mouth watered at the sight.

"I've been thinking about this all day, Adam."

I rolled her chair toward me. "Baby, brace your legs on my armrests and then touch yourself."

She put her feet on the armrests. I placed my feet around the base of her chair to keep her from scooting away.

"Now, touch yourself, baby. Make yourself come. Watching you fall apart is going to make me lose myself."

My words gave her whatever push she'd needed as she touched herself. I grabbed my cock and rubbed it as I saw her rosy pussy. She glistened as she entered her body, and she threw her head back at the feeling.

She moaned, "Adam...Adam...Adam..."

Those words on her mouth did something to me. My name was getting her off behind her closed eyes. She vigorously rubbed herself, and I stroked my cock, harder and faster. We were going to come together. Any second, she was going to go.

"Ainsley, look at me when you come. Watch me come."

Her eyes snapped to mine and then zeroed-in on my hand rubbing my dick. It was ready to blow. She panted hard and came. I let it go and erupted on the floor as we watched each other fall apart. She was a goddess as she slumped back in her chair. I leaned back in the chair and watched her.

She's mine.

Her legs were still propped on the armrests with the evidence of her arousal still on display. I caressed her feet.

"I'll play Twenty Questions anytime you want."

Ainsley smiled coyly at me. "I love that game. I can't—"

There was a knock on the door, and Ainsley abruptly tried to scoot back, which caused the chair to start tipping back. I went to grab it when I heard the door opening.

My voice thundered as I yelled, "Do not come in here!"

The door slammed shut.

Shit, I forgot to lock the door.

First, I made sure that Ainsley wasn't going to fall. She kept glancing toward the door. There was cum all over the floor.

"Baby, get dressed. No one will see you. Let me step out in the hallway."

Ainsley still looked half-startled. "I guess that will teach us to leave the door unlocked again."

She tried to make light of the situation, but I was on edge. Someone had almost seen her exposed in all her beauty.

I gave her a chaste kiss. "I'll be back."

As I walked to the door, I zipped myself back up, and I opened the door enough for me to slip out. Snake was about seven feet from the door. He was a smart guy not to give me a knowing grin.

"What's up, Snake?"

Snake ran his hands through his hair. "I need another walkie-talkie so I could talk with all the guys. Mine died."

He held up his nonworking one. This was another reason I hated those damn things.

"Let me get you another one. I'll turn one on too, tonight to help. Stay out here."

Snake nodded, and I went back into the room. Ainsley

was dressed, and she was cleaning up my mess.

"Baby, I'll get that. I just need to get this walkie-talkie to Snake."

She smiled sweetly up at me. "I wanted to. I'm almost done."

I grabbed a charged walkie-talkie, went back out into the hall, and handed it to Snake. He took it from me, turned it on, and headed off toward the bar.

He called over his shoulder, "Thanks, man. Let me know if you need anything."

"Will do."

I went back in and Ainsley threw away the last of the paper towels.

"Thanks, baby."

"Anytime."

She wagged her eyebrows up and down, and I chuckled.

I went to the desk, sat down in the black leather chair, and looked at all the screens again. All looked clear. Ainsley came and sat on my lap. I moved her hair over so I had access to her neck as she leaned back.

She played with her ring. "Are you still okay about going to my mom's friend's thing tomorrow? I found out it's actually a congratulations party for her daughter. She got admitted late into medical college. I told my mom that I'm seeing someone, but there's no pressure to come."

I continued flipping through the screens as I gave Ainsley's neck a kiss. "Yes, I want to go. What time do we need to be there? Do you like Donna and her daughter?"

"It starts at seven, and it's a dinner thing. Donna was a supposed friend of my mom's when I was growing up. We should only have to stay a couple of hours at most."

There was a slight vulnerability in her voice that cut to the quick of me. I wanted her to trust me enough to talk about what had happened to her.

"We'll leave around six thirty to get there on time, if that sounds good. Do you want to talk about it?"

I kissed her neck again and wrapped my left arm around her waist. She settled in a little closer, obviously needing the connection.

We sat in silence for a few minutes.

Then, she talked solemnly. "My dad was a horrible man. This supposed friend of my mom's used to tattle to my dad, and it would cause problems for her. My mom is the type of person to look for the good within people even if there isn't any. She stayed with my dad until he left her, and honestly, I think she is still under some delusion that he'll come back. She's always been there for me, and she's protected me, but we don't talk about any of it. It's as if what I remember as a kid never happened. Sometimes, because of all the denial, I question if any of it was even real."

With her anguished voice my curiosity was at an all-time high. Ainsley stayed silent as she looked into the distance with her eyes unfocused. Since we had met, it seemed Ainsley enjoyed the silence at times. That was something we both had in common. Feeling the need to touch her, I kissed her neck again, and Ainsley leaned into it. As the silence continued, a lone tear fell down her cheek. My right hand came up and brushed it away.

"What did he do to you and your mom, baby?"

Ainsley sat up and turned toward me. Her blue eyes were on the brink of tears. It was the saddest I had ever seen them.

"I've never talked about this to anyone. It's always been something I've kept hidden, and I've dealt with it myself."

I knew I should be paying attention to the monitors.

Things could go bad at a moment's notice. *Fuck my club at this point. Ainsley needs me. I am here for her. She is important to me.*

I picked her up and carried her over to the couch. After what we'd shared, we had something more between us. I could feel our bond growing.

I turned her toward me, making sure she saw my face, as I spoke. "Ainsley, you don't have to tell me, but I'm here if you want to talk about it."

She looked down at her ring and softly spoke. "I don't want to go into detail right now, but he used to beat my mom at night. If either one of us did anything wrong, she would be punished. He was a horrible man."

Ainsley looked away, and I pulled her to me. I knew the significance of what she had shared with me. She trusted me enough to tell me something she had never told anyone. The meaning of that was not lost on me. There was one thing I had to know.

Barely above a whisper, I asked, "Did he ever hurt you? Did he ever touch you?"

She shook her head. "No, not physically."

Mentally, I sighed with relief. Ainsley was done talking, and I wasn't going to push her. She yawned, probably from mental exhaustion. Slowly her eyes got heavy. I held her until she fell asleep, loving the feeling of her being mine, and then laid her back on the couch. Draping a black blanket over her small frame, I stared at her, lost in all the feelings I continued to develop for her. Her breath came out even and I knew she was different from all the other girls I had been with. In sleep, Ainsley's lips were a pale pink. She looked beautiful as her chestnut hair was splayed across the pillow. Thoughts of what had happened played through my mind. I hoped I could give her what she needed in a relationship. Part of me knew I would fuck it up at some point. Hopefully, I was wrong.

As I walked back to my security post, my phone vibrated again. It was a text from my sister, and she asked about the party. I ignored it and decided I'd respond back tomorrow. I went back to the desk to watch the screens. I still didn't know what I was going to do about being at a party where Selena and my brother would be.

I kept glancing over to make sure Ainsley was okay. I noticed that the deep hurt I normally felt when thinking about Jake and Selena lessened. I had Ainsley, and what had happened to me was no longer controlling me.

Ainsley was important to me.

She was the most important thing in my world; the only thing that mattered.

Ainsley

L AST NIGHT HAD been intense, both sexually and emotionally. I had shared a bit of my past with Adam, which I had never done before with anyone. Telling Adam what had happened to my mom and me had been both liberating and terrifying at the same time. It had been liberating in the sense that I felt like now that my secret was out. I wasn't drowning in the pressure of my self-condemned silence. I was terrified for leaving myself so exposed, knowing I had given yet another piece of myself to Adam that I might never get back if things ended. That was still highly probable, considering his past and all the warnings he had given me.

I wondered if my mom had told anyone about what my dad had done to her. The memories had to haunt her while she still lived in the same house where all the abuse had happened.

Each and every time I went back home, it would feel like all hell would break loose at any second, and I would be sent to my room. I shook the memories that were trying to come to the forefront of my mind.

I was in the shower, getting ready for tonight's dinner event. Adam had dropped me off earlier since I didn't have my clothes at his place. Adam had gone to the club to work, and he would be picking me up in about half an hour.

Getting out of the shower, I wrapped a towel around my body and then worked on drying my hair. Tonight, I was going to wear my blue baby-doll dress with some strappy nude sandals. My mom had gotten the dress for me last year for my birthday. I liked the simplicity of the dress.

My phone pinged, and I saw it was Nora.

Nora: Hey, girl! Is it okay if I stop by? I'm in the area.
Me: Of course.
Nora: Okay. I wanted to make sure that you weren't taming the one-eyed snake.
Me: I'm ignoring you.
Nora: Ha-ha!

Nora was such a free spirit. It hadn't bothered her in the slightest that I was seeing someone. She wasn't the jealous type, and I thought that was why we got along so well.

There was a knock at the door. I opened it, and Nora came breezing in. She wore the punk-rocker look today with torn tights, a short mini skirt, and a tight T-shirt that said, *Try Me.* She went toward the kitchen, and I followed.

"Hey, chica! I'm thirsty."

"Make yourself at home. You know that."

Nora knew her way around my place. While she had been

in between places, she had lived with me for a few months last summer while she saved up some money for a new place. I had offered for her to stay longer, but she needed her own space.

Nora took out a glass. "You look cute. Oh shit, I forgot Adam is picking you up for that dinner thing. I'm gonna skedaddle."

I leaned against the counter. "Don't be silly. I missed hanging out with you this week, but I know you had to work."

She continued with getting herself some water. That was one thing Nora and I had with each other—the truth. We were always straight with one another.

Nora still had red tips on the ends of her black hair as she filled her glass with tap water. "I know. I've been beat from picking up the afternoon shift at the diner. They had an opening, and I jumped on it. There are only a few more weeks before fall semester starts, and the extra money will help in case something happens to my car, or you know, any of the normal day-to-day sucky stuff."

I nodded my head. "The offer still stands to come and stay here. My rent is paid for."

Nora put her lips together and gave a big kissing sound. "I know that, and I love you for it, but you know me. I need space. Speaking of money, did you have anything to do with the raise I got at Club Envy?" She arched an eyebrow at me.

Ah, this is why she made sure to stop by.

I looked her straight in the eyes. "I had nothing to do with it. I would never interfere like that."

Nora gave me a smirk and then a little nod. "Good. I didn't think so, but I had to make sure." She took a drink of water. "So, you and the man-friend are getting all cozy with each other still?"

I rolled my eyes. Emilyn must have told Nora about my

term for Adam.

Nora laughed. "I love that name 'man-friend'. Ha-ha! Where on earth did you come up with that? And why the hell did you not tell me that term? I'm dying here. I choked on my food from laughing so hard when I put two and two together after Emilyn had been talking about it. Now, come on, spill. How's it working with taking the relationship outside the club? Everyone at the club is talking about how different Adam's becoming with you."

"Everyone's talking? Different?"

Adam seemed the same to me. *Why was everyone talking about us? Did Adam know everyone was talking? What would he think?* My anxiety inched up.

"Slow your roll down. It's not bad. Yes, everyone's talking. Before you, Adam was all business, business, business and no fun. Even his previous partners were appointments. He never lit up like he does when you're around, and quite frankly, he's almost insufferable when he hasn't seen you for a while. My dear, I think you've pussy-whipped your man-friend. Are you picking up on what I'm putting down?"

My mind was going a million different directions with all the information Nora had unloaded on me. "Um...um...I honestly don't know what to make of all that. We're together. We don't have titles with each other per se, but I feel a stronger connection forming."

She played with the red tips of her hair. "I can see it. That's good though. Titles and expectations can be stifling." Nora stretched as if the thought put her in a small prison. "As long as he's still treating you right and not pulling those dick-wad moves he did that day when you left his place, the man-friend and I will get along smashingly as friends. Otherwise, it's going to suck to work for such a prick."

"You're the best. Are you still seeing that guy from the bar the other night? Isn't his name Jude?"

She shrugged. "Yeah, we see each other here and there. You know how it goes. It's fun, so we'll see."

Nora generally would see a guy for a year or so, and then they would both move on. She rarely had any drama when it came to relationships. She gravitated toward people like her.

There was a knock at the door. I opened it, and Adam stood there in flat-fronted khakis with a button-up shirt. The sleeves were rolled up at the elbows. He even gave the preppy look an edge when combined with his bad-boy look.

"Hey, baby. Sorry I'm a few minutes late. You look beautiful."

I opened the door wider, and he saw Nora sitting at the table.

"Thank you. You're quite dashing yourself. Nora and I were catching up."

Nora gave Adam a serious look as she spoke. "Hey there. You'll be happy to know that your nuts are still safe. Seems like you're keeping *my* girl happy." She stood and took her glass to the dishwasher.

I glanced back at Adam, and one side of his lips were quirked. Adam looked at me when he spoke. "Good to know *my* girl is satisfied."

My cheeks reddened as I bit my lower lip. Nora laughed, probably at Adam's possessive comment, as she came walking up to me.

She gave me a kiss on the cheek. "Gotta roll. See you later. Tell your mom I said hey."

"Will do. Bye, Nora. Tell Jude I want to meet him some time."

She threw her right hand up as she walked to her car. "It's

a date. Bye guys. Take care of my girl."

Adam called after her. "She's mine."

Nora laughed as she got into her car. I loved being important to someone. I kissed Adam on the cheek. "I'm yours, don't worry. Let me grab my purse, and we can head out."

"I'm going to tell her you said that."

I was genuinely happy. My heart felt lighter than it had in years. The self-sentenced prison of silence disappeared. Grabbing my purse and keys, I headed back toward the door to lock up. We got in the car and made our way toward the Buckhead Club.

It was a hot day today, even in the early evening hours, and there wasn't much wind. The car windows in Adam's black Camaro were tinted and nearly black. It was like a one-way mirror looking out to the world.

An idea formed, and I licked my lips, wanting to embrace this new sexually open side that Adam had uncovered. At his house one time, he had mentioned how he wanted me to give him a blow job. I had tried to do that with my ex, Jarrod, a few times, but all he'd wanted to do was have quick sex and then go to sleep. I hadn't honestly known what I was missing.

"So, what did you do today after you dropped me off?"

We were flying down the road as he drove. "I contacted a staffing agency to find a new security guy to watch the cameras at night. Hampton is also seeing if he knows anyone who would want the job. Brandt and I need to get someone in place. I'm not dealing with what I had to last night when I could have been alone with you."

I grinned at his words. "It'll make it easier on you guys."

I worked up the courage to give him a little something extra as he drove. I eyed his belt buckle and then looked back up at his eyes.

"That's the plan, baby."

Adam kept glancing over at me. He could probably tell that something was up. If I didn't make my move soon, the moment would be gone. I unbuckled my seat belt and leaned over to his belt buckle.

"What are you doing, Ainsley?"

I peered up at him from my leaned-over position. "Well, you said that you wanted my dirty mouth to suck you off. I think now is a good time, don't you?"

The instant the words were out of my mouth, he hardened underneath his pants. I worked on freeing him.

"Hell yes, baby. Wrap those luscious lips around me and suck me in deep."

That spurred me into action. Leaning over the console, I brought his tip into my mouth. The engine revved, and I went deeper, tasting his shaft. As his tip hit the back of my throat, I went further, thankful my gag reflex was not bad. I took him in all the way and he filled my mouth completely.

"Fuck, Ainsley. That feels so good that deep. Move, baby. Move fast."

I moved up and down, taking him all the way on each slide down. His hips flexed and the purr of the engine combined with the feeling of having Adam in my mouth was a hedonistic combination. Being on the road while pleasuring him was a thrill that I had never experienced before in my life. He was getting harder, which was a sign he was about to come. I slowed down my pace, drawing out his pleasure as he had taught me.

"Ainsley! Fuck!"

Adam liked absorbing the drawn out pleasure. My tongue played with him as it continued a slower paced slide. Hearing him moan had myself getting worked up sexually as I pushed my legs together to try and keep the ache at bay.

The car shifted into park. One hand came down to the back of my head, grabbing my hair and taking over the speed. I relaxed my throat completely. Adam had reached his limit and had taken back control. I kept my lips firm, feeling each and every bulging vein as my mouth worked him. The ridge around the head was my favorite part to touch as I sucked him hard.

"I'm going to come, baby. Take me, take all of me."

I wanted him, all of him.

Warm liquid filled my mouth, and I swallowed and tasted the salty essence of Adam. His grip relaxed on my hair and he slumped back into the driver's seat. Giving him one last lick, I rose, and I loved seeing the satisfied look on his face.

I touched my lips with my tongue as I gathered any escaped cum. "I think I'll love car sex."

A devilish grin appeared on his face. "Baby, I'm going to give you some fan-fucking-tastic car sex in a moment."

I nodded. "Yes, I want that."

I kissed him briefly, and he kissed me back before I sat back down.

I realized we were in a Starbuck's parking lot. "Are we getting coffee?" A small giggle escaped my lips.

He revved the engine and reversed out. "You're the only fix I need, Ainsley."

"I guess all those practices on my lollipops paid off."

"I'd say they more than paid off. Lucky lollipops."

He pushed a button, and a low rhythmic melody came on the speakers. It was erotic and reminded me of the club. As we merged back onto the highway, he grabbed my hand. More and more, Adam would do these types of small gestures and I loved it. He meant more to me than anyone else ever had.

He was still unzipped and free in the driver's seat.

It was hot, looking at his semi-erection. "Do you want me to zip you back up?"

"No. I want you to scoot your seat back as far as it can go and then lean back."

I did all that he'd said.

Once I had finished, he continued. "I want you to take your panties off, lift up your dress, and start touching yourself. Don't come. You're going to watch as my cock comes back to life, getting ready to enter your sweet little pussy."

His words were raw, powerful, and dominating. I liked when he would take control of me sexually. It allowed me to find myself—the person that I was meant to be but had hidden all these years.

I pulled my panties off and tossed them on the floor of the car. Next, I put my fingers to my clit and touched it. Little throbs of pleasure pulsated out.

"Ainsley, pull your dress up. Expose yourself to me. I want to see you."

That voice had me moaning as I lifted my dress. I ran my hands up as more moisture gathered and I slickened myself. I wanted him badly.

"That's right, baby. Spread your legs farther. Get it good and wet."

His words fueled my actions as I moaned, thinking about having car sex. I slid my legs as far open as they could go. I was so close to coming.

His hand came down on mine. "Slow down, baby. We're almost there, and then I'm going to take you—hard."

Adam's hand crept up under my dress to my right breast. His fingers slipped underneath my bra and slightly traced the area of my nipple while I continued to touch myself. The teasing touch had me desperate.

I slowed my fingers down as I whispered, "Hurry. Please hurry. I need you."

"Ainsley, focus on the pleasure." His voice was stern, commanding.

My mind eased and I let my body do the thinking. I looked over and saw his dick twitch and focused on the sensations. I felt desired, needed, naughty, and sexy.

The engine roared again. A few minutes later, the car slowed. Through the front window, I could tell we were entering a parking garage. I kept touching myself and then a concrete wall came into view.

"Ainsley, lift your dress over your head."

My dress came off in the next instance. Adam moved his seat back, and I could see his throbbing erection as he crawled over the console and faced me in the passenger seat. On top of me, he scooted my body up the seat until there was enough space to fit his dick underneath me. He pulled down the cups to my bra, binding my breasts up. Adam leaned down and bit the tip of one nipple and then the next, causing me to arch off the seat. As I came back down from the sensation, he impaled me.

"Adam…"

"I almost ran off the road while watching you touch yourself. I've got you. Shh…"

Just when I thought I would cry if I didn't get the friction I needed, he moved. Lips migrated to the side of my right nipple, and he sucked the flesh of my breast deep into his mouth. There would be a bruise left on me. I wrapped my legs around his back as he increased the pace to a raw, carnal speed.

I took my hands and ran them down his back as we both screamed out, toppling off into a black abyss. As I surfaced, stars danced across my eyes. Adam collapsed on me, kissing me possessively, as he held me and continued to move inside me. I loved having him inside me, knowing part of him moved within me.

He pulled back. "I hope to hell you love car sex as much as I do now."

The way he would act when we had sex was as if everything we did was new and exciting to him. Whether he made love to me or fucking me, sex seemed like it was more special because it was with me.

"I'm thinking that you'll need to take me on all available surfaces in this vehicle."

"I like that idea—a lot."

He laid his forehead on mine and we both closed our eyes.

"Can you feel our connection growing, Ainsley?"

Softly, I murmured, "Yes. Are you okay with it?"

He brushed his lips over mine. "Yes, I am. I want this with you."

We stayed wrapped in each other for a few more minutes.

He pulled away. "We need to get going. It's almost time for dinner to start. I don't want you to be late."

"Okay, hop out and let me get dressed real quick."

He gave me one more kiss and then got out of the vehicle. I found my underwear and then worked on righting my bra. There was a huge hickey where he had been sucking. That mark would be there for days. I touched it and smiled. After finding my dress and putting it on, I got out of the car where Adam waited for me expectantly. Car sounds echoed through the parking garage.

We intertwined our hands and walked to the elevators that would take us to the floor where the club was.

As the elevator doors closed, I announced, "I love my mark."

Adam's brown eyes shot down to the place on my breast where the hickey lay underneath my dress. "Good. I like my mark on you, and I like knowing the fact that my cum is in you right now."

"I like knowing it's there, too."

He gave me a heated look. A shiver ran through my body. Adam was right. Our relationship had grown to something more.

The elevator doors opened. I stopped and looked around as a thought occurred to me making sure no one was around. We were about to see my mom. "Do I look normal? I don't look like I had an intense orgasm in a car in the parking garage, do I?"

He chuckled. "No baby. You look beautiful."

That was the affirmation I'd needed as we continued to the entrance of the Buckhead Club.

A waiter dressed in a black suit greeted us. "May I have your name?"

"Ainsley Pearson."

He looked through his list. "Oh, yes, here you are. You and your guest are going to be at table fourteen."

"Thank you."

We continued through the doors and entered into a lavishly decorated room. White flowers filled the room with purple accents. A fruity smell drifted through the air.

I spotted my mom. "I see my mom. Are you ready?"

"Let's do this."

Adam watched everything closely as his brows scrunched together. He looked a little nervous.

"Adam, you know there's nothing to be worried about,

right?"

He nodded as we continued to make our way to my mom. We were almost there when my mom turned. She was in a suit skirt with a long-sleeved, button-down silk shirt. Her hair was put up in a French twist. She was an exact replica of me with her pale blue eyes and brown hair, but she was older. Her figure was still slender.

I gave her a hug. Seeing mom outside of her home was easy. I always tried to talk her into meeting me someplace in town, but rarely would she agree to leave her home.

"Hey, Mom. This is Adam. Adam, this is my mom, Christine."

Adam extended his hand. "Nice to meet you, ma'am."

My mom extended both her hands and took him into a quick hug. Pulling back, her kind smile showed. "Nice to meet you, Adam. Please call me Christine. I'm so glad you were able to come."

Adam seemed to relax as he pulled me back to his side. "Me, too, Christine. You did an incredible job of raising such an exquisite daughter."

With those words, I knew I wanted to be the one he would want to keep...forever.

Hopefully, in time, he would feel the same way.

Adam

DINNER HAD GONE well, even with all these pretentious people. They were so far removed from reality. This is why Brandt and I wouldn't do shit like this even though we were bringing in a significant amount of money each month. Some people were surprised we dressed in jeans and T-shirts at the club, but it was who we were. The group of people here were a bunch of fake people, all gathered to congratulate themselves on a job well done. Currently, it was mingle time before the presentation part of the dinner began—at least, according to the schedule of events I had been presented with.

Ainsley, Christine, and I were standing and talking.

Ainsley excused herself. "I'll be right back. Would you get me some water if you have a chance?"

"Sure thing, baby."

Ainsley smiled and walked off, her brown hair swaying behind her.

Hell, she rocks my world.

I wasn't sure how to classify what we had, but it was more than anything I had shared with anyone else, including Selena. My self-protection told me to pull back, but I fought it. I knew what it felt like when I was without Ainsley. Putting myself out there was worth the risk.

Christine spoke to me. "It's quite heartwarming to see you so taken with Ainsley. The two of you are good together. I'd love to have you over for dinner. I'll check with Ainsley and see if this Wednesday works. Does that sound good?"

"I'd like that, Christine. Thank you."

She smiled and then someone tapped her on the shoulder. Christine turned and spoke to the person. She was kind and soft-spoken. She was the epitome of manners and niceties.

My phone rang and I excused myself to the corner of the room. "This is Adam."

"Adam. Hampton here. We've confirmed that it's Roach in Alpharetta. He's gotten a job at a strip club that has a no-camera policy. I assume they have the same gig going on there, too. He gets his sidekick in past security, and they take pictures. How do you want to handle it?"

Roach turned into a huge pain in my ass. "I don't want to get mixed up with this unless I have to be. I want to find out who it is, get the pictures gone, and forget about this whole deal."

"Sounds good. You've always gotten involved in the past. I'm glad you're letting me take care of it. I'll get it handled and get back with you and Brandt. I sent you a couple of re-sumes for the security system. There's a guy named Matt that I think would be especially good."

My mind went to Ainsley. She was the reason I didn't want to be so involved in the drama. I scrubbed a hand down my face as the fear of commitment tried to surface. I beat it back with the biggest stick I could find. Ainsley wasn't asking for me to stop being so involved. I wanted to step back. There was no reason to fill my time with stupid shit like this anymore when we had someone more than capable to handle it.

"Thanks, Hampton. We'll be waiting."

"Will do. Give me a few days. Talk to you then. Bye, Adam."

"Bye, Hampton."

I need a drink.

I walked over to the bar and got Ainsley a water and myself whatever beer they had on tap.

"Adam Ryker?"

I turned and saw a man with black but slightly graying slicked-back hair. He looked familiar.

"Gerald Pearson with S&P Associates. You normally work with my partner, Henry Smith. This is my wife, Lydia."

She was a petite woman who had a kind smile. Lydia was significantly younger than Gerald. She had blonde hair with brown eyes. She looked sad, the kind of sadness that had penetrated her so deeply that it had no place to go but to the surface.

Aw, hell, he's from my law firm. What a place to run into these money bloodsuckers.

I held out my hand. "Nice to meet you, Lydia. Good to see you, Gerald. Brandt and I have an appointment to talk with you guys this week about a few things."

He had dark coal eyes that were almost eerie. He reminded me of a greasy car salesman.

"I saw that. I'm going to be sitting in on the meeting with Henry. Club Envy has become one of our top accounts."

I didn't care about all this bullshit schmoozing.

He asked, "Are you friends with the Stevensons?"

The Stevensons were throwing this party. I was glad I didn't know them.

"No, I'm here with my girlfriend. She's a friend of the family."

Ainsley spotted me and came my way. She was graceful and confident as she walked through the room. She had a strong presence, but around me, she had become laid-back and comfortable.

She walked up to me, and all I could think about was my mark on her right now.

My mark. My Ainsley.

I was about to introduce her when she stiffened and looked like she had seen a ghost. Her face turned pale.

Gerald spoke. "Ainsley, it's good to see you. It's been a while. How are you doing?"

Lydia was next to speak with more life than I thought she could have at this point with how defeated she seemed. "Oh, Ainsley. It's wonderful that I'm finally getting to meet you. Gerald has talked so much about you. I hate that you haven't been able to come over for dinner yet."

Who the hell is this guy? And why is he so familiar with my girl?

Ainsley stood there shocked, unable to move as her eyes widened. Adrenaline pumped through my veins as I prepared myself for whatever Ainsley needed. I glanced back at Gerald, who looked between Ainsley and me.

Her voice was small as she said, "Adam, please get me out of here."

I grabbed her by the waist to escort her out when Gerald reached out and touched her arm. I would have thought he'd electrocuted her with how she jumped back. I moved her behind me, and she latched on to the back of my shirt as if she was afraid something else was about to happen.

I stepped in and adopted my no-nonsense tone as I said, "Gerald, I suggest you not touch my girl again. It's apparent she doesn't want to talk to you. If you push this further, I can guarantee I will be the one to end it. I don't know what is going on, but you need to stop."

Gerald stopped looking at Ainsley and turned his attention to me. His eyes became even darker, if that were possible, like a volcano brewing, waiting to erupt. "She's my daughter. I think I have the right. You might be dating her, but she's not yours."

What.

The.

Fuck?

The first thing I needed to do was get Ainsley out of this situation, and then I'd get all this shit sorted mentally. Ainsley had become mute beside me. I brought her to my side and wrapped my arms around her.

I said, "You have one thing wrong. Ainsley is mine to protect."

We were starting to get an audience. It was time to go, so we left. Ainsley tried to hold it together as her world was slowly unraveling.

Hell, she's tough.

We were approaching the exit when Ainsley stopped.

"My mom. We have to get my mom out of here. He can't get near her. Adam, I have to find my mom."

Her voice was urgent. She turned and frantically scanned

the room. I looked over at Gerald, who was otherwise engaged, talking to someone else. He was still occasionally watching us. I wanted to pummel his ass into next week.

"We'll find her, baby. Don't worry. He's not going to hurt either one of you."

She wasn't listening to me, and she must have spotted her mom because she took off at almost a jog. The room swarmed with people, and the conversations felt deafening as this situation unfolded. I kept glancing back to Gerald, who was now out of our line of sight. Hopefully, he'd stay put.

Ainsley made it to her mom. She pulled her mom out of a conversation with another woman.

"Ainsley, please, your manners—"

She cut her mom off. "Mom, he's here. We need to go. Dad's here." Fear laced her voice.

Christine's eyes looked scared as she glanced around the room, but then she nodded to Ainsley. I glanced back, thankful the fucker still couldn't see us.

I stopped both Ainsley and Christine when they turned to walk back toward the exit that Gerald was near. "Let's go out the back exit over here, so we don't attract extra attention."

They headed for the back exit as I walked behind them. Ainsley held her mom's hand for dear life as we left the banquet hall. My body geared for a fight if one was needed. *That shithead isn't going to get near either one of them.* The shutting of the banquet hall door muffled the music noise as we left. I checked, and we were alone in the red-carpeted corridor.

Ainsley was frantic. "Mom, come stay with me for a few days, please."

I looked at Christine's hand, and it shook ever so slightly. Other than that, she seemed that she had pushed away whatever fear had taken over a few minutes ago. "I'll be okay, sweetie. I need to get home. Don't worry."

"Please come home with me."

I was two seconds from dragging Christine home with us from the sound of Ainsley's voice.

Christine kissed Ainsley on the forehead. "I had mentioned dinner to Adam. I'd like to see you both again. Does this Wednesday work?"

Ainsley looked stunned into silence. Hell, I was speechless from watching her mother act as if the man who had beaten her countless times wasn't standing on the other side of those wooden doors. It was as if Christine wasn't comprehending the situation.

Ainsley was desperate. "Mom, yes, I'll come this Wednesday. Please call me if you need something. Please don't let anyone in the house, Mom. Set your alarm."

"I will. Sweetie, you worry too much." She turned to me. "Take care of my baby girl. She means the world to me."

I took Christine's offered hand. "I promise. I won't let anything happen to her."

Christine hugged her daughter. "I love you, Ainsley."

"I love you, too, Mom."

Christine turned and made her way to the parking garage. I didn't know what to do as Ainsley watched her mom disappear behind the elevator door. I was at a loss. I touched her shoulders, and she turned to me, her eyes filled with water. She grabbed me by the waist and sobbed into my chest. The muffled cries filled the hallway we were in.

"Shh...I've got you. He's not going to touch you, Ainsley. He'd have to kill me first."

The sobs continued. "Don't let me go. Please don't let me go." Her cries tore through me.

"Ainsley, I'm not letting you go. Baby, you're mine."

She sobbed harder as I picked her up and carried her to the car. I didn't want any of these assholes seeing her affected like this.

Who the fuck invites someone like Gerald to the same event as his ex-wife? Ainsley had been right on her assessment of Donna. Bitch.

By the time I had my girl back in the car, she was working on getting her emotions back under control, like I had seen her mother do in a matter of minutes.

Ainsley needed to talk. She needed to let it out.

Her eyes were swollen as she said, "I'm sorry I lost it back there. My family is all sorts of messed up. I panicked the moment I saw him. I haven't seen him since he walked out on us."

"You're not the only one with a messed-up family. It's okay to be vulnerable with me. I think after what we've shared over the last two weeks, you'd know how important you are to me."

She nodded and looked out the window. "I do."

It felt good to put my emotions out there. Saying that helped quiet the beast trying to convince me to pull away, the one afraid of getting injured emotionally again.

I pulled the car out and decided to take her back to my place. In fact, I wanted Ainsley to stay with me until we saw if her dad was going to make further contact with her.

I needed to talk to Brandt to let him know I wanted to fire Gerald's law firm. There was no way I could let them continue to represent us.

Asshole.

Ainsley was reflective the entire ride home, and I didn't push her to talk as I played some low soothing music to mask the silence and give her privacy. She stared out the window. I pulled the car in to the garage, and robotically, she got out and headed for the door into the house.

At a loss for words, I racked my brain on what to do. The distance that was between us felt like a canyon. I needed to feel her. I wrapped my arms around her waist as the garage finished closing.

"Hey, baby, do you want to talk?" I nuzzled her ear.

She turned in my arms and grabbed me tightly, wrapping her arms around my neck. "Yes. You should know what you're getting into. I'll understand if you want to stop seeing me."

The thought of walking away from her wasn't even an option at this point. I put my finger underneath her chin and brought it up, so I could see her beautiful face. "Ainsley, I'm not leaving at the first sign of trouble. I'm committed to this, to us. I thought we shared something deep together?"

She nodded. "We did. I'm just…I just…"

I kissed her briefly to silence her. There was no reason for her to explain herself. I led us into the house and straight to my bedroom. She kicked off her shoes and crawled underneath the blanket. I followed and brought her against my body. She traced the dragon tattoo on my forearm.

As her hands made their way down the body of the dragon, she said, "My dad would come home each night, and if things didn't go exactly as he wanted down to the minute, he would say, 'Christine, you and I need to talk this evening.' That always meant that he was going to punish her. As the years passed, it was rare when I didn't hear those words at night. Almost thirty minutes after my bedroom door shut, I would hear my mom's muffled cries along with occasionally hearing what I assumed was her body being slammed into something. After the beating was done, he would come to my room and stand in the door while I pretended to sleep. I don't

181

know what he would have done if I had stirred. I never slipped. When I would come down for breakfast in the morning, my mom would greet me like nothing had happened. The only way I could tell was from the slight wince or limp she would have at times."

Ainsley stopped for a second as she closed her eyes and took a deep breath. I looked at her features and imagined a little girl hiding under her covers, scared to death, as her mother was hit repeatedly in the next room.

She continued. "My dad came in one evening, shortly after receiving a huge promotion at work, and let us know he was leaving us. He went upstairs, packed his bags, and left. It broke my mom almost worse than the beatings. She barely got out of bed for weeks until one day she snapped out of it, and everything resumed as if my dad never left. We never spoke of him leaving. I don't know why. The moment I was able to move out for college, I did. In the last four years, she's gotten better, and she doesn't conform exactly to the old schedule. I only go back home for her birthday and Christmas. I can barely stomach being there. It's like a tomb of bad memories."

A tear rolled down her face. When she blinked her eyes, two more followed down her cheek. "I've always felt like a coward for pretending that huge elephant in the room, knowing my mom was repeatedly beaten, doesn't exist. When Mom and I are together, we act as if nothing ever happened, and I had the perfect childhood. I should have helped her at night instead of hiding beneath my blanket. She deserved someone who would try to protect her."

Ainsley took a deep breath and continued before I had a chance to say anything. "I don't expect you to have to deal with what happened today or even go to my mom's house this Wednesday. For so long, I've pushed it aside, and it feels like after seeing my father today that all those wounds reopened all over again."

I rubbed her hip through the fabric of her dress. Her eyes looked exhausted.

"Baby, I think you're one of the bravest people I know to have endured what you have and still be who you are. I still want to go with you on Wednesday."

She refocused on my dragon tat. "It's only courageous when you stand up for those who are incapable of standing up for themselves. It's easy to stand on the sidelines and watch."

My childhood and family had been great, and I couldn't possibly imagine what I would have turned out like if I'd had to endure what Ainsley had. I had no idea what to say, and then I remembered something my mom had told me as a kid.

"If it was done again, would you fight for what you believed?"

"Yes."

"Then, baby, I think that's what matters. You can't right what's been done. It's happened. It's in the past. But you can change the wrongs when they're done in the future."

Ainsley seemed fascinated with my tattoos. When we had first met, she seemed like she would like to get one herself one day. I liked the thought of ink being on her perfect body. I continued to rub soothing circles on her hips.

"That makes sense. I agree. It's easier said than done though."

I was about to speak when she asked, "What does your dragon tattoo mean?"

Ainsley changed the subject, and I let her.

"The word dragon is derived from two Greek words. One of those words means a huge serpent or snake, and the other means seeing clearly. When I learned the meaning, it seemed like the perfect tat to get."

Being with her like this, only the two of us, in our own world was heaven to me. She shivered, and I pulled the blankets further up on us. She snuggled in deeper to me.

"Does that tattoo have to do with the drama in your family at all? In the car, you made it sound like you had a messed-up family, too. Is this why you got this tattoo?"

Hell, I hate talking about what happened with my brother.

After a few reflective moments, I decided to share this piece of me. "Yes. I told you about Selena, my ex. On the night that I was going to propose to her, she left me after I found out she had cheated on me."

She nodded.

"Well, turns out that the guy she had been cheating on me with was my brother, Jake, who is two years older than me."

Her eyes got big as she gasped. "Your brother?"

I nodded. "Yes, my own fucking brother. We don't speak anymore, and I haven't seen him since I found out. The ironic thing of it all is that she left me to get married sooner, but they're still not even engaged."

"I'm sorry. Do you wish things had turned out differently?" Her voice was solemn as she spoke.

For some unexplainable reason, it was freeing to talk to Ainsley about what had happened. It was like a weight being lifted off my chest. "Not anymore."

She smiled and those baby blue eyes sparked to life from their melancholy state. "I like that answer."

"Me, too, baby. Me, too. If she hadn't, then I wouldn't be lying here with one of the most amazing women I've ever met."

Ainsley's lips came to meet mine and we kissed slowly as we savored each other. Today, we had given each other more than we had given anyone else in both body and soul. I held her to me, giving her the comfort she needed. Her breathing finally evened out as I cherished her.

Ainsley was the one woman who made me want things I hadn't dreamed of having in years.

Ainsley

I T WAS WEDNESDAY, the day we were going to see my mom. I was a nervous wreck. I wasn't sure if I'd absorbed anything in class this morning. Instead, I'd wondered what dinner was going to be like, especially after seeing my dad this last weekend. Each time I closed my eyes, his cold dark pupils would emerge into my mind, trying to permanently sear the picture behind my irises.

Blinking the image away, I looked down at my watch, and I had approximately ten minutes left on my shift at the library. I worked the science fiction section today, making sure everything was in the proper order. After this, there was only the religious section left. Between all the interns, we had almost completed the entire library. We were about three weeks away until the fall semester started in September. I was so close to being done with school. I only had two more semesters. Finals for the second summer session were next week, and then I'd have a couple of weeks off prior to school starting.

I pushed the book cart back to the closet and I tidied up the area. My boss, Angela, sat at the desk reading emails.

"Night, Angela. I'm going to clock out and then leave unless you need anything else."

She turned my way. Her smile reached her warm caramel eyes. "I don't need anything, but thanks for checking, Ainsley. Do you have any plans tonight?"

"My boyfriend and I are going to see my mom tonight." I gave a small smile and wished I hadn't mentioned my mom. Thinking about going to my childhood home only made me more nervous.

Angela knew I had started dating someone from one of our previous conversations last week while I had been working, so she didn't press me for more information. "Have a wonderful time, Ainsley. Tell your mom I said hello."

"Will do, and thanks. You have a fun night with the hubs and kiddo."

"Thanks, Ainsley."

I walked out into the Georgia sun and felt the summer heat pressing in on me. My phone vibrated. It was Adam texting me.

Adam: Are you heading back to my place?
Me: Yes, if you want me to.
Adam: Yes, I do. I'll be by to pick you up at five. Dinner is at six sharp, right?
Me: Yes.

Just the thought of having dinner at six was hard. It was the time that my father had demanded to have dinner each and every night for as long as I could remember. A minute before or a minute after had meant problems for my mom that night.

I hate my dad.

The hate felt like it bubbled over with everything that he had done to us. He had robbed something from my mom and me that we would never get back.

I got in my car and drove to Adam's place with my AC working as hard as it could go. My cell phone rang as I was halfway there.

"Hey, Nora," I answered.

"Hey, chica. Are you going to Club Envy this weekend?" It sounded like Nora was munching on chips as she talked.

"No, I have to study for finals. What did you have in mind?"

It sounded like she put more chips in her mouth as she continued crunching. "I wanted to go hear The Thrillhammers again. We can have some girl time and dance. What about the following weekend?"

I grinned. "I'll be free from school. It's a date."

"Awesome. I can't wait. I'm out. Gotta go get ready for work. Good luck with your mom tonight."

"Thanks, girl. I'll talk to you later."

"Sounds good. See ya."

"Bye, Nora."

I hung up the phone as I pulled into Adam's driveway. I got out and made my way inside where I was greeted by Lindy. Her gold fur was soft as I petted her.

"Hey, girl. I've got a few hours of homework. Do you want to help me?"

Her tail wagged as we made our way to the couch in the

living room and sat down. She leaned her head against my legs as I got out all of my books. I lost myself in my studies, pushing the thought of dinner with my mother to the far recesses of my mind.

The door opened and Lindy's ears perked up, but she remained by my side. Adam strolled in, wearing khakis and a button-up shirt.

"Did you have a meeting?" I asked.

He walked up to me and gave me a kiss. "Yes. I had a business meeting about club legalities. How was your day? Are you done studying?"

"Almost. Give me ten more minutes and I'll be done for the evening."

Adam sat down in the chair and gave a pouting huff. I knew what he wanted. I wanted it, too, but I had to finish studying.

"I promise that you can have your wicked way with me after I'm done. You know, you've been having your way with me all week since I've been staying with you."

He gave me a cocky grin. "I know. Those damn books might as well be called cockblockers."

I giggled. "Well, you've successfully been evading the cockblockers all week. My assignments are due tomorrow. The cockblockers demand their time."

"I'd rather you suck my cock."

I looked up from my book. The last few days, he had successfully distracted me from my studies. Dinner tonight at my mom's would be stressful, and I wouldn't want to finish my homework prior to class tomorrow.

"Adam, you're not winning this round." I gave a no-nonsense look. "I have to get this done before we go to my mom's. Tomorrow's my last day of classes before finals. I promise, I want nothing more than to be wrapped around you."

He stood and gave me a kiss. "Well, at least the cock-blockers don't hold your interest."

I pushed him away as I laughed. "No, they don't. Go feed Lindy."

He winked at me and walked toward the kitchen as he said, "Come on, Lindy, let's get you fed."

Lindy stayed glued next to my side, and Adam gave her an incredulous look from the kitchen door. I pressed my lips together as I looked back down at my books. Nonchalantly, I patted Lindy's head.

Adam went further into the kitchen and called, "You've turned my dog into a traitor."

"She loves me."

He mumbled something about mine and I giggled.

"Good girl," I cooed lowly as Adam poured dog food. I gave Lindy a command. "Go eat, sweetie. I'll still be here."

Lindy took off toward the kitchen. I could hear Adam telling her what a good girl she was for staying loyal.

Well, what he doesn't know won't hurt him.

I turned my attention back to my studies, trying to hurry.

Maybe there would be time to get a little action in prior to leaving.

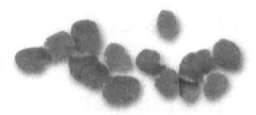

We were in Adam's car, headed to my mom's for dinner. We were almost there, and my stomach got heavier with each passing block. Adam's hand grazed my leg and I jumped, letting out a little yelp.

I looked over at him and placed my hand on top of his to keep it from retreating. "Sorry. You startled me."

Behind his shades, he glanced my way. "It's going to be okay, Ainsley. I'll be right there with you the entire time."

"I know. I get this way every time. I'll be okay. At least my mom doesn't adhere to the exact same schedule that she used to when she was married to my dad. She hasn't done that in years. It makes it bearable."

Adam squeezed my hand. "We'll make it through tonight, and then I'll take you home and make love to you all night long."

My teeth grazed my bottom lip. "I'd like that. I hate that we didn't have time before we had to leave. If Mom wasn't so persistent about being on time, then we—"

Adam interrupted me. "I want nothing more than to lose myself in you, but this is important. There's no reason to stress your mom out."

I squeezed his hand in response. The blinker turned on, and I noticed that we were turning into my old neighborhood filled with large homes in Buckhead. Adam didn't say a word as the GPS took us closer to my childhood cage. Every time I entered the neighborhood, it felt as if the world collapsed in on me, trying to suffocate me and eliminate me from existence. Adam slowed the car as we pulled up to the large red brick house with black shutters. The lawn was manicured perfectly.

"Is this it?" Adam's voice seemed to echo through the car.

My mind felt like it was in a tunnel, trying to distance itself from all the memories invading my brain. I nodded. He parked the car, exited, and came to my door to let me out. I grabbed his hand and we made it to the front door. I felt like a stranger here as I rang the doorbell.

The door opened, and my mom stood there with her hair perfectly pulled up while wearing her red apron that she had worn since I was a kid. My stomach knotted.

"Hey, sweetie. It's good to see you, Adam. Dinner will be on the table in two minutes. Go ahead and take a seat."

I walked in the door and gave my mom a hug. My voice was low as I said, "Hey, Mom."

Adam spoke from behind me. "Thank you, Christine, for having me over."

She gave me a pat on the back prior to quickly walking back toward the kitchen. "I'm so glad to have you. Hurry up and sit. I don't want dinner to be late."

We followed her and I glanced up at Adam. He smiled and I tried to return it, but something was up with my mom. She acted like she used to when my dad lived here. Four places were set at the table.

I continued walking into the kitchen. "Hey, Mom. Are we expecting another guest?"

She pulled a salad out of the fridge. "Don't be silly, Ainsley. Go ahead and take a seat. I'll get the main course."

We both sat down, and I felt for my ring that my grandmother had given me on my right hand.

Mom stopped, glanced at the clock, and then checked her phone. "Your father is working late tonight. I'll make something else for when he gets home. Let's go ahead and eat."

"Mom, Dad doesn't live—"

"Ainsley, why don't you tell me about your day? How's school?"

My mouth was dry as my mom opened the oven. This

was a replica of what life had been like all those years ago. Mom went to the docking station and played "Requiem in D Minor" by Mozart. My heart thundered in my chest.

Something happened to Mom since I last saw her at the party.

I was speechless as I watched this scene unfold. I couldn't say anything as she walked over with a loaf pan in her hands. Adam said something to me, but it sounded distant. My breaths were coming faster as I watched my mom put the loaf pan on the trivet in front of me. The smell permeated my nose and my worst nightmare came to life as I stared at the meatloaf.

Meatloaf Wednesday.

My chest heaved as Adam put his hand on my shoulder.

I felt numb as I pictured my father walking in the door and throwing his stuff down at any moment. I had to keep blinking rapidly in order to know that the image wasn't real.

Mom sat down and said, "Shall we say grace? Adam, you're in for a treat. Ainsley and her father love my meatloaf."

Mom said grace.

Adam leaned toward my ear. "Ainsley, baby, are you all right?"

I shook my head as my mom finished praying. The moment the knife cut into the meatloaf, I lost it and tears streamed down my face.

"Mom, Dad doesn't—"

She cut me off again. "Ainsley, hand me Adam's plate."

Robotically, I reached for his plate, and Adam's hand came on top of mine.

He whispered, "Do we need to leave?" The concern in his voice was evident.

Before I had a chance to process and respond, Mom grabbed my plate. The moment the meatloaf hit my plate, the smell became more pungent and the bile rose in my throat.

I need air. I need to get out of this house.

My stomach was about to revolt on me if I didn't get away. I pushed away from the table, causing my chair to make a terrible noise as it moved in protest. I ran to the door leading to the backyard, to my freedom. My fast pace brought me off the patio and into the grass. I took in cleansing deep breaths, trying to right the image that was inside those walls. Those walls held so many dark secrets.

I didn't notice Adam until I felt his hand on the small of my back.

"I'm here. What do you need, baby?"

Tears streamed down. "It's like when I was a child. Something happened to her. She needs help, Adam. I don't know what to do."

My mom's voice called from the door. "Ainsley, Adam, dinner is getting cold. Come on back into the house. I'll need to start cleaning up here shortly."

Ice spread through my veins, and I shivered. As a child, dinner ended at six forty-five each night. If I hadn't been done eating, then I would go without. Mom had to have the kitchen completely cleaned by seven fifteen. Remembering my father's inspections had me wanting to curl up into a ball like I used to as a kid at night.

What happened to my mom to make her act like this? Did my dad talk to her?

Adam's voice broke through to me again. "Ainsley, what do you need?"

I closed my eyes and took a deep breath, finding the strength I had used to forge through all the years. The strength chased away the cold as I let it run through me.

I turned and looked at Adam as he watched me with his

brown eyes, concern etching his face.

"I need to go talk to her. Will you stay out here for a minute? If you want to leave, I'll understand."

Adam put both of his hands on my face as he looked earnestly at me. "I'm in this for the long haul, Ainsley. I'm not leaving. Go talk to your mom. I'll be here. Whatever you need, it's yours."

Leaning up on my toes, I gave him a quick peck on the lips. My heart overflowed with how connected I felt to Adam. "Thank you."

I pulled away and walked toward the door. I entered the house and Mozart still played. My feet felt like they were in quicksand. Part of me wanted to leave and pretend this wasn't happening, but I had a chance to help my mom.

Mom sat at the table, eating her meal. Her head kept glancing at the clock hanging on the wall right in front of her. My eyes kept blinking as I tried to keep my world clear of this fuzzy falsity my mom had built.

I sat next to my mom. "What happened, Mom? Why are you acting as if Dad still lives here?"

Her eyes glanced toward the clock, and mine followed. It was six thirty-eight. Per my dad's standards, we only had seven more minutes until dinner would be officially over.

My mom smiled sweetly at me as the same blue eyes I had stared at me. "Sweetie, I don't know what you're talking about. Hurry up and eat. Dinner is almost over. Are you nervous about your tests next week? I know that business law class has been giving you problems. Your dad will be able to help you with that when he gets home."

A few tears slid down my face, thinking about how broken my mom seemed. "Mom, Dad left us. He's not coming home. Why are you saying all these things?"

My mom's face crinkled, and then it cleared as she patted my arm. "Ainsley, will you help clear the dishes tonight?"

"Mom, stop. Please stop. Dad's gone. I know what he did to you, Mom. I know he used to beat you at night."

My words seemed to bounce off my mom as if I hadn't said anything, and she continued to eat.

"Mom, did you hear me? I know what happened to you. We are better off without Dad being here. What happened? Why are you acting like this?"

I knew I pounded my mom with questions that caused her to flinch slightly. However, she recovered quickly, and the impenetrable mask was back in full force.

Finally, after finishing her bite of meatloaf, which had me practically gagging, she responded. "Ainsley, don't say things like that. You don't understand. He loves me. He doesn't mean to do it. I think you need to leave before your father gets home."

"Mom, he's not going to hurt you anymore. He's gone. Please snap out of it." I pleaded with her to listen to reason, to come back to reality.

My mom's face looked like my words were registering, but then she shook her head and spoke, "He loves me, Ainsley. He loves us. We need to listen to him better. He's trying, but we don't do as he asks. We can do better, Ainsley. You need to go home. I'll take care of everything."

"Mom—"

She looked at me sternly. "Ainsley, I love you, but it's time to leave."

I focused on being rational versus emotional.

This isn't my mom. My mom would never ask me to leave. Never.

It was as if her poor mind had collapsed in on itself and

altered everything that was real and true.

She needs help.

I needed to research what options she had.

I gave my mom a kiss on the forehead. "I'm sorry, Mom. Everything is okay. We're going to leave so you can get everything cleaned up unless you need some help."

We both glanced at the clock. It was six forty-four.

"No, sweetie, I've got this. Go ahead and go. Tell Adam I said thank you for coming over. I'll call you tomorrow. Love you."

"Love you, too."

I headed out to the backyard where Adam was on the phone. As soon as he saw me, he hung up and looked at me expectedly.

"How's Christine?"

My body felt heavy and my mind was tired with what it was trying to process. My emotions kept wanting to go back to the past while my brain fought to stay in the present.

Dad does not live here.

I looked back at the house as I saw my mom rushing through the kitchen. "Something snapped within her. I don't know if it's from seeing my dad at the party or if he's contacted her, but she's living in the past right now. I need to research what I can do and where I can get her help. Can you take me home?"

He grabbed my hand and walked to the gate that led to the front yard. "Ainsley, we'll get this figured out. Let's go to my place first to make a plan."

"Okay."

I nodded my head as I pushed down the swelling tears. This was not the time to have a breakdown. I needed to be strong like I had all those years when I was living under the same roof as my father. Just because Adam was in my life didn't mean that I could let the emotions spew from me like an erupting volcano. If I could find someone or someplace to help my mom, maybe we could finally be free of the prison we had both self-sentenced ourselves to since before my dad left.

I prayed I had the strength to help my mom.

Adam

WE PULLED INTO the garage of my house. What a fucking disaster tonight had been over at Christine's house. I looked over and Ainsley was deep in thought.

My girl is strong.

I couldn't imagine what I would have done if I had been forced back into my worst nightmare. Her mom had completely lost touch with reality, and I wondered if part of it was because of me.

Brandt and I had fired Gerald's law firm today, and it hadn't gone over well. Gerald had been present, and he had slightly lost his temper until he'd regained his composure. I could see him as an angry man.

I balled my left fist as I put the car into park, imagining

him tormenting Ainsley and Christine.

Bastard.

Ainsley turned toward me with her hand on the car handle. "Hey, I'm going to look at some centers and call them to see what we can do to help my mom. I need to see what my options are. Earlier you said you weren't leaving, and I'm not doubting you, but if you want me to go home to do all this, I can."

The stoic, analytical, and straightforward Ainsley who kept everyone at a distance was present right now. I thought it was a safety mechanism she had adopted after all those years of enduring what she had to. It was the version of Ainsley that I had met her first night at Club Envy, and I hated it. I wanted my girl back, the one who opened up and gave me everything she had unconditionally.

"I want you here."

She gave me a small smile. "I want to be here."

I blew out a small breath. "I need to tell you something. I had planned on telling you tonight when we got back home. You were stressed about heading to your mom's, and I didn't want to add to it before we left."

She swallowed hard and fixed her body posture ramrod straight. "What do you need to tell me?"

I scrubbed a hand down my face. "I met with your father's law firm today and we fired them. We told them we had found other representation. Your dad got mad but reined in his temper."

Ainsley chewed on her bottom lip. Then, she looked me straight in the eye. "Did he mention my mom or me? Did he give you any indication he was coming back into our lives? Did he know you were firing him prior to this afternoon?"

I soothingly rubbed her hand. "No, or I would have told

you. Brandt and I made the final decision today after we found someone else to represent the club. Nothing about you came up. Brandt handled the meeting, and he was actually the one to tell them, so it wouldn't come across that you or your mom had anything to do with it. But, Ainsley, after I found out what he had done to you, I was not going to support his business or take a chance that he'd be there when you were."

The tension from her shoulders seemed to lessen. "Thank you for telling me. I need that honesty from you, Adam. Mom has been acting weird for the last few days when I've talked to her on the phone. I don't think it's because of you firing him today."

"I know you need honesty, baby. Let's go inside, so we can look to see what help is available."

She got out of the car, and I followed her into the house. I was determined to be there for her in whatever way she needed.

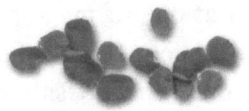

Ainsley had been talking to counselor after counselor to get advice on what to do. Her mom would have to admit herself voluntarily unless she was a danger to society or to herself. Ainsley rubbed the back of her neck as she pleaded with someone to help her. My heart broke that she wasn't making any progress.

I remember the feeling.

When I'd been alone in her mom's backyard, I'd called Brandt to see if he knew anyone who could help from his stint at a facility. I hoped he called me back with good news.

"I appreciate your time. I understand. Thank you." She hung up the phone and sighed. Then, she said to herself, "Why won't anyone go over there with me and talk to her?"

She looked down at the next number and dialed it, not giving me a chance to say anything. She had been like a machine, making phone call after phone call.

My phone vibrated. It was Brandt calling. I nonchalantly walked out of the room.

I answered the phone. "Hey, man. Do you have anything?"

A door closed, and then Brandt's voice came over the phone. "I talked to my buddy, Jason, the interventionist. He says if Ainsley's willing to call him and talk to him, he'll come help and do whatever he can to try to convince Christine to admit herself. This is going to be tough on your girl. It'll only get worse before it starts getting better."

"I know. I'll be by her side the entire time. Can you vouch personally for Jason?"

"Yeah, I met him at one of my support group meetings. He's a recovering addict, too. I think they make better interventionists than someone who doesn't understand what it's like."

Putting Ainsley in the room with a recovering addict that I didn't know bothered me. I'd trust Brandt with my life, but Jason was a stranger.

Brandt must have sensed my struggle as his voice came over the phone again. "I promise, Adam, I would never put Ainsley in harm's way. I know what she means to you even if you haven't fully accepted it yourself. Jason has been clean for over ten years. He's in his thirties. This isn't a Roach thing where I'm doing something for another buddy to help out a friend of a friend. I promise."

The sincerity of Brandt's voice helped assure me. "Text me Jason's number, and I'll let Ainsley know. Thanks for covering for me at the club."

"Anytime. You know that, man. I'll send the number as soon as I hang up."

I walked back toward Ainsley. "I'll check in with you in a bit."

"Sounds good."

I hung up the phone as Ainsley pressed the End button with a little more force than necessary.

She muttered, "I don't understand why it isn't easier to find help."

I knelt beside her as my phone vibrated with what I assumed was the number from Brandt. Ainsley glanced up with a determined look on her face.

"Brandt has someone, an interventionist, who is willing to come out to your mom's house. His name is Jason. He's going to help get her placed if she wants to go somewhere. He's a recovering addict, but Brandt has personally vouched for him."

Ainsley was already nodding her head as she sprang into my arms. "Thank you! Thank you! Thank you! Adam, this means so much to me."

We fell back onto the floor, and I held her tight.

"You're welcome, baby. Call Jason and talk to him. See what he has to say, and then we'll go from there. Here's the number."

She took my phone and dialed the number from the text into her phone. She paced the room as she waited for Jason to pick up the phone.

"Jason. This is Ainsley Pearson. Adam Ryker gave me your number. Yes, something's happened to my mom. She regressed back to the time when my dad lived in our house."

She paused and took a deep breath. "He used to repeatedly beat her at night if one of his rules wasn't followed. If she was perfect, he would invent something new that she had done wrong."

She listened and walked. Lindy was followed her every step. My dog loved her. Each time Ainsley would stop walking, Lindy would lean against her, and Ainsley would pet her head before resuming her laps around the living room.

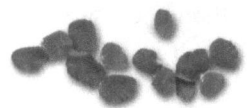

A few hours had passed while Ainsley and Jason talked on the phone. I worked on my laptop since Ainsley kept looking at me and asking if I was still okay. When I started working, I thought it had eased her mind. Ainsley had answered question after question for Jason. From Ainsley's talks with me, I'd known most of it but not all the smaller details. Ainsley and Christine had been through hell.

Ainsley and Jason's conversation came to an end.

"Thank you so much, Jason. You have no idea how grateful I am to you. Yes, that sounds good. I will see you there."

She hung up the phone and came to sit beside me. I set my laptop aside, and Ainsley curled into me. She twirled her ring at record speed as a few tears fell down her face.

"We'll get through this. What time are we meeting Jason over there?"

"Nine in the morning. I gave him the address, and he's going to meet me there. Jason thinks that it would be best if I did this alone. Having someone else there who doesn't know my mom well might put her more on edge." Her voice was soft and tired.

Irritation loomed in the back of my mind at the thought of some other guy spending time with Ainsley without me there. I was an asshole, and I knew it. She lifted her head, and I pushed the feeling aside as I saw the relief in her eyes.

"Sounds good, Ainsley. I'd still like to drive you and wait out in the driveway, regardless of how long it takes."

She hugged me. "I'd like that."

She yawned, and I sat us up. "Let's go to bed. You've had a long day."

Ainsley rubbed her eyes. "Now that I've found someone to help my mom, I'm exhausted."

We stood and headed to bed. Ainsley quickly put on one of my T-shirts and laid down. I took all my clothes off, got in bed, and brought her to me, needing to feel her against me. Her sweet floral scent surrounded me. Soon, Ainsley's breaths evened out.

I closed my eyes and thought about what I had found when I least expected it.

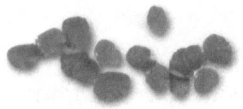

We were almost to Ainsley's house to meet Jason. She had been on the phone most of the morning while Jason prepped her for the upcoming meeting with her mom.

She had gone to my office to write a letter to her mom that described her feelings. It would hopefully cause her mom to want to get help. It was a standard technique to use during an intervention. Since coming out of the office, Ainsley hadn't talked about the letter. I would never ask to read it. That letter contained every raw emotion she had as she was going to plea for her mother to choose life. Her delicate fingers kept making an infinity symbol on the letter she held.

"Ainsley, don't be surprised if your mom is resistant at first. Just know that she might say things that she doesn't mean. Follow the interventionist's lead. He'll know how best to handle the situation."

Her head cocked to the side, and I knew what came next.

"You seem to know a lot about this process."

I nodded as we turned into her neighborhood.

"How do you know so much?"

We pulled into her driveway.

"Brandt."

She looked shocked, but she nodded her head. I knew she wouldn't ask any more questions about what had happened to Brandt. It wasn't my story to tell, but he'd made a mess out of his life for a bit.

A black Honda Civic pulled up to the curb of the house shortly after we did. A tall man with glasses and a zipped polo got out of the car. I jumped out of my vehicle before Ainsley could stop me. I needed to meet this Jason character before he took my girl into the house.

Confidently, I walked up to him. "Jason, I'm Adam Ryker, Ainsley's boyfriend."

I shook his hand firmly while his grip was loose.

Good.

"Nice to meet you. Ainsley talked about how supportive you've been."

"I'd do anything for her."

Jason gave a genuine smile. "I know what you mean. I feel the same way about my wife."

Jason and I are going to get along great.

Ainsley walked up to us. She had put on jeans and a T-shirt this morning and thrown her hair up into a ponytail. She looked tired. Her sleep last night had been restless at best.

Jason turned his attention to Ainsley as he adjusted his glasses. She had that impenetrable mask on. In moments like this, I realized how much more of herself Ainsley gave me than anyone else.

Ainsley spoke. "Adam is going to stay in the driveway and come in if we need him. I have my letter. Is there anything else you need from me?"

Jason gave her a fatherly smile. "You've done everything you can. Remember, it's up to your mom to decide if she wants help. Follow my lead, and we'll do everything we can to get your mom help. Do you have any questions?"

She shook her head. "No. I want to get this over with."

Jason adjusted the zipper on his polo shirt. "Okay, let's head on up and do this. You're going to be great, Ainsley. Just stay focused like we talked about."

"I will. My mom is what matters." Her voice sounded confident.

I knew my girl though, and she was scared as she twirled her ring. She gave me one last look with a half-smile prior to following Jason up to the house. I got in my car before they rang the doorbell. Within a minute, Christine answered the door and welcomed them in the house, almost in the same manner she had with us last night. I hoped she cooperated. For Ainsley's sake, part of me was tempted to drag Christine's ass to the clinic if she didn't agree to go.

I settled into my seat, preparing for a long wait.

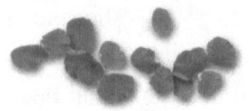

Over an hour had passed. I guessed it was a good sign that they hadn't been kicked out when Christine was confronted with the truth. I stretched my limbs that were getting restless, and my phone vibrated. It was my sister, Jessica.

Jessica: Have you decided if you're coming to the anniversary party?

Me: I haven't. The party isn't for another five weeks, Jess.

Jessica: Okay. I just want you to be a part of it.

Me: I know, Jess, but you need to stop pushing.

Jessica: I love both my brothers, and it's hard for the family to be divided.

Me: I love you, too, sis. I'll let you know. As far as I'm concerned though, Jake and I aren't family.

Jessica: I know, and I understand. But I still feel like I need to try to fix us.

Me: I'll be in touch.

Jessica: Okay.

For the first time in a long time, I didn't feel complete and utter anger for what my brother and Selena had done.

I have Ainsley. She is mine.

Selena paled in comparison to what Ainsley and I shared. I still wasn't sure if I wanted to attend the party. My brother was still an asshole for what he had done. He had committed one of the ultimate betrayals in my book, and I'd never trust him again.

I touched the steering wheel and changed the XM station

to get the sports highlights. My phone vibrated again. It was Brandt.

Brandt: Gerald called and asked to speak with you. He won't say about what, but I'm sure it's because we fired his law firm. He might be calling your cell. I told him you were out for the day.

Me: He's an asshole. I'll deal with him later. Thanks for the heads-up. I'm not going to take his call today. It's the last thing Ainsley needs, and I won't hide it from her.

Brandt: Understood. Any word on her mom?

Me: Not yet. They've been in there for over an hour.

Brandt: Remember how long we had to talk before I agreed to go?

Me: Yes. Hopefully, she makes the right choice and decides to get help.

Brandt: If she's ready, she will. Keep me posted. I've got everything under control here.

Me: Thanks. Ainsley has class after this, and then I'm going to take her somewhere for her to relax.

Brandt: I'm glad you got your head out of your ass, and you didn't fuck up this good thing you've got going with her.

Me: Me, too. Let me know if anything happens at the club.

Brandt: Take care of your girl. I've got it.

Me: Roger that.

I took a deep breath as my mind thought of something special I could do for Ainsley. If Christine agreed to go, Ainsley could not have contact with her mother for thirty days. I scooted my seat back to try to stretch my legs as I had a thought of what to do for Ainsley. I opened the yellow pages app on my phone and searched for what I hoped would help my girl take her mind off all the shit happening with her mom, even if it was only temporary.

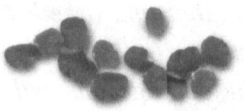

After two more hours, the front door finally opened. Jason came out first, followed by Christine, and then Ainsley. Ainsley stood tall, but her eyes were red from what looked like excessive crying. With her slumped shoulders and downward-cast eyes, Christine looked like her world had been taken from her. Jason held some luggage.

I released my pent-up energy through a long breath that I didn't realize I had been carrying all this time. On instinct, I went for the door handle to comfort Ainsley, but I pulled back when I remembered that it could negatively impact the situation if Christine were to feel like everyone was watching.

Pride was a terrible and powerful thing at times. I remembered how hostile Brandt had been the day of his intervention.

Ainsley put her arm around her mom's waist. The wind blew Ainsley's hair as she looked to be saying soothing words to her mom. With shaky hands and a nod, Christine grabbed Ainsley's free hand.

Jason was patient and unhurried as they walked toward his car. He was good, much better than the asshole who had done Brandt's intervention. We'd almost lost Brandt that day until I had taken that asshole of an interventionist out in the hall and set him straight.

My eyes stayed trained on Ainsley as she walked past me. She glanced my way and gave me a sad but relieved smile. Hopefully, after class today, Ainsley would be able to relax with what I had planned.

I looked in the rearview mirror as Ainsley hugged her mom. Then, Christine got in the backseat of Jason's car. She looked forlorn as the door encapsulated Christine to what would hopefully be the journey to her mental freedom. She was going to have a tough road ahead of her. Ainsley nodded and responding as Jason said something. After a few minutes, Jason got in his car and took off. The moment Jason's car was out of sight, I got out and walked up to Ainsley. She stared off into the distance in the direction of where her mom had gone.

"Hey, baby."

I wrapped my hands around Ainsley's waist, and she turned to me and grasped me tightly. I rubbed her back as she took deeper than normal breaths. A strong gust of wind blew and she shivered.

"Do you want to get in the car?"

"Just hold me for a sec. It was tough in there. I watched my mom break down when she realized what she was doing and that I had known what happened to her. When she agreed to go, we had to get the house in order first. She wouldn't go otherwise. We had to empty the fridge, get all the laundry done, and put up the dishes before we got her packed. I'm sorry it took so long, but she seemed afraid that my dad would find the house in what she considered a mess. I'd left my phone in the car, or I would have told you what was going on."

I kissed the top of her head and held her tightly. "Don't apologize. Your mom is going to get help, and that's what matters."

She nodded her head. "Yes, it was hard, seeing her broken like that. I don't know what caused her to break. She wouldn't talk about it. Hopefully, she'll tell me eventually."

Ainsley pulled back, and the redness from her eyes was

still present, but it began to fade. "Thank you for being here for me."

My thumbs went up to her cheeks where a couple of tears had escaped. "There's nowhere else I'd rather be. Do you still want to attend class? Or do you want to go somewhere else for a bit?"

She looked down at her watch. "My first class is starting. It's the last day of new material. My other two classes required us to email our assignments instead of attending, and I did that this morning."

I turned us to the car and walked to the passenger side of the vehicle. A bird sang a melodic melody. As I put Ainsley into the car, I thought about how my whole life was right here in front of me and not in the past.

She was my light that brightened any dark night.

Ainsley

A
S CLASS CAME to an end, I handed in my paper. I was ready to go curl up somewhere and go to sleep. The day had been emotionally draining, and I was thankful for the three-day weekend I had coming. My professors had given us Friday off to study. I had three finals next week, but right now, all I cared about was shutting my mind off. Adam had insisted on waiting for me on campus versus dropping me off at his house to get my car.

The campus was nearly vacated as I sluggishly made my way out to the parking lot. I smiled to myself as I saw Adam sitting on a bench, engrossed in his phone. He was probably working on getting caught up on emails from the club.

I was falling for him more and more every day. We still hadn't said that we loved each other, but it felt as if it had been trying to leave my tongue lately. We weren't ready, and I'd told him I would never pressure him for more than he was willing to give, but the feeling was starting to make itself known.

He looked up as if he could sense me near him. He smiled under his mirrored aviator glasses. *I could get lost while looking at him.*

"Hey, baby. How was class?"

I adjusted my backpack. "Good. There wasn't much new material, but I'm glad I came. The professor gave us a few clues as to what would be on the test."

Adam grabbed my backpack from me and we walked to the car. It was sweltering, and I picked my ponytail up off my neck.

"I want to take you somewhere. Are you up for it?" he asked warmly.

He watched my response closely. Adam had been attentive, which helped. I never had anyone to lean on before as I had always depended on myself. The vulnerability aspect of trusting someone enough to be there for me was terrifying, but it made me feel cared for at the same time.

He opened the car door, and I sat down in the passenger seat. I enjoyed the smell of hot leather.

"I'm exhausted. Can I take a rain check?"

"It'll be relaxing, I promise."

The hope in his voice caused me to capitulate to his request. "Okay, sounds good."

He grinned at me as I got into the car and then strolled over to his side. The car roared to life and we were on our way. My mind kept going back to the moment reality had taken effect in my mom's mind.

Jason sat in the blue wingback chair that was next to the cream couch. My mom was in black pants and a dark-purple long-sleeved shirt. The smell of pine was pungent in the house. My dad had insisted on having that smell throughout our home.

I mentally scoffed at the word home.

We had never had a home. Being here again, after what had happened last night, made the bile in my stomach turn, causing an acid flavor in my mouth.

Jason spoke. "Christine, Ainsley has prepared a letter for you that she'd like to read to you."

My mom smiled. "I'd love that. I need to set the meat out for tonight's dinner in twenty minutes. Gerald requested pork chops and mashed potatoes."

My eyes closed, and I took a deep breath as I prepared to read my letter to my mom. I prayed it would take root and bring her back to me. Having her stuck in the past pained me. I opened my eyes and turned to face my mom. It was as if I was staring at a broken version of myself as her pale blue eyes met mine.

She gave an encouraging look. "Go ahead, sweetie. I'm listening."

I cleared my throat, unfolded my letter, and tried to blink the words into focus since tears kept trying to take over. After the fifth try, I saw what I had written. Tears from when I had written it earlier stained the paper.

I looked down and read.

Mom,

I love you. You've always been a model for strength and unconditional love, regardless of the personal costs to you. I don't know what happened since the party, but you're hurting inside, and you have gone back to a dark place in our past. When I came over here last night for dinner, I thought I had been transported back to the days of my childhood.

Mom, I know what Dad did to you all those years. I heard him beating you. I saw the remnants of the injuries the next morning as you would limp around the kitchen while fixing breakfast. I know, Mom. I know what happened. Dad can't get you any longer. You're safe. I'm safe. We're both safe. You don't have to protect me by overshadowing any of my wrong-doings with yours in order to keep the attention on you.

Jason is here to take you to A New Beginning Domestic Abuse Center. They are going to help and give you the tools to effectively process what was done to you—to us, really—for all those years.

Mom, please accept this gift. I want to have a healthy relationship with you. I want to be free of the chains of our past. I want to come visit you and not be consumed by the over-whelming guilt of what happened to us. We deserve happiness, Mom. We deserve to be loved freely without consequences.

Please come back to me, Mom. I love you.

I finished the letter and looked at my mom. She blinked rapidly as if the real world tried to break through. A tear streamed down her face. I said a silent prayer that my words had penetrated her thoughts.

"You knew what was going on?" Her shocked voice tore through me.

A sob escaped me. "Yes. I'm so sorry I didn't help you."

Jason came into the conversation with a soothing tone to his voice. "Christine, I'd like to take you to the center. It's a place to teach you how to cope with what has happened to you and to heal. Will you accept this gift?"

My mom scrunched her eyes shut as if she battled some-thing within her own mind. What she'd thought was her reality was turning into fiction.

"Ainsley, baby, we're here." Adam's voice brought me out of my deep reflection.

I turned toward him. "Sorry. I was thinking about when I read my letter to my mom this morning and how I had to watch her struggle as she tried to reclaim what was real. Jason was unbelievable as he slowly coaxed her into agreeing to go. I hope they can help her. He's going to call me tomorrow to update me on everything. I hope she's in the best hands."

Adam looked down at my right hand and smiled. I followed his gaze and saw I touched my grandmother's ring. I knew that was my nervous tell.

"Brandt said this guy was the best."

"Thank you for calling him. Please tell him how much I appreciate it until I'm able to see him again."

"I will."

Looking down at my hand, I asked, "Do you want to read my letter to my mom sometime?"

He gave me a smile. "I'd love to, but there's no pressure, Ainsley. I understand how personal it can be."

"I want you to."

He kissed my hand.

I looked out the window and saw a blue-and-white striped awning with the words Nubiance Spa printed in black. It was the premier spa in Atlanta. Two green spiral trees in stone planters were placed on each side of the door. My mom's friends used to talk about coming here for massages. I looked back at Adam and then back at the spa, wishing that I could afford a massage here.

"Let me give this to you, Ainsley. It's a gift from me to you."

Turning back to him, I said, "Thank you."

I was too tired to argue, and quite frankly, I was grateful for his thoughtfulness.

Adam smiled at me as he got out of the car and came over to my side to let me out. "After this, I'm going to order food to be delivered to the house. We'll have an easy night in. I thought we could order in from your favorite Italian place, Luigi's."

"I'd love that. Thank you. Thank you for everything."

"You're welcome. I would do anything for you, Ainsley."

His words warmed the chill that had been in my body since yesterday. As he opened the spa door, the eucalyptus smell from the spa invaded my senses and tension ebbed from my body. White candles were lit throughout the room.

A beautiful Asian woman in a white wraparound dress stood beside the counter. Her skin was like porcelain and she had pale red lips. Her coal-black hair was done in a bun. "How may I help you?"

We walked up to the counter.

Adam addressed her. "Appointment for Ainsley Pearson. My name is Adam Ryker. I called earlier and made all the arrangements."

She gave him a smile. "Yes, Mr. Ryker. We've made all the arrangements you requested. Miss Pearson will receive the premier package."

"Perfect."

I glowed inside with how thoughtful Adam had been.

The receptionist walked around the counter. "Miss Pearson, please follow me, and I'll show you to your room to change. Fresh cucumber water will be delivered to you momentarily."

"Thank you. I'll be right there." Before leaving, I reached up and kissed Adam. "You're the best. I think you definitely deserve something special for this."

He caught on to my sultry tone and gave me a crooked grin. "I'll hold you to that."

"I'm sure you will."

Feeling lighter from the day's heavy emotional weight, I walked behind the receptionist. I pushed away all my thoughts for what the future held aside. I was going to lose myself and be in the moment.

My mom is safe.

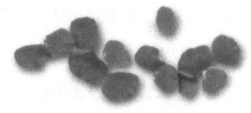

I was in heaven as the masseuse massaged my body. A waterfall was in the room. I listened to the water cascading down the wall. Low soothing sounds came through the speakers lining the room. The masseuse's hands were magical as the oil glided over my skin while she worked through the tension in my muscles.

I wish I could afford to do this every week.

All too soon, the woman gently said, "Please rest for a few minutes, Miss Pearson. I will come back with a refreshing mango drink."

I sleepily said, "Okay."

A door lightly opened and closed. The ambience absorbed into every fiber of my being as I rested and existed. My mind was shut down, at ease, and void of worry. The door opened, and internally, I groaned, dreading that my spa time was over.

I tried to savor the last few minutes before the masseuse gave me my drink.

Then, the blanket was lifted off my feet and up to my butt.

Oh, maybe, it isn't over yet, and Adam added something. He deserves a huge thank you after this is over.

The blanket was brought down from the top of my back, exposing it. Only my butt was covered now. Light touches trailed across my back, and they felt familiar. It was Adam's touch. I bit my lip and turned my head. His hand came to the back of my head and stopped my movement.

"Stay put, baby. I'm going to make you feel even better."

I gave an appreciative moan as he walked toward the other end of the table. His fingers brushed the soles of my feet. They curled while a delicious tingle spread to my calves and up my leg. He left a trail of fire as one of his hands moved to the inside of my right leg before making its way farther up my body, inch by inch. My sex clenched as I anticipated his touch.

"Adam, I need you."

"You're mine, Ainsley. I'm going to take care of you first, and then I'm going to take you."

I moaned as my legs moved wider apart, beckoning him inside. He shoved his fingers in deep as his thumb touched my clit. I moved over him. I grabbed the sides of the table and lifted myself until I was on all fours and could move back over his fingers with force.

"Fuck. Do you want it hard?"

Breathily, I panted, "Yes…"

I turned his way for the first time, and I noticed he was naked. His defined muscles and tatted arms had me craving him.

"Ainsley, I'm going to take you rough from behind, and then I'm going to make love to you on this table."

"Just hurry." I had turned into a crazy, wanting mess, and I didn't care where we were at the moment.

I need him.

I want him.

I desire him.

Adam got on the table behind me. The moment his tip teased my entrance, I pushed back, and my mouth opened as I embraced the pleasure from his hardened length entering me. My walls clenched down on him as he rammed inside me, hard and deep.

"Adam…"

"Feel me, Ainsley. Feel all of me. You're so fucking perfect."

I cried out as he pounded relentlessly into me. The sound of flesh meeting flesh filled the room as that indescribable feeling built within me, wanting to be free and demanding to escape.

"I can feel your pussy tightening, Ainsley. Come for me, baby. Let go."

After he gave two more deep thrusts, I came and screamed. Before my orgasm had ebbed, he flipped me over onto my back and positioned himself between my legs. My body was slick with oil as he intertwined our hands above my head.

Adam's chocolate eyes made contact with my eyes as his lips descended to mine. We were connected on a deep level. I wasn't sure either one of us understood the depth of the level at this point. With our heavily scarred pasts, maybe neither of us wanted to understand it.

We moved, our bodies naturally syncing as if they knew each other on an atomic level. My legs tightened around Adam, needing to feel as much of him as possible, as he slid in and out of me.

He pulled away from my mouth. "Ainsley, don't close your eyes. Stay connected with me."

I nodded as the feeling of ecstasy spiraled through my body. Adam hardened, and I felt his warmth spreading through me as we kept our intense eye contact with each other. It intensified the orgasm before we came down from our high.

"Adam…"

"I know, Ainsley. I feel it, too."

He put his head to mine, like he had in the parking garage. "Something real is happening between us."

My hands came up to the sides of his face. "I know. It's foreign and indescribable."

I didn't know what else to say. The moment spoke for itself. We lay in silence until Adam leaned down and reverently kissed me. Our hands found each other as we sealed and strengthened what had happened.

He pulled back. "Let's get dressed and head home. I want you to myself."

I gave him another kiss back. "You're a dream come true."

He kissed me again. "You've changed me, Ainsley."

After we got dressed, we headed out the front, and I kept my head down. They probably knew what we had done in the massage room, and I didn't want my flushed color to confirm it. Once we were out in the daylight, I froze on the sidewalk as a thought occurred to me.

"You fulfilled my wish from Twenty Questions. We had sex in a public place."

He put his shades on his face. "Was it exhilarating?"

I jumped into his arms and kissed him. "Yes. I'm putting that down in a definite repeat column. I'd say that was some incredible sexilicious sex."

He laughed as he set me back down and opened my car door. "Hell yes, it was."

We got in the car and headed home. The world seemed brighter versus the monotone colors I had seen earlier.

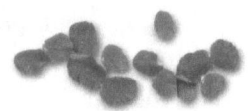

We pulled into the garage. My body was limber. As we walked into the house, Lindy greeted us.

I patted her head. "Hey, girl. I missed you. Want to come with me?"

Adam called from behind as Lindy and I walked to his room. "You've turned my dog into a traitor."

"She has good taste."

I giggled as I made it to the bedroom. I opened a drawer and then slipped on one of Adam's T-shirts. Lindy followed me back as I went to the couch and laid down. I could hear Adam filling the automatic dog-food dispenser.

I called out, "I love how relaxed I feel. Thank you for the wonderful afternoon."

Lindy laid her head on my stomach and I spoke to her. "You're my special girl, Lindy."

I pet Lindy as I closed my eyes.

Adam sat down and moved my legs on top of his lap. "Are you comfortable, baby?"

I peeked one eye open. "Very."

Adam massaged my feet.

"Oh…that feels good. How's the club doing without you being there so much with the problem you had mentioned?"

"Brandt has got the club under control and Hampton is handling the other problem."

I didn't pry or push for information. I liked it when Adam gave me pieces of himself of his own accord.

He reached the arch of my foot and it felt so good. My moan elicited a smile from Adam as he watched my reaction.

"Someone was in my club, taking pictures of people and then selling them on the Internet. It was an inside job. We found out who it was, and the site is in the process of being taken down. Our new lawyers are scaring the shit out of the college kid who was doing it. Our previous employee has his own fallout he's dealing with after all the contracts he violated within his terms of employment. I found the good news out while you were at the spa."

I sat up, and Adam released my feet.

I laid my head on his shoulder. "Congrats. I'm sure that's a huge load off your mind. Was it only a two-man team?"

He scrubbed his hand down his face. "Yes. This asshole named Roach gets the job at the place and then lets this college-aged kid in to take pictures. Then, they'd load them up on a server where users would subscribe and download the pictures they wanted for a fee."

People were weird. Adam traced my kneecap.

"How did you find out?"

"An old fu—a former member of the club found out. Her boyfriend brought it to my attention, and then we got it handled."

He glanced over at me, and I schooled my features into an impassive expression. I knew he'd had multiple past partners, but it didn't stop the small stab of insecurity from occurring as I thought about how I was a way to pass the time, something more than a pleasure buddy to him, but it was still undetermined what he could give me. I quickly moved past it though when I remembered what we had shared today.

"I'm glad that's over and done with," I said.

"Me, too, baby. Are you doing okay after everything you went through today?"

I looked down at my ring on my right hand. "Yeah. I'll be ready to see my mom at the end of the month. I'm curious to know what happened, what made her go back to the time before my dad left. I hope we can patch that missing part of our relationship. Part of me wants to ask my dad if he contacted her this last week, but I won't. I don't want him to think he could affect Mom like he did."

Adam looked like he remembered something. "Your dad called the club, looking for me today. Brandt thinks he's pissed about us firing his law firm. I'm sure he wants to try to convince us to come back. He'd be the hero of the office if he did."

My eyes got big at his words. "Did you…did you talk to him?"

"No, Ainsley. I'll tell you when I do, I promise. I'm going to have to speak to him, or it's going to look suspicious. Brandt technically fired them. As far as your father is concerned, you and your mom had nothing to do with the decision. It was business."

"I believe you. Thank you for telling me."

His hand lay on top of my right hand.

"We'll get through this together. I'm here for you, Ainsley."

Together.

I like the sound of what that means.

With how deeply I felt about Adam, it was getting harder to drown out the word that tried to make its way to the surface.

Adam

IT WAS THURSDAY. It had been a long week for Ainsley since she was unable to contact her mom. Ainsley was currently taking her last test at school before working at the library for a couple of hours. Then, she would be coming here to the club. I had a surprise for her—for us really—as the last of the furniture was being delivered. I turned the bedroom connected to my office into our own private quarters. We would no longer need the Afterburn room. I wanted our own place in the club, not a place where a ton of people had fucked before.

Trigger walked in with Snake. Both were carrying a new white leather Tantra Chair.

Snake asked, "Where do you want this, Adam?"

I pointed over in the corner. "Right over there. Thanks,

guys."

They set it down.

Trigger pulled his hair back. "Brandt radioed us and said the flower guy would be here in about thirty minutes. Is there anything else you need?"

"Nah, I've got this. Text me when Ainsley gets here."

At the same time, they both said, "No problem."

I was sure they thought I was some pussy-whipped fool, but I didn't care.

Before Trigger left the room, he turned and asked, "You've still got the Afterburn room booked. Do you want me to unbook it for you? If you don't want it, do you mind if I take it tonight?"

I gave him a nod. "Yeah, go ahead and unbook it for me. I won't need it anymore. Have fun tonight."

Trigger chuckled. "Oh, I plan to. Honey Pie and I are going to burn up the sheets." He held up his hands before I had a chance to say anything. "Those damn names girls give themselves when they want to stay anonymous suck. But she makes up for it when she's wrapped around my dick. Hell, I'll call her whatever she wants if she rides me all night long."

I didn't miss having sex with no strings attached, and it surprised me. Hearing Trigger talk only reminded me of Ainsley and how badly I wanted her here with me.

Dipping my head and adjusting my ball cap, I replied, "Well, you and Honey Pie have fun."

Trigger shook his head as he muttered about damn anonymous names.

My phone rang, and I answered it without looking.

"This is Adam."

"Adam, Gerald with S&P Associates. Do you have a second?" His voice sounded forced and on the verge of unfriendly.

Shit.

Hearing him brought back the desire to pummel his ass into next week.

Might as well get this over with and talk to him.

I responded, sounding detached, "I've got about five minutes before my next meeting."

"Good. That's all I need. We want the Club Envy account back Adam, and we'll do whatever is needed to earn it." Gerald reminded me of a greasy car salesman.

Fuckwad.

I sat down on the edge of the bed and lied, "Gerald, this was a business decision for the club, and it's the direction Brandt wants to go. We appreciate everything S&P did, but I have to respect my partner's decision."

I would let Brandt know what I'd told Gerald. Brandt would go along with it to protect Ainsley. It made sense since he was the one who had broken the news to S&P.

"Okay. I appreciate your time, Adam. I'll talk with Brandt. Do you have any complaints that would keep you from switching back to S&P?"

"I'm a business partner, Gerald. I'm going to support my partner like you support your law firm. I trust Brandt's decision." My tone was businesslike and unattached.

"Thanks for your time, Adam. On a personal note, I wanted to check on Ainsley. I know she was upset at the party. It's been hard on her since her mother and I split."

Here came more lies as anger bubbled beneath the surface of my mind. I hated sugarcoating shit and playing nice. I wanted the situation to be handled and dealt with, but in this case, it would cause problems for Ainsley.

"Gerald, divorce is hard for anyone. I think it takes time

to adjust."

He was pleased. "I thought you'd understand. I appreciate your time, and I'm sure we'll be in touch soon after I talk to Brandt."

No fucking way.

Matching his tone, I said, "Thanks for the call."

"Good-bye."

I hung up the phone and texted Brandt. I didn't want him to be caught off guard, and I needed him to keep up this lie. If Gerald thought Ainsley was the reason, I was afraid it would cause her unneeded stress.

Me: Gerald might call you. I told him that it was the direction you wanted to go. I hate pussyfooting around the topic, and I would rather tell the bastard where he can go, but I don't want Ainsley to get any heat from my decision.

Brandt: No problem. I won't take his call until we talk.

Me: I appreciate it.

Brandt: Anytime. He's an asshole.

I went to work on the room and put new red satin sheets on the bed. I had added a Tantra Chair, sex swing, and a chest that had a few essentials, such as cuffs and rope. Ainsley and I could add to the collection as we found additional toys we liked.

My phone vibrated.

Trigger: Flower guy is here. He's a little out there. I'm sending him back with Snake.

Me: Someone said he was the best for this sort of thing. Thanks.

Trigger: Put me down in the negative column for getting

pussy-whipped.

Me: Fuck off, asshole.

Trigger: That's what I'm planning to do with this sweet piece of ass.

For whatever reason, a smile emerged on my face.

Bastard.

Before I had a chance to respond, the flower man came back, wheeling a cart full of white flowers from the florist.

"Mr. Ryker?" He had a strong French accent.

I gave him a nod. "Yes, that's me."

The dark-haired man with a mustache looked around the room. "Is this the place we are setting up for your mademoiselle?"

I pointed to the room. "Yes, I want flowers covering every surface."

"Oui. This is going to be beautiful for your girl." He kissed his two fingers together as if he could already picture what he was going to do.

I rubbed my hands together as the nerves sat in. It had been a while since I put myself out there like this. "I hope so."

The florist arranged the flowers. He sprinkled white rose petals on the red satin sheets, floor, and every other surface in the room. Vases of flowers were arranged around the room. I had to admit that he was good at his job. The mood of the room changed from a sex haven to a lovers' nest.

He turned to me after placing the last of the unused flowers on the cart. "Does this meet your expectations, Mr. Ryker?"

"Yes, it does. Thank you."

"Thank you, Mr. Ryker. I'll send the bill in the mail. We will go unless there is something else you need."

"I've got it from here. Have a good day."

He gave a nod. "And the same to you and your mademoi-selle."

He left, and I made a few last-minute adjustments when Brandt strolled into the room and whistled.

"Whew, you're going all out tonight. What time is Ains-ley due here?"

Looking down at my watch, I responded, "About two hours. What's up?"

Brandt had one of those shit-eating grins on his face, and I rolled my eyes.

"You've got it bad for this girl. I think she's good for you. She came by before her test today to thank me for giving you Jason's name. She said she had tried to stop by earlier in the week, but I wasn't here."

I walked back into my office to get a drink. "Yeah, she texted me that she was finally able to see you."

Brandt sat down and threw his arm over the back of the chair. He wore a Thrillhammers T-shirt that had hammers go-ing around in a circle.

"Have you decided what you're going to do about your parents' anniversary party?"

I sat down, too, in the chair across from him. "I think I'm going to go, but I'm not ready to commit yet. I'm thinking about bringing Ainsley with me, but I don't know since Jake will be there. I still have four weeks."

Brandt cracked his neck. "Do you not trust her?"

"Yeah, I do, but I don't want that asshole touching any part of my life. Ainsley and I are in a good place. Jake has al-ways tried to ruin things for me." I scrubbed a hand down my face, thinking about all the shit he was probably going to try when he knew I had someone.

"Yeah, he's a prick. He's always been jealous of you. When we opened up the club, I lost count of how many times he tried to report us. I get it, but at some point, Ainsley's going to want to be a part of your whole life."

When I thought about taking my relationship with Ainsley to the next level, it terrified me. I liked when the progress naturally happened and wasn't planned.

"Yeah, I'll cross that road when it comes. We'll see. Have you thought anymore about telling Nikola you're better and explaining what happened, like your counselor suggested?"

He cracked his neck to the other side. "I royally fucked up. I heard she's dating someone. Nikola deserves to be happy. You know what I put her through—hell, what I did to everyone. It's what I deserve. Let's not talk about it."

I held up my hands in surrender. I could always tell when Brandt's mind was made up. "That works. It's your decision. Just keep your options open."

I knew he still thought about her. It was why he had only slept with one person since their horrendous breakup. I knew he still loved her, but that was for them to sort out. I'd keep nudging Brandt to talk to Nikola, and it would either happen, or it wouldn't.

Brandt stood up and ran his hands down his jeans. It was a nervous habit of his. Obviously, thinking about Nikola had put him on edge.

He changed the subject. "On the Gerald thing, you need me to decline going back to his law firm for some bullshit reason that has nothing to do with you or Ainsley, right?"

"Yeah, I don't want her to get blamed for something I decided. I'm sorry to put you in that situation."

He gave me a don't-be-ridiculous look. "You're not putting me in a situation. I don't want Ainsley getting any unnecessary shit either."

"Thanks."

He stretched in a way that caused his back to pop. "That staffing agency is sending over three candidates. Also, that Matt guy Hampton recommended will be here in twenty minutes. Do you want to interview them with me?"

I stood, too. Brandt knew the answer to that.

"Yeah. I know you're against having someone else for security because you like doing it, but we need some additional help if we want lives outside this club."

Brandt didn't comment as we walked toward the security office. He knew I was right, but he liked hiding behind the work versus dealing with what bothered him—Nikola.

I left the interviews for the security position. We had one good candidate out of the four we had talked to. Matt had a background in law enforcement. The ones from the staffing agency had been a no go. The agency said they had a few more for us to talk to, so we would see what we ended up with for potential employees. At least we would have someone, so I wouldn't have to deal with that shit when Brandt couldn't do it again.

I looked at the clock. Ainsley should be off work and on her way over by now.

Between what had happened with her mom, her studies, and watching Emilyn a couple of times this week, we hadn't been at the club together in over a week. I still couldn't escape the name *man-friend* from Emilyn, Nora, or their mom, Nancy.

Getting back to our new room, I put Ainsley's congratulatory gift on the bed. Technically, it was for me, too.

My phone vibrated. It was Ainsley.

Ainsley: I'm on my way. Had to stop and get something. Be there in ten minutes.
Me: What did you stop and get?
Ainsley: A surprise for you. I hope my Pleasure Buddy is charged up and ready. I've missed being at the club.
Me: Hell yes, I am. Hurry your sweet ass over here.
Ainsley: Yes, sir!

Her calling me her Pleasure Buddy reminded me of when we'd first gotten together. Things had definitely changed. I positioned the champagne bucket off to the side of the Tantra Chair. Then, I grabbed the silk piece of cloth and put it in my back pocket. Giving the room one last look, I was pleased with how it had turned out. Ainsley deserved to be treated special.

Walking toward the exit, I glanced into the lounge area. Trigger was helping arrange tables as Honey Pie tried to hang all over him.

He looked my way. "Hey, Adam. Snake should be at the door in a second. Nora needed help in the cooler, and asked if I could help with the tables. Snake locked the side entrance since no one was there. He has the handheld monitor if anyone does come."

Trigger and Snake knew I liked someone at the door all the time. They had received an ass chewing for not being there the night Ainsley had a near run in with the drunkards. I checked my pocket for my keys in case Snake wasn't there yet when we came back to the door.

"Sounds good. I've got my keys. I'm going to get Ainsley. Consider me unavailable unless it's an emergency."

Trigger gave me a cocky grin as Honey Pie's hands were getting higher on the inside of his leg. I had never messed with her as she was one who wanted multiple partners. As I thought about it, most of my partners no longer came here once we had gone our separate ways even though they were welcome to.

Grabbing his walkie-talkie out of his back pocket, Trigger said, "I'll let them know, but I'm pretty sure they figured that one out."

I shot him the bird, and he laughed.

Bastard.

As I walked out the door, Ainsley was getting out of her car across the street. I wished she would park closer, but I wasn't going to press it. She gave me a little wave before pulling out a gift bag with that tissue paper stuff that people put in presents. She walked over and met me. Her blue eyes pierced me. The outside world and traffic faded when she came near me.

I gave her a kiss. "What's in the bag?"

"A present for you. You can open it when we get to our Afterburn room tonight." She gave me a wink.

Little did she know we were headed straight to our own room.

"Congrats on finishing your classes. Are you ready to celebrate?"

She nibbled my lip as a familiar Ford Explorer pulled into the parking lot. My arms were around Ainsley, and her back was to the parking lot as I brought my mouth to her ear. Right before I spoke, I recognized who was driving. It was my sister, Jessica.

Fuckity, fuck, fuck.

I didn't want her to meet Ainsley yet. I wasn't prepared

for Jessica to go back home and blab to the family that I had a girlfriend.

I tried to sound unaffected as I softly said, "Let's get inside."

Ainsley took my hand and led us to the door. I looked back. Jessica had parked, and she was getting out of the vehicle as Ainsley and I cleared the entrance. Snake was there.

"Baby, hold on. I need to talk to Snake for a second. Will you wait for me by my office door? Don't go in."

Ainsley gave me an adorable grin and shook the bag with my surprise as she walked backward. "Sure. Your surprise will be waiting."

"I'll be right there."

The moment she was out of earshot, I spoke to Snake, who had gotten off the bar stool, "Jessica is outside. Hold her at the door, and I'll be back in a minute."

"Will do."

Shit. I do not want to have this conversation with Jessica tonight.

I jogged back to the office where Ainsley waited outside the door.

"Is everything okay?" she asked.

A few stray pieces of brown hair had escaped her ponytail, and I tucked them behind her ear. My mind was going a million different directions.

I readjusted my baseball cap. "I have a small issue to handle, and then it's me and you, baby. Will you wait for me at the bar?"

Ainsley watched me closely. "Would it be better if I came back later? I don't want to get in the way of your work."

"Fuck no. Just give me five minutes, and then it'll be us for the rest of the night."

She leaned up on her tiptoes and gave me a kiss. "Now, that sounds like a fair trade-off. Take as long as you need. I'll talk to Nora. I don't want to be in the way."

We walked to the bar. The place started to fill up. I looked over and saw that douche bag Tyler was here.

Shit.

This night was not going as planned. We should have been in our room. I gave Tyler that don't-you-dare-think-about-it look and then turned to give Ainsley a quick kiss.

"I'll be right back."

She smiled. "I think you're going to owe me an extra orgasm for making me wait. Did I mention I don't have any panties on?"

Nora coughed, and Ainsley's face reddened when she realized her friend had overheard what she said. My dick was hardened. Ainsley was about to see what happened when you stoked the fire.

Loudly enough for Nora to hear, I responded, "This man-friend is good for at least two extra orgasms after making his girl wait." More lowly for only Ainsley to hear I said, "I'll be exploring to see if you're telling the truth when I get back."

Ainsley pushed my shoulder. "Stop. Go. Hurry."

She giggled. As I walked away, I heard Nora say, "Well, hot diggity dang, someone is getting lucky tonight."

I smiled to myself as I walked up to the side entrance.

Yeah, we're both getting lucky tonight.

Snake nodded. "She's right outside."

Slapping Snake on the shoulder, I said, "Thanks, man."

I walked outside as the sun set. Jessica was leaning up against the wall. Her long brown hair was pulled up into a messy bun on top of her head. She wore a casual red summer dress.

She pushed off the wall. "Hey, how are you doing? I know you're busy, but I need to talk to you."

My sister was sweet and always tried her best to keep the peace in the family.

"Hey, I'm good. I know I haven't gotten back with you on the anniversary party. I will soon, I promise."

She checked her phone. Her brows crinkled. She was upset about something. "I'm meeting some friends in ten minutes for dinner a couple of blocks away. I saw you standing outside, and I figured I'd tell you the news in person. I've been debating on how to tell you all day."

Cautiously, I prompted her to continue, "Okay, I'm listening."

Jessica chewed her lip. "We have a mess with the family on our hands."

"Are Mom and Dad okay?" My mind tried to go in a million different directions, and I willed it back into focus. It never did any good to react with emotions until I had the complete story.

She nodded. "Yes, yes, they're fine. They're trying to talk some sense into Jake."

The mention of his name made me mash my teeth together. I took a deep breath. Jessica knew how I felt about even mentioning him.

Jessica looked me in the eyes. "I know you don't like to talk about him. You know I don't agree with what he did, but he's still our brother. Anyway, Selena's pregnant, and he left her, claiming the baby isn't his. Mom and Dad are beside themselves. Selena is calling everyone to help her. Jake isn't taking anyone's phone calls. It's a mess. I wanted you to know what was happening."

I massaged my temples. Selena was pregnant and probably with Jake's baby. I tried to process all this information, but the anger and hurt I'd expected never came.

"Jake is an asshole. He always has been and always will be. I don't know what to tell you, Jess. Selena made her choice. I have no influence on Jake at all."

Jessica kicked a couple of rocks around. "I know. I guess I needed someone to talk to about it. Selena asked that I reach out to you for help. She's going to be a permanent part of the family now with the baby. I'm trying to help. I don't want Mom and Dad not to know their grandchild."

Grabbing Jessica, I gave her a hug. "I'm sorry, sis. I hate that you're in the middle, but don't get me involved. I don't want that for Mom and Dad either, but you can't fix this. Don't mention to Selena that we talked. There's nothing I can do. I hope they figure their shit out, but that's it."

My sister pulled back, and the stress in her face was evident. "I like to fix things. You know that. You seem different, Adam. I thought this would hurt you deeply, and I wanted you to know before you found out through the grapevine. You seem like you're moving on though. Are you seeing the woman I saw you with when I pulled up? Is she an actual relationship or the same ole, same ole?"

After giving her a chaste kiss on the forehead, I pulled back and walked toward club. "I have a situation brewing in there. Have fun at dinner. This is Jake's problem to fix. He needs to own up to his shit. I hope he does."

She called after me. "Thanks for letting me talk to you. Love you."

"Love ya, too, sis."

I turned and jogged back into the club.

How the hell did Jessica pick up that I am moving on?

The thought of Jake knowing about Ainsley caused my

heart to start clenching in pain as I thought about him taking Ainsley from me. He had succeeded in doing it before, and I wasn't prepared to go through that heartache again.

I entered the club. As twilight set, the club lighting became more pronounced with the different colors coming through the frosted glass. There weren't any windows. It was an auto setting we had put into place.

My mind raced with all this new information Jessica had told me.

Selena is pregnant. Jake abandoned her.

Jake is available now. Selena is available now.

Shit.

Regardless of what they had done to me, that was a shitty hand to be dealt to Selena, but that mess was for them to figure out.

I wanted Ainsley and no one else. I needed to get my head into the game and give her the night she deserved.

Ainsley was still at the bar, chatting it up with Nora. Ainsley needed to know about Gerald, and I wanted to tell her before we got to the rest of our evening.

I walked up behind her and wrapped my hands around her waist. Nora went to a customer who had walked up to the bar.

"I need to tell you something."

Ainsley turned and looked at me in concern.

I continued before her mind had a chance to race out of control, "It's nothing bad. Everything has been handled, but your dad called, wanting us to hire them back."

Fear shot through her eyes.

"I'm not hiring him back. He asked why I had let them go. I told him it was Brandt's decision and that I support my partner. Brandt knows, and he is going to go along with it. He wanted those fuckers fired anyway. Nothing is going to come back on you."

She swallowed hard. "Did he say anything else?" Her blue eyes searched mine.

"He tried to prod my thoughts about your run-in with him at the party. He blamed it on the divorce and said you were having a hard time adjusting to it. I said that divorce was a hard adjustment and left it at that. Ainsley, I promise you, everything is okay. He's already called Brandt."

She let out a big sigh. "I trust and believe you. Thank you."

I needed something to take the edge off after dealing with Gerald and now my latest family drama. "Want to do a shot before we head back?"

Ainsley tilted her head to the side. "I've never done a body shot before. Should we try it?"

I gave Ainsley my answer as I ordered. "Two shots of tequila, limes, and salt, Nora."

Nora responded with a teasing tone. "You're good, Ainsley. Coming right up, boss man."

Ainsley giggled as I looked around to make sure we didn't have any direct onlookers. We were in the dark part of the bar area. I spun Ainsley around to the side facing the wall as Nora set down the salt, limes, and two shots of tequila. Ainsley took the shot, downed it, and then sucked on the lime. She scrunched up her nose as the alcohol burned her throat. I couldn't help but laugh.

"You forgot the salt, baby."

She coughed a little bit. "Ugh, that is harsh. Oh, gosh."

Nora came up and handed her a napkin. "I have done a disservice to you, my friend. You need shot practice. It gets better with time."

Ainsley took the napkin. "The problem is enduring the

time it takes to get used to it. Oh, I forgot how gross tequila is."

"Oh, give your man his body shot, so you can get to those orgasms he promised you. Be prepared for shot lessons soon." I gave Nora a look to give me privacy. She winked at me and turned her back and went to tend to another customer on the other end of the bar.

Ainsley and I were semi-alone now.

"Are you ready, baby?"

In response, Ainsley dipped two of her fingers into the tequila. Delicately, she ran it from the middle of her cleavage to the jawline of her neck. Her nipples pebbled underneath what had to be a thin bra. She had on a low-cut tight shirt and a short skirt that flowed out.

Damn.

Her mouth was slightly ajar as she grabbed the salt and covered the path of the tequila with it. I placed my hand on the inside of her leg, and I traced small circles as I made my way up higher on her inner thigh. She raised her eyebrow, challenging me to check. *Oh, baby, I'll be happy to oblige.* I looked around again, and everyone else was otherwise engaged with their fuck choice for the night. I noticed Tyler was with Jasmine again.

Ainsley looked me in the eyes. "I hope you're ready to take me to the Afterburn room after this. I'm in need of some serious attention."

My hand went up her skirt and I felt that she was bare like she had said. "I think you need a little attention right now, while we do the shot."

She gasped as I made contact with her clit. My hand played with her folds as she tried to encourage my hand to go inside her with small squeezes from her legs.

"Finish setting up the shot, and we'll be on our way."

"Wh-Wha-What?" she responded.

The more we were together, the faster Ainsley let go of her mind and put her body in command instead, ultimately letting me take control. It was one of the ultimate signs of trust. I treasured the feeling.

Her eyes were cloudy and I repeated, "Finish setting up the shot and we'll be on our way."

I pushed against her clit harder as she grabbed the tequila shot, nearly dropping it as her mouth opened in an O. I let up on the pressure as she put the shot in between her breasts. Ainsley placed the lime in her mouth. My finger barely touched her and she leaned her head back against the stool, opening up her neck for my lips to touch. The pulse in her veins was chaotic. The club music was low, but added to the ambience of carnal need. I leaned down to start sucking the trail of salt on her skin up to her jawline. Ainsley made small little noises as the intensity of my touch continued to increase minutely every few seconds.

As I finished tasting her sweet skin, I moved to the shot between her breasts. In the same moment, I stood and downed the shot while my fingers plunged inside her, giving her more. She let out an audible gasp around the lime as I continued to finger-fuck her in the corner of the bar while I watched her become clay in my hands. My thumb pushed on her clit as my middle finger stroked her walls while I put the shot glass back on the bar.

She was close to coming and I pushed her sweet spot just right. That made her bite down on the lime and I encapsulated her mouth with mine, sucking it dry. Her orgasm rolled through her body while I continued to massage it out. I loved feeling her around me while she came.

244

I pulled back and discarded the lime in the shot glass. "Did that take the edge off?"

Ainsley was still in the aftereffects of her high as she responded, "Yes. Did it for you? You seemed a little edgy."

"I'm more than good. I'm going to blindfold you now, Ainsley. I want to surprise you with something."

A smile spread across her face as she picked up the gift bag she had brought into Club Envy. She gave it a shake, reminding me that I had a surprise, too. "Okay."

I took the black silk blindfold out of my back pocket and placed it over her eyes. "Can you see anything?"

"No. I love the feel of silk."

"I know you do. I'll take it slow."

Grabbing her hand, I walked us back to my office, locked the door, and then led her into my bedroom—*our* bedroom now.

"Are we in your office? It would have taken us longer to get to the Afterburn room." Her voice was inquisitive.

My ever analytical girl.

I stood behind her and let the blindfold go. The gift bag dropped on the floor as she looked around.

A hand went to her mouth. "What is all this? It's beautiful, breathtaking."

She turned to me, and I grabbed her hand.

"It's our own room for when we're here at the club. Everything is new, including the mattress, even though I was the only one who had ever slept on the previous one. I hope you like it."

"I love it. Thank you. I'm speechless. No one has ever done something like this for me before."

Ainsley turned and hugged me tightly. Her words warmed my heart. She deserved the best of everything. I nodded toward the Tantra Chair. "Did you see I got us one of our favorite pieces of furniture?"

Her eyes lit up, and she left my grasp. She walked over to the chair and lightly touched the champagne bottle in the bucket next to it. She kept looking at the entire room in disbelief.

When she looked at me, the joy in her eyes told me how happy she was. She was happy with me. She wanted me.

Ainsley ran back to me and put her hands around my neck as she kissed me. The kiss became heated as my hands drifted to the zipper of her skirt. Then, I remembered we had her gift to open.

Fuck, I want her now.

I struggled with what to do as I unzipped her skirt and it bellowed down to her ankles. My hand traced down her flat stomach.

She pulled back from my lips slightly. "Thank you for making me feel special. Take me. Make me yours again, Adam."

I retracted my hand slowly when I was about to reach her sex. She started to protest as I walked us back to the bed. "There's a gift for you on the bed, baby."

"Don't stop."

Her breasts were heaving. My hands went to the hem of her tight shirt and I pulled it over her head, leaving a paper-thin bra that only accentuated her nipples. I traced the hardened points through the fabric. She pushed her breasts into my hands, needing more. She learned more about absorbing the desire to make it better.

As I touched her, I said, "You'll like your present. Go ahead and open it."

She only pushed harder into my hands. "Adam…"

I stopped touching her. "I want our first time in our new room to be special."

My words and lack of connection through our touch seemed to clear some of the fog. Ainsley gave me a gorgeous smile as her powder-blue eyes danced with excitement.

She crawled up onto the middle of the bed. I liked seeing her happy even though all I wanted to do was get on the damn Tantra Chair. She undid the big red bow and lifted off the box lid. She peeled back the tissue paper stuff with the red paper rose petals the store had added. I would never understand all that extra shit people added to presents since they were thrown away afterward. Her eyes lit up as she ran her hands along the silk. In the box was a blue-and-black corset set.

Her eyes met mine. "I love it. I've never had anything this beautiful. Thank you."

"You're welcome, baby. You're more beautiful than the lingerie could ever be, and you're going to look sexy as hell."

Her tight body was going to be hot in that getup.

Her fingers caressed the fabric. "So beautiful." She turned to me, still on the bed touching her new lingerie. "Open your gift."

I took the gift bag off the floor and pulled out all the frilly paper shit. In it was a rope. I looked at her questioningly.

"I want you to tie me up to the Tantra Chair while you take me."

She was making my fantasy from Twenty Questions a reality.

Fuck.

Me.

18

Ainsley

THE ROOM WAS filled with flowers.

Our room.

That term kept echoing in my mind, and I liked the sound of it. I was overwhelmed as I took in everything. No one had ever done something like this for me. The feel of the blue-and-black silk corset set was luxurious. I was hardly able to speak because a word Adam wasn't ready to hear bubbled to my lips every time. He had possessed me and made me his in a way I never knew possible.

A few feet away, Adam watched me with a fire that was ready to consume everything in its path. I was glad I had taken that shot to put some alcohol in my system, so I wouldn't focus on trying to analyze Adam's gesture as love.

I stood up from the bed and walked over to Adam a couple of feet away. "I need to change. Give me ten minutes and come back." I'd never worn one of these before, and it looked like it would take me a while to get into it.

"I could help you change." His voice was low and sultry.

Slipping my hands underneath his T-shirt, feeling his hardening muscles, I responded, "I know, but I want to surprise you."

If we continued to touch each other, I wouldn't have a chance to try on the blue corset. I took a few steps back to distance myself from Adam, and he looked as agitated as I felt.

"You've got two minutes, and then I'm coming in and taking you, Ainsley." His voice was serious.

My hands went to the front snap of my bra, and Adam took another half-step toward me.

"No. You have to leave first."

"Fuck that shit, Ainsley."

I unsnapped my bra. "Go. Give me a few minutes. I'll make it worth your while. The anticipation will make it better."

He blew out a breath as he looked down at my now bare breasts.

I encouraged him to be patient. "It'll be worth the wait, Adam."

Without a word, he turned to walk out of the room, and I changed quickly.

From his office, he called out, "I'm a dying man in here, Ainsley. Hurry up. Two minutes, and I'm coming in."

I giggled and yelled into the other room, "All good things come to those who wait! Be patient."

"I bet good things would still come to me if I went ahead and came in." He sounded a little pained.

"You said you wanted our first time in here to be special."

I heard him curse in the other room, and I smiled to myself, trying to squelch the laugh. After snapping the last garter to my corset, I walked over to the Tantra Chair and sat down with one leg bent.

I took the blindfold and tied it over my eyes before calling, "Come on in."

The world was black, but I heard the door open, and then the lock snapped into place. A moment of silence ensued. I normally welcomed the quiet, but I was nervous as to what Adam thought.

Does he like what he sees?

His voice was low and sultry as he said, "Don't be nervous, Ainsley. You're beautiful. I want to savor you and sear this vision into my mind forever."

I tried to lie perfectly still as I felt Adam undressing me with his eyes. More footsteps followed, and then a soft, hypnotic melody filled the room. It had a soothing, erotic sound with the low pulses. A drawer opened, and then there were more footsteps.

His voice broke through the sound feeding the growing desire within me. "I'm going to tie you to the Tantra Chair, baby. If you want me to let you go at any time, say so. Don't think you have to see this through because of me."

I arched my chest up, pleading with Adam to touch me. His fingertips touched the top of my corset where the tops of my breasts were visible.

I shivered. "I promise. I want this with you."

"I'm going to put handcuffs on you and then use rope to tie the other end of the cuff to the chair. They're padded, so it shouldn't hurt if you need to pull on it. Okay?"

I nodded and then the cuff went around my right wrist. A few seconds later, my hand became stretched in a downward angle toward the floor.

"Move your hand. Is that okay?"

I tested the restraint. It was comfortable but secure. "Yes, it's fine. Hurry."

He walked over to the other side and repeated the process. "I'm not going to hurry. Feel the desire building, baby."

My left hand became bound, and I licked my lips in anticipation.

"Are you thirsty, Ainsley?"

Before I had a chance to answer, the cork from the champagne made that popping noise, and I heard liquid splashing on the floor.

"Open your mouth, baby."

I complied and opened my mouth, and then the champagne slowly trickled in. The bubbling liquid was cold and deliciously sweet. Some slipped out the side of my lips, and a trail of champagne made its way to my breast.

"I think you spilled some. Let me help."

His tone caused my stomach to flip-flop as he shifted his body to sit between my legs on the small curvature of the Tantra Chair. My feet were slightly behind his back on the upward hump of the chair, leaving my silk-covered sex the focal point.

Adam unbuttoned a few buttons from my corset, which allowed my breasts to begin spilling out. My nipples hardened at the cool breath he blew across them. As he scooted forward against me, I felt his erection along my lower abdomen. *He was naked.* He was so close but so far away from being inside me. I wanted our connection, that feeling of oneness and belonging.

"Adam…"

Cold liquid dropped on my nipple, and his mouth quickly lapped it up as soon as it would touch my skin. Goose bumps formed on my body as Adam sensually took control. I loved completely giving myself over to him. He moved to the next nipple, abandoning the champagne, and sucked it into his mouth.

Pulling back slightly, he murmured against my skin, "My mark is getting light on you, Ainsley. It's time to freshen it up a bit."

I moaned as he sucked the part of the inside of my breast that had been marked since our car sex in the parking garage. With how hard he sucked, this mark would last for a long time. I reveled at the thought of having it with me. I imagined touching it in the morning. The tender pain that would occur had me wrapping my legs around Adam, encouraging him to suck harder.

He pulled back and put his lips against mine as he spoke, "I think it's time you see one of the advantages to this outfit that you look so fucking gorgeous in. I'm about to take you, mark you, and make you mine again, Ainsley."

"Yes." My voice sounded as if it was a prayer on my lips, wishing it to be true.

Snaps erupted in the room as my sex became bare. The fabric was still on me. I had noticed how the underwear snapped in the middle, and this was most definitely an added bonus. Adam's tip teased my entrance. I tried to move my hands, to grab him and pull him into me, but they were tied. I gave a frustrated grunt as Adam's hardened length barely slid in.

"You're greedy for my cock to be in you. I can feel how you're trying to pull me in."

"Yes!"

He moved farther in, and I tried to use my feet to encourage him. He was seated in the part of the chair that dipped, and there was no moving him from this angle.

"Please, Adam. Please."

In one quick movement, he pushed in so deep that I called out incoherently. My body instinctively moved as my feet used the small hump as leverage.

I love this chair.

Our bodies were in a dance. Each time he entered me, the penetration became deeper.

"That's right, baby. I can feel you tightening around me. Take me, take all of me."

He removed the blindfold. On the down stroke onto Adam's dick, my body erupted with Adam's. We rode out our orgasms as his lips touched mine softly. Our eyes stayed connected and we were one.

As our breathing leveled out, Adam put his forehead to mine. "Thank you for giving yourself to me completely, Ainsley."

"You're the only one, Adam."

In this moment he owned me, body and soul.

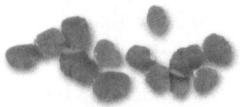

It was Friday. Later tonight, Nora and I were going to head to Club Envy to hear The Thrillhammers play. This would give us a little girl time together before our guys joined us. I had wanted to meet Jude, and he was going to come an hour or so after we got there. At that time, Adam would join us too.

Adam and I were in my bedroom. He leaned over and gave me a kiss on the cheek. "If you need anything at the club, ask anyone. They'll get it for you."

I continued to brush my hair. "Adam, that's not necessary."

"I know that, but I wanted you to know." He slipped on his gray T-shirt, obscuring his fine body. He chuckled. "I like how you look at me."

"Well, you're pretty easy on the eyes, if I do say so myself. I'm going to put my hair up before we end up in activities that will for sure make me late. I don't want Nora walking in on me taming the one-eyed snake."

He smirked and put on his shoes. On my way to the door, I glanced back, and he gave me a wink.

"At least it's not those cockblocking books stopping us this time."

I shook my head while giving Adam an endearing smile, and then I went to the bathroom. In the end, I decided on a simple updo for the night of dancing I had ahead of me. I pulled my simple black halter dress off the hanger and slipped it on. The dress fit my body like a glove. I always got compliments when I wore it. I had gotten a bargain on this when the department store had a major sale.

I added a bit of lip gloss when Adam walked by and asked, "Are we going to stay in our room at the club tonight?"

"Like all night?"

Adam put both his hands on the doorframe. "Yes, so I can peel that dress off of you and make love to you all night long. You're sexy, Ainsley."

I walked up to him and ran my hands along his chest. "Will you be watching me on the monitors until Jude gets there?"

"All. Night. Long." He kissed me between each of his words.

A slight thrill went through me from knowing Adam would be watching me. The doorbell rang.

I yelled from the bathroom, "Come in!"

The walls were thin here. I heard the door open.

Nora called out, "Hey there, guys."

I walked out to the living room, and Adam followed. Nora had on ripped red hose with a black leather mini skirt. Her shirt was black with slashes that showed red underneath the open areas.

Nora gave me a wink. "Hey, chica. You're rockin' it. Are we ready to have some fun tonight?"

I shimmied my hips. "I'm ready."

Nora gave Adam a cheeky smile. "Thanks for loaning your girl out for a bit until Jude gets there."

He laughed. "Damn straight, she's my girl. Tell your man-friend to hurry to the club, so I can get her back."

I giggled at that idiotic term. "I'm never going to escape that nickname."

Nora responded. "No, Adam's not. It's a great word." She turned to Adam. "Take a chill pill. You get her almost every day. It's time to share. Sharing is caring."

"Nora, I'm grandfathered in on the sharing is caring rule. I don't have to share. I'm excluded from that rule when it comes to Ainsley." Adam turned his attention to me, leaning down and giving me a kiss. "I'll see ya at the club. I'll be watching. Be good."

I bit my lip. "No promises. I'll see you there."

He gave me another chaste kiss before walking to the door. Nora and I went back to my bedroom to get my shoes.

She sat on the edge of my bed. "So, no confessions of love yet?"

I found my comfortable strappy black heels and sat down

next to Nora to put them on. "No. I've almost said it a couple of times, but I catch myself. I meant what I said about not pushing him, but when he does romantic things or looks at me like I'm the only thing that exists, it makes it hard not to say it. I feel that I do, but he's not ready to hear it. I don't even need for him to say it back because I can sense how he feels about me."

I loved times like this with Nora when we were able to catch up. She was always on the go lately with all her jobs. Plus, she had her new guy, Jude.

"I get it. I do. I think it's good that you aren't hung up on all that, but I think your man-friend is feeling the same way. You've got his dick in a choke hold." To emphasize her point, she took her index finger and made a ring around it with her other hand.

I pushed her backward, and she lay on the bed in a fit of laughter, saying something incoherent, which caused me to start laughing. As the giggles subsided, we both lay on the bed and stared up at the ceiling. It was a reflective-type silence.

Nora was the first to speak. "How's your mom?"

"I spoke to Jason, and she's doing good. She wants to have a session with me at the end of the thirty days when she can have visitors. It's only three weeks away. I'm anxious to see how she's doing, but I'm nervous about what she's going to talk about."

"I understand." Nora stood as if she felt claustrophobic.

"How's your mom's new boyfriend?" I asked.

"Oh, he seems all right. You know how Mom is. She meets and falls hard for the guy, and then he leaves when he realizes Emilyn and I are part of the package or when she gets sick. I guess it's part of the joy of being a single mom. She had her doctor's appointment yesterday, and she's still in remission, so no sign of cancer."

I stood up and gave her a hug. "That's wonderful. I knew Nancy was stressed about going back to the doctor when she came to pick up Emilyn the last time."

Nora paced. "Earlier this week, Mom and I updated her Will with the lawyers, just in case. She didn't want Emilyn ending up in a state facility if her parents decided to come out of the woodwork and try to claim her." She stopped in the mirror and fixed her lipstick that wasn't out of line. "Okay, enough of the heavy. We need to go have some fun, let off some steam, and pull out our inner wild girls."

I stood and grabbed my purse and keys. "Do you mind if I ride with you? I'm going to stay at the club tonight."

"Of course not. I think Jude is being dropped off by a friend, and then we are going back to his place afterward." She shrugged. "We'll see."

Not having a definitive plan was the Nora way.

The club was hopping as we entered. This side of the club seemed more like Adam with the street signs and metal walls while the sex club was sensual and erotic. Both sides of the club suited Adam in different ways.

The bouncer, Jethro, greeted us. "Hey, ladies. It's going to be a full house. Adam has a table saved for you near the stage. Enjoy the show."

I gave him a warm smile. "Thank you. We will."

Jethro was like a giant teddy bear. It was hard to reconcile his sweet demeanor with him being a bouncer. I was sure though that he could handle his own, or Adam wouldn't have him in that position.

Nora rubbed his bald head. "Jude's coming by. Don't give him hell like last time."

Jethro gave her a fatherly look. "I have to make sure he's good enough for you. It's in my job description. Ask Adam."

I was sure my eyes went wide, wondering what he thought about me.

He gave me a wink. "Don't worry, Ainsley. I think you guys are perfect for each other."

I liked Jethro, and I gave him a warm smile. "I'm glad I passed."

We had only talked a few times, but he and Nora were tight. Nora gave him a big kiss on the forehead. "Don't worry, big guy. He's good to me."

Jethro gave her another look as she winked and blew him a kiss. He had a deep belly laugh. Nora grabbed my elbow and took me into the club toward what I assumed was our reserved seat since there were not any other vacant ones. The bar was hopping as the place continued to fill.

Before we sat down, Nora asked, "Do you want a drink?"

I had to raise my voice for her to hear me. "Sure. Surprise me. Something sweet."

Nora nodded and walked to the bar. I sat down and looked for the video cameras that I knew were in here from the times I had been in the security office with Adam. I spotted the camera and blew a kiss up into the lens, knowing he watched me. The new security guy, Matt, hadn't started yet, and Brandt wouldn't pay any attention to it.

Nora set my drink down in front of me. "Sex on the Beach. They didn't have a Sex on the Tantra Chair version."

I rolled my eyes and chuckled before taking a drink. It

was fruity and cold. "Once you try the chair, you never go back."

Nora laughed. "Touché."

I held up my drink. "I like it. Thanks."

"You're welcome."

The music continued to play and reverberate through the walls. Nora moved to the beat as she sipped her drink.

I leaned in closer. "Is that The Divas playing up there? Adam mentioned he was getting another band since the demand for The Thrillhammers was high."

"Yeah, it's their last song. I saw Chris from The Thrillhammers up at the bar, and they're going to start in about twenty minutes. This place is going to go crazy. Greg, Wayne, and Shannon from the band are getting ready in the back. I like their sound. It's chill."

Nora took a drink of whatever and closed her eyes as she let the music absorb into her.

The song ended as the lead Diva said, "Thank you, Club Envy. It's been a fucking blast. The Divas have loved playing for you. Hold tight as The Thrillhammers will be on here shortly, and they have a hell of a show for you guys."

Everyone applauded as The Divas took a bow. I'd have to remember to tell Adam that I liked their sound. As the music died down, I knew I only had a few minutes before they cued up some other music while The Thrillhammers got ready to perform.

I leaned in closer to my friend. "Nora, I meant to ask you something at the house. I know we haven't been spending as much time together lately since I started seeing Adam, and I want to make sure we're okay."

In true, typical Nora fashion, she gave me a big air kiss. "We're totally fine. You and me are like peanut butter and jelly. We work together. We've both been crazy busy, and I have a new fella I'm twitterpated with at the moment, so I know how it is. But you'd be there for me if I needed something."

"True, true, and true. Okay, good. Twitterpated, you say?"

I raised my eyebrow as she laughed.

"Oh, that's all you're getting out of me for the moment. I'm going to the restroom. Be back."

Nora stood up and walked away. I knew she liked Jude a lot, but she wasn't ready to admit the depths of her feelings.

My phone vibrated. I smiled because it was Adam.

Adam: You look gorgeous. If I see one more guy eye-fuck you, we're going to have problems.
Me: I like knowing you're watching me.
Adam: I can't wait to taste your body again.

I smiled at the phone, thinking of a response, when he sent another text.

Adam: I'm going to taste you all night long as I fuck you.
Me: I'm already wet for you.

I smiled at my overly open, sexual text. As I hit Send, a tall blond approached. He was the same guy from the other night in the sex club.

Tyler something?

He was the son of one of the partners at my father's law firm. He sat down and made himself comfortable.

"Ainsley, right?"

I swallowed, squared my shoulders, and responded as a familiar rock song played. "Yes."

Simple one-worded answers normally got the point across. My phone vibrated in my hands again, and I glanced down.

Adam: I'm on my way.
Me: Okay.

Tyler's blue eyes were looking me up and down, and I was glad Adam was on his way.

"Well, we don't have to worry about that bracelet bullshit over here. I like how you look, baby. And I think you feel the same way about me. Why don't we go grab a bite to eat and get to know each other better?"

The fact that he used the endearment that Adam sometimes called me had my stomach turning.

He is disgusting.

I looked him straight in the eyes as The Thrillhammers took the stage. The band made a few adjustments.

"Tyler, I'm Adam's girlfriend, regardless if I'm in the sex club or out of it. Going forward, I would appreciate it if you would stay away from me. I have no interest in you."

Tyler gave me a cocky smile. "What would your dad think if he knew you belonged to a sex club?"

I lost my patience with this arrogant ass as he threw his arm over the back of his chair and took a sip of his beer.

"Tyler, I could give a rat's ass what my father thinks. He already knows Adam is dating me, so I'm sure he's put two and two together."

My insides were shaking at the fact that this man would bring my father into this. Thinking about my dad and what he had done to my mom had my heart racing. The memories were fresh as if a knife had reopened the scar I had long ago tried to forget. A hand came down on my shoulder, and my body relaxed slightly. *Adam is here.*

Tyler's eyes narrowed in on what I assumed was a very pissed off Adam behind me. "Is she the reason you dropped my dad's law firm? It's obvious she has daddy issues."

Adam came around and stood beside me as I was about to respond. When I glanced up at his face, he looked furious. His muscles were defined as he positioned himself in an authoritative stance. "You've crossed the line for the last time, Tyler. I don't give second chances. I'm going to ask you to leave my establishment and never come back. Your membership for the club is officially revoked."

Tyler stood up and matched Adam's stance. I stood in case something happened. My palms sweated as the air became thick, and the feeling of a fight permeated the atmosphere.

Tyler spit out, "You think you're some badass motherfucker who can dictate who I can or can't talk to. Last I checked, you didn't own the bitch, so she can fuck whoever the hell she wants."

Shocked, I looked at Adam to see his response. He was still in control of himself, which helped keep my heart from jumping out of my throat.

Coolly, Adam said, "Are you going to leave the premises?"

"Make me, asshole."

Tyler reminded me of my father. The music was still playing in the bar, but all activities had stopped, and everyone watched us. For the first time since this had started, I noticed Trigger and Snake standing a few feet behind Tyler. Adam nodded his head, and they both came to each side of Tyler and took him out of the club.

Nora came up beside me, and she took in the scene in her carefree way. "Jude's on his way. What's going on?"

Adam looked back at me. "Stay here. I'll be right back."

I walked, and Nora followed me. Tyler spit profanities at Adam.

I hurriedly said, "That guy Tyler tried to start something."

Nora looked at me as her eyes widened. "I always miss things when I'm in the pisser. Your man-friend is going to whip his ass."

Chastising her, I responded, "Nora..."

Jethro called out above the crowd, "There's nothing to see. I suggest you all go back to doing what you were doing. If you leave now, you're out for the night."

I still continued to push through the crowd as the crowd turned and refocused themselves on what they had been doing before the Tyler incident. I was only a few feet behind Adam as Tyler continued to yell.

As we crossed the threshold, I heard Chris from The Thrillhammers say, "Let's get this party started. How's everyone doing tonight?"

Snake and Trigger released Tyler once outside. He stumbled forward a few steps.

Adam said, "Don't choose the hard way, Tyler. Just leave. Make the right choice."

Brandt came up and stood a few feet from Adam as Tyler walked toward us.

"You've got all your cronies here. I don't think it would be a fair fight."

Fight.

I kept telling myself that a fight was not a beating.

Adam is giving him a choice.

Adam spoke. "Tyler, they aren't here to step in. They're

263

here as witnesses in case you try to make it into something it's not. This will not end pleasantly for you, but I will defend myself. Go on home."

My eyes danced to Adam, and he was completely confident and collected. He didn't seem like he looked for a fight, but he was willing to stand up for himself—or me, for that matter.

Tyler continued his path to Adam. "I'll be telling her father all those dirty little rumors circulating about you and her at the club, motherfucker."

The threats Tyler made didn't bother me. He could tell my dad anything, and I couldn't care less.

"Tyler, go." Adam's voice was laced with ice.

I shivered from the chilling essence it left within me.

Without notice, Tyler sucker-punched Adam in the jaw.

Adam took a few steps back, stunned. His hand came up and rubbed his jaw as he regained his balance. "That's the only shot you're going to get, asshole."

Tyler started to throw another punch, but Adam blocked it and hit him square in the face. Blood erupted from Tyler's nose as he sank to the concrete crying out in pain.

Adam turned and saw me standing there. He'd obviously expected me to have listened to his previous request to stay in the club. His face looked upset. He kept glancing back and forth between me and the douche bag laid out on the concrete.

Tyler cried out in pain, again, mumbling about how Adam would pay. My mind was prepared for the flight response to kick in, but it never came.

Adam came to me and yelled over his shoulder. "Get him a towel." He turned to me and touched my shoulder. "I need to speak to you." There was worry in his voice as he looked me over.

I nodded as Nora said, "Jude will be here in a minute."

"Okay, Adam and I will be back in a few." I said.

I hoped whatever he needed to talk about didn't have anything negative to do with us. Brandt was still out here, and he tossed a hand towel from his back pocket onto the pavement for Tyler.

Adam

S^{*HIT*} *HIT.*

I hadn't wanted Ainsley to see me dealing with a situation like this, especially with it only being a week since her mom had been admitted. Between this incident with Tyler and the pressure to make a decision regarding my parent's party, I was tired of all this bullshit, and I wanted to lose myself in Ainsley and find our escaped reality. First, I needed to make sure Ainsley and I were okay. With Ainsley's violent past, I wasn't sure how she would feel about what I had done. Ainsley still looked cautious.

Shit.

She glanced over at Tyler as the boys were asking if he wanted medical attention. They were standing around, watching him. I didn't give a fuck if he lay there all night and cried like the pansy-ass he was. He should not have pushed me when it came to my girl. I wrapped my arm around her waist and brought her closer to me. I felt calmer having her in my arms.

"Let's go inside and talk, baby. Then, we can come back to the bar to join Nora and Jude."

"Sure."

I wasn't able to tell what she thought as we walked inside. She wasn't showing her emotions, and her mask was in place.

Double shit.

The Thrillhammers were doing their thing as they sang "Wirehead." I guided Ainsley back to my office on this side of the club. We were nearing capacity.

I opened the door. "After you."

She nodded and walked inside. When the door closed, I walked up to her and brought her to me.

Her head tilted up to me. "What's bothering you, Adam? Is it about you fighting with Tyler?"

"Yes, that's always the last resort, Ainsley. I don't want you to think I go around doing that. I would never hit you."

Her fingers came up and grazed my cheek. "I know that. I'll admit, conflict like that makes me nervous, but I watched you, and you were completely in control, Adam. He struck first, and you ended it. I'm not upset with you, and I don't think you would do anything to me. You're not my father."

Hearing those words from her lips was how I had hoped she would feel. "I'm glad. I never would, Ainsley. I promise. You mean the world to me."

"I know. I feel the same way." Her sweet smile was a soothing balm to my self-inflicted torture. "Are you ready to head back out to the club?"

Part of me wanted to bend her over the desk, but I decided to wait until we got back to our room.

"Yes." She gave me a sweet kiss. She started to speak, stopped, and then said, "Adam, thank you for standing up for me earlier."

I leaned my forehead against hers. For me, touching her that way intensified the connection. My feelings were spiraling into what I now knew was uncharted territory for me. I thought I had loved Selena, but what I felt for Ainsley wasn't even remotely the same. She was my everything. My heart wasn't ready to make that type of declaration. Ainsley and I were good where we were at. She had a shitstorm she was dealing with, and all she needed was my support.

My thumb traced her lips. "Ainsley, I protect what is mine. And, baby, you're at the top of what I consider mine."

"I feel the same way, Adam."

I kissed her again. "Let's go see Nora and Jude. Then, I'm taking you back to our room where I'm going to make love to you all night long."

"I like being in your arms. It's safe."

Her words continued to reach parts of my soul that had never been touched.

I grabbed her hand and rubbed my thumb against hers. "I like you in my arms, too." I couldn't say anything else even though there was so much more I wanted to say.

We moved out into the club as The Thrillhammers were in full swing. Jude and Nora were dancing on the other side of the dance floor. Ainsley gave a smile toward them and then turned to me. We moved to the song. Her body melded to mine. I put my leg in between hers and ran my hands up and down her body. Ainsley and I were sync'd as one, and I could feel myself getting worked up. She moved her hips and touched me as our bodies sweated from the heat.

The band continued singing "55-Gallon Drum."

I was a rock I liked to roll
Full of myself, full of soul
Kept my lid tight, held down in school
No use for the law, even broke the golden rule
In a slick twelve gauge steel
Hard and cold and rolled like a wheel
When I was young and slow to learn
I took a few bullets but it helped me burn
I'm a fifty-five-gallon drum
Got a bellyful of fire and an iron lung
Yeah, I'm a fifty-five-gallon drum
I'm past my prime, but I just got rollin'
Glowing red, ashen white
Blind beacon in the night
So gather 'round I'm smoking hot
Take what you give, give you all I got

The song ended, and lust had become the dominant feature in Ainsley's eyes as we stared at each other. They started the next song, "Ain't That a Shame," and I leaned into her ear.

"Let's get a drink. I think Nora and Jude went to the bar."

She looked torn. I knew she wanted to go back to our room and be together. I had that intense need also. After what had gone down today, we needed alone time. Making love seared in our feelings, branding them into our very being.

"Baby, we'll go back to the room soon. I have the same need. Trust me."

We made our way to the bar where Nora took a shot.

Nora looked our way. "Hey, guys. Jude, this is Adam and my girl Ainsley. You guys, this is Jude."

I cocked my eyebrow to Nora and mouthed *my girl*. She laughed as I extended my hand and I sized Jude up. He had a pierced lip with shaggy black hair. He seemed like an all right guy.

Jude greeted us. "Hey, mate. Nice to meet ya, Ainsley."

Nora wagged her eyebrows up and down as he spoke with his Australian accent.

Girls and accents.

Ainsley extended her hand and smiled sweetly. "Nice to meet you too, Jude."

He put his arm around Nora. I was glad to see that he only seemed to have eyes for Nora. He hadn't given Ainsley a second look. That was going to make getting along with him a hundred times easier.

Jude brought his beer to his lips. "I like this band. They have a good sound."

I responded, "Thanks. They pack the house every time they play."

He sat his empty beer bottle down. "I can see why. I hate to bounce with my girl, mates, but this was the only way I could surprise her. I made some plans to celebrate some good news she got. We'll plan something soon, so I can chat with you guys a bit more, if that's okay."

Nora looked shock. "We are?"

He leaned toward me as if he was going to tell me a secret. "See, us blokes need the element of surprise every once in a while to do that swoon thing I hear about from my sister."

We laughed. Nora looked like she glowed within.

Ainsley beamed as she said, "Well, Jude, you made me swoon. Nora told me about the good news, and I couldn't agree more." Ainsley turned to Nora. "I want deets on what Jude does."

"Sure thing. Looks like it's time to roll."

Jude laughed as he walked away with Nora. "I'm not sure

I'll ever get used to your American colloquialisms."

They were out of earshot when I leaned down into Ainsley's ear. "You ready to get out of here?"

She nodded, and that was all I needed. I pulled her from the bar, and we walked back to the sex club side. The crowd tried to press in on us as we made our way toward to my office that had the connecting door to the sex club.

As I unlocked the door, I asked, "What was Nora's good news?"

"Nora's mom got another clean bill of health. Her cancer is still in remission."

She was slightly breathless as anticipation built. The outline of her nipple showed through her dress.

I opened the door and pulled Ainsley through. "That is excellent news. Jude seems good for her."

"I think so, too. I think she likes him a lot."

The moment we stepped into the sex club side, the air shifted to desire. I needed her closer, and I picked her up. She wrapped her legs around my waist.

"Adam—"

My lips cut her off as I walked. She caught on quickly, and her arms laced around my neck. The sound on this side of the club was pulsing and erotic, and my dick throbbed. After dodging a few people, we made it to my office where I locked the door behind us as we continued to lose ourselves in the kiss. My hands moved Ainsley's dress up higher on her thigh. I readjusted her in my arms, so I could make my way to her panties. A snapping sound broke through the silence, and Ainsley grinded her hips against my dick.

Shit, I need her.

My fingers grazed her entrance as I kept walking. As she made little noises, we tumbled into the bed. We fervently worked on undressing each other. Clothes were flying until I felt her skin against mine.

I ran my hand along her hip bone and up to the curvature of her breast. "I'll never tire of this feeling. I'm about to savor you."

"Adam—"

In a quick movement, I had Ainsley underneath me, and I hovered on top of her. I brought our bodies up to the center of the bed on the satin sheets. Our breaths mingled as we kissed. There was a faint taste of alcohol. I intertwined our hands, and I brought them above her head as I moved inside her at the same time. We fit each other perfectly, and as I pushed in and out, our bodies synchronized.

I wish this feeling of complete bliss could be drawn out into infinity.

She began to pulsate, and I knew we were close.

"Look at me when you come, baby."

She broke the kiss and opened her eyes. Her back arched, and I kept stroking her on the inside as her body felt the pleasure from her orgasm. I erupted inside of her as we kept our eyes locked.

I am never letting her go. She is mine.

I stayed inside her as I rolled underneath her, and Ainsley lay on my chest. Silence fell on us for a bit as our hands roamed over each other's bodies. She traced the tattoo of an old weighing scale on my arm.

"I'll never tire of how you make me feel, Adam." She gave me a light kiss.

"I'm going to make you feel like that always."

She laid there for a few minutes as she touched my arms, before saying, "I think I understand this tattoo more after tonight. I see the characteristics in how you act." She traced it again. Last week, I had explained most of my tattoos to her. "You said that this helped remind you to keep everything in balance even when you wanted to tip to the extreme. You try to assess the situation first before reacting to it."

I kissed her swollen lips. "That's exactly what it means."

Ainsley

I WAS ON my way to A New Beginning Domestic Abuse
Center. It was hard to believe a month had passed since
my mom agreed to get help. This was the first day my
mom was allowed to have visitors. With the new semester
starting, I had to take a later time in the day to meet with my
mom. So far, classes had been intense with it being my senior
year.

Jason had called last night to prepare me for today. He'd
said that the first few sessions would be with her counselor
too. I was comforted and intimidated by the fact that someone
would be in there, listening to everything we would have to
say. In the end, I was grateful someone would be there to facil-
itate our discussion.

Adam had offered to drive me, and I had taken him up on

it without hesitating. I could only imagine how emotionally drained I would be after today. He was safe, and I felt like I could trust him with myself. I was reflectively looking out the window as I twirled my ring.

"We're almost there, baby. It's going to be okay. Jason told you that your mom was making good progress."

I nodded. "I know, I know. It's just…I don't know…a little nerve-racking, I guess, knowing that my mom and I are going to be talking for real today. In the past, we've always had this distortion field that kept the truth slightly blurred. We had lots of truths, but the omissions overshadowed them."

His hand came on top of mine. "You'll be with someone to help guide you. Do you want me to tell you what it's like?"

I still wasn't sure what had happened to Brandt that had caused an intervention. Adam had never offered it up, and I hadn't asked. I respected Adam for not sharing a story that wasn't his to share.

When gossip ran rampant at the library, my boss, Angela, always said to all the employees, *A story has a beginning, a middle, and an end. Be sure to insert yourself in the right spot within the story. Sometimes, your role is solely as an observer who reads the story. Sometimes, you should close the book, put it on the shelf, and walk away. And sometimes, you're the lead character.*

Those words always resonated in my head when my curious nature wanted to dig deeper and analyze the situation. This was Brandt's story, and if he ever wanted me to know what had happened to him, then he would tell me or let Adam.

"Yes, I'd like to know what you felt like when you were there for Brandt."

He scrubbed a hand down his face. "It's like being there with someone you've known your entire life, but you're not sure what's going to happen since your last meeting with that person was stressful. You're going to face some hard truths, and then you'll start finding your way. Eventually, a balance will happen where you'll sync with each other again. It helps having someone in the room with you to navigate your way."

We pulled into the parking lot. My biggest fear was that my mom would be mad because I never protected her or that her eyes would be opened from a veil of false realities, and she wouldn't like the person I had become.

"Okay. I understand." I was going to have to find my confidence.

Adam put the car in park. "She's still your mom, Ainsley. Just like Brandt was still Brandt. They are on a self-discovery journey after all the damage they did to themselves. She's still going to love you."

I nodded as I looked at the center. Since my mom had left to get help, I had longed to see her again. Now staring at the white brick building and realizing the moment was here, I was afraid of what was behind the hypothetical curtain. Adam opened his door and came to my side. He had his laptop bag over his shoulder as he held his hand out to me, and I took it.

"Thanks for being here for me."

He squeezed my hand as the breeze blew over my skin. "There's no place else I'd rather be right now."

I took a deep breath and stopped him outside the entrance. There was something I wanted to give him while I was with my mom. It was a piece of me—a raw, exposed part of me that I knew he would keep safe. I pulled the folded piece of paper from my purse.

My lips suddenly felt dry. "If you want to read the letter that I wrote to my mom, here it is. There's no pressure though."

He took the letter as if it was sacred. "I want every piece of you that you'll let me have. Thank you."

We walked toward the doors, and they automatically opened.

A woman dressed in scrubs sat behind the counter. She was elderly but had a friendly smile. "How may I help you, dear?"

She was the type of person I wanted to read me bedtime stories at night.

"I'm here for an appointment with Christine Pearson."

The nurse's name tag had Clarice imprinted on it. "Hey, Ainsley. Your mom has been excited to see you. I'm Clarice." She looked warmly but inquisitively at Adam. "I don't show another visitor for Christine."

I responded, "He's going to wait in the waiting room. I called and spoke to Sarah, who said it would be okay since he drove me here and back. His name is Adam Ryker."

Clarice stood. "Of course, my dear. Adam, the waiting room is right through that opening. I'll be back to see if you need anything as soon as I take Ainsley to the Ocean Room."

Adam looked at Clarice. "Thank you." He turned to me and gave me a kiss right below my ear. "I'll be waiting for you. Remember to be true to yourself. It will help you both."

I turned my head and gave him a quick kiss on the lips. That small amount of contact helped soothe the butterflies swarming in my stomach. I followed Clarice through two large brown metal doors. The hallway was colorful and calming with the tranquil colors of the sea. It further helped soothe my anxiousness. We walked up to a room, and there was a blue wave insignia with the name of the room.

I stared at it as I awaited my fate on the other side of the blue door, wondering what the future held.

"It's okay, Ainsley. Go on. This is an excellent part of the recovery process."

Clarice's words helped spur me into action. I squared my shoulders, took a deep breath, turned the knob, and opened the door. I walked inside and saw my mom sitting in the chair. She now had shoulder-length hair. She was in shorts and a purple cotton tank top. She never wore summer clothes. I had always assumed she avoided revealing clothing to conceal the bruises that my dad had given her.

My mom stood. "Ainsley, you look beautiful. I love you."

She opened her arms, and I ran straight into them. Tears seeped from my eyes. There was something indescribably secure about being in my mother's arms.

"Mom, I have you back. I love you, too."

My mom's arms cocooned me, and the tears fell faster and faster. She seemed so much better than the last time I'd seen her.

After a time, a voice cleared from behind us. "Ainsley, I'm Doctor Jacobs. Thank you for joining your mother and me in this reconnection session."

I pulled back and smiled at my mom. As I wiped the tears, I turned. "Hi, Doctor Jacobs. Sorry about that. It's wonderful to see my mom this way."

The doctor was relaxed. I liked her demeanor.

"There's no need to apologize. It's hard to be away from someone we love for a while. Why don't you both sit on the couch, and we'll start? Christine has something she'd like to say."

I nodded my head. "Yes, yes, I'd love that. Whatever we need to do."

My mom led us to the couch, and I took my seat about a foot away. She was different and still my mom at the same time. Adam was right. I felt like a stranger, but it was somehow familiar.

My surroundings were starting to come into focus. The room was a soft blue, and pictures of the sea hung on the walls. A seashell lamp was in the corner on the table.

I glanced over at Doctor Jacobs. She was about my mother's age with dark black hair that was pulled back into a ponytail. The doctor wore white capris with a light blue top. Dark-rimmed glasses framed her eyes.

"Christine, why don't you read the note you wrote for Ainsley in our last session? Then, we can go from there."

The doctor discreetly wrote something down in her notebook.

My mom took a note from the white wicker table and turned my way. Her hands were shaking slightly, and a tear fell down her cheek. Besides the day of the intervention, this was the most emotionally exposed I had ever seen her.

She cleared her throat. "Ainsley, the other day during a session with Doctor Jacobs after all my learning and self-discovery, I was challenged to write a note to you. The subject was left open, and it was up to me to write whatever I thought. So, this is my note to you."

My mom unfolded the note. I didn't know what to say as insecure thoughts raced through my mind.

"My dearest Ainsley, you have always been the light of my life, even on the dreariest of days. Each morning, when you would come down the stairs, you were my sun even though my nights had been storms. After you came with Jason for my intervention, I know that you knew about all those stormy nights and what your father had done to me. Ainsley, yes, your father abused me both physically and mentally. We were married for one week before he hit me for the first time. He begged and pleaded for me not to leave him. Finally, I agreed to stay. It was three months later before he struck me again. The cycle repeated itself until I got pregnant with you."

"Then, it stopped, and I thought whatever beast tormented your father had been soothed with the news of the new life we had created. For a year after you were born, things were good between us. We were a family."

"Then, my father died, leaving a sizeable amount of money along with the deed to our house to me. My dad, your grandfather, was a powerful man. See, Ainsley, the house and all the wealth was from my side of the family. Gerald was adamant that you never know about the trust fund I had received from my father. A stipulation in the trust stated that as long as I stayed married to Gerald, I would only receive enough to pay the bills each month. My father detested Gerald and repeatedly tried to get me to leave him after seeing a bruise on my face. That was when Gerald stopped hitting me in places that people could see. Once my father died, Gerald threatened my mother, saying if she ever stepped over the line, you and I would be taken from her forever. We were all she had left, and she loved us dearly."

"So, from there, the beatings happened on a regular basis. At first, I fought back and threatened to leave him, but then he threatened to take you from me. Gerald said he would disappear forever, and you would call someone else mommy and never know the difference."

"When you're in the situation, it becomes murky as to what is up and down. You begin blaming yourself for all that is happening. That's not the case though. I realize now that I'm not at fault."

"Ainsley, I had prayed that you would never know what happened, but now that I know the truth, I should have noticed how you were deteriorating throughout the years as the realities of what was going on took root in your mind. My one and only goal in all this was to keep you safe. I didn't want you tainted from all the ugliness."

"When you showed up with Adam, I saw the spark that had been missing from your eyes for all those years. He's ignited something within you, Ainsley, and I couldn't be happier."

"In one of our group sessions here at the center, we watched videos as to what children of abuse thought of themselves, and my heart ached. There was one common theme that occurred with all the videos. The children blamed themselves for not helping the parent who was being abused. They thought they should have fought for their parents, that they should have done something to help. Sweetie, I can see you doing that, and I want you to know that none of this is your fault. You and I are both innocent bystanders in all this. There was nothing you could have done."

Tears were streaming down my mom's face, and my vision had become blurry as the truth was being said out loud in the open. The truth felt like it set us free, and all those years of being sentenced to our silent prison seemed as if they had led to this moment of clarity and healing.

"Mom—"

My mom gently cut me off. "Ainsley, I have one last bit to read, and then we can talk. I want to get it all out in the open."

I nodded, and she wiped her eyes.

"At the party, when I found out your father was there, I panicked. My hair and outfit had not been what he would have allowed me to wear. It was too colorful and bright. I violated so many rules that I knew something was going to happen, and I slipped into old habits. Then, two days after the party, your father called me and asked what poison I had put in your head against him. He asked if I remembered what used to happen when I disobeyed him. That caused me to regress, and I retreated to a time when I followed the rules precisely."

"I hate that Adam had to witness that, but in the end, I'm thankful that I'm now getting the help I need. I love you with my entire heart, Ainsley. I always have and always will. I look forward to being a part of your life as me, the real me. I want to see you grow in your love and be there when you get married and have babies of your own. Thank you for saving me."

I leaned over and grabbed my mom. In between sobs, I said, "I love you. Thank you for keeping me safe. Thank you for coming here. I have you back."

Her words had been beautiful, raw, and honest. They were the epitome of what I craved in a relationship in order to have trust. The wounds that had cut bone deep seemed like they were beginning to close infinitesimally.

Doctor Jacobs spoke. "That was beautiful, Christine. Before today, I hadn't heard what your mom wrote, Ainsley. I wanted you to know that all those words were from your mother's heart without any feedback or discussion from anyone else. How does that make you feel, Ainsley—hearing those words from your mom?"

I sat right next to my mom, and we grabbed each other's hands.

"I was relieved and happy because it feels like my mom and I are finally admitting that there are skeletons in our closets versus the rosy childhood it felt like I was being told I had. There were times I thought I was crazy, and I had imagined what my father did to my mom. I was sad, thinking about everything she had gone through. And I truly feel loved by her. The honesty in her words resonated within me. I'm confused because this is my mom, but it feels as if I'm seeing the real her for the first time in years. I used to get glimpses as a kid, but she faded away with time."

Doctor Jacobs wrote something down and then looked at me. "Those are all normal feelings, Ainsley. Your mom wanted help, and that makes a huge difference. Do you blame yourself, Ainsley?"

I looked down at my ring before looking back at the doctor. "Yes. I know it's not rational, and hearing the words from my mom has helped, but anytime the memories try to haunt me, I imagine there will always be a small piece of me that wonders what if I had done something."

My mom squeezed my hand, and another tear fell from her cheek.

"Christine, that is completely normal for Ainsley to feel that way. Our regrets and mistakes shape us. The scars of what you both went through will always be present, but they can become unnoticeable, small blemishes with time and healing.

Ainsley, your mom has made remarkable progress."

I nodded. "I can tell. This is one of the best days of my life."

My mom kissed the side of my head. "Me, too."

The sound of the pen on the paper made noise. Doctor Jacobs looked up and smiled. "You guys are blessed to have the love and bond you share. Christine, did you want to tell Ainsley the decision you came to this morning?"

My mom removed her hands from mine and angled herself my way. "I have decided to sell everything inside the house, except for my parents' memorabilia in the basement I was able to save and anything else you might want. I think a new beginning is what we both need. I plan on getting something smaller. As long as you're okay with it, I'm going to get it listed."

This day could not get any better. "I think it's a wonderful idea. Besides Grandma's things, I took everything that I wanted when I left. How much longer are you staying here? Is there something I can do to get it listed for you?"

She gave me such a genuine smile that my heart soared. "I've elected to stay here for at least another thirty days to continue with my counseling. We're discussing in what capacity and if I'll enter the half-way program. I'd like for you to start coming once a week for us to make sure we have a solid foundation. In regard to the house being put on the market, a realtor is bringing by some paperwork for me to sign, and it will be listed."

Doctor Jacobs added, "Everyone is feeling positive and wonderful right now. That's an excellent thing. Studies have shown that if you continue the healing process, you make life-long changes, so when your instinct is to go back to your comfort zone, you have the tools to keep yourself from doing that."

It was information and emotion overload as I tried to take it all in and analyze it. "I'd love to do that, and I think it's an excellent idea to come see my mom every week."

Doctor Jacobs stood, and my mom and I followed suit.

"I think we have made some excellent progress today. Ainsley, you were given a lot to process, and I would imagine as you sort through everything your mom has said, you might have some questions. Does the same time next week work?"

My heart was sad that my time had been so limited with my mom, but I kept on my brave face. My mom needed this time to get better, and in the process, I would heal, too.

"Yes, that works great. Thank you, Doctor Jacobs." I turned and gave my mom a hug. "I feel like I just got here, but I am so happy right now. I'll be back next week. I love you."

She returned the hug. "Love you, too, sweetie. Go spend some time with your guy."

I remembered that I hadn't told my mom what he did. "Mom, I want you to know what Adam does."

My mom held up her hand. "I already know. Your father told me when he called. Ainsley, if he makes you happy, that is all that matters to me."

"He does, Mom. He really does."

"Good. I'm happy for you."

We walked toward the door, and Clarice was there, waiting, as if she knew we would be leaving. Mom and I hugged and said good-bye one last time. Then, I followed Clarice to the front entrance. I felt like the puzzle pieces in my life were finally falling into place. Adam waited at the desk, and I bounded into his arms.

He kissed the top of my head. "How did it go?"

I was practically beaming. "Perfect. She's so much better. I'll tell you all about it on the way home."

We walked back to the car.

As soon as we got in the car, Adam turned to me. "Your letter was beautiful, baby. Thank you again for sharing that piece of yourself with me."

I smiled. "I'm glad. I wanted you to be a part of it."

On our way to Adam's, I couldn't stop talking about everything that had transpired with my mom. "You were right. It was different and odd, but for me, it was refreshing, too. I don't know what happened with Brandt, and I'm not asking, but with my mom, I never knew her without the fear looming over her. She's free and discovering herself. It's a beautiful thing."

He pulled into the garage. "I'm happy for you, baby, and for your mom. You are in a different situation than what Brandt's was." He scrubbed a hand down his face and looked at me. "There are very few people who know Brandt had an intervention. He swore me to secrecy, or I'd tell you. He did say that it was okay for me to tell you about the intervention in general and what I had experienced. I don't want you to think that I don't trust you."

I leaned over and kissed him. His whiskers tickled my face. "I know, and I'll never pressure you for information that doesn't belong to me."

He gave me a loving smile. "Let's go inside."

We walked into the house he had filled the living room with flowers.

"Are these for me?"

Adam turned me around and grazed his lips to mine. "Each petal represents how many times I thought about you today."

"I love you." The words had come out of my mouth without any warning.

Adam

I WAS SUCH an ass. Ainsley had told me she loved me last night, and the words had died in my throat when I tried to talk. So, instead, I had tried to show her by making love to her among all the flowers in the house. I hadn't been able to tell what she thought. When I'd kissed her instead of speaking, I'd seen the hurt flash across her face momentarily, but she hadn't pushed me for the words. However, now it felt like there was a big fucking elephant in the room between us. The last time I'd uttered those words to a woman she'd put my heart into a blender. Ainsley had the power to do much worse damage.

Ainsley had been normal this morning, but hell, I was paranoid at this point. It was lunch time, and I was at the club, handling all the administrative shit to get my mind off of that stupid-ass elephant that wanted to be dealt with. There was a knock at my office door.

"Come in."

"Adam?"

Fuck.

I stood and came around my desk. "Selena, what the hell are you doing here?"

She looked the same as she had four years ago. I hadn't seen her since I walked into the family function where my asshole of a brother had decided to tell—no, show me that he was with Selena. Her black hair was longer, but she still had those green cat eyes. There wasn't a bit of me that was attracted to her. Relief coursed through my body.

Have I been worried about what I would feel when I saw her? Was I afraid that I would still have feelings for her? Is that why I refused to give Ainsley that last piece of me?

Yes, it was.

I love Ainsley.

There was nothing between Selena and me.

Nothing.

She walked toward my desk. "I know Jessica filled you in on Jake leaving me when he found out I was pregnant."

Regardless of how I felt about her, she was still in a shitty situation. "She did." My voice was without emotion.

She walked a little closer until about three feet separated us. I stepped back.

"I need your help, Adam."

I laughed in disbelief. "That's pretty funny coming from you Selena. I don't have time for this shit. I'm sorry for the situation you're in, but it's not my place to get involved."

She gave me a sad look. "Just pretend you are interested in getting me back. Jake wants whatever you have. He always has. I made the wrong choice all those years ago, Adam. He's only kept me around because he thought you wanted me. But I guess he doesn't think you'd want me with a baby on the way. He promised me marriage, a family, and a beautiful life. I've gotten none of that. I only have heartache and pain. I wish I had made a different choice, but I love him."

My fears were confirmed. Jake would try to get Ainsley if he knew I loved her. I needed to let her know how I felt. I stepped back farther. I was not telling Selena I had someone in my life. It would spread like wildfire through my family.

"Selena, I'm sorry Jake did this to you, but I'm not getting involved. It took me a while, but my life is where it's supposed to be. If it were me, I'd be glad he was out of my life. Don't waste several more years falling prey to his games. I wish the best, but I'm not a pawn in your chess game."

"Adam—"

"Go, Selena. I'm not your guy anymore. You chose Jake. Try to work it out with him if that's what you want." The plead in her voice made me feel sorry for her, but it didn't make me want to move heaven and earth for her like I once had.

A few tears trickled down her face. "The Adam I knew would have done that for me."

"I'm not the Adam you knew."

I stood there without wavering or any emotion on my face. If she sensed any empathy, she would become a bigger problem and potentially a problem for Ainsley. I needed to explain all this to Ainsley before Jake found out about her.

I looked at my watch. "Selena, I have a meeting. It's time to leave. Let's not make this ugly."

She nodded, and the venom I used to hate when we fought came back. "You can be an asshole at times, Adam. I needed a favor. Me leaving you happened years ago. You need to get over yourself."

I didn't say a word. It wouldn't do any good. She turned and left, slamming my office door behind her. I waited a few minutes before I headed to my car. No one guarded the damn door, and it wasn't locked. Pulling out my phone, I sent a text to the team, including Brandt.

Bastards.

Trigger, Snake, Brandt: Someone needs to either lock the door or fucking guard it like they're supposed to. My ex just came here.

They all sent me back individual texts:

Trigger: Fuck. I'm sorry, man. I stepped away for a few to show the new beer delivery guy where to go.
Snake: I'm on it. I was on the bar side.
Brandt: I'll deal with it. Are you okay?

I only responded back to Brandt.

Me: Yeah. Selena wanted me to pretend to want her, so Jake would take her back. I'm going to the gym and then getting some lunch.
Brandt: Shit. I'll get after them. Unacceptable. You said no, right?
Me: Of course. Ainsley is my future.
Brandt: Good to hear. Maybe you should tell Ainsley that.
Me: I plan on it.

Now, I needed to wait until this evening to get Ainsley to the club. I'd take her somewhere special and tell her how I felt.

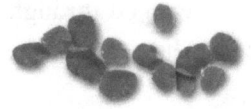

I was on my way back from grabbing a quick bite to eat after my workout when my phone rang. It was Jessica. I thought about silencing her, but she'd probably show up like last time while Ainsley was there, and then I'd have a bigger mess to deal with.

I hit Answer. "Hey, Jessica."

"Can we talk? I'm near the club."

I looked at the clock, and it was three hours until Ainsley was supposed to be there. She always texted me when she came to the club.

"I'm sure this is about Selena. I'm pulling into the club now. Jessica, I'm only giving you five minutes on this subject, and then it's closed between us forever."

A blinker sounded in her car. "I'm pulling in, too. Five minutes is all that I need, and then I won't mention it again."

Hell, that is worth five minutes versus multiple days of dealing with talk of Selena.

I saw my sister's SUV pull into the lot across the way. I made it to the door as she did. Jessica looked like she had come from yoga class. Trigger stood post as he opened the door.

About fucking time he did his job.

He said, "Adam—"

"Not now."

"But, Adam—"

"Trigger, I'm busy. I'll come deal with whatever you have to say in a minute. Stand your fucking post this time."

My patience was at the end of its rope with all this shit

raining down on me. We walked through my office door. Jessica was like me, and she didn't waste her time with pleasantries.

She put her purse on the table. "Selena called me. She's upset."

I stood there, staring at my sister. I loved her, but she was walking on thin ice.

She held up her hands. "I know, I know, I know. You don't have to sleep with her. She wants your help to spur Jake into taking responsibility."

I scrubbed a hand down my face.

How the hell is this my responsibility?

Jake was his own person, and we didn't speak.

"Jess, listen, you guys all need to open your eyes and realize that I am not the answer to this. Let's say I pretend to try to win Selena back. I give in and actually do it. It's not going to do a damn bit of good in the long run, and you know it. If I'm the only reason he's with her, then he'll bail the moment I meet someone. I'm done with that part of my life." My tone grew insistently more impatient.

Jess stopped, and she looked at me for a few seconds. "You've met someone, haven't you? It's the woman I saw you kissing a few weeks ago in the parking lot. You've moved on. Oh, geez, Adam. I would never have come here if I had known you were in a committed relationship. Mom and Dad are going to be so happy. I'm so happy for you."

Images of my parents telling Jake and Jake seeking Ainsley out came to mind. Jake trying to steal the one thing I now breathed for was unbearable. Until I was able to tell Ainsley, she didn't need to exist to them. I swallowed the bitterness that came to my tongue as I said what I needed to say to get Jessica off of Ainsley's trail.

Jessica had tears in her eyes as she walked toward me, but I stopped her.

"Jessica, that woman you saw me with is nothing but a fuck buddy I use for pleasure. She's like the rest—a great piece of ass. You know the score." The words were acid on my tongue.

My sister kept watching me. "Well then, it shouldn't—"

I held up my hands. "Regardless, I'm not helping. I don't want there to be problems between us, but if you keep pushing, you're going to cause a major rift between us."

She scratched her forehead as she comprehended everything I'd said. "I'm sorry. Thanks for listening. I like to try to keep the family together. You know how it is. I know what I asked you to do was a Band-Aid, but I keep hoping he's changed." She looked around the room.

I wished Jessica could learn how to let things go that she couldn't control.

"I know this is a sensitive subject, but are you coming to the party?"

She looked resigned as she grabbed her purse from the chair, like she knew I would say no, and it would be another thing to add to her list of problems to solve.

I nodded. "Yes, I'll be there."

She stopped and dropped her purse as she looked at me. "You will?"

Regardless if Jake was there or not, it was time for him to stop dictating my life. "Yes, I'll be there. They're my parents, too, and I want to be there for this event. I don't think it's necessary for me to do my own thing anymore."

I had always gone the day before or after to spend time with my parents for special events. Back then, seeing Jake and Selena together had been like a knife to the chest. Now, I had a different future.

Jessica came up and engulfed me in a hug. "Thank you, Adam. Thank you."

I hugged her back. "You're welcome, sis. I'm sorry it took me so long to answer."

She squeezed me tightly. "All that matters is that you finally did." She pulled back and wiped a tear from her eye. "I need to go. Selena is going over to mom and dad's house. They don't need the stress. I know it's not my problem, but it's my nature to fix things."

We walked toward the door. "Take care of yourself."

"I will. I promise."

Snake passed us in the hall. "Snake, will you show Jessica the way out? I have something I need to do."

Snake gave me a knowing nod. "Sure thing."

Jessica gave me one last hug before following Snake. I needed to piss and get my head back in the game. I had called a hotel and reserved a room for Ainsley and me. We would have a romantic dinner on the balcony overlooking the city before I gave her my heart. It was time, and I was ready.

After using the restroom, I headed to Brandt's office to decompress before Ainsley came to the club. Brandt sat at his desk, commanding security from his computer screens. Our new security manager would start next week, and Brandt was not happy with it. He liked hiding behind the camera. Maybe this new freedom would force him to face some things he had been avoiding.

Brandt turned toward me with his hair pulled back as I sat on the couch.

"What the hell did you do?"

Well, shit, this isn't decompressing.

My eyes flicked to the screen out of habit. Everything

looked fine. I rested my hands on my knees and leaned forward. "Jessica stopped by. She pressed me to help Selena."

Brandt looked at me in confusion. "Did you agree to help? Is that why Ainsley ran out of here less than five minutes ago? I was surprised you didn't go after her. What happened?"

I stood up. "What the fuck are you talking about? Ainsley isn't due here for a while."

My chest tightened as I tried to fit the pieces together.

Brandt stood. "Shit. Ainsley was in your bedroom off of your office to surprise you. She texted me to let her in the back way. Trigger was supposed to tell you. She got here about thirty or so minutes ago while you were at lunch."

"Fuck."

Brandt didn't know what to say as I turned and ran toward my office. That means she had heard everything I said to Jessica.

Every. Single. Fucking. Word.

What have I done?

Ainsley

A few minutes prior…

TEARS STUNG MY eyes as I sank to the floor in the room off of Adam's office. His words devastated me as I heard him tell his sister what he thought of me. It felt as if a hot poker burned my eyes. My confession of love to him now felt foolish. I had given him my heart, and he had tossed it aside. It was no wonder he'd looked startled last night when I had let the word *love* slip. My mind had been exhausted from the meeting with my mom, and it had escaped without me realizing it. I had been holding it down so much that it was bound to escape at some point, like a captive waiting to break free.

As he continued to talk to his sister about his ex, Selena, I put my fist in my mouth and bit down to silence the cries trying to break free. I wasn't able to concentrate on anything else he said. My world was shattered.

Finally, I heard his office door close. Even though the best thing was always to stay and talk it out, self-preservation won out. I knew his true feelings now. They hadn't changed since the time on the Tantra Chair in his house when he had said that we were fuck buddies. I should have known that he wouldn't have changed. All those special moments I'd thought we shared were lies.

Grabbing my purse, I ran out the front where Snake guarded the door.

"Ainsley—"

I didn't answer as I went to my car. Tears were beginning to fall from my face, regardless of how hard I tried to push them to the side until I was somewhere safe. Cranking my car, I pulled out as quickly as possible, and my tires squealed in protest. I didn't know where I was going.

As soon as the club was out of sight, uncontrollable sobs racked my body while I drove. I attempted to blink the tears away enough to see the road, but the hurt continued to spread through my body like a poison. I clutched the steering wheel in a death grip, forcing my attention on the road. My mind kept going back to what I had done today that led me to hearing that awful confession.

I came to the club to surprise Adam since my class had gotten out early, and Angela had given me the night off. After confessing I loved him last night, I wanted to lighten things up. I had bought his favorite dessert of cheesecake and had made a picnic on the floor, so we could relax without the pressure I had put on our relationship. I meant what I'd said, and I would never push him for more.

The door to our bedroom had been left open, so I could

hear him approaching. The conversation played out as questions raced through my mind.

How long has Selena been talking to him?

My mind processed everything I heard. Selena and Jessica were pressuring him to pretend to still be interested in his ex in order for his brother to still want her. It was totally screwed up. He refused, and then I was mentioned.

"Jessica, that woman you saw me with is nothing but a fuck buddy I use for pleasure. She's like the rest—a great piece of ass. You know the score."

For as long as I lived, those words would forever be ingrained to my being as they flashed through my mind. They echoed through my head like a bell resonated through an empty town square.

Fuck buddy.

Use for pleasure.

Piece of ass.

The words continued on a loop as my heart disintegrated into a million ice crystals. This is what a broken heart felt like. It was as if my soul had been ripped from me and left in its place was a skeleton.

The memory was acute and I tried to shut it out by focusing on something else.

Money. I need money to go stay somewhere for a few days.

I had over two hundred dollars in my bank account, but I needed that for bills.

My mom's cookie jar.

She always kept money in there, and I had a key to get into her house. I'd pay her back and explain everything later. Right now, I needed to get my head on straight, analyze the situation, and stitch my heart back together. My phone vibrated, and Adam's name flashed across it.

Seeing his name was hard, but I let it roll to voice mail. Next, a text message showed on the screen. I didn't want to read what he had written, but he needed to know I wasn't coming by tonight and that I had heard him.

My relationships all ended because I was being used for something, and it had happened again. Jarrod, my ex, had used me to try to get a connection with my father. Adam had used me for sex. I felt like a dirty whore. Maybe my past was too much to overcome to live a normal life like I desperately wanted.

The phone was like a beacon as it continued to light up with call after call and text after text from Adam. I pulled into my mother's driveway and brought up the text message screen, refusing to read his texts. I had heard the truth, and any lie he'd told me wouldn't obscure what I had heard.

Me: I heard you talking to your sister. I know where we stand. I can't have that type of relationship. I wish you had been honest with me. Bye, Adam.

I shut off my phone and went into the house. Everything was as we had left it when my mom had left for A New Beginning Domestic Abuse Center. My feet faltered, and I stopped for a second to get my balance. Looking at the inside of the house caused another sob to escape me as I imagined my father coming in night after night from his day at work. That would be followed by his infamous words...

Christine, you and I need to talk this evening.

Another sob erupted, and tears cascaded my face as I was reminded of how much hate had existed here. Maybe that was why only my mom loved me. I wasn't whole enough to keep around.

I need to get out of here. My mind was in a bad place, and this house was like a cancer that would continue to consume me if I didn't leave. I hurried to the cookie jar in the kitchen cupboard to the right of the sink. I opened it, took out all the cash I could fit in one fistful, and stuffed it into my pocket.

After shutting the cabinet door, I ran to the front door as quickly as possible. This place was toxic. I'd never know how my mom had survived here all these years. As I put the key in the lock, I fumbled with locking the door as I tried desperately to escape. The key wouldn't come out of the door. It was as if the house tried to make me stay. To carry the memories of all the things that had happened within those walls would be a heavy burden to carry. Finally, I was able to free the key, and I went to my car. I prayed I would never have to come back to this place.

My car was my safe haven as I got in and hastily backed out of the driveway. Picking any direction that led me from here, I drove for about half an hour out of the city until I came up to a small motel. In bright neon letters, the sign said *Vacancy.*

My pale blue eyes were red-rimmed and bloodshot. I decided to put on my sunglasses to hide my blotchy face. Taking deep breaths, I reached down deep to the far shadows of my being to find the strength to get through these next few days.

I am strong enough. I can do it.

I'd email my college professors to get what would be discussed, and I would bury myself in my books. I was far enough ahead that a few days wouldn't hurt me. The first thing I needed to do was get a hotel room.

A lone tear slipped down my face as I kept replaying the conversation in my head.

Fuck buddy.
Use for pleasure.
Piece of ass.
I was nothing but a whore to him.
I am worthless.

I got out of my car and walked up to the desk where a middle-aged pimply-faced guy with a red shirt and black pants stood behind a counter.

My voice sounded more confident than it had any right in sounding at the moment. "I need a room for four nights, please."

He opened his books. "Would you prefer a TV with a queen-sized bed or a king-sized bed only? The TV with the king-sized bed is broken."

"The king-sized room will be fine."

I didn't need the sound of a TV. I would embrace the silence and let it cover me in a protective blanket while I became stronger. At least if it were silent, nothing horrible would be happening.

He wrote in his book and then got a key from under the table. "That'll be one hundred and twenty dollars for the three nights. Do you want to pay cash or credit? I'll need an ID also."

I took out the money and my ID as he'd requested and gave them to him. "Cash, please."

He wrote down some information and then handed my ID back to me.

"Thank you. Here's your key. You're in room twelve."

I nodded and took the key. Walking to my room, I noticed the red paint peeling off the exterior walls that had been battered with time. In truth, it was how I felt on the inside. It didn't matter. It was a place off the map.

I opened my door and stepped in. The sound of the door closing behind me felt as if all hope was truly lost for Adam and me to find our way.

Two days had passed, and I was lost in my books that had been in my car since I had come straight from class to the club to surprise Adam. I was a few days ahead in my classes. I needed one more day, and then I would force myself back into the living world.

I'll go to school the day after tomorrow.

I needed clothes. I only had two spare sets in my car, and I needed two more sets if I was going to stay for two nights before heading to class. This room had become my safe haven. There was a fast-food restaurant across the street. I would go over there about once a day to get food of some sort. That was about all I could stomach at this point. Most of my one meal a day would be thrown away when I couldn't force down another bite.

Forcing my thoughts back on the task at hand, I knew I couldn't go home, not yet anyway. I wasn't strong enough to deal with the memories.

Clothes. Where could I get clothes?

I didn't have enough cash left. There were clothes at my mom's, but I didn't want to go back there with how it had affected me the last time. I had no choice but to get my act together. I needed to be strong for my mom, too.

Nora.

Nora would help me and not tell anyone where I was at.

I went across the brown carpet to the red floral bedspread where my backpack laid. I pulled out my phone and turned it on. There were over ninety-nine notifications. I cleared them out and pulled up Nora's name.

Me: Can you do me a favor?
Nora: Yeah, I tried calling to see if you wanted to do lunch, and it went to voice mail. Are you okay?

Adam hasn't told her we're over? What did people know?
I figured she would have known what was going on by now. My mind didn't know what to make of this.

Me: I don't want to go into it, but Adam and I broke up. I need clothes. Can you bring them to me? I'm not ready to face the world yet. I've been locked up, studying.
Nora: I'm sorry, Ainsley. I'll crush his balls if you want me to. And of course I'll get you some clothes. Where can I bring them?
Me: Sunshine Motel. Room 12.
Nora: What time do you want me to drop them off?
Me: Whatever is easiest for you.
Nora: Okay, give me a couple of hours to swing by your place, and then I'll come to you.
Me: Thanks, Nora. I'm going to turn off my phone again.
Nora: Anytime. You know that. Okay. I'll call the motel if I need you. Things will get better, I promise. Have you talked to him yet?
Me: No. I'm not ready to. I have to get my things from his place, but I'll figure that out later.
Nora: I understand. See ya in a bit.
Me: Thanks again.

I shut off my phone and crawled underneath the covers as a fresh wave of tears hit. Regardless of what I'd told myself, it was going to be a long time before I healed completely from the loss of Adam. Texting Nora had shown me how far I still had to go with moving past the hurt.

I would focus on the second I was currently living in until I was able to be in the minute, then the hour, then the day. Eventually, the sharp pain would become a dull ache, aches I could live with. The covers were pulled over my head like they used to be when I'd tried to drown out the world when my father would hit my mom over and over again. It was hard thinking that Adam had written me off and not told anyone about us.

It was a fresh cut to my already battered self.

Adam

I WAS A fucking mess, a disaster. I hadn't slept in over two days as I'd tried every which way I knew to find Ainsley. I had gone to all her classes, her mother's house, her place, the library, and anywhere we had ever been. Every place I'd tried was a dead end. She had disappeared, and I hoped that she was okay. My girl had every right to react the way she had without knowing everything that was going on.

I need Ainsley back. I love her, and I am ready to tell her how I feel.

Shit, where could she be?

Nora came running into my office. "She texted me. I know where she is."

I stood. "Where? Is she okay?" Relief washed through my body, knowing she had made contact with someone.

She gave me one of those looks. "Yes, she's alive, but she's not okay. She's heartbroken. Adam, I have never led her astray like I did over texts. You'd better not make me regret helping you get her back. If you're going to try to win her back, make sure you know that you want this and not the chase. I understand what happened with her overhearing your convo with Jessica, but so help me if you are lying to me—"

"Nora, I swear I'm not. I love her, and I'm never letting her go. Ever." There wasn't an ounce of doubt in my mind. I hoped my voice conveyed the same sentiment. "Please tell me where I can find her, Nora."

Nora looked me over for a second, and I met her gaze head-on, not backing down. I was so close to seeing Ainsley again.

Nora nodded to herself and then said, "I believe you, but first, you need a plan."

"A plan? No, I need to see her now." My voice sounded strained.

I only need Ainsley.

Nora walked over to the desk, and she drummed her fingers on the glass top. "Yes, a plan. For starters, you need a shower and some fresh clothes. You're getting ripe. Second, you need to sweep her off her feet, show her how you feel, and how much you love her. You're going to have to do something to get her to let her guard down. I don't know if she'd talk to you if you were waiting outside her motel door."

Scrubbing a hand down my face, I knew Nora was right. Ainsley needed me to give myself, my entire being to her. If I'd heard those words that I said to Jessica, I would have been devastated after everything we had shared. Ainsley had never asked for anything in return, except for honesty from me.

I messed up.

I sank back in the chair as my mind raced with thoughts. I had to do something that would take Ainsley off her guard for a moment in order for her to see the truth behind my words, something that would cause her to be open enough for me to slip in. That incessant drumming from Nora's fingers drove me fucking mad. It was like a dog constantly nipping at your heels.

Dog.

Lindy.

I stood. "I have to go. Can you go get her some clothes and meet me back here in two hours?"

"What do you have planned, Casanova?" One of her eyebrows was cocked.

Grabbing my keys from the desk, I made sure with my other hand that I had my wallet. "I need to get a few things. When I meet you back here, I'll explain, but I have a plan."

She made a shooing motion. "Hurry. Skedaddle. I'll meet you back here in two hours."

I was already out the door. "Sounds good." I stopped. "And, Nora?"

"Yeah?"

"Thank you."

She gave me a salute. "You're welcome. Just don't let her go again."

"Never."

I made my way to my car and headed to my house. I thought back on the events that had led up to this moment. Nora had been a hard case to convince to help me.

Brandt had informed me that Ainsley was in my office the entire time I talked to Jessica. I ran out to the parking lot, and there was no sign of Ainsley's car. Pulling out my phone, I dialed her number as I looked in all directions, trying to spot her vehicle. My mind was chaotic as I tried to think of where she could be. My heart felt as if it was being crushed.

It rung.

I muttered into the phone, "Come on, baby, pick up. It's not what you think."

My pulse raced, and thoughts of never seeing Ainsley entered my mind.

Her voice came on the phone. "Hey, this is Ainsley. Leave a message, and I'll call you back."

Damn it. Damn it all to hell.

"Baby, call me. Let me explain. What you heard is all lies."

I typed out a text, not knowing what to do or where she was going.

Me: Ainsley, baby, call me. What you heard is not true.

I ran back into the club as I tried to call her repeatedly.

Snake was at the door. "Adam, Ainsley—"

"I know. Did she say where she was going?"

Snake shook his head. "No, man. I asked if there was something wrong, and she didn't respond."

I had the phone up to my ear, getting Ainsley's damn voice mail again. I walked and called over my shoulder. "Call Nora. Let her know I need her to come in. Have her come to my office."

Snake didn't question my direction.

Why did I not listen to Trigger when I walked into the club? This is all my fault.

As I typed out another text, Snake called after me. "I'm calling right now."

"Tell her to hurry."

*Not bothering to close my office door, I went to our bed-
room and saw a blanket with a champagne bottle and cheesecake on the floor.*

A picnic for two. Fuck.

*I glanced over toward the bed and saw a pink envelope
peeking out from under my pillow. I called Ainsley again, and
it went to voice mail. She was on redial. At this point, she had
shut off her phone, so I texted her incessantly.*

Me: Please call me.

*Me: Ainsley, it's not what you think. That's not how I feel
about you.*

Me: I want to tell you how I feel in person, not over text.

*My heart ached, knowing how much my girl was hurting
right now. I walked over to the pillow and pulled the envelope
out from underneath the pillow. On it was my name written in
Ainsley's handwriting.*

I stared at it for a few minutes. I wished I could turn back the hands of time and tell her everything before this whole mess had broken out. One drop in the balance of things had caused a ripple effect that changed everything. I opened the envelope as I sat on the bed, and I read the words Ainsley had written to me.

Adam,

I know I said something last night that you weren't ready to hear or say. I will never push for anything you aren't ready to give, and I don't expect it. I know and can feel how deeply you care about me, and that's enough. It's more than I ever wanted or dreamed I would receive from someone. What we have is unlike anything I've ever known, and I've never felt something this strong. You have my heart, forever and always. I love you exactly for who you are.

Ainsley

It felt as though a knife stabbed repeatedly into my heart. I loved Ainsley. Now, it was too late to tell her she had all of me, too, just like she had given herself to me. I vowed to never miss an opportunity to tell her how I felt again.

Nora knocked on the bedroom door. Then, my phone vibrated. It was Ainsley.

Ainsley: I heard you talking to your sister. I know where we stand. I can't have that type of relationship. I wish you had been honest with me. Bye, Adam.

My heart went to my throat as I typed a response, hoping she would not turn off her phone again.

Me: Ainsley, I love you. I didn't want to tell you this over text. Please come back to me, baby.

I sat there and stared at my phone, waiting for a response. Seconds seemed like hours. Her phone had to be off. I knew she would have responded to that text even if it was to confirm we were over. I was getting desperate.

"Hey there, boss man. Where's the fire? Snake said to get here."

Nora's voice startled me as I stood. I put Ainsley's letter in my pocket, wanting a piece of her close to me.

"Let's talk in my office."

Nora had blue-tipped hair this week. She went to the chair and lounged back in it with her arm thrown over the back. I sat down beside her.

"Who killed your puppy?"

She was joking, but when I looked at her, she sat straight up.

"Is Ainsley okay? Shit, what happened?"

"I fucked up."

She folded her arms over her chest. "I'm Ainsley's friend, Adam. I'm going to support her. I've already helped you once. Do you remember what I told you I'd do if you hurt her again? I need this job, but I will follow through with my threat."

"I love her, Nora, and she doesn't know it yet. She thinks I'm using her." My voice sounded defeated as I cradled my head in my hands. I felt defeated.

Why did I doubt her feelings for me? Why did I let Jake win again?

Nora shifted in her chair, and I assumed she leaned forward.

"Why does she think that?" Her voice softened some, but there was still a note of accusation as she spoke.

I had two choices—either give her the whole truth or a piece of the story. Raising my head, I chose the whole story. I couldn't risk Nora not helping me. If Nora suspected any foul play, she'd walk, and I'd be on my own. With Ainsley's mom being at the center, she'd eventually reach out to Nora. Each minute that slipped by meant that Ainsley distanced herself from me more, and that would make it much harder to get her back. Nora was key to have on my side.

After telling Nora everything, I said, "I need to find her. I need to tell her how I feel. Will you help me?"

Nora sat there for a minute as she thought everything through. "I believe you. Yes, I'll help. If she contacts me, I'll let you know. If I start contacting her, she'll know something is up. We aren't clingy friends." She stood and walked toward the door. As she was about to cross over the threshold, Nora turned and looked at me. Fire flashed through her eyes, and her tone was a warning. "Adam, don't screw with her head.

Either give her all of you or let her be. I mean it. She needs someone who will give her everything and not a convenient piece."

"I'm going to give her all I have, Nora. Everything."

She nodded and left. Grabbing my keys, I headed for the car to look for Ainsley anywhere and everywhere I could think of.

Thinking back on everything that had happened since Ainsley left helped me process where all I had gone wrong. It was a long list. Pulling into my garage, I hopped out of the car. Lindy greeted me at the door.

I kneeled down and petted her head. "I need your help, girl. I messed things up with Ainsley, and we're going to get her back. Will you help me?"

Lindy barked.

"Good girl, Lindy. Let's go get our girl back."

This had to work. I was betting the rest of my life on it because I was nothing without Ainsley.

Ainsley

TIME DREW NEAR for Nora to drop off my clothes. I knew she would keep everything we talked about light until I was ready to talk to her about what had happened with Adam. The events were still too raw in my mind to verbalize.

I tried to figure out what I was going to tell my mom when I went to see her in two days for therapy. She didn't need the extra stress of my life, but I didn't want to put up another front. We finally had the truth. I decided to tell her everything.

My book was splayed on my lap as I read further ahead in Econ. A knock sounded at the door, and I threw my covers off my lap, displacing the book to the side. I was ready to hug my best friend, and see something from my life outside of these walls.

Without looking out the peephole, I opened the door. The sun's brightness greeted me, and I had to close my eyes for a second as they adjusted from the glare of the sun. No one was there, and then I heard a dog bark from below. I looked down, and my mouth dropped open. Lindy sat at the door perfectly poised with a big red bow on her collar. A paper note was clipped to it.

"Hey, girl. What are you doing here?" My heart raced as I looked around, but I didn't see Adam.

He has to be here.

Am I ready to see him?

Yes, I am even if that means more torture for me.

Lindy walked into the room, turned, and sat down, facing the door. I looked back out, and no one was out there. I didn't even see his car in the parking lot.

I walked over, knelt in front of Lindy, and rubbed her coat. "How did you get here, girl? Where's Adam?"

She barked, and then she shook her head. The letter came out of the paper clip and fell to the floor. On it was my name.

Biting my lip, I opened it with shaking hands, praying this wasn't a dream or a cruel joke.

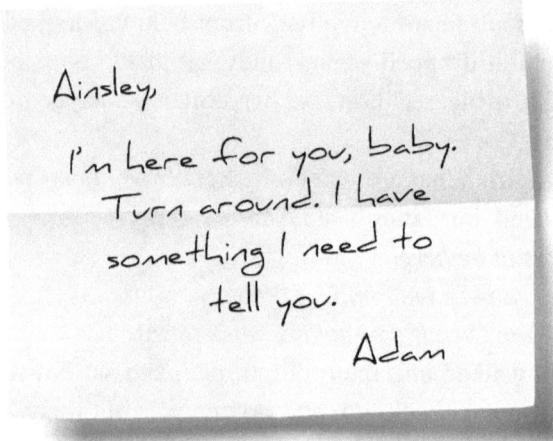

Ainsley,

I'm here for you, baby. Turn around. I have something I need to tell you.

Adam

I turned around, and Adam was there, holding a bouquet of white roses. My heart dared to hope, but the hurt was still present as I maintained my distance.

Why is he here?

I tried to make sense with what he had said and his actions now with bringing Lindy. What he'd said to his sister at the club completely contradicted what he was doing now. My brain felt like it was about to overheat.

"Ainsley, I love you." He never stopped looking at me as his words echoed through the room.

My lip trembled as I tried to stay centered. I was speechless.

He took a step toward me as he repeated what he had said, "Ainsley, I love you."

Afraid that I'd wake up from this dream, I forced myself to respond, "But…you told your sister that I was nothing but a fuck buddy, a good piece of ass. You have a family celebration you're going to that I knew nothing about."

He took another step closer. "Ainsley, I'm going to explain everything. Can we talk? I needed you to know how I feel first. I've been in love with you for a while as I suspect you've been with me. I was too scared to admit it."

I blew out a breath and waited for him to continue, trying to remain open-minded and not distance myself from fear of being hurt again. If he gave me his love and then took it away, I'd be devastated.

He continued. "My sister has been trying to get me to agree to come to my parents' surprise anniversary party since before we met. The night I showed you our new room, my sister showed up at the club earlier in the evening. It was while we were outside kissing. I wasn't ready for her to know about us, so I took you inside before I came back out to speak to her."

I know my eyes reflected shock from his last statement.

He scrubbed a hand down his face. "Ainsley, it had nothing to do with you and everything to do with me. I didn't want Jessica running off to my family and telling them about us until we were ready because of Jake. My brother always tries to get in the way of anything that makes me happy, and you baby, make me very happy. The moment Jake finds out about you, he's going to try something. I know it. I've been fighting the depths of my feelings for a while, afraid of what you could do with that type of power over me."

"I would never leave you for someone else."

Adam nodded solemnly. "I think I know that, but he's done it before. He's taken something that I thought made me happy, but all along, I was waiting for you to come into the picture. Nothing compares to what I feel for you. I didn't...I couldn't take a chance in losing you. Our connection is deeper baby, but my fear took over in this case. I wasn't ready to share you with my family until you knew everything. You're too important to risk. When Jessica told me in the parking lot that Selena was pregnant and that Jake had left her, I felt nothing but pity for Selena. There were no residual feelings. You are my present and my future. You know the rest of the story with what you overheard. Saying that about you, about us, was a lie. You're not my fuck buddy or a piece of ass. You're my life."

I closed my eyes as the scene that I had witnessed from the other side of the door reemerged in my mind, and a tear slipped out. His words that explained what had happened soothed me and mended my once obliterated heart, but I was still scared to let myself hope too much.

"Ainsley, when my sister asked about you in my office, I panicked. I lied to my sister, so she'd drop it. I wanted to wait until you came to the club that evening, so I could tell you that I loved you. I want to be your forever."

I watched him and his body posture, and it seemed like he was telling the truth, but I needed to think. I needed to process. My reality was altering from what I had conditioned myself to accept for two days, and now, that wasn't the case anymore. My mind was a mixture of emotions.

I looked over to Adam. "Can I have a few minutes to think?"

"What?" His voice sounded shocked.

"I need a few minutes to think this all through. We've done this before, Adam. Please let me think." The words felt wrong coming out of my mouth, but my protective measures in place refused to retract them. I looked down at my knotted hands, thinking about both times I had been reduced to feeling like a whore.

He looked utterly lost as he stood there, and then he walked out the door without a word. My heart ached as I let what felt like my true love leave. I was left in the room with Lindy as she cocked her head to one side, looking at me like I was the world's biggest idiot.

I am an idiot.

Adam had come here and professed his love, and I had asked for a few minutes to think.

I love him. I know I love him.

What have I done? Oh my gosh.

Adam is here. He loves me. He loves me. He loves me.

My heart raced with excitement. Still barefoot, I ran toward the door as Adam came bursting back through with a determined look on his face.

"Ainsley, I'm not letting you go. You're mine. I should have never walked out that door. I know I fucked up. Hell, I've fucked up a lot. But you're mine. Damn it, you're mine. I fucking love you. You're my everything."

He breathed rapidly, and seeing him be this honest shifted everything into focus.

"I want you to be my forever, too. I love you, Adam."

Adam closed the gap between us, and his lips came to mine. He kissed me as both hands touched the sides of my face. His thumb stroked my cheek as his lips sought mine as if he was starved for me.

"I want to take you somewhere. Will you leave with me, baby?"

"Yes, can we drop off my car somewhere?"

His lips touched mine again for a brief second. "Brandt and Nora are going to swing by and pick up Lindy and your car. Then, I want to take you somewhere."

"That sounds perfect."

His nose ran down my jawline. "Perfect is going to be when we make love again."

My hand went down to the hem of his shirt, and I reveled in the fact that he was in my arms again.

He pulled out his cell phone and typed a message. "They'll be here in a few minutes. Let's get you packed."

He kissed me again as he faced the room.

"Did you have them on standby?"

"Yes. There was no way I was going to be separated from you after being apart for two days. Let's get you packed."

"Okay." This was all going so fast, and I tried to memorize every second of Adam coming to me, fighting for me, wanting me.

Packing consisted of Adam putting everything haphazardly into my backpack. There wasn't much here, and he was done before my laptop finished shutting down.

"Anything else, baby?"

I looked around the room. "No, I think I have everything. I need to return the key to the front desk."

Adam put his hands around my waist. "Let's go. This place is a dump." We walked toward the door as Adam issued a command. "Follow, Lindy."

Lindy was by my side instantly, and the three of us made our way to the front office. Adam slipped on his aviator sunglasses. He looked intimidating.

He glanced down and smiled at me. "I'm glad to have you back in my arms."

"I'm glad to be back in your arms."

The same manager came out that was here when I'd checked in. "Sir, pets aren't allowed on the premises for upkeep purposes."

Adam stared blankly at the hotel manager, and the man

swallowed. Adam looked down at me. I received a warm smile as he took the key from my hand and handed it to the hotel clerk.

"We're leaving."

The manager cleared his throat and looked around. I had noticed that Adam could generally make people nervous with his demeanor.

"Um…okay…I'll need to check the room for incidentals since you had a dog. I didn't know when she checked in. My boss would write me up."

Adam took his free right hand and pulled out some bills from his jeans pocket. "My dog didn't cause any damage, but this should more than cover anything you might happen to find."

The guy looked stunned as he took the bills that probably amounted to a few hundred dollars.

"Yeah, thanks. That should cover anything I find." He folded the money precisely.

We walked.

Adam called out, "If you don't find any damage, keep the money for yourself."

Inside that tough exterior of the man I loved was a sweet, gentle caring man. We were about ten feet from the car when Brandt pulled in with his black SUV. Nora jumped out of the truck, wearing jeans and a T-shirt. Her hair had blue tips now, which made me smile.

She walked up and gave me a hug. "I'm sorry I misdirected you. He told me everything, and I knew you loved him. I hope you're not mad."

I hugged her back. "Not at all. Thank you for telling him." I lowered my voice as I said, "He loves me, Nora. He loves me."

"I know, chica."

Adam called out, "Lindy, load up."

Lindy was by my side, and she nudged me. I let Nora go and pet Lindy's ears the way she loved.

"We'll be back later, sweetie. I promise. Go load up."

Lindy took off and jumped in Brandt's passenger side. Adam smiled at me as he walked toward my side. Brandt petted Lindy and then came to stand by the front of the car.

I handed Nora my keys. "Thank you."

"Your car will be at Adam's house unless you want us to take it somewhere else." She jingled the keys in her hands.

My eyes shifted to Adam as I said, "That'll work. I don't plan on being anywhere else."

Nora walked back toward the car as gravel crunched under her feet. "We'd better leav, Brandt, before these two spontaneously combust from nookie need."

Brandt chuckled as Adam ushered me to the passenger side of his car.

I waved. "Thanks, Brandt."

He winked at me. "Anytime. Go give your guy some attention. He's been worried about you."

A grin emerged on my face. "I plan on it."

I ducked into the car, and Adam closed my door. Taking a deep breath, I memorized his scent. I had been without it for too long. He jogged over to his side and opened his door. Through the tinted window, I saw Brandt walk up to speak to Adam. With the door cracked, I was able to hear what he said.

"I'll take care of everything. Shut off your phone. Spend time with your girl."

"Thanks, Brandt. I plan on not letting her out of my sight for a while."

Brandt gave him a manly slap on the shoulder. "I'm glad

you didn't make the same mistake I did."

Adam nodded but didn't respond. Brandt sounded sad, and I realized that he must have lost someone he loved.

Maybe that was what caused him to need an intervention?

It made sense now why I hadn't seen him with any girls. He was such a decent guy, and I wanted him to get his happily ever after.

Adam got in the car, encapsulating us in our own world.

As we pulled out of the lot, I asked, "Where are we going?"

"It's a surprise if you're up for it." He glanced my way and looking down at my hand as he drove.

"I am. As long as we're together, that's all that matters." My actions from two days ago felt foolish. I should have known to get all sides of the story before reacting. "I'm sorry I ran like I did. I should have faced you and dealt with it."

"I should have told you what was going on with my family. I won't make that mistake again. I can assure you of that. There's no more running from what I've been afraid of. You're getting all of me, baby." His hand moved to the top of mine as he spoke.

His touch calmed me.

"Were you unsure of what we were? Is that why you didn't tell me about your parents' anniversary party?" I looked down at his hands as I ran my index finger along his skin.

The blinker came on, and Adam pulled off onto the side of a dirt road. He put the car in park and then turned my way.

"I want to get this all handled before we get to where we are going. I don't want you mistaking what I'm telling you because of lust. The moment we're alone, our need for each other is going to take over."

"Okay." I knew he was right.

Adam pulled his glasses off of his head and tossed them on the dashboard before looking straight at me. "I was afraid of getting hurt and of also hurting you. Our relationship exploded and I had no control over it. You came into my office, wanting to try the sex-club thing, and from that moment, you owned me. From the first time that I had you, I craved you on a level I never knew before. I fought it. Everyone, meaning my family, always thought I was waiting on the sidelines until Selena and Jake broke up. When he didn't propose to her like he'd promised, it was evident that he was using her. Until you, I refused to put myself out there again. You captured my heart, Ainsley. I knew I loved you before Selena came to visit me, but in that moment, something freed me that allowed me to admit it to myself. I used the hurt from my past as an excuse to protect myself, which almost cost me you."

I understood what he was saying. I had been cautious with him about my triggers of fighting also. It wasn't until I'd seen him handle himself with Tyler that I knew he could control himself in a moment of anger.

"It makes sense. Are you going to tell them about me now?"

He nodded. "Yes. I told my sister I was going to their party. It'll be the first family get-together I've been to in four years. I want you to come with me. Will you go?"

"I'd love to. Are you sure?" Part of me was still afraid he was reacting to me leaving, so I had to make sure.

"Ainsley, I've never been surer of anything in my life. Jake is—"

I put my fingers to his mouth. "It doesn't matter what Jake does. I'm yours completely."

He kissed the part of me that touched his lips. "I believe you. I'll never hide anything from you again, regardless of what it is."

Running my fingers along his cheek, I said, "I believe you."

He leaned into my hand. "That's all I can think of to tell you, but if you ever have questions, ask me. There are no secrets between us. Is there anything else you want to ask?"

"No, but I promise I will. You know that I thrive on honesty."

"I do, baby. Let's go spend some time together."

"Yes, just me and you, no one else."

Adam turned the car around, and we drove into the city. We were both quiet and a little introspective as we passed mile marker after mile marker. I leaned over the console putting my head on his shoulder. It wasn't the most comfortable position, but my body wanted to be near him. There was a peace that settled in over us as we held hands. After some time, we pulled up to a tall white stone hotel, the Mandarin Oriental in Atlanta. I sat up, stunned at where we were.

I turned to Adam. "We can't stay here. It's one of the nicest hotels in Atlanta. We can go to your place."

He got out of the car without responding and gave the keys to a valet. Adam came over to my side and opened the door.

I stood up. "Adam, really—"

I was silenced as his mouth descended on mine, and my focus ignited into a need for him. I had been without his affection for over two days, and I was starved for him. The way his tongue moved in my mouth made me think he felt the same way. My hands traveled down his chest.

Breaking the kiss, he pulled back. "I want some uninterrupted time with just us. I want it to be special, so we never forget it. Tonight is our first night of forever."

"I'd love that." My insides jumped with happiness.

After we walked through the glass doors, a woman greeted us, wearing a gold and black suit. "Here you go, Mr. Ryker. Please insert the key card into the elevator and push the button for the ninth floor. You're in room nine-one-nine. All arrangements have been made. Please let us know if you need anything."

How did she know who he was? He took the key. "Thanks. Please make sure we are not disturbed."

"Understood." Her hand was displayed to show the way to the elevator.

We entered the elevator, and the doors closed. Adam brought me closer to him as we ascended toward the ninth floor. We got off the elevator, turned left, and headed to our room. Adam didn't say a word as he put the key card into the door. He turned the handle.

Before pushing the door open, he turned to me. "We're about to lose ourselves in each other. I need to feel you."

"Yes."

He opened the door, and I gasped.

I love him irrevocably.

Adam

STANDING BEHIND AINSLEY, I watched her reaction as she took in the room. A canopy had been added to the bed. Rose petals were sprinkled in a trail from the door. Lighting had been adjusted low. Flameless candles were on every surface. The windows had sheer curtains, and the skyline of Atlanta was set against the twilight of the evening. The room smelled of Lavender.

She turned to me. "This is beautiful. I love this. I love you."

"I love you too, Ainsley. I'm so sorry I almost lost you, lost us."

Her fingers came up to my lips. "Shh, love always finds a way. Now, there'll never be any doubt that our feelings are real for each other."

There had never been truer words spoken.

I pressed closer to Ainsley, staying only a breath away from touching her. "Is there anything else you need to know, baby, before I make love to you?"

"No…"

My hands went to the edge of her shirt and pulled it over her head. Her pants followed. I was transfixed on watching her as her toned body was illuminated in the light.

I took a step back, shucking my shirt and pants off. She took off her undergarments. We stood there, staring at each other, bared to each other.

"Ainsley, you're gorgeous."

She was mine, only mine. I planned on keeping it that way…forever.

She took a deep breath. "Thank you." A blush crept on her face.

I slowly prowled toward her as she backed up toward the bed. The hotel had changed the sheets to silk. I loved how her body felt against mine with that material surrounding us. The back of Ainsley's knees hit the bed and I got close enough for my erection to touch her stomach.

Without losing eye contact her hand came down and stroked me. The warm touch of her fingers massaging my stone dick was heaven. I bent down to taste the sweet nectar of her lips.

The kiss was slow and savoring as my thumb caressed her cheek. I leaned her back on the bed and scooted us up to the middle, surrounding us in silk. Pulling back and sitting on my heels in between Ainsley's legs, I started at her feet and kissed my way up the inside of her thigh. Her body twitched underneath me as it bowed off the bed, anxious for me to make it to my destination.

"Adam—"

Pulling my head back, I watched my girl squirm for a second before answering, "I know."

Wanting to make sure she was ready, I licked her core savoring her essence before making my way to her navel. Ainsley writhed beneath me as my cock brushed against the inside of her leg, knowing it was close to where it wanted to be, inside Ainsley.

"Adam—"

Around her nipple, I murmured. "I know."

This would be a night I would forever remember as I gave someone my true heart for the first time. My mouth found her lips. Ainsley's tongue came out and tempted me closer. It worked as mine entered her mouth and tangled with hers. I lined my dick up, teasing her pussy a little.

"Adam—"

I finally gave her what she wanted as I sunk into the tightest, warmest, most exquisite place on earth. She fit me perfectly as I slid in and out of her slick heat. Her hands ran down my back as if she tried to memorize my body.

Ainsley's legs wrapped around my ass as we both got closer to the most perfect ending. An ending that pushed everything else aside, except for the one person that meant more to you than any person in the world.

We came as we swallowed each other's cries of bliss. After I pulled out, I rolled to the side and brought her close to me, legs entwined.

"This does feel like the first night of our forever." Her words were shy.

I brought her closer to me. "It is our first night of forever. I'll love you forever, baby."

She trailed her fingers along my chest and over my heart.

"I don't think I'll ever tire of hearing you say that. I still feel like this is a dream. I'll love you and treasure your love forever."

I put my forehead to hers, pressing her hand harder against my heart. "I thought I had lost you. I'll never make that mistake again." I needed to ask her something that had been on my mind for the last couple of days. "Ainsley, do you want to get married someday?'

She pulled back, and I held her to me, not letting much room come between us even though she tried.

"Adam, I…Adam…" She stopped and took a breath. "I'm never going to push you for something you don't want. Having you is enough. We don't need to rush this."

I pressed for an answer. "But if it was your choice, is that something you would want eventually?"

Her blues eyes were watching me. "If it was my choice, yes, it's something I'd want down the road…when we're ready…after I'm done with school. I'm not one who needs a title to know I'm yours."

Her words made me want to put a ring on her for the ultimate claim. My lips came down to chastely kiss her. I liked the thought of her becoming Ainsley Ryker. I could feel her thumb playing with her ring against my chest. "What are you thinking about, baby?"

"Adam, I don't want you to change yourself for me. I fell in love with who you are, not with what you think I want. I'm not leaving you."

I waited for her to look at me. She always did if the silence lasted a little long.

"Ainsley, this is what I want. We'll know when it's right for us, but I want a life with you and whatever that entails. I want it."

My fingers resumed their path of trailing up and down her back as we both lapsed into a comfortable silence.

"Adam?"

"Yeah, baby?"

She propped herself up on one elbow. She was probably trying to get a better view of my reaction. "Would it be possible to meet your parents ahead of their surprise anniversary party? With everything else going on with Jake, I'd like them to meet me when tensions aren't so high."

"I think that's a good idea. They're going to love you."

She lay back down and cuddled into me. I could feel her smile on my skin. We lay there for a while, wrapped in each other's arms. She yawned. "I have something I want to do tomorrow. I don't have to be in class. I'm ahead on my work, but I'll need to go the next day, and I have therapy with my mom, too."

I rubbed my hand down her back as she nuzzled into me.

"What do you want to do tomorrow? Name it, and we'll do it."

"I want to get a tattoo."

"Do you know what you want?" Imagining ink on her perfect body turned me on.

"Uh-huh. But it's a surprise."

Her hand drifted down to my dick, and it stiffened.

"I'm about to make love to you again, Ainsley."

Rolling her beneath me, I slipped in and spent the rest of the night claiming her and loving her until exhaustion overtook us.

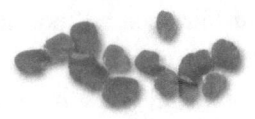

I sat in the parlor of the tattoo shop I'd used as Ainsley was getting her ink in the back. She had asked that I stay up in the front while she was tattooed. Moon, my tattoo guy, knew me well, and he'd had Chastity do the work on Ainsley. I was understanding, but another man looking at Ainsley was a no-fucking-go zone.

From pictures on the desk, Moon was working on a huge job and doing a life-sized human skeleton on someone. They were working on the back rib cage this evening per the girl at the counter. I loved the sound of the hum from the gun. It was addictive to feel that sting hitting skin to create a piece of art. I looked at the clock Ainsley had been back there for about thirty minutes.

My phone rang. It was my mom. I had called her this morning and left a voice mail while Ainsley had been changing.

"Hey, Mom."

I heard a door closing on the other side. "Hey, Adam. Sorry it took me a while to call you back. It's been crazy, and I heard you found out about the baby."

Here goes nothing. "Yeah, Jessica and Selena stopped by to tell me what is going on. You know how I feel about that, Mom. I don't want to get involved. It's their life."

"Oh, I know. I wish they hadn't tried to make it your problem. Jessica always tries to solve it all. We've been talking to Jake while Selena has been staying with us."

Selena's parents lived in California and rarely came to see her. In a way, it was sad that she didn't have family like I had to lean on. I still hated that my parents were so involved. They were getting older and this seemed like unnecessary stress for them always having to help clean up Jake's messes.

"That's nice of you guys. Hope it works out for them."

"You sound different, Adam. Whenever Selena or Jake has been brought up, you've always changed the subject, and became short."

This was something I loved about my mom. She never pushed. She only supported her family.

Here goes nothing. "I am different. I've met a girl. We've been dating for a while. I'd like for you guys to meet her."

My parents didn't know about their surprise party, so hopefully, they would be able to meet before the weekend. "Well, Jake is coming over here to talk to Selena. Your dad and I are going to step out for lunch. Do you guys have plans?"

"No, we don't. Ainsley is getting a tattoo right now. Do you want to meet at our usual deli?"

The door opened, and I could hear my father's muffled voice on the other end, but I couldn't make out what he said.

My mother responded. "We're going to meet Adam and his girlfriend for lunch while Jake comes over. Go get your shoes and change your shirt. We need to make a good impression, Tom."

My dad mumbled something, and it made me chuckle. He probably had on one of his worn Falcons T-shirts.

"Ainsley should be done in a few minutes. We can be there in about thirty."

"We'll see you there. We can't wait to meet her. She must be special to you."

It was time to put it all out there and to stop being a fucking pussy. "I love her, Mom. She's the one, but we aren't rushing into anything. She still needs to finish college."

My mom sounded choked up as she responded. "I can't wait to meet her. I know she's going to be perfect. She already is if she has won your heart. I'm going to go freshen up. We'll be there, and please tell her not to be nervous."

"Sounds good, Mom. See ya in a few."

"Bye, Adam."

Ainsley emerged from the back with a huge smile on her face as her eyes found mine.

I stood, matching her expression. "Did you go through with it?"

"I did." She walked up to the heavily pierced receptionist with purple hair. "What do I owe?"

Smacking her gum, the girl behind the desk responded. "Nothing. Moon said it was on the house for you taming the untamable."

I wanted to punch the shit out of Moon for saying that. People needed to have tact. I went to speak when Ainsley laughed.

"Tell Moon thanks," she said.

"Sure thing, doll." The receptionist went back to looking at her magazine.

The bell to the door chimed as we walked out of the shop and to the car.

"So, do I get to see what you got?" I asked.

"Eventually."

"When?" I wanted to see what she had chosen.

She smirked. "When we're in a place where it's okay for me to pull my pants down a bit."

I cranked my car. "Hell, I'm glad Chastity did it. I'd have to beat the shit out of Moon if he had seen any part below your waist."

She cocked her head to the side. "He's a professional. I'm sure he's seen a lot more than that."

"Maybe so, but he won't be seeing you...ever." The thought of anyone seeing something that was meant for my eyes only had my mouth tasting metal as my anger simmered.

She smiled from ear to ear as I reversed out of the parking spot.

"Where are we going?"

I slowed down as we were nearing the edge of the parking lot, and then I turned down the alley. I wanted to see her tattoo, and I also needed to see her reaction when I asked about meeting my parents on such short notice. If she wasn't ready for it, I would postpone the lunch date, no questions asked.

"First, I want to see that ink."

Ainsley giggled and laid back her seat. She unbuttoned her pants, and a white bandage became visible.

I stopped her. "Let me."

She dropped her hands to the side. When I pulled the white gauze back, there were two As, one delicate and one more masculine, interwoven together below her hipbone.

She watched me closely as she explained. "It's for us, two As coming together as one. I hope you like it." Her eyes got wide. "Oh, man, I hope you like it since it's permanent."

I covered up her fresh ink and then kissed her roughly. "I love it. Eventually, we'll get an R on there."

The thought of Ainsley being permanently mine was something I was going to want to do sooner rather than later. Waiting until she was out of school was going to be hell.

"I like that idea."

We were both smiling at each other like two crazy people in love. I moved back to my side of the car as Ainsley buttoned her pants up.

"So, where are we going to now that you've seen my ink?"

"I talked to my mom while you were getting your tattoo. I told her about you, about us, and what you mean to me. She wanted to know if it was okay to do lunch. We can do it some other time, but you mentioned wanting to meet them prior to the surprise party."

Ainsley's face lit up. "I would love to."

"Perfect. We're going to our favorite deli." My world was falling into place perfectly. It was as if the puzzle pieces all made sense and the picture of my future came into focus.

We went across town to the deli about twenty minutes away. Her ring moved at an unprecedented speed.

"What's on that mind of yours?" I asked.

"Do you think that it's going to bother them that I come from a broken home? Sometimes, parents can have ideals of what they want their kids to end up with. Our relationship must appear rushed to them, considering they just found out about me. I'm not nearly as accomplished as you."

Guilt crept in my mind for giving Ainsley any feeling of insecurity about us. That was a reason I had kept her from my family.

"They're going to adore and love you because I do. My parents are like your mom. They want what makes me happy. They don't care about any of that other shit."

"Okay." She gave me a tentative smile.

"It'll be fine, and honestly, it doesn't matter."

Her mouth gaped open. "Of course it matters. They're you're family."

I merged onto the highway. "No, it doesn't because I love you regardless. No one can change that fact. Would it have changed your mind about me if your mom didn't like tattoos?"

"No." She didn't hesitate, and her voice was confident.

That confirmed what I already knew.

We love each other.

Before long, we were pulling into the deli. Ainsley stared ahead at the red awning. I got out of the car and opened her door. My parents were near the window, watching us. I could see my mom touching my dad on the shoulder.

Ainsley shielded her eyes from the bright sun as she'd left her sunglasses on the dashboard. A family passed us with two little ones. As I let my mind go down the road, a world of possibilities opened up for me, and I enjoyed every thought.

Ainsley gave me a big smile. "Here we go."

I gave her a quick kiss on the lips. "Here we go. This is our story—no one else's. Don't worry."

We walked as she reflectively said, "I like that. This is our story. I love our story."

"Me, too."

We walked into the deli. My mom had to force herself to stay seated until we were a few feet away. She rose, wearing a white lace top and black capris. As suspected, my father was not wearing his Falcons T-shirt. He was in a green polo.

"Mom, Dad, this is Ainsley Pearson. Ainsley, this is my mom, Melanie, and my dad, Tom."

Ainsley reached out her hand, but my mom pulled her into a hug.

"It's a pleasure to meet you, Ainsley. We've been waiting for this day for Adam for a long time."

My dad stepped up and gave her a hug. "Welcome to the family, sweetie."

Ainsley's blue eyes danced with happiness.

The waitress came up. "Is everyone having the usual?"

My parents and I responded, "Yes."

The waitress looked toward Ainsley. "What can I get you, sweetie?"

"Turkey sandwich and chips."

"Will do."

The waitress turned and headed back to the counter to

place our orders. The sweet smells from the dessert counter were mouthwatering. We took our seats, and I grabbed Ainsley's hand under the table, giving her a reassuring squeeze. I was surprisingly not nervous. This felt right, which further confirmed it was the right step for us.

My mom started it off. "Adam says you're finishing school. What's your major?"

From that point forward, we lapsed into easy conversation as our food was delivered, and we ate. My mom and Ainsley hit it off , talking about my mother's love for quilting. I came to find out that Ainsley had always wanted to learn how to do that. My father seemed captivated with her, too, like she was already a daughter. My world seemed complete.

I paid for lunch, and we made our way to the door.

My mom grabbed Ainsley's hand. "I'm so glad he has someone as wonderful as you. Let me know when you want to start your quilting lessons."

Ainsley gave a small little jump. "I will. I thought that would be a good Christmas break project."

"Perfect. I'll start gathering some fabrics." My mom gave her a hug. "Thank you for loving our son. I can see it in your eyes and actions."

Ainsley looked straight at me. "I do. I really do."

I had all I needed right here.

Ainsley

I WAS WITH my mom at our next therapy session as I filled her in on the ups and downs of my week. We were meeting in the same room with Doctor Jacobs. Being able to talk honestly and openly with her was a breath of fresh air. My mom wore shorts again, which was going to take a little bit to get used to.

"Oh, Ainsley, I'm glad you and Adam worked it out. When I get my new place, I'd like to have you guys both over, if you are willing to try it again." There was worry in her voice as her eyes cast downward.

"Mom..." I waited for her to look at me.

I could only imagine how intimidating the next meeting would be with Adam after having an almost complete stranger witness her breakdown. She looked up at me, and regret filled her eyes. My heart broke for her. She had so much to deal with, and I should be the last of her worries.

"Mom, we would love to come. Just let us know when would be good for you, and we'll work it out. Adam understands. He went through this with his friend, Brandt, who gave us Jason's number."

She nodded, but she still didn't look convinced. "Okay, good. I'm glad, sweetie. The one thing I've always wanted was to be a part of your life. I'm still anxious about everything, but I will try not to stress."

"Well, you are a part of my life, Mom. You always will be. I promise. I like how you tell me how you feel now." My words were warm and gentle.

My mom smiled as if she had won some sort of prize. "Doctor Jacobs has been working with me on self-expression since I was always pretending my world was perfect. I'm feeling things I haven't felt in a very long time. It's refreshing and scary."

I beamed back at her. "Well, I love it."

"Me, too, sweetie."

The tranquil blue walls were still as soothing as the last time we had been here.

Doctor Jacobs wrote a few notes, and then she addressed me. "You seem to be doing well with all this, Ainsley. Are you finding these sessions helpful?"

I smoothed down my skirt as I faced the doctor. "I am. I probably should have done counseling a long time ago. It's helped my mom, and we've found our way back to each other by dealing with the hand we were dealt. For that, I'll be forever grateful. I want to continue coming with my mom."

Doctor Jacobs adjusted her dark-rimmed glasses. "That's wonderful, Ainsley, and very insightful. Christine, would you like to share what decision you've come to this last week?"

"Yes." My mom bit her lip as she thought about something for a minute.

I loved seeing my mom act natural instead of like a robot.

"I've decided that I'm going to do a halfway program here at A New Beginning. With that, I'll be able to do some part-time work. I sent my resume to a bookstore when I looked through the classifieds section of the paper. They called and want me to work there part-time. After talking with Doctor Jacobs, I decided I'm going to take it. For the next few weeks, I'll be working three days a week for four hours a day. I think it's going to help me adjust as I start finding a new niche in this world."

I gave her a hug. "Oh, Mom, that's wonderful. Did you hear back from the realtor?"

"Yes, the house is officially on the market as of yesterday. I'm selling far below market value, so I think it's going to go quickly." She took a cleansing deep breath. "It feels good to do all this. It's also intimidating, not knowing what's going to happen, but that's good. I think that means I'm finally living."

"I'm so proud of you, Mom."

My mom kissed my forehead. "I'm proud of you, too. I couldn't be prouder with how you've turned out. I love you, Ainsley."

"I love you, too."

Doctor Jacobs looked at her watch. "Our time is almost up, Christine. Do you still want to do what we talked about?"

My mom stood. "Yes. If it's okay with you, Ainsley, I'd like to say hello to Adam and give him a glimpse of the real me. Hopefully, it will make the transition easier when we're together again."

I practically bounced out of my seat. "I'd love that. He'd

love that."

We stood as Doctor Jacobs opened the door.

My mom looked relieved as she said, "Good. I think it will help when you guys come over."

This was something my mom needed, and I wasn't going to argue that it wouldn't matter to Adam, that he would still love my mom because I did. To her, seeing Adam did matter, and that was what was important. We made our way to the reception area, and Adam was bent over his laptop, closely scrutinizing something. As if he could sense my presence, he rose and folded down his laptop as he gave me a gentle, loving smile. I walked up to him, and his hand came down around my waist.

"Christine, it's wonderful to see you again." His voice was warm and melting.

My mom's fingers were fidgeting slightly. "Hey, Adam. It's wonderful to see you, too. I wanted to come out here and thank you for everything you've done for both Ainsley and me."

Adam released me and then extended his hand. My mom turned it into a quick hug.

"Christine, you're more than welcome. You have an amazing daughter that I love."

She patted my shoulder. "I know you do and thank you. I need to head back for a group session, but I can't wait to have you both over for dinner."

"I look forward to that. Once you and Ainsley decide on a date, I'll clear my schedule."

"That sounds great." My mom looked relieved.

I hugged her. "Love you, Mom. Let me know if this same time works for you next week."

She turned and follow Doctor Jacobs, but then she looked

back. "It should. If something changes, I will let you know since I'll be working. Love you, too, Ainsley."

They disappeared behind the door, and I sank into Adam.

"She's doing so well. I'm proud of what she's accomplished." There was pride in my voice.

"You should be proud of your mom. It's tough to change a lifetime's worth of habits."

I looked down at my watch. "Can we stop by my place? I need to get a dress for the surprise party tomorrow night. I also need more clean clothes until I have a chance to return to my place to do some laundry."

Adam's brows scrunched together for a second and then smoothed. "Yeah, we can stop by your place to get some stuff."

We walked out to the parking lot. *My mom is going to be okay. I am going to be okay.*

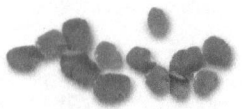

We were at my place. Adam sat on my bed as I pulled a couple of dresses out of the closet. I had a duffel bag on the bed, and I had put a couple more days' worth of clothes into the black bag. Considering how much time we spent together, not having a drawer at each other's houses felt ridiculous.

Adam played with the bag straps as I threw in a pair of shoes.

He got up. "I'll be right back. I need a drink."

"Okay."

He seemed a little nervous, but it was probably because he was going to see Jake for the first time in a long time at the party tomorrow night.

I finished grabbing a couple of necklaces that I could wear with almost anything.

Facial wash. I need facial wash.

Adam came in and resumed his spot on the edge of the bed.

"I'm almost done. Let me get something from the bathroom, and I'll be right back."

Adam smiled. "Sounds good. Hurry back."

He acted strange as I left the room. Adam's leg bounced a million times a minute. I flicked on the light and opened up the cabinet below the sink to grab a new bottle of facial wash. When I stood up, a sticky note caught my eye. I leaned closer to make sure I wasn't seeing things.

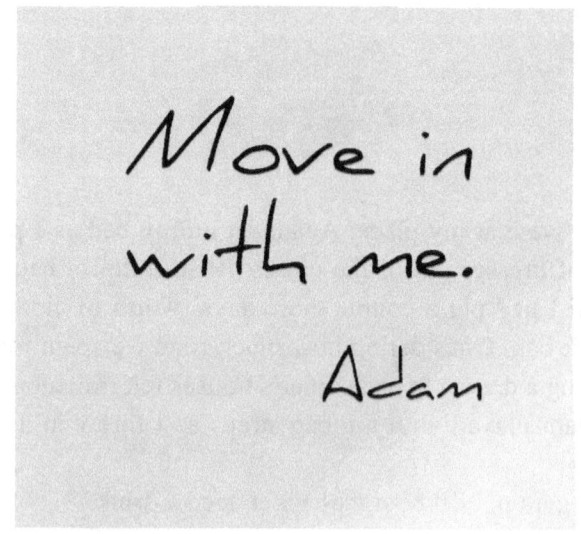

I stared at the note for a second as my heart jumped out of my chest in excitement.

Is it too soon? Are we ready?

Moving in with Adam felt right. Even though we had recently said *I love you*, we were ready for the next step. Adam had asked me. He wasn't being pressured to take this step. He wanted this, too.

I tried not to overanalyze it, and I went with what my heart was telling me. Giddiness filled me as I sprinted into the bedroom where Adam was perched on the corner edge of the bed. His eyes searched mine before I jumped into his arms. He was caught off guard, and we went tumbling toward the floor. I yelped as Adam stuck out his arm to brace the impact, and then he rolled me on top of him.

I laughed as I raised my head. "I think you know my answer from my graceful entrance."

His face lit up. "Really?"

"Yes, I want to move in with you."

We'd talk later about me contributing what I could to the bills. I wasn't going to take a free ride even though there was no way I could pay half with my current financial status. He had known that though, and he still wanted me to move in with him. It wasn't worth mentioning right this minute.

He flipped me underneath him, pushed up my dress, and spread my legs. He snapped my thong from my body. His tatted arms were flexed as he held his body above mine. "I like that answer a lot. Can we get you packed tonight?"

One of his hands had gone to his zipper, and he freed himself. He slowly aligned his tip at my entrance. I tried to move into him, but he pulled back to keep himself out of reach.

"What's your answer, Ainsley?" He enjoyed playing with

me, as his teasing tone implied.

I felt Adam's tip tickle my entrance again.

"Will you give me what I want and not make me wait if I tell you?"

He smiled. "Yes."

"Yes, we can pack up my stuff tonight." Adam, pushed into me, filling me.

Adam was all I wanted.

All I needed.

All I had ever hoped for.

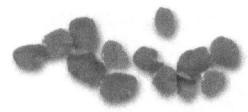

We were getting ready for Adam's parents' surprise party. I put on a light blue tank dress that had a slim, easy fit. It hit right below my knees. It was comfortable, and I needed comfort with what I imagined was going to be a pretty intense evening. I put on jeweled silver gladiator sandals as Adam came into the bedroom.

"You look beautiful. Are you about ready to go?"

He had been pacing the house the entire time I was getting ready.

I grabbed my silver hoop earrings from the dresser. "Almost." I put them in. "Now, I'm ready."

Adam scrubbed a hand down his face. He hadn't shaved today, and he had a five o'clock shadow that matched his brown hair color. He had opted for slacks and a button-up black shirt that was rolled up at the sleeves.

"Okay, let's go. We need to get there before my parents do."

"Okay, sounds good."

I looked at the clock, and we were leaving with almost forty minutes to spare. It wasn't worth bringing up and adding to his stress that we'd be there in plenty of time since he seemed to need the extra time.

Grabbing my purse, I followed him out to the car and got in. He drove out of the neighborhood, drumming rapidly on the steering wheel with his thumbs. In moments like this, I always wanted to be left alone, and I believed Adam did, too. The restaurant we were going to was about ten minutes away. I was about to talk to Adam when my phone rang. It was my mom's new number.

"Hey, Mom."

She sounded like she was in a car. "Hey, I'm headed to the bookstore and wanted to let you know. They asked if I could come in today to get all the paperwork out of the way after they close along with their other new hire. The center approved since classes are done for the day. I'm taking a cab to the house to get my car, and then I'll be at the bookstore for an hour or so. I'll call you on my way back to tell you how it went. Wish me luck."

She sounded so happy.

"Good luck, Mom. You're going to do great."

"Thanks, sweetie. I'll call you as soon as I leave."

"Sounds good. Bye, Mom."

"Bye."

Adam focused on the road and didn't say a word. His knuckles were white from gripping the steering wheel so hard. I knew being around Jake was going to be hard for him.

Maybe he needed a little reassurance. "Adam, it's going to be okay. Jake can't do anything to us."

He continued staring out the window as a vein in his neck

pulsed. "I don't want him near you, Ainsley. I don't want him even looking in your direction."

"I'll stay by your side the entire time."

He took a deep breath and nodded. I let Adam get mentally prepared for the personal demons he was going to have to face at this party. He had the reassurance from me. Now, he had to believe it.

We pulled into the parking lot, and Adam sat there, watching the building as if it were dangerous. I gave him his time as I sat quietly in my black leather seat. He turned off the car, and the warmth of the day seeped in, raising the temperature slowly. He blew out another long breath, and then in one fluid motion, he extricated himself from the car.

I met him at the hood of the car on my side. He grabbed my hand stiffly, and we walked toward the entrance at a brisk pace. We were eating at Ruth's Chris Steak House tonight for the anniversary party. The air smelled savory, and my mouth watered.

Adam opened the door, and we entered. We were headed toward the hostess's podium when I noticed a restroom off to the right. I pulled his hand, and he responded by following me on this small detour. Adam needed a distraction and something to focus on. Taking the lead, I took us about ten feet down the hall.

"Where are we going, Ainsley?"

I was winging this as I went. I didn't respond as the main restroom door made a slight creaking noise. To the left was the men's, and to the right was the women's bathroom. Ahead of us looked like some type of supply closet. The supply closet seemed like the better choice. I opened the door and brought us both into the tight dim quarters. The faint smell of cleaning supplies was present.

"Ainsley—"

I stopped his sentence as my lips pressed to his. My hands went to his pants, and undid them. Adam's erection sprang free and I stroked it hoping my touch kept him from stopping this.

"Let me do this," I said as I sank to my knees.

The stress of this night had affected him more than I had thought. My tongue came out to taste the bit of pre-cum that had come out of him. The tip of his dick was smooth as I swirled my tongue around while massaging the rest of his length.

"Hell yes, baby. Take it all." Adam's words were raw as he spoke.

His hands fisted in my hair and my hands braced themselves on his leg as he pushed himself deeply in my mouth. Adam hissed as he entered all the way in.

Barely covering my teeth, I lightly raked them across his skin giving Adam the pleasure pain combo he gave me at times for one stroke.

"Fuck, yes!" he cried.

Adam thrust his hips into me, quickening the pace. He fucked my mouth, and I loved it. He grabbed more hair and increased the force as I made a tight suction around him, causing him to moan. It wasn't going to be long until he came.

"Ainsley…"

My name was reverent on his lips. Hot liquid spurted into my mouth as I swallowed every last drop. He stopped moving for a brief moment before bit by bit he pulled languidly out. I stared up at him as he looked down on me with a lazy grin on his face that was barely visible from the dim light above the door. His thumb softly caressed my cheek.

"Thank you, baby." He tucked himself back in and then zipped his pants up before he pulled me up into his chest. I wrapped my hands around his waist.

I listened to his heartbeat. It was steady and strong, like us. Adam's hands made their way down my body. I stopped their progress. *This would help reassure him.*

"Wait until we get home so you can make love to me. This was about you. Each time you think about Jake doing anything, know that it's going to be you satisfying me at the end of the night. You're going to be the one inside me, Adam, no one else but you. I need you. You're the only one."

He put his forehead to mine. "You're perfect for me, baby."

"We're perfect together."

Our breaths mingled and created a sweet smell.

Adam pulled his forehead back and grabbed my hand. We came out of the supply closet as someone passed by. I looked down, and as we entered the corridor and slight giggle came out.

"They probably knew what we were doing, Adam."

He wagged his eyebrows at me as his chocolate eyes melted me. "I'm sure they figured it out."

I gave him a slight hit on his stomach with my free hand. Adam's grip was less aggressive than it had been prior to coming into here.

Mission accomplished.
We could do this.
I would be here for him—always.

Adam

MY BODY FELT the low drug from my orgasm as Ainsley and I made our way back to the front of the restaurant. Ainsley had given me what I didn't know I needed. My mind no longer felt like it was running a marathon as I imagined different scenarios about what might happen.

Ainsley was mine...completely. Jake could go to hell. His tactics wouldn't work on Ainsley.

I hated that the restaurant was dim with dark walls. I wanted to be able to see everything when I was in tense situations. We came up to the hostess.

Wearing a white shirt and black pants, she looked up from her podium. "Do you have a reservation?"

"We're here for the Ryker surprise anniversary party. My

sister, Jessica Ryker, made all the arrangements. She'll be bringing my parents in about fifteen minutes."

The hostess's finger went down some list. "Yes, you're in the private dining area. Rachel will show you the way."

A waitress, assumedly Rachel, appeared to the side. "Follow me. Everything is set up as Ms. Ryker requested."

"Thank you."

I became highly aware of everything going on in my environment as the brunette walked us to a room off the side of the main dining area. Glasses clinked, lovers whispered, and a couple argued in the corner.

Ainsley stood supportively beside me as she held my hand and leaned into me. She looked gorgeous in her dress, and I was proud to have her on my arm as my girl. The waitress opened the door, and the room was filled with family and friends. Most looked surprised that I was here, which quite frankly, I would be, too, if I were them.

I scanned the room and found Jake to the left, so I veered Ainsley and myself to the right. There was no reason to poke the beast. I didn't want a scene in front of my parents. The last time we had been in the same room, I had pummeled his ass. Jake watched us closely. Selena stood beside him, and she looked at us also. *What a pair those two made.*

The room was filled with rectangular tables that sat approximately six people each. Each table had name cards on it. Jessica had told me that Jake and I were sitting across the room from each other. That was for the best.

I was surprised that the hate I'd normally felt wasn't there for him. We'd never be okay, and I'd never trust him, but I thought we could at least be in the same room without killing each other. Ainsley and I went and stood next to Gertie and Marty, my parents' card-playing partners. They were older and slender with graying hair.

Marty patted me on the back. "Glad to see you here, son. Your parents will be, too. Who's this lovely lady you've brought with you?"

Ainsley extended her hand as I said, "This is my girl-friend, Ainsley Pearson. Ainsley, this is Marty and his wife, Gertie, that are friends of my parents."

"It's nice to meet you both." They smiled at Ainsley's words.

Light whispers radiated out from around me. I was sure they were talking about Jake and me being in the same room together. Plus, I had a girlfriend. All those combined were un-precedented for me.

From there, people were rotating up to us. I knew the main thing was that everyone wanted to meet Ainsley. She was the first girl they had seen me with since Selena. I kept my eyes on Jake the entire time, and he watched me. Ainsley handled herself with a calm confidence, but her sweet demeanor had the people I had known all my life falling in love with her.

Brandt came in at the last minute. We slapped each other on the back.

"Glad you made it, man."

"Traffic was a nightmare, and there was a small incident at the club."

I was about to start asking questions.

He held up his hands. "It's been handled, so don't worry. It was a slight misunderstanding. One of the rooms was double booked. Snake gave up his for the night, and I gave him one for the next three nights he's off, which more than made up for it. The computer at the front had a glitch and let people double book. I've taken it offline, and I'll get our tech support team to fix it."

"That works."

Jake called out, "They're here. Jessica texted me."

An excited silence descended on the room. I glanced over at Jake, who stared at me again before glancing toward Ainsley.

Fucker.

A cocky grin spread across his face as Selena stood by his side. Brandt had told me of rumors that he had heard of them both cheating on each other through the years. Apparently, Roach and Selena had some sort of past. They all disgusted me. I stared back at Jake with an impassive look on my face.

Ainsley nudged me, and I looked toward her.

She brushed her lips against mine before whispering, "I love you. Remember, he can't do anything. I'm leaving with you, only you."

"I know. Love you, too."

Her words did soothe me as the door slightly creaked open. A loud unified word was yelled throughout the room. "SURPRISE!"

My parents looked around in shock and awe as my dad put his hand on my mom's shoulder. I mentally laughed. Mom had made him wear khakis with a polo shirt tonight. Fifty bucks said that he had on one of his heavily used Falcons T-shirts underneath. My parents made eye contact with me and smiled when they saw Ainsley beside me. It made me feel good that so many family members had reached out and accepted me—well, us—as if I had never distanced myself. More than ever, I wanted the happiness my parents had.

Jessica beamed behind my parents as she wore a pink-and-white striped maxi dress. My parents made their rounds as we took our seats at the assigned empty table where small name cards were placed with our choice of entree. On the

RSVP card options for dinner, we had been given choices for steak, chicken, and fish. I had sent my response to Jess via text since I had responded so late.

I scooted Ainsley in when Jake and Selena took the seats across from me.

Fuck.

Before I spoke, I saw my parents were still across the room. Jake gave me a cocky grin, and his eyes darted toward Ainsley. My natural instinct was to spout off a slew of obscenities. I choked it down when Jessica walked up. Brandt was on guard beside me.

My sister sweetly said, "Jake, you are supposed to be seated across the room. Please don't start anything. This is Mom and Dad's day."

I hated that Jake and I looked alike. Jake didn't have the tattoos, and his hair was slicked over in the greasy car-salesman way. He worked at a sales company that sold electronics to major retailers.

Jessica turned to Ainsley. "It's nice to finally meet you. Mom and Dad went on and on about you on the way here. I'm happy for you guys."

Ainsley stood and gave a friendly embrace to my sister. Waiters were beginning to shuffle with trays.

"It's nice to meet you, too, Jessica. Thank you. Your brother makes me very happy."

Jessica looked toward Brandt and then walked to him. "Where has my favorite guy been hiding? It's good to see you."

Brandt and my sister had always gotten along well. "Good to see you, too, sis."

A waiter approached. "Ms. Ryker, they're serving the appetizer. The maître d' asked when you wanted the cake to be brought in."

Jessica turned toward us. "I'll stop by again. Let me go talk about Mom and Dad's cake."

My sister was off as Ainsley took her seat again. Selena watched us closely. She had on a dress similar in style to my sister but in red.

Selena spoke first. "Are you and Adam...dating?"

A shit-eating grin spread across Brandt's face. Ainsley took her napkin and placed it on her lap.

Before responding, she gave me a look of love. "Yes, we have been for a while. He asked me to move in with him a couple of days ago, so I guess it's a little more serious than dating now."

Selena and Jake both looked shocked. Salads were placed in front of us. Selena was now staring at me intently.

"Can I talk to you Adam?"

Ainsley and I were both mid-bites when our forks hovered in the air as Selena's spoken words registered.

Jake hissed, "What do you need to talk to him for?"

Selena's green eyes shimmered as she watched us, not answering Jake. She was playing some sort of game with her Cheshire grin she gave.

"We said everything we needed to say at the club." My tone was matter-of-fact.

Jake looked at her. "Why the fuck were you at his club?" His voice rose.

I warned him. "Jake, this is Mom and Dad's day. Nothing happened. She told me about the baby. Congrats by the way."

Ainsley had put her fork down at this point, and took the scene in with her head cocked to the side.

Jake pressed on, "Why were you at the club, Selena? Damn it, answer me." He turned toward Ainsley. "He'll never be faithful to you. He goes through women like water on some never ending quest because he wants what's mine."

I looked around to make sure no one watched. I'd leave before I let him ruin Mom and Dad's party even if it made me look like the bad guy. We were still undetected. Brandt had his fists balled, but he looked toward me. I gave a slight shake of my head. There was no need for reinforcements.

"Jake, you and I are going to have problems if you keep this up. It won't be tonight, but if you don't cut the fucking crap, I am going to address it. All you and I have to talk about is the weather. Focus on your pregnant girlfriend. You're about to be a dad. Grow the fuck up, and get over yourself." My voice was low and hard as steel.

Jake looked toward Ainsley. "Did you know about his little rendezvous with my pregnant girlfriend?"

Bastard.

Selena sat there with a smug look on her face.

Bitch.

She was using this opportunity to make Jake jealous.

I was about to tell Jake not to speak to my girl.

Instead, Ainsley said, "Jake and Selena, I'm not one to beat around the bush. I like honesty and directness, so I am going to give you the same courtesy. I don't want to cause problems, but you both need to understand something. Adam and I aren't playing whatever little game you guys get off on. We're in love and happy. Pulling this adolescent move tonight is having no impact. Whether I do or don't know about their meeting is none of your business. You have a child on the way. Focus on that."

A silence fell on the table, and my mouth quirked up in a smile as I watched Jake look back and forth between us. Brandt chuckled. I was sure Jake and Selena weren't done with their shenanigans, but as long as we took away the power they tried to hold over us, they would be ineffective. Ainsley's hand found my knee, and she squeezed it as she took another bite of salad, seemingly unaffected.

Dinner progressed in silence, and the cake was served. All of the food was fabulous, but I wanted to get out of here. Regardless of how strong Ainsley and I were, I didn't like her near my toxic brother.

My parents walked up to the table. This was my time to escape.

I stood. "I think we are going to leave and head back home. Happy anniversary, Mom and Dad."

Brandt stood with us and echoed my sentiments, "Happy anniversary, Mum and Dad.

Ainsley stood, too, as my mom went to hug her. "Thank you all for coming. This meant the world to me. Maybe we can do lunch next week?"

My girl's smile lit up the room every time I saw it. "I'd love that. Thank you for having me. Happy anniversary to you both."

Mom went over to Brandt and gave him a hug. She whispered something in his ear, and he nodded. My dad told Ainsley good-bye. Next, Mom came over to me.

As her arms went around my shoulders, she whispered in my ear, "I'm glad you found your way. She's perfect for you and loves you like you deserve."

"Thanks, Mom. She's my world."

We walked out as Jessica came up. "Thanks for coming." She turned to Ainsley. "I'm glad to have finally met you. I'll call Adam, so maybe we can get together soon." She poked Brandt in the chest. "Don't be a stranger."

We responded. Jessica was on cloud nine, having had an

event with little drama.

As we walked out to the car, I said, "You handled Jake well."

"Hell yeah, she did. You have a feisty one on your hands." Brandt gave Ainsley a hard sisterly pat on the back as she laughed. Before we had a chance to respond, Brandt continued. "Well, I'm going to split and head back to the club. I'll see you guys later."

Ainsley and I both called out in unison, "See ya."

The night had set in, and the crickets were beginning to make their presence known. The car was in the back corner of the lot, and the parking light was out. She began talking, and I realized it was in reference to my earlier comment about handling Jake.

"I think when you refuse to play the game, it eventually gets boring playing all by yourself. Jake's jealous of you, and Selena found a way to still play her cards. If it works for them, that's their thing, I won't participate though and be a pawn in their game."

We made it to the car, and I opened the door.

"Agreed, baby. Let's get home, so I can sink inside you."

"I would love nothing more."

She gave me a quick kiss before getting in the car.

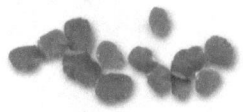

We were halfway home when Ainsley's eyes were slowly starting to drift shut from the party. Her head began to bob as I put on low soothing music in the car to further lull her to sleep. She hadn't been getting much sleep lately between class work and my incessant need to have her. I was half-tempted to sleep in our room at the club since it was closer, but we'd do that another time. Staying there, would end up in a long marathon of love making. I wanted her home and in our bed.

After fifteen more minutes, we were pulling into the garage as Ainsley's phone rang.

She sleepily pulled it from her purse and yawned as she said, "Hello?"

Silence filled the car as Ainsley sat erect. "Where's she at? Is she stable?" Her voice cracked on the last word. "Okay, I'm on my way."

She hung up the phone and sobbed. "Adam, we have to go Northside Hospital. That was the police. They found my mom almost beaten to death on her living room floor. Adam, hurry. They say she's in critical condition."

I reversed the car out of the driveway, put it into drive, and took off, the tires squealing. "Ainsley, it's going to be okay. We'll get there."

Please let her mom be okay.

Ainsley

I FELT AS if my entire world caved in on itself as the police had told me the news of my mom. Adam drove fast as I held on to the door while the same thoughts kept circulating through my mind.

Please let my mom be okay. Please. Please. Please.

I knew my dad had something to do with this. Down deep in my core, I knew he had caused this. *We'd deal with that once my mom got better.*

Adam's concerned voice filled the interior of the car. "What can I do? What do you need?"

Tears were beginning to leak from my eyes as I tried to remain strong for my mom. She needed strength.

"Just get me there. I can't lose her, Adam. I can't. I just got her back."

I bit my lip painfully to stop my words and to have something to focus on besides the heavy brick crushing my chest. Guilt washed over my body when I realized my mom had never called me like she'd said she would earlier. I should have known something was wrong. Sobs erupted from me before I had a chance to push them down into a lockbox.

"Ainsley, baby, we'll be there in five minutes."

"She was supposed to call me, and I forgot. Adam, she should have called me a couple of hours ago, and I didn't remember. If she dies, it could be my fault that I didn't go looking for her." My head slumped forward and my body racked itself with uncontrollable sobs.

A hand came down on top of mine. "Let's get to the hospital and see what's going on. We'll talk to the doctor, see what he says, and then do whatever we can to make her better."

"O-o-okay." My mind was numb as I thought about my mom in pain.

As soon as we pulled up to the hospital, I jumped out of the car before it had come to a complete stop, and I ran toward the door. Adam would find me. I ran up to the nurses' station. I ran so fast that I had to put my hands out to the counter to stop me. An older woman with blue scrubs sat behind the counter.

"I got a call that my mom, Christine Pearson, was admitted and is in critical condition. Where do I find her?" My face was wet as more tears made fresh tracks down my face.

"I'm checking. What is your name, sweetie?"

"Ainsley. Ainsley Pearson."

I heard the automatic doors open and close behind me. I felt Adam's presence. He came up and placed his hand on my lower back.

The nurse looked up and gave me a gentle smile. "She's

in surgery. Go to the second floor and the nurses there will show you where to wait. I'll let them know."

I took off toward the elevator as I called out, "Thank you."

Pushing the button repeatedly, I tried to make the doors open faster. The long-awaited ding finally sounded. As soon as the doors opened, I made my way in and pressed the number two. Adam was right there with me as his hand made long strokes up my back.

"Come on, come on, come on."

The elevator wouldn't close fast enough.

Adam calmly pressed the doors closed button, and then the elevator climbed at a turtle's pace up to the second floor. My mind felt like a bobbled mess as I tried to sort out all the thoughts racing around in a circle. I refused to think about anything negative. My mom needed positive thoughts. The doors opened, and I ran up to the nurses' station on the second floor. A young woman around my age with blonde hair and blue eyes sat behind the desk.

"I'm Ainsley Pearson. My mom, Christine Pearson, is in surgery. The nurse on the first floor was supposed to phone and say that I was coming."

I talked quick and jumbled that I was surprised the nurse was able to hear me.

"Yes, she did. Your mom is still in surgery, and updates have not been posted in the system. I will keep checking back and let you know. As soon as the doctor is out, he'll come talk to you, too. The waiting room is right across the hall. The vending machine and coffee pots are in the room next to it. If there's anything else you need, let me know."

My voice was hoarse. "How much longer until they're out?"

The nurse clicked a few things on her computer and then smiled at me. "It depends on what they find. There's nothing specific in the system yet."

My face tried to return the smile, but the weight of worry was heavy. Adam guided me to the room and we sat on a pink love seat.

He put his arm around the back of my head, and I laid my head on his chest as he rubbed soothingly on my back.

"Can I get you anything, baby?"

I shook my head. Antiseptic smells filled the air as I focused on counting the number of squares on the carpet. I didn't know how much time passed when I heard a familiar voice. It was Doctor Jacobs from the center.

"Hey, Ainsley. Is there any word yet?"

I peered up to see my mom's therapist looking tired and worried.

"No. As soon as the doctor is out of surgery, he's supposed to come talk to me."

Doctor Jacobs came to sit beside me. "I was in a session when the bookstore called and asked if Christine had changed her mind. I knew how excited she was to get this job. I called a friend at the police station and asked him to swing by your mom's house. He found the front door open and your mom was in the living room. He called me to get your contact information after the ambulance had arrived."

My lip trembled. "Th-Thank you, Doctor Jacobs."

Her hand came on top of mine. "Are you okay?"

"I should have...I should have known something was wrong when she didn't call me a couple of hours after checking in. If I had remembered, she wouldn't have suffered for so long." The truth hurt, and the guilt ate me alive.

"Ainsley, you have a life, too. There is no way you could

have known this would happen. Your mom wouldn't want you to blame yourself like she doesn't blame you for what happened to her before, remember? The only person to blame is the one who committed the crime." Her voice was warm and soothing like it had been in our sessions.

My father. I knew it was him, but I kept quiet until we had some sort of proof. Adam was still stroking my arm.

"I know. I'm trying. Once I have some answers, it will help."

I knew she was right. Whatever had happened to my mom was out of my control. Once I heard she was okay, the guilt would lessen.

Doctor Jacobs pulled out a piece of paper and wrote something down. Extending her hand, she said, "This is my number. I have to get back home to my baby as he'll be hungry here in about thirty minutes. I can come back in between feedings. Please call me the minute you hear something if I'm not back yet. Are you able to stay with Ainsley the entire time, Adam?" Every time she mentioned her child, an involuntary smile graced her lips.

Adam took the piece of paper. "I'll be here. I'm not leaving. Thanks for stopping by. I'll keep you posted."

I hadn't known she had a baby. I turned to her. "Thank you for everything. Please wait until we call you at your home. There's no reason for you to be away from your little one if nothing is going on here."

Doctor Jacobs stood. "Adam, could you text me your number, so I can check to make sure you guys don't need anything?"

He was already pulling out his phone. "No problem. I'll do it now."

"Thank you. If you need anything, Ainsley, I'm a phone

call or text away."

I nodded. "Thanks, Doctor Jacobs. I promise I will contact you if I need anything."

Doctor Jacobs yawned and then walked out of the room. I laid my head back down on Adam's chest.

"I'm here, baby. I'm here. What can I do?"

"Just hold me."

He pulled me closer to him. I was glad he hadn't filled my head with, *It's going to be okay.* No one knew how this was going to turn out. I forced my mind to focus on the sound of the second hand on the clock.

Tick.

Tick.

Tick.

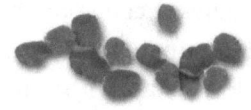

"Ainsley, baby, the doctor is here."

Adam's voice awoke me. I shot up and shook my head to try to clear the sleepy fog.

I walked toward the doctor a little stiff while extending my hand. "I'm Ainsley. Do you have an update on my mother, Christine Pearson?"

Adam was right behind me.

The doctor wore green scrubs. His face mask was pulled below his chin while his hair cap was still in place. He extended his hand. "I'm Doctor Thompson. I performed the surgery on your mother. She's currently stable and in recovery. Ms. Pearson had a cerebral hemorrhage. We had to perform surgery to stop the bleeding. In addition, she has six cracked ribs, a broken wrist, and severe bruising over her entire body."

My stomach dropped and I closed my eyes, taking in all her injuries. "When will she wake up?"

"That's up to Ms. Pearson. We're keeping her in an induced coma for the next day while she stabilizes and the swelling recedes in her brain some. From there, we'll monitor her progress. The surgery went well, and I'm pleased with the results." His tone was informative and without emotion.

"Will my mom...will she...will she be like she was before this?"

"That's hard to say. If the trauma had been deeper on the brain stem, the chance of full recovery would decrease significantly. I'm optimistic in this case. If she had been left unattended much longer, I believe the injuries would have been fatal."

There was so much to process. I'd come close to losing my mom tonight. "Okay. Can I see her?"

The doctor's pager went off. "It's another emergency. Your mom is still in recovery, and someone will come get you when you can see her."

"Thank you, doctor."

He was already turning and jogging to wherever his next emergency was. I put both hands up to my face.

Adam came up beside me. "Let's get you something to drink."

I headed over to the love seat as I repeatedly swallowed, trying to clear the lump in my throat. "I can't leave in case the doctors come."

Adam's brows were scrunched together in worry. "All right. I'll get you a drink from the next room. I'll be right back."

Once I could see my mom, I would feel a million times

better. I sank into the couch.

Within minutes, Adam returned with a ginger ale. "Drink some of this."

I drank the ginger ale as I let my mind process all the facts again. I knew my dad had something to do with this, and Doctor Thompson had said this could have been fatal. If my dad had hit my mom hard enough, he might have thought he'd killed her.

My eyes became wide as I grabbed Adam's arm. Panic lacing my voice, I said, "Can you call that guy Hampton who you used to find who took photos at the club and have someone watch over my mom here at the hospital? I know my dad did this, and he probably meant to kill her. I know it, Adam. He's going to find out he failed, and I don't know what he'll do. The police won't believe me. I can't tip him off that we think it's him until my mom wakes up, and she can prove it. I'll pay for it. I'll figure out a way."

He stood. "Don't worry about money, Ainsley. Let me call him and get the ball rolling to get someone up here."

My mind felt better, and I wasn't leaving this hospital until someone was here to watch over my mom. I drank the ginger ale. I took small sips, again listening to the second hand of the clock pass away the time.

Tick.

Tick.

Tick.

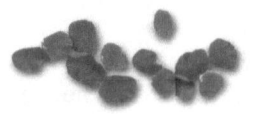

An hour later, a nurse came, and I stood.

"Ainsley Pearson, you can see your mother now. You can only stay for five minutes. You can come back tomorrow and see her again for the entire visitation period. The doctor is limiting it for tonight."

"Okay. I'll take whatever I can get."

Grabbing my purse, Adam and I followed the nurse. We entered into a hallway lined with rooms that had glass windows. All the patients looked immobile. We came to a door and I could see my mother through the window. The nurse opened the door and I walked in.

The gasp that left my mouth was audible. Her face was black and blue. Her wrist was in a cast. She looked so fragile, so weak, so vulnerable in this state.

Multiple machines were hooked up to her. The smell of disinfectant was strong. The only sound in the room was her heart rate monitor and some sort of accordion machine that made a pumping noise. Tubes flowed from her in every which way.

Pushing back the tears that were brimming, I found my inner strength. My mom didn't need to worry about me. She needed to focus on healing.

I came up to the side of her bed and touched her good hand. "Mom, I'm here. They're going to keep you sleeping for a day or so, but I wanted you to know that I love you, and I'll come here as much as I possibly can. I can't stay very long tonight, but I'll call and check on you regularly. Adam's with me, Mom. He hasn't left my side. I love you."

I stood there and rubbed my mom's hand until the nurse came in.

"It's time, Ms. Pearson."

Leaning down, I gently kissed my mom's hand and whispered, "I love you, Mom. Please come back to me."

As we left the hospital, Adam pointed to a guy in the waiting room. "He's going to make sure your mom is okay, baby."

They both nodded at each other.

"Thank you, Adam."

"Anything for you and your mom."

The proverbial clock kept ticking in my mind, passing the time until I was able to see my mother again.

Tick.

Tick.

Tick.

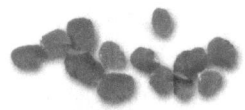

A week had passed since my mom was admitted. I was sitting in her room while she slept, working on my homework. She still hadn't woken up. I was now allowed to stay for a few hours a day. For the past few days after class, I would come here and work on homework. Adam was working, but he always stopped in about thirty minutes before I had to leave to say hey to my mom. He had been beyond supportive through this entire situation. I barely slept, and when I did, it was restless.

The night before last, someone questionable had come asking questions about my mom. When the security guy that Adam had hired approached him, the man had run out of the hospital. He had been wearing sunglasses and a hat in the dead of night, and he had yet to be identified. As soon as Adam had gotten the call, we had driven up here, so I could see my mom through the glass window.

My mind still raced with fear, wondering if my dad would find a way to get to my mom. I had a constant prayer in my head to keep her safe.

Until my mom woke up, the police had zero leads as to what had happened to her. Hampton had agreed with us that it was best not to tell them my theory until my mom woke up. Doctor Jacobs had agreed to also not say anything. Plus, she was bound by doctor-patient privileges. The doctors still remained optimistic about my mom's progress, which was good.

Opening my math book, I spoke aloud, like I had all the days before. "Shall we learn about statistics tonight, Mom? My homework is on probability theories. It's going to be an exciting afternoon of homework for you and me."

When I was in here, I kept my voice cheery and upbeat as I updated my mom on all my life's happenings. Out of habit, I paused and looked up, encouraging a response, but I got nothing.

"Looks like the first theory up is central limit theorem. This one is about normal distribution in nature."

I paused and looked up at my mom. Her fingers twitched. I dropped my books and went to her side.

"Mom, move your fingers again. You can do it."

My eyes didn't leave her hand, and then her index finger curled all the way in. I hit the call button, and the nurse came on speaker.

"It's Ainsley. My mom's finger moved twice." I spoke in excitement, practically jumping.

"That's good news. We're coming."

My mom's eyes fluttered and then came open to look into mine.

"Mom, you're awake. Oh, Mom, you're back."

She tried to smile but she was weak. "Ain…Ains…"

"Shh…Mom, it's okay. Don't speak. The doctor is coming."

Doctor Thompson came in. My breaths were coming fast as I felt my mom returning to me bit by bit.

"Good afternoon, Ms. Pearson. I'm Doctor Thompson. We're going to check you out, and then your daughter can come back in."

"Mmmkay…" Her voice was small.

I patted my mom's good hand. "I'll be right outside the door if you need anything."

She nodded as she let out a long, tired breath. I had my phone in my hand and hit the speed dial for Adam.

He picked up on the first ring. "Hey, baby. Everything okay?"

Excitement bubbled from my lips. "She's awake! Adam, she's awake! She came to while I taught her statistics. The doctor is with her now. Adam, she's alive! My mom is alive!" My voice cracked as the happiness consumed me.

I heard the sound of a large metal door opening on the other end. "Best news yet. I'm on my way."

"Okay. I love you, Adam."

"Love you, too, Ainsley. I'll always be here for you."

The curtains were drawn in my mom's room, and I paced ten steps down before turning and taking ten steps back. I was going to wear a hole in the tile when my handsome man came through the doors. Sweaty, he wore gym shorts and a T-shirt. I ran straight into his arms and he picked me up.

"Are they still with her?"

"Yes."

He set me back down. "I'm glad I made it in time. I was getting a quick workout in at the gym."

Doctor Thompson came out with a clipboard in hand. "Evening, Miss Pearson. Your mom seems to be recovering nicely. Her movement is slow and delayed, which is to be expected. With a little therapy and continued healing, I do believe your mom is going to make a full recovery. Until she's able to speak more, we won't know if she sustained any brain injuries."

I took the doctor off guard as I hugged him. "Thank you. Thank you for everything."

He awkwardly patted me on the back, and I pulled away. "I'll be in touch with a treatment plan as soon as your mom gets additional rest, and I can do a full evaluation of her. Your mom was asking for you."

I was already walking toward the door before he finished. I peeked in the room, and the nurses were rearranging her. She looked exhausted.

Both nurses were leaving.

The one with red hair said, "We'll be right back with some pain medication that will help with her discomfort."

"Okay, thank you."

I moved to stand beside my mom. I looked back, and Adam was at the foot of the bed.

"Hey, Mom, everything is going to be okay. The doctor is very pleased with your progress."

She closed her eyes, and I needed to confirm if my suspicions were correct.

I pulled out my phone and pushed record. "Mom, I'm taping you, so I can tell the police. Who did this to you?"

She swallowed several times. It was the strongest I had heard her voice since she woke up. She fought to stay awake as she said, "It was your father...Gerald."

Adam

Middle of December (A Few Months Later)

I T WAS COLD as I went to the car from the club. Ainsley was on Christmas break from school. Currently, she was with her mom at her house, getting ready for today.

Her father, Gerald, was being sentenced for attempted murder. He deserved whatever they were going to throw at him and more. I had hired the best prosecution lawyer to work with the state. His main job was to keep from allowing any plea-bargain shit.

As I cranked the car to get the heat going, a tap happened on my window. It was Brandt. I rolled down the window. He was crazy for being out here without his coat on.

"Hey, man, good luck. Give Ainsley and Christine a hug for me. Let me know if you guys need anything. I hope that fucker gets what he deserves."

I scrubbed a hand down my face. It had been a stressful few months. "Me, too. I'll give the girls a hug for you. Thanks for everything, Brandt. My schedule will lighten up a lot, so I'll be able to work my normal hours."

He shrugged his shoulders. "I'm glad I can help. You know that. She's more important than the club."

"I know. Thanks, man."

He took a step back and then stopped. "Did you get it yet?"

A smile emerged on my face. "Not yet, but the jeweler called, and it's ready. I'm going to get it tomorrow while Ainsley drops her mom off at the airport. Christine's going to see her great aunt, Marge, out in Arizona. Then, Aunt Marge is going to come here for a couple of months to help out. By then, we're hoping that Christine is fully recovered."

Marge, Christine's long-lost aunt, had heard about Gerald through the grapevine. Shortly after Christine had been released from the hospital, Marge had reached out and rekindled their relationship. During their marriage, Gerald had succeeded in isolating Christine from her entire family, especially after her mom had died.

"Good luck, man. You guys need a little time to yourselves."

I let out a long breath as a few flurries fell from the sky. "I couldn't agree more. I'm ready for this to all be over. It's taken a toll on Ainsley, but she's strong."

Brandt kicked at some rocks on the pavement before he looked back up at me. "I'm glad they're still going to counseling."

"Yeah, me, too. I think it's helped them put the past in the past, so they can live out their present and future without those ghosts. Today is going to determine a lot." I was stressed, wondering what the day was going to bring.

If they let that motherfucker walk free, I wasn't sure what I would do.

Brandt tapped the roof of my car. "Yes, it is. Go get your girl."

"That's where I'm headed."

I drove to Christine's. Christmas wreaths hung from the light poles, and the businesses all had Christmas lights adorning their establishments.

Ainsley had talked us into putting a tree up on both sides of the club. I'd tried to tell her that people were at the sex club to fuck and not be jolly, but she wouldn't hear of it. Both our bedrooms, at our home and the club, had trees in it, too. She loved Christmas. In the end, I'd smiled and helped get all the trees decorated. Snake and Trigger had made whipping sounds as I hung tinsel. Ainsley had scowled at them and then laughed. In the end, Ainsley had made it up to me as she let me bend her over the Tantra Chair and fuck her senseless multiple times.

I pulled into Christine's driveway.

She had lived with us for the first month after she was released before moving into her new home. When the time had come, Christine had been ready to be independent, but Ainsley had worried about her mother since all her motor skills were still returning slowly. At the time, Christine had only been at about seventy percent of her normal self. The doctors had expected a full recovery, but it would take time. As of two days ago, the doctors had estimated that she was about ninety percent recovered.

As I sat in the driveway, I thought about hearing Christine's statement to the police in the hospital room.

Ainsley was seated next to her mom where she stayed anytime her mom was awake. I stood beside Ainsley. I felt better standing in situations like this. It made me feel more prepared and able to react.

Christine had been attacked twelve days ago today. Since Ainsley had gotten the phone call to come to the hospital, it had been an emotional roller coaster. There were times when I hadn't been sure that Christine was going to wake up, and my heart had broken for Ainsley.

Once Christine did wake up, she wasn't able to talk for long periods which made it difficult for the police to get a confession. The doctors had limited her visitors, not wanting to cause stress since the first few days were critical to recovery.

She was stronger today and we believed we'd be able to finally get her account of all the events in one setting.

Christine's hospital bed was tilted into an upright slanted position as two detectives sat on the other side with their notebooks and voice recorders.

The slightly balding man wearing a fitted suit asked, "Ms. Pearson, can you tell us what happened?"

He and his female partner, who had a tight bun on her head, looked like they were sharp and a no-nonsense team. That was what we needed.

Christine's black-and-blue face nodded. She was still weak, and her speech was slow. Breathing was sometimes painful with her broken ribs. She closed her eyes as if she was conjuring the scene from that night.

"I went home to get my car, so I could drive to the bookstore and then back to the center. As I crossed the living

room to the garage, Gerald came out from the kitchen area. He asked why I was still trying to ruin his life. I didn't know what he was talking about. He said I had poisoned our daughter against him, and that caused him to lose one of his biggest accounts. I assumed that account was Adam's club. He lost the partnership, and he walked out on his only source of income after a heated argument."

She paused and opened her eyes for a second before closing them again. *"His partner's son—Tyler, I think—had gone to his dad and told him that Gerald's daughter had cost them hundreds of thousands of dollars. He said she had daddy issues. Gerald blamed me for that. He threatened this was going to be the last time I ever got in the way, and he was going to finish things once and for all. He threw me against the wall where he repeatedly hit and kicked me until I could no longer stand. I tried to fight him off, but he was too strong. He told me how worthless I was and that I was a waste of space. He was livid and out of control, more than I had ever seen him."*

She took a few minutes as she closed her eyes. The officer with the tight bun asked, *"Are you able to continue?"*

Christine nodded. I was glad. It was time to get things rolling so that motherfucker could get what he deserved.

Taking a deep breath, she winced. Ainsley was patting her head and about to say something when Christine continued. *"When he picked me up and shoved me across the room, I tried to grab a candlestick, but he pushed me and then stomped on my wrist so that I would drop it. I knew he wasn't going to stop this time.*

"I saw my life flash before my eyes. The pain turned me numb, and the world became fuzzy. I tried to stay awake, but eventually, my body shut down. As my eyes were closing,

something heavy hit my head and my world went black. The next time I woke up was with my daughter sitting beside me."

Ainsley had a few silent tears as she sat stoically support-ive next to her mom. She had an inner strength unlike anyone I knew.

After her mother had survived surgery and Ainsley and I had gone home from the hospital, she had sobbed into my chest until exhaustion claimed her.

After that, Gerald had been arrested, and the trial process had started. We never received a confession as he'd pleaded the fifth and refused to talk to anyone. Hampton had tried to track down the guy from the hospital who had come to visit Christine, but the guy had never looked into the camera and had left on foot.

Since then, I'd had both Christine and Ainsley on con-stant surveillance. Christine had insisted on paying for it out of her trust fund. It hadn't mattered to me as long as they were safe. There hadn't been any questionable activity since the night of the hospital.

Last week, both Christine and Ainsley had testified in front of a jury, which had been emotionally exhausting and stressful for both of them, but they had survived. The defense had been trying to spin a story that Christine wanted Gerald back. When Gerald had refused a reconciliation, Christine had nearly killed herself for revenge.

Total bullshit.

It had taken everything I had within me not to climb over the railing separating the spectators from the actual proceed-ings. My teeth ground together as I remembered seeing Ains-ley defend herself against that dickwad of a defense attorney.

Ready to get to the courthouse to get this over with, I texted Ainsley.

Me: I'm here. Coming to the door.
Ainsley: I see you. We're on our way out.

I got out of the car. Christine's home was a small two-bedroom cream-colored bricked house with black shutters. Overall, it was perfect for her and easy to manage. I met them on the sidewalk leading to the front door.

We would be taking her mom's Buick Enclave. The height of the car made it easier for Christine to get in and out. The wind was chilling as I ran up to Ainsley. She was bundled up with a red scarf wrapped around her neck. Her brown hair blew as she shivered.

"Hey, ladies. Your chauffeur has arrived." I leaned down and kissed Ainsley on the cheek. "Go ahead and get in the car, baby. It's cold. I'll help your mom. I don't want you to get sick."

Ainsley went ahead and opened the passenger door. She then reached in to crank the vehicle before getting into the backseat. Less than a minute later, Christine got into the vehicle without any help. She was getting stronger each day, but at times, she would get shaky on her feet. Having someone walk beside her was more precautionary than anything at this point.

I jogged over to the driver's side of the car, and an introspective silence descended on the car as we made our way downtown to the courthouse. I glanced in the rearview mirror, and Ainsley looked out the window. Her thumb touched the finger with her ring. She wasn't able to twirl it with her gloves.

I imagined we were all thinking about the events that had led up to this moment—at least, I was. The endless questioning, the prepping with the lawyers, and the trial—it had all been tough.

We arrived at the courthouse as our lawyer, Joe, walked out. He wore an Italian-made gray suit with a pale pink shirt.

He greeted us. "Sentencing is in one hour. Let's head inside and get this over with, shall we?"

Ainsley responded, "Thanks, Joe, for everything." Her teeth were beginning to chatter.

Joe raised a dark eyebrow that matched his hair color as he put his hand on Ainsley's shoulder. "You can thank me *when* we get this asshole convicted."

She nodded as Joe gave her a comforting smile.

"I'm going to go speak to your mom as we walk in. Let me know if you need anything.'

"I will."

Ainsley's eyes moved over to the right, and Nora came walking up.

She hugged Ainsley. "Hey, chica. How ya holding up?"

"Good. Ready to get this over with and move on. How's Emilyn? I hated that I had to cancel on her for the last few weeks."

Ainsley's head was nervously moving up and down as the cold seeped into our bones. During the fall semester, Ainsley would have a date to hang out with Emilyn every other week. Ainsley had been spreading herself too thin, trying to be there for everyone. With the intense prepping for the trial over the last few weeks, something had to give.

Nora ran her hands through her hair. Last week, she had changed it to black. I'd assumed it was for the trial since she wanted to be there for Ainsley. Joe had asked her to.

The wind continued to blow as Nora answered. "Emilyn's good. She watches that damn movie you got her, *The Last*

Unicorn, over and over again. I feel like I'm about to break out into that stupid butterfly song at any minute."

She looked at me, and I nodded toward the door. Ainsley was freezing.

Nora continued. "Let's get inside before we freeze to death."

"S-sounds g-good. I'm glad she likes the movie." Ainsley stuttered as she responded.

She hated the cold more than I did.

Nora laughed. "*Like* is a bit of an understatement."

I rubbed my hand briskly up and down Ainsley's arm as we walked in. Joe was beside Christine as they entered the waiting room.

Here's to hoping the next hour goes by quickly.

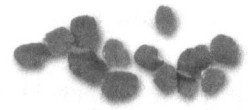

Joe walked into the small room we had been waiting in to the right of the actual courtroom. The room was bare, except for tables, chairs, and pictures of previous presidents hanging on the walls.

"It's time. Does anyone have any questions?" Joe asked.

We responded, "No."

Joe had done an excellent job in preparing us for each step of the way.

We made our way into the courtroom. Ainsley sat between Nora and me on the right side behind the wood railing separating us from where all the action would take place in the courtroom. Christine and Joe took their seats in front of us to the right of the state prosecutor.

The room smelled stale. I looked at our national symbol behind the judge and hoped that justice would be done today.

A small movement to the right caught my attention. I glanced down and saw Ainsley's ring making quick circles as she twirled it now that it was freed from the confines of her glove.

The side door opened and Gerald came walking in with cuffs on. His overweight, greasy asshole of a lawyer waited for him at the table adjacent to Christine's. Gerald stared at Christine. It was as if he dared her to look at him.

During the trial so far, Christine had not looked over once. I believed that had shown she was truly breaking the psychological hold that monster had on her.

Ainsley leaned in to me, and I held her closer to me as the jury filed in. They knew the fate of Gerald, and I was ready for the sentencing to commence. I glanced again at our national symbol and mentally pleaded that Gerald would receive a guilty verdict.

The bailiff came forward. "All rise. Court is now in session. The honorable Judge Roberts is presiding."

We stood, and Ainsley grabbed my hand, abandoning her ring twirling. Her fingernails dug into me as the judge came out in his black judicial robe. Judge Roberts was completely gray-haired. His serious expression looked like it had been etched onto his face permanently.

The judge sat in a mahogany stand at the front of the room and calmly stated, "You may be seated."

The sound of everyone retaking their seats filled the silence of the courtroom, which only increased my anxiety as reality set in that this was the end of the road one way or another. I lovingly squeezed Ainsley's hand as she chewed on her bottom lip.

The foreman of the jury stood and the bailiff took a piece of paper from him. I needed to see what was on that paper.

Did they agree he's guilty? Will Ainsley and Christine be safe? Will we be able to finally rest at night, knowing Gerald is behind bars?

My mind kept circulating through these questions as the bailiff handed the judge the verdict. Time slowed, and seconds became years as the piece of paper was unfolded.

The judge turned to the jury. "Mr. Foreman and members of the jury, have you reached a unanimous verdict?"

The well-dressed, lean foreman answered, "Yes, your honor."

Finally, it was the moment of truth, the moment that would hopefully return a guilty verdict, the moment we could be free of this horrible nightmare.

Without hesitation, the judge read the decision of the jury, "In the court of the fourth judicial circuit in and for Forsyth County, Georgia, in case number one-four-nine-two-zero-D-A-X-M, the state of Georgia versus Gerald Pearson, we, the jury, find the defendant guilty of attempted murder. I assess for punishment the confinement in the institutional division of the Georgia department of criminal justice for fifty years without chance of parole, so say we the jury in Forsyth County."

The gavel sounded.

Ainsley stood and wrapped her arms around my neck. "We won, Adam. We won. My mom is safe now. We're safe." Her voice was choked and full of emotion.

Christine hugged Joe as I turned Ainsley's back to her father. She didn't need to see her father if he looked this way. Nora wrapped herself around Ainsley. Gerald turned my way, and I pressed Ainsley tighter against me. Rage boiled inside but then simmered as I remembered he was getting his due.

Gerald's coal-black eyes stared at us without any emotion. I stared at that asshole right back, not backing down. His contempt for me grew, and I didn't care as long as it was directed away from Ainsley.

The policemen came to Gerald's side and escorted him out the side door. Gerald kept turning toward us, hate emanating from his expression.

I held Ainsley, thankful I had her safe in my arms. I kissed the top of her head. "It's over, Ainsley."

"I know. He's gone. My mom is safe."

Ainsley is safe.

I could feel the stress from the last few months beginning to evaporate. Together, we had survived what life threw at us.

"I need to go hug my mom." Ainsley had tears in her eyes as she went to the rail.

Leaning over, they embraced each other.

Christine had tears in her eyes. "I love you, Ainsley."

"I love you, too, Mom."

Finally, justice was served.

With Gerald being put away, the slate felt cleaned, like we had a new beginning in front of us.

Ainsley's mom was currently on a plane, headed to Aunt Marge's.

I was taking Ainsley somewhere special in the middle of nowhere, so we could have some uninterrupted time together. We needed it desperately. The cabin was prepped for our special week, a week I hoped that we'd remember forever.

Lindy was in the backseat, content to be tagging along, as she laid down and slept. Lindy had practically become Ainsley's dog since we moved in together. I had Ainsley take Lindy a lot with her whenever she could. I knew she would protect Ainsley if anything happened.

One night, Ainsley had told me about the dog her dad had thrown out when she was a child and my heart had broken for her all over again. With the amount of hurt and damage that asshole of a father had caused, the sentence he had gotten didn't seem like enough.

We turned down a dirt road that was lined with pine trees.

"Thank you for being patient with me these last few months." Ainsley's voice was soft as she spoke.

Ainsley had been worried that she wasn't satisfying me with enough adventurous sex. We'd had a hell of a lot of sex, but it had been less uninhibited. However, sex with Ainsley was always perfect. She had needed more lovemaking than hard, sensual fucking, and that was what I had given her. I'd be there for her, however she needed me.

"Ainsley, there was nothing to be patient about. You're it for me."

She sighed a contented sigh. "I love you."

"Love you too, baby."

A faint cedar smell filled the car. The dirt road was bumpy as we had to slow the car down. After a few minutes, the cabin came into view. It was an old-fashioned styled log cabin that had a wood wraparound porch. Four rocking chairs sat on the left side and a wooden swing to the right of the door.

"It's beautiful. Thank you."

We needed this. "Anything for you." A smirk spread on my lips as I thought about all my plans for Ainsley. "You're going to be thoroughly fucked by the time we head back home in seven days."

She gasped. "Seven days? I get you alone for seven whole days. No interruptions, no appointments, just us…for seven days?"

Our schedule has been nonstop for the last few months.

"Yes, it's all ours. The place is stocked with food so we won't have to leave. They left the key under the mat for us."

Ainsley leaned over and kissed me as her hand came down to the front of my jeans. She leaned across the console and kissed my neck while unzipping my pants.

"I like where you're going with this, baby."

The feather light kisses tickled my skin as I felt her smile against me. Her fingers wrapped around my cock and played with the tip.

From the corner of my eye, I saw movement as she lifted her dress. Her free hand drifted downward.

Hell, this was going to be hot watching her pump my dick while she touched her clit. When she made contact with her sex, her teeth sunk into my flesh.

"Mmmm…" She was moaning louder.

She is mine…forever.

She kept a steady pace causing a slow climb. The tip of Ainsley's nose then trailed up and down my neck. She drove me mad. I wanted her to go faster, but I focused on the pleasure letting her stay in control this time.

"Ainsley, I'm going to wear you out these next few days. I'll make your body sore, so when you move, you'll be constantly reminded of me."

She lightly bit me again. "Bring it, my man-friend and Pleasure Buddy. Now come find me."

Her words confused me. The cold air rushing in from the door opening woke me out of my blissful haze I had entered. Ainsley was out of the car with Lindy following before I realized what she had done. I opened my car door and stood, shocked. "You left me hanging."

Ainsley and Lindy were almost to the front door as she giggled and turned back for a brief second. "Hurry and get the bags. I'll be waiting to be fucked." Her tone was teasing as she crooked her finger for me to come after her.

The wind blew. It was cold. I zipped myself up.

My dick does not need a case of frostbite.

"I'm going to fuck you hard, Ainsley, when I find you."

They had made it to the door and Ainsley put the key into the front door. She turned and yelled. "I'm counting on it."

The thought of chasing her down had me harder than hell. Lindy was by her side the entire time, and then they disappeared behind the front door.

I grabbed the two bags and practically ran up to the cabin. It was a medium-sized three-bedroom cabin with a screened-in back porch overlooking the lake. I was sure Ainsley was going to explore everything before I got in there finding a place to hide. I was glad that I had asked the owners to lock the master bedroom. The key was under the vase on the table in the hallway for what I had planned later.

The grounds were clean and manicured. It was isolated and perfect for us. I planned on spending most of this next week naked and buried inside of Ainsley and taking care of her. I opened the door and set our bags down. My eyes scanned for any signs of my girl. My dick was still rock hard, waiting to find its home.

A cedar smell greeted me. In the corner was a Christmas tree, like I had requested. Ainsley loved Christmas, and I'd wanted her to have a tree everywhere she stayed.

Where is she?

The place was as nice as the photos had been. To the left appeared to be the kitchen, and to the right was the living room where a fire crackled and two plaid couches sat in an L-shape.

"Ainsley, where are you?" My voice was slightly hoarse with need.

Lindy appeared in the hallway and laid down. As I walked her way, I heard in a soft voice, "I'm in here."

The sound came from behind me. I turned and walked toward the couch. On the floor was a white fur rug and a naked Ainsley with a blanket casually draped over her hips. Her breasts were perky, and her hair spilled out onto the rug. Instinctively, my shirt came over my head, and my pants followed right after. I leaped over the couch, and I was on top of Ainsley in two seconds flat about ready to plummet inside of her.

Her hand went up to the bandage over my heart which stopped my movement. "What happened?"

This morning, while I had been running errands, I had stopped by Moon's. "Peel back the bandage and find out."

Inquisitiveness filled her features as she gently pulled back the white gauze. The moment she saw the tattoo, her eyes went to mine. It was the same as the one she had gotten on her hip—two A's entwined, one masculine and one feminine, for myself and Ainsley.

"I love it, Adam."

"We're forever, baby."

She put the bandage back in place and then leaned up to kiss it. Lying back down, she said, "Make love to me first."

Her words melted me each and every time.

"This is turning out to be a fan-fucking-tastic vacation already."

She giggled. "Remember your promise to make me sore?"

My legs were already moving hers apart as I tossed the blanket aside. I positioned myself and barely pushed in.

"Oh, I remember, and it's a promise I plan to keep. I'll be fucking you later for that stunt of yours."

My words had her biting her lower lip. "Good."

I sank into her, and her body responded.

I would never tire of this feeling, being inside Ainsley.

Ainsley

I LAY BONELESS next to the fire with Adam nestled up to my back as we watched the flames dance around the new log that Adam had put on. The crackling sound was calming. The cabin smelled of cedar, which added to the overall ambience. Adam's finger traced the curvature of my body. I had lost count of how many times we had been together this afternoon. It was as if we were wild animals, craving each other. I had missed having this part of our relationship since my mom's break down.

With my father in jail for the next fifty years, my mom was free and could now live her life. She was much better, but the road had been hard.

As I'd dropped her off at the airport, she'd told me, *Ainsley, the journey of our life makes us who we are. There are sour spots, sweet spots, and scary spots. Regardless of what spot you're in, take it, embrace it, and live it. It's only through our emotions that we truly know we are alive.*

Her words were true and wise. My mom and I were going to be okay.

Adam kissed my shoulder. "Is my girl finally feeling satiated?"

I looked up at him. "I don't know if I could ever have enough of you."

He kissed me again. "We're going to need to eat. There are supposed to be some premade meals in the fridge. I'll go start one."

"Okay, sounds good. Hurry back."

He got up, and I heard his feet pad into the kitchen.

My eyes went back to the flames as I watched them lick the wood and sway with the air. My mind went through the perfect memories of the day and settled on what had been underneath the bandage of his heart. His tattoo was perfect, and the significance of where he had placed it was not lost on me. I was his heart, his forever.

Without Adam's body heat, I pulled up the blanket.

A cold nose nudged my shoulder.

"Hey, girl."

I turned over to face Lindy, and she wore a big red bow with an envelope, like she had at the motel. A smile from the memory involuntarily spread across my face. I sat up and tucked the blanket underneath my arms as I grabbed the envelope with my name on it.

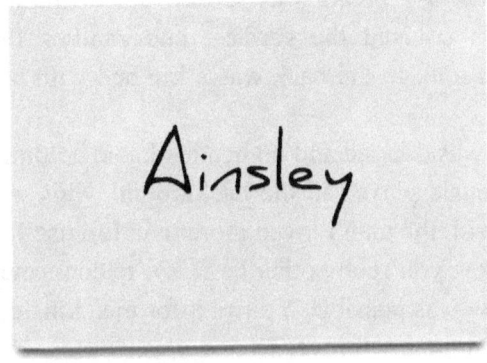

I took out the note, my heart racing with excitement.

I wrapped the sheet around my body as I looked for him. At the beginning of the hallway, rose petals made a trail to one of the bedrooms. It was the door that had been locked earlier when I did my quick scope of the place before getting naked on the fur rug. I had assumed it was where the owners kept their personal belongings.

My feet were traveling faster on the wooden floor. The door was barely cracked open. I pushed it farther open and peered inside. My breath was sucked out of me at the sight. Fresh petals covered the surface, and candles flickered all around the room. In the back was a big bed with a white bedspread.

Adam was dressed and on bended knee, holding out a ring box. Soft music played in the background. This was a dream come true with the man I loved more than life itself.

"Ainsley, you're my other half. We're connected in a way I never knew was possible. You're it for me, Ainsley. Will you marry me and be my forever?"

I was on my knees in front of him as joy pumped through my body, and my eyes moistened with happiness. "Yes! You're my forever, too."

He hugged me to him and then gave me a deep kiss until he pulled back. All my dreams were coming true. "I want to put your ring on you and see what it looks like. I'm publicly claiming you with a symbol of eternity. I want the entire world to know you're mine."

My hand shook slightly as he slipped the ring onto my finger. It was a princess-cut solitaire on a platinum band. I kissed him and he stood with me, leaving the sheet on the floor, as he brought me over to the bed. He laid me down.

"Adam, you brought me to life. You're my happily ever after. You love me like I never knew I deserved. With you, I feel complete, and I feel loved. I know you're my forever."

He looked at me like I was the air he needed to breathe. "You're my beginning and my ending, Ainsley."

"You're my happily ever after, Adam."

Thinking back on everything that happened in our lives, I knew that… *Every event in our life causes a ripple effect that we never truly understand until the waters calm and everything reveals itself. In that moment, we truly see.*

Epilogue

Brandt

New Year's Eve

ADAM, MY BUSINESS partner and best friend since childhood, and I were the only ones at Club Envy. We always closed on New Year's Eve so we could go out and have some fun. The club lost a shit-ton of money, but our employees appreciated it, so what the hell? I hated having the bar closed since losing Nikola. It meant I had to find something to fill the hours. For the fifth time, I made sure all the cameras were working before I headed to Adam's office. Since it reminded me of the girl I'd lost in a bout of stupidity, I rarely used my office. Instead, I'd taken over the security station within the club. I peered through the open door and saw Adam focused on his computer.

I knocked. "Hey, man, you need anything?"

Adam hit a few more keys then closed his laptop. "Nah, I got it done. I'm about to leave. You still going with Trigger tonight?"

Adam and Ainsley had invited me to hang out with them. But hell, that was like salt in the wound. I was happy for my friend, but there was also a tinge of jealously. I'd had that happiness once but had thrown it away. New Year's Eve was not a good time to be around a newly engaged couple. They'd be involved in a complete shag-fest tonight.

I cracked my neck. "Yeah, he's convinced we'll get more ass by teaming up. I figure I'll see if anything catches my fancy. May get a quick fuck in. Who knows?"

Adam gave me that look, so I headed it off before he could bring up...her. "I know you think I should contact Nikola, but after what I put her through with my addiction, she deserves to be happy."

Adam stood to leave. "I know. I'm not going to say anything about it. You know what I think, but you're your own man. It's your life. I think you need to take your own advice— you know, what you told me about Ainsley. That's all."

Adam knew I wasn't going to respond to that statement. We'd been friends for too damn long.

We were in the bar area turning off all the lights when Adam asked, "Where are you going tonight with Trigger? Is it that girl bar he prowls when there isn't anything here he wants to tap?"

I chuckled. "Yeah, Coyote Ugly. He says it's the best place to get a piece. You still taking Ainsley into the city tonight?"

We walked out of the club and I locked up, rechecking everything as we went. Outside, it was cold enough to see our breath in the night air.

"Yeah, after all the family time we had over Christmas, I wanted us to have some uninterrupted us time. She's with our moms, baking."

Ainsley's mom had come back for Christmas and was leaving tomorrow to go back to Arizona to be with her aunt for a little while longer. The past week had been nothing but celebration after Adam and Ainsley announced their engagement. I was happy for them, I really was, but it hurt—I wanted that, too.

We walked a few steps as Adam added, "I think we've about figured out a date. Sometime this summer after she's done with school, before she starts working."

Adam had asked me to be his best man the moment he told me he'd asked Ainsley to marry him. Of course I'd agreed. I was honored. "Sounds good. I'm happy for you, man. You deserve it."

I veered off to my SUV and ended the conversation. "Have fun, Happy New Year. Are you guys still coming over tomorrow for the traditional collards and black-eyed peas at my mum's?"

"Of course we are! Ainsley talked to your mom and is bringing some sort of dessert she's baking. Happy New Year to you, too, Brandt. See ya tomorrow."

As I closed the door I said, "See ya."

I put the key in the car and cranked it, cursing to myself. I hadn't used my automatic car starter. I hated the cold, but I hated wearing a coat even more.

Trigger texted me.

Trigger: You ready? I'll meet you there. I'm about two minutes away. My buddy texted and said there's gonna be pussy a-plenty.

Me: I'm on my way.

As I pulled out of the parking lot, I tried to tell myself that I'd be fucking someone senseless tonight. Maybe that would get this restless feeling out of my system. I made a mental note to call my sponsor this week. I needed to talk to him. He helped keep it real and understood me in a way that you can't unless you're a recovering addict.

A few minutes later, I pulled up to the bar. In pink neon letters was the name of the bar.

I opened my car door and headed inside. Rock music blared and there were girls dancing up on the bar. I saw potential ass in here, but every time I tried to think about fucking someone, Nikola's face flashed in my mind. That was always the problem that kept me from pursuing anyone else. I couldn't go through with it. The one time I had, guilt had plagued my thoughts for days. I spotted Trigger across the bar at a table with two ladies.

Obviously, everyone was on the prowl tonight, looking for hookups. Lust filled the air as bodies ground against one another. Some rubbed against me. Nothing happened in response; I wasn't interested. Hell, I felt like a pansy.

I went over to the table. "Hey, man."

Trigger looked like as if he'd already been hitting the booze pretty hard. I drank in moderation these days. I'd learned the hard way that anything in excess led to trouble.

"Hey, Brandt. This is Amy and Lucy."

They were both gorgeous. I tried to force my mind to get in the game. Nikola wasn't an option, so I needed to make the most of what was left of my life: empty meaningless sex. Amy licked her lips, and I decided to go for her since Lucy already had her hand on Trigger. Amy had blonde hair and vivid blue eyes. She wore a tight, black mini skirt with a sparkly blue halter top. The outline of her nipples showed through the top. She'd be a good distraction—I hoped.

"What's your poison, Amy?"

Amy leaned in closer to me. "Cranberry and Vodka."

"You got it."

I signaled and the waitress came to the table. "Guinness for me, cranberry and vodka for the lady."

The waitress nodded and took off toward the bar.

Amy put her lips to my ear. "How about you and I go somewhere and start the night right before our drinks come back—there's not room for two of us under the table. I want to take turns getting each other off all night while we ring in the New Year."

Well, she was forward. Trigger gave me a wink and took a swig of his beer. I leaned over slightly to see that Lucy was under the table giving him head. Fuck. The girls were horny tonight, that was for damn sure.

I looked at Amy and decided some space was needed while I tried to push Nikola to the far recesses of my mind. "Give me a minute. I'll be back."

I pushed away from the table and headed to the bar to intercept my beer. She called after me, "Hurry back."

Without bothering to reply, I kept walking. There was a very good chance I would not be coming back to the table. I might leave. I was messed up. I'd definitely be setting up a meeting next week with my sponsor. Decision made, I started toward the bar. I'd take a shot, pay for the drinks, then leave. The music rocked around me, but I wanted to be home. Making it to the bar, I laid my hand on the cool counter.

When the bartender came over, I said, "Shot of tequila."

"You got it." She went to work, barely speaking as the throng of people kept moving toward the bar. The place was packed.

I pulled out a twenty and handed it to her. "Keep the change."

"Thanks." She stuffed it in her pocket and went to the next customer.

Someone pushed past me as I was about to down the shot.

"I'm so sorry. It's packed."

I froze. That voice. I turned and the auburn-haired, green-eyed goddess I'd only dreamed about seeing again stared back at me. She had on leather pants and a low-cut red shirt. I remembered how good those breasts felt in my hands. My cock was fully erect now at the sight of her. I still wanted her. I still loved her.

"Nikola—"

"Brandt—"

Her eyes searched mine, and I saw it—the flicker of emotion between us that I'd thought was dead. She still had some sort of feelings for me. But to what extent?

I set my shot back on the counter. "How have you been?"

"Good, how about you?" She swallowed hard, and I could feel something crackling between us.

Before I had a chance to respond, hands came around my waist. "I was missing you at our table. I think it's time we found ourselves some privacy. I want you."

Fucking hell.

Nikola walked backward. "I can't do this. I need to go."

She turned and rushed into the sea of people. I called after her. "It's not what you think."

Fuck.

I took Amy's hands off me. "It's not going to happen."

She pouted, but I turned away, searching for Nikola. I needed to find her and explain what she'd seen. A new determination to fight for her— for us—filled me. I hoped she'd listen to me.

Pushing through the crowd, I saw the top of her auburn hair at the side door. Not caring about anyone else, I pushed harder to get through. If she'd give me a chance to apologize, to make things right, we could take it slow. The metal door was heavy as I shoved it open. Nikola stood there, waiting on the curb.

"Nikola…wait. It's not what you think."

She turned, an alarmed look in her eyes. "That's what you always used to say when I'd catch you with drugs."

Her words knocked the breath out of me. Nikola was the one who'd been the most affected by my drug addiction. "Nikola, I don't know what to say… I've changed. Can we talk?"

Her lip trembled and it looked as if she was about to capitulate when a black sports car pulled up beside her. Some dark-haired, built asshole got out of the car. He looked me up and down, sizing me up. A possessive rage boiled within me as he put his hands around Nikola's waist. It was an instinct that had been ingrained in me—she'd been mine for so long before I'd lost her. I reminded myself she wasn't mine now. Whoever this guy was, he leaned down and whispered something in her ear.

I gave it one last shot. "Nikola, two minutes of your time."

She looked at me with tears in her eyes as the guy brought her closer. She shook her head. "I can't, Brandt. Not right now. I hope you're better, but I...I...I need to go."

The asshole opened her door and said something else. She shook her head, and he shut the door. He glared my way. "Brandt, I think you've caused her enough grief. Leave her the hell alone. She doesn't need someone who can't be depended on."

I was stunned, not knowing what to say after that low blow. I deserved it, but it still felt like shit. I had changed and was clean. The guy looked at me like he had Nikola's best interest at heart. I wondered if she'd moved on with him. If I was too late. Am I too late? The Nikola I remembered was full of life, happy. In the past, she'd have run into my arms and I would have kissed the life from her. We'd been each other's everything. The Nikola that I'd seen had looked broken and sad. All I wanted to do was chase her and explain that I was better. She'd been changed by my decision to use. This was all my fault. The red lights faded as the car drove away with the love of my life in the passenger seat.

Enjoy an excerpt from

Stand alone Novel

1

BANE

Six Years Ago

I WAS DONE. Finished. Out.

For the past seven years, I belonged to a division of the government that wasn't on the books. I operated alone. There was a mission: I either failed or succeeded. If I failed, that meant I was dead.

After all the shit I'd seen, done, caused—I had survived. It was a fucking miracle.

I was the best at what I did, but there were times I saw my life flash before my eyes. But when you're the government's covert assassin, what else was there to expect. If I was captured, I didn't exist. If I died, I didn't exist. If I succeeded, I was assigned my next mission.

The plane wheels screeched as I touched down in Alaska.

Finally, I was where I wanted to be.

At times, I wasn't sure I knew who I was anymore. My identity was erased from the system long ago. For the last three months, I'd been working on getting released from the program. It was a slow process with how deep I was in with Black Division.

Those suits knew I wouldn't share anything I'd done. Hell, half the time I wanted to forget. After three months of debriefing, the government let me out. Of course, there was an underlying threat.

If we so much as suspect you've betrayed this country, consider yourself dead, Mr. Bradley.

Yeah, nothing else was new. I wasn't an idiot. I knew I'd be monitored for years to come, but they wouldn't find anything.

In all the dark bullshit that swirled around me, there was one person who kept me grounded over the last two years … Jasmine. She saved my soul before it would have been lost completely to the animal beckoning to take over within me. Finally, I was going to spend the rest of my life with her.

The cabin of the plane dinged and the pilot came on to thank us for flying. Who the fuck cared? All the passengers wanted the same thing—to get off. The only thing I wanted was to see my girl.

Jasmine, the love of my life, waited for me at the front of the airport. I carried only a duffel bag. That was all I'd wanted from my previous life. Everything else I set fire to and tried to forget it. There was nothing good about my past besides her.

The last time I'd seen Jasmine had been a little over six months ago on my last furlough. I always flew her to different places to meet to maximize our time together, but the last time, I'd come here and fell in love with Alaska. Yeah, the winters were shitty, but it was isolated and away from the fuckedup-ness in the world. There was a true peace. Maybe I'd heal enough to be worthy of Jasmine.

Jasmine knew me as Bane Bradley. On the fly, I'd used it when we met at a local bar two years ago in New York. It stuck. And now, it would be my name for the rest of my life. I liked it.

The government hadn't even known about that name. All the names of my previous identities blended together, morph-ing into one. My mother called me *bastard* my entire child-hood. That name was also fitting for the shit I'd done. Some-times a person became a product of where they came from.

The cold air hit my face, and I debarked from the plane at the small airport. It was almost time to see my girl—Jasmine.

I was here. I was home. *Home.* The word lightened the load as I practically sprinted to the front of the airport. Over the phone yesterday, Jasmine said she had some news for me. Her voice shook minutely, which meant she was nervous. When I'd asked, *do you still want me to come?* The resounding *yes* was all I needed. We'd make it through anything else.

Until yesterday, when I'd been released, we hadn't talked since I'd last visited. But the moment I heard her sweet voice on the end of the line, I knew she still loved me. Jasmine knew I worked for a secret agency, although she thought about it more along the lines of James Bond type shit.

Nothing was further from the truth.

But, it kept her from asking questions and that was all that mattered, which, in turn kept Jasmine safe. As of that moment, all the other shit was in the past and didn't matter.

A secret smile formed as I thought what I had planned for us. Getting somewhere private was priority—another reason I insisted on Jasmine picking me up at the front versus coming in.

Outside the airport sat the love of my life in her old, tan four-wheel-drive SUV. Another bitter gust of wind hit me, but I made it to the vehicle in record time. As soon as I got in, her subtle vanilla scent greeted me. Oh how I missed that smell.

Jasmine leaned over. Our lips touched as she whispered against mine. "Hey, baby."

All the countless lie detector tests, questioning, and debriefing were worth it in that moment. First, I had to taste her. As I cupped her face, her soft skin was a soothing balm against my callous palms.

Her lips formed to mine. My tongue sought entry in her mouth, and she opened to me, intensifying the kiss. That sweet little moan had my cock as hard as a rock. We needed to get out of here before I took her in the parking lot. As soon as we got somewhere, I was sinking deep within her—for hours on end.

A car honked behind us. Jasmine giggled and whispered against my lips, "Are you ready to go home?"

"Yeah, baby. Take me home."

Home. There was that word again.

I'd never had a home. Ever. There was no way the shithole I'd grown up in could be considered a home. As soon as I turned eighteen, I enlisted in the marines. Within two years, I was recruited to the Black Division. Life expectancy in the program was three years. I'd lasted seven fucking long years.

As Jasmine drove, I couldn't take my eyes off her honey-blonde hair and dark-chestnut eyes. She had a body made for worshiping that was hidden underneath her oversized thick coat. I was never going to have to let her go.

Glancing my way, she asked with a knowing smile,

"What are you looking at?"

"You. It's always you. I'm sorry it took me so fucking long to get home to you."

Her hand came out and held mine. "You made it. That's all that matters. And, you're here for good?"

"I am." A tinge of guilt raced through me. There had been several times through the last two years where I'd stood her up because I was on a mission in some hellhole. It was a miracle she'd stayed with me through it all.

While we were apart, I called as often as I could, but sometimes it was weeks before she heard from me. I craved to hear her voice like an addiction. Honestly, it was a miracle I got to date her. When you signed up to be an operative, there were no ties to the world. However, I'd disclosed our relationship as soon as it became one. After intensive monitoring and background checks, Black Division was satisfied and gave me the all clear to continue the relationship.

Driving to the small apartment complex in town, Jasmine parked. I'd only been here once, but with my photographic memory, I knew where we were. Jogging to Jasmine's side of the truck, I grabbed the keys out of the ignition and cradled her in my arms. The squeal of delight rang through me. I spun us around, earning peals of laughter. I had my girl in my arms, and I was going to spend the rest of my life cherishing her.

As we walked to the door, I kissed her slow. With my right hand, I managed to unlock the door while never taking my mouth from hers. I needed to know this was real and not a dream. Over the last year, I'd dreamed of being with Jasmine and having a child. Time would give me both.

I wanted it all—the white fence, the wife, the kids … everything. And for the first time in my life, I believed I deserved it.

The door closed with a loud thud as I kicked it. The atmosphere intensified as I plunged deeper into her mouth. A small moan of acceptance came from Jasmine as she held me firmly to her.

The next stop was the bedroom.

"Bane—"

Cutting her off, I murmured, "Later."

If she pushed me away, I'd stop. But right now, I needed her to know this wasn't a dream. Jasmine was here and pliant in my arms. It was tempting to fuck her hard in the living room, but the first time home, I was going to make love to her. Savor her. Adore her.

Sitting her down, I pushed the coat off her shoulders. Jasmine grabbed the hem of my shirt and together we took it off. A finger trailed down my abdomen eliciting a shiver.

"I missed this. I missed you." Jasmine's words fueled me as I reclaimed her mouth.

My cock ached to sink into that perfect pussy of hers. Going to her stomach to take off her shirt, I touched the soft skin. Jasmine's abdomen wasn't flat but had a bump to it. I took a step back. My eyes shot to hers.

Was she?

Both of her hands came up and caressed her stomach. "I wanted to talk to you first before we had sex. But then, we got in the moment." A beautiful flush crept on her cheeks. "Bane, I'm pregnant."

I nearly staggered back. Jasmine was pregnant. My girl was pregnant. With a baby. We hadn't been together for almost six months. Fuck, I wasn't sure how this worked. The baby had to be mine. Our baby.

She took a step closer. "Bane, it's yours. We're having a baby. I'm six months along. There was no way to contact you.

I wanted to tell you in person."

My hand shook as I touched her stomach. "We're having a baby."

The dream was becoming reality. A child. Jasmine as my wife. It was all real.

An unknowing feeling of love toward someone I'd never met flowed through me. I was connected to this little person already, and I'd known about her for less than a minute. It was a girl. I knew it.

Sinking to my knees, I kissed her stomach where *our* child grew. Instead of causing death, I'd helped create a life. If my soul was too damaged, I knew I'd never be given the responsibility to be a father. Maybe this was the world telling me I deserved to be happy.

Jasmine's hands came out and touched my shaved head. "Yes, the last time we saw each other. I found out about two and half months ago. It's a girl."

"We're having a baby girl." I swallowed hard as I remembered the little girl in pigtails on the swing from my dream. I couldn't stop giving little kisses to her stomach. My rough palms caressed as I whispered to our daughter, "I love you, little girl, with my whole heart. I will love you and protect you, little one. Always."

Glancing up to Jasmine, a tear came down her face.

What if she isn't ready to have a baby? What if she isn't happy about this?

Standing, I cupped her face. "Are you okay with this?"

She sniffled. "I love the thought of having your child. I was worried you would think I cheated on you. I've been so nervous."

"Never, baby. This is a miracle. Our miracle."

Bringing Jasmine to me, I felt her soft body meld to mine.

I smiled against her lips as the baby bump touched my stom-ach.

I was going to be a dad.

"I'm going to take you to bed and make love to the moth-er of my child."

"I want you, Bane." As she spoke her breathy reply, I walked her back to the mattress.

From this moment on, I'd never be the same.

CHAPTER

2

BANE

ON THE BED, I watched Jasmine sleep with her hair fanned out around her face. Peace. That was an odd feeling for me, but I had it. Finally. Through all the mayhem and destruction I caused in nearly every country of the world, I'd found a form of forgiveness through the child growing in Jasmine's stomach. I couldn't stop touching her.

Almost everyone I'd killed was a motherfucker. Knowing that was the only thing that kept me from completely losing myself to the darkness that tried to drown me.

In all the years I'd been part of the Black Division, I ended the life of five innocent people on accident. They were called casualties of war. I called it murder. That burden would be on me forever. The faces of the innocent haunted me when I closed my eyes. The motto of the agency—their deaths had been a sacrifice to the greater good. Bullshit. Everyone deserved a chance at life.

Those innocents had been someone's child and the regret of what I'd done hit me harder than before.

I am so sorry. So very sorry for the sins of my past. I will spend every day for the rest of my life trying to make up for it.

Whoever I mentally spoke to, I hoped they heard my promise.

Thinking back to the night I'd met Jasmine, I'd been at a bar drowning my sins away with alcohol. I'd killed my fifth innocent person and was on leave. Who would have thought that night would change my life forever?

For the next three weeks, I was off until my next assignment for who-the-hell-knows how long to some forsaken shithole. All I planned to do was drink, fuck, and sleep. Simple.

The bartender approached and I slid my glass to him. "Another one."

Bourbon, of any kind, was my drink of choice. As long as it was amber and got me fucked up—I didn't care. Numb was numb and that's all that mattered.

New York was a good place to take a three-week hiatus. The city never slept and there was pussy galore. The stool next to me moved and I glanced that way. I always wanted to know everything that was going on around me. It was part of who I was now. Outside of the Black Division, I was a ghost.

A beautiful blonde that I could fuck into next week, if given the chance, sat alternating glances between her watch and the door to the bar.

She looked my way. "Excuse me. Is this the original Finnegan's everyone talks about? I'm meeting my girlfriend here and she's late."

For all that was holy, she had the voice of a goddess that would sound amazing screaming my name while I fucked her into oblivion.

The bartender sat my glass down and took an order from the girl. She liked girlie cocktails as she ordered a Cosmo. I brought my glass up in salute to the girl with the mile-long legs beside me. "The one and only original Finnegan's."

Fuck, I had no clue, but it sounded good if that meant she would stay.

"Oh, good." The gorgeous girl let her shoulders relax. "I'm from Alaska, so this big city is a bit intimating."

I took a small sip of the liquid heaven. "What brought you to New York?"

"I've always wanted to see the world. I've been saving up to come here for years. My friend from New Jersey is meeting me here to catch up while I'm in town."

Here was to hoping little Miss Alaska was at the wrong bar.

That first night we'd met there was no sex. Instead, I'd gotten her number and taken her on a proper date the following night. Shocked the hell out of me. I had to work five long days to get between her legs. The wait was worth it. The moment I sunk inside her for the first time, I was gone. Changed forever.

My life was perfect.

Sitting at the kitchen table, I sipped on my coffee while Jasmine finished eating the breakfast I'd cooked for her. I didn't care for breakfast. Maybe it was from all those years of waking up starving with my mom, only to be denied. I took another sip, letting the warmth of the liquid keep me from going to that dark, cold place called my childhood.

I loved seeing Jasmine's healthy appetite as she nourished our unborn child. Testing the waters, I threw a thought out there. "I thought we could look for a house today."

Watching her closely, she paused mid bite. "You want to buy a house together?"

It wasn't a no, and sounded hopeful. This was good. This was very good.

Not wanting to give her surprise away, I shrugged. "Yes. I figured it would be nice to have a place of our own, maybe get a dog."

Yeah, I was going for the whole fucking caboodle in this new life. I'd always wanted a dog. Jasmine's apartment was nice and felt homey, but I wanted us to have a home that stood by itself in its own yard. All my life I'd lived in apartments, hotels, or in some desolate place.

Thoughtfully, Jasmine rubbed her stomach. "You're not doing this because of the baby, are you?"

Scooting her chair out, I placed my hand on top of hers, touching her stomach while kneeling. She needed to hear and see my earnestness. "I promise. Baby or no baby, I wanted to get a house together. You'll see."

Quirking an eyebrow, I knew I slipped. Jasmine knew something was up, but I stood and gave her a quick kiss before taking my seat. To hide the slight curvature of my lips, I took another sip of coffee.

Biting her lower lip, she said, "I love the idea. It'll be nice to have a real home and family again."

Having Jasmine happy was all that matter. She'd lost her parents a few years back in a dog sledding accident. The dogs broke free when a bear came out of nowhere. The sled tumbled down the mountain with her parents still on it. They were found dead two days later. Up here in Alaska, it's beautiful but brutal. I knew how lonely she was, and it nearly killed her having to sell her parents' house. What was harder for Jasmine was seeing the new owners tear down the only place she thought of as home. Otherwise, I would have bought her parents' home for our place.

Taking her plate to the sink, Jasmine rinsed it and put it in the dishwasher. I couldn't take my eyes off her perfect body. I wanted her again and it hadn't been an hour. Fingers trailed along my shoulder. Jasmine leaned in and whispered, "I'm going to take a shower. I think there's room for two."

Seeing that ass sashay out of the room, I bounded out of my seat. Silently, I followed. My girl was as insatiable as I was. The shower curtain sounded as she got in. Quickly, I shucked my clothes and walked into the room as it steamed.

Pushing the shower curtain aside, Jasmine reached for the shampoo and glanced at me from over her shoulder, clearly pleased I'd followed her. "I thought you were going to stand me up."

I engulfed her in my arms. "I'll always be there for you."

After getting ready, we were in the car. Jasmine sat in the passenger seat, rubbing her stomach with her right hand while her left one settled on my leg. The early-afternoon sun was in the sky beginning its descent. Nights were long in Alaska during the winter months. The sign for *Fish Hook Road* was up ahead. I turned left and saw Jasmine look at me confused from the side. The driveway at the end of the street was where Jasmine's surprise awaited her.

"What are we doing here?" I didn't say a word as I parked in the driveway. Jasmine continued to talk. "Oh, Bane, I love this house. It's not for sale, though." There was longing in her voice as she looked at the two-story home. When I'd been here before I left Black Division, she showed me around town; Jasmine pointed out this house as one she'd always loved. There was no denying the dreamlike tone she'd spoken with.

Trying to stay nonchalant, I said, "I know, but thought we might look around to get some ideas."

"That's a good idea."

The snow crunched beneath our boots as we made our way up to the pale-yellow house. The smell of smoke filled the air from nearby fireplaces. Our breaths came out in little puffs. Jasmine danced about in front of me as she made her way to the front porch. I wanted to stop her, but figured being a crazed, overprotective guy this early was not smart. Jasmine had been fine for nearly six months. *Six months.* I'd missed over half of the pregnancy. When we had another kid, I vowed to be part of everything.

Touching one of the front poles, Jasmine said, "I saw them painting this a couple of months ago. I think it's my favorite shade of yellow."

I touched the door handle and turned the knob. "Bane, we can't trespass."

Opening the door anyway, I shrugged. "We're not going to harm anything. Let's take a look around."

Jasmine still protested, but I walked in. The living room was as I'd imagined it. Glancing back at the door, my girl stood at the threshold.

"Bane, it's wrong."

With a devilish grin on my face, I prowled toward her.

"Bane, no—" I ignored her and picked her up as she chortled. "You always get want you want, don't you?"

"Yes, because I got you." Jasmine gave me that soft look, filled with love, as her hand touched my cheek.

The builders followed the specs I provided perfectly. The

floor plan had been opened up. Bright colors were on the walls.

In my arms, Jasmine gasped when she looked from me to the sign on the wall.

WELCOME TO YOUR NEW HOME, JASMINE!

"Bane, this is ours?" Her voice was unbelieving. "You bought us my favorite house and had it redone?"

I could tell she was beginning to get excited as the reality sunk in.

"I did. For you, me, and now our little girl. Do you like it?"

Glossy eyes looked at me, on the verge of tears. "It's incredible." She kissed me. "I love you. I love you so much. We're going to be so happy together."

This was all I needed. Ever. "Let me show you what they did in the bedroom."

Bane is available now
at your favorite online book retailer.

Paul – You are the love of my life. My happily ever after. Thank you for all your support in making my dreams a reality. I love you infinity factorial.

Makaela – I treasure each and every day we spend together telling stories, playing princesses, cuddling as we watch movies, and all the silly things we do throughout the day. Your love of stories makes my heart soar. I love you. I love you more. I love you the most.

Gehrig, Janet, Kathy, and Tim – Thank you all for all your unconditional love and support. I'm lucky to have four incredible parents.

Kelly – My sister from another mother. What would I do without you? From the bottom of my heart…thank you! Love ya!!! But most of all…thank you for giving me Lark!!! Oh, Lark, how I love thee. #LarkIsMine

The Thrillhammers – Thank you all for letting me use your awesome lyrics in Ripple Effect. You guys are an awesome band.

Nikola – I love ya, girl! Thank you for being the absolute set of eyes that see my book. Your attention to detail is incredible. But above all, I am blessed to have you as a friend.

Betas: April, Maren, Brandy, Heather, Jemma, Kelly – Thank you guys for all that you do and the time that you take in reading my stories and giving me back honest feedback. I love each and every one of you guys. I'm incredibly blessed to have friends like you.

Heather Davenport (Book Plug Promotions): Thank you for all that you do in coordinating all the events in releasing my book. I'd be lost without you.

Kristin's Korner – Each and every one of you guys means the world to me. Thank you for making the Korner such a special place day in and day out. You know you love me dearly as your #informationprovider. I love all of our banter and will treasure the memories forever.

Damien's Darkside Divas – Your kindness and love knows no bounds. Thank you for all that you do for me. I will forever treasure the friendships and memories you guys have given me.

3 K's and a J – Ladies, you guys mean the world to me. Thank you for all that you do and your daily support. I love you infinity factorial!

Sarah – I love you and your brilliant personality. Man friend will forever be associated with you. Loved being part of your special day. I meant each and every word of the speech I gave at your wedding.

Alyssa – Thank you for proofreading my book. You have an excellent eye for the details. I look forward to continue working with you in the future.

Jefster – Thanks for all the laughs and friendship. You're an incredible boss and even a better friend. There's over 5,000 commas in her for you to enjoy.

Readers – Thank you for all your support through this journey and allowing me to share a piece of me with you. Each and every one of you mean the world to me. Thank you from the bottom of my heart!

Available Now

The Trust Series

Trust Me
Love Me
Promise Me
Full-length novels in the TRUST series are also available in audio.

The Effect Series

Ripple Effect (Book 1 of the Effect Series)
Domino Effect (Book 2 of the Effect Series)

Stand Alone Novels

Dissipate
Bane

Joint Collaborations

Predestined Hearts

Coming Soon

Innocence

To join my newsletter to for up-to-date information:
http://tinyurl.com/mcppuhn